CT

Cheryl Taylor

GONE TO GROUND

GT

Cheryl Taylor

Copyright 2014 Cheryl Taylor
FIRST EDITION January 2014

Cover Design by Cheryl Taylor
Cover Photograph by Kathy McCraine

ISBN: 978-0615945163

Printed in the United States

Published by:
CT Communications
9535 E. Marilyn Ln.
Dewey, AZ 86327
cfaytay@gmail.com
cherylftaylor.com

To Mom

Note:

The towns described in the book exist, though maybe not quite as described (it is set in the future, after all). The ranch land where most of the action takes place, also exists, and is much as described. However, the actual ranch names, camp names and specific geological features are fictional. While it is rough land, broken by several deep canyons, the Adobe Canyon described in the book is fictional.

Unfortunately, the challenges that ranchers face from some recreational land users is not fictional, and should you decide to explore this area of Arizona, remember that we all share this land, and should do our best to care for it. Please pack out what you pack in, stay on roads, leave the waters the way you find them, do not harass the cattle (they have a right to be there, too) and please, please, please if you open a gate, close it behind you. Also, remember that not all this land is public, in spite of how empty it seems, and respect signs forbidding trespass.

T he man sat in the shade of the large, shaggy bark juniper tree watching the distant rider traverse the steep canyon side, following a small group of cows and calves. He saw her horse hesitate and look up in his direction. He held his breath. His horses dozed in the shade further back in the juniper thicket where the rider couldn't see them, even if she happened to look that way. He was fairly certain she wouldn't be able to see him either, sitting in the deep shadows, and dressed in dark shirt and jeans, tan face shaded even more deeply by his gray felt hat.

He knew where she was heading. He'd grown up in this brush filled Arizona wilderness, ridden its many empty miles every day from the time he'd been able to sit a horse, until he left the ranch at age fifteen. He nodded in approval. The canyon would be a safe refuge. He'd been on his way there himself, sure that no one else was left alive who knew about the lonely camp. He'd been wrong, apparently.

The cattle and rider moved out of sight, heading down the narrow side canyon toward its junction with the main rift. The man rose to his feet, dusted off his jeans and headed back to where his horses were waiting. He pondered the question of the woman and how she'd gotten here. Who was she? He was sure he knew who, or what, she was hiding from, but how did she know about Hideaway? No one but the cowboys, past and present, who worked the ranch knew about that lonely little camp, hours from the headquarters, and even further from any other form of civilization. Those cowboys were all gone now. All except him.

Well, he decided, it was time to answer some questions. Maybe the woman would be just what she seemed, a refugee from a world that had descended into chaos. Maybe she'd be agreeable to having another living within the sheltering walls of Hideaway. Life would be easier with two to share the chores of survival. He'd been assuming that if

1

he managed to get away, he'd be living the rest of his life alone. He didn't mind that too much, but he decided he didn't mind the idea of company either.

If she wasn't agreeable to sharing, well, there were ways of dealing with that, too.

2

It has been a year, Maggie thought as she rode through the rocks and brush, headed for home. *Only a year since the world came to an end. The world as we knew it. Where people had begun to believe that things like shiny cars, soda, TVs and video games were as necessary to life as food and water. Now that was all stripped away and the world came down to the essentials that had been there since the beginning of time: food, water, shelter, family.*

Suddenly her horse stopped, head up, and looked alertly toward the opposite side of the narrow canyon, ears at rigid attention. Maggie shaded her green eyes and looked in the direction the horse indicated, but didn't see anything. Probably a javelina or a deer. Stray wisps of honey blond hair, pulled loose from the thick braid dipping below her slender shoulders, floated on the light updraft from the canyon until catching in the light sweat that covered her face and neck from working in the hot sun all day. The dark gold hair stuck, giving her an uncomfortable, sticky feeling, and making her think longingly of the cool stream and water hole waiting at home. She nudged her horse into movement and they continued down the narrow canyon after the small herd. Her mind began to wander again, rambling down oft traveled roads, looking into the past.

No, she corrected herself, thinking back. *It wasn't just a year. The last year may have been the culmination, but the downward slide began a number of years ago. Maybe with the World Trade Center, maybe even before. We seem to have tangled the world up in truly spectacular fashion,* she thought ruefully, *and now we have to deal with the mess we've created.*

The first two decades of the 21st century had been marked by increasing violence and disorder across the world. Famines, plagues, genocides, wars, terrorism, gangs, wildly changing climate, wildfires on a scale unheard of only a short time before, and an increasingly unstable economy: None of these things were exactly new, but the degree to which they intruded on the average American hadn't been seen in an extremely long time, if ever.

Okay, she conceded to herself, *maybe the two World Wars and the Vietnam War altered the pattern of people's lives, and changed the direction of the country. Maybe the Great Depression left its imprint on millions of people. And alright, the Black Death in the 1300s certainly had a dramatic effect on the culture of the planet.*

But never before had so many disasters happened in such a short amount of time. They crushed and wrenched the pattern of people's lives across the world to such an extent that it would be a profoundly long time, if ever, before the pattern would return to a semblance of what had been considered normal such a short time earlier.

Maggie let out a huge sigh that caused her horse to twitch and swivel its ears back in her direction. She didn't dare become so caught up in her reverie that she lost sight of her small group of cows in the bush. She'd spent most of the day finding them and getting them headed in the right direction, and the constant stress of watching for the cattle as well as keeping an eye out toward the skies for seekers, the small orb-like, silvery electronic drones used by the Enforcers to monitor more remote areas, had caused her neck and shoulders to tighten and a headache to play behind her eyes.

It was unlikely that seekers would be sent out this far into the unpopulated wilderness, but you never knew. The Enforcers took their jobs seriously, and their job was to make sure that the people left populating the country stayed where they were told to stay. She couldn't be the only one who had decided to escape from the ever tightening militaristic governmental fingers, and surely some of those others had tried to make their escapes by heading into empty rangeland in hopes of living off the land.

She was positive, however, that the greatest concentration of seekers would be around the perimeters of the Authorized Population Zones or APZs; those places where the government decided to concentrate the people left alive. The official explanation was simple; there were too few law enforcement agents and soldiers to protect and guarantee safety to the population if everyone was living in far flung areas. The authorities maintained that people were not being deprived of their homes and property, only being relocated temporarily until a reliable form of law enforcement and government could be reestablished.

Maggie let out a short laugh that again startled her horse. Concentrated for their own good, *yeah, right*. Every journalistic fiber in her body rebelled at the thought. Throughout time people had been locked away for *their own good*, and frequently absolutely no good came of it, except for the people trying to control them. Even then it often backfired. Just look at the Japanese internment camps of the early 20th century for goodness sake.

The problem was that many APZs quickly became hotbeds of chaos and crime in their own right. Food and goods were still in short supply and those ruthless enough to take what they wanted had a ready crop of people, shell shocked from disaster and grief, to prey on. In order to maintain control, the Enforcers had to enact rigidly structured systems of operation and stomp hard on any of those inhabitants inclined to buck the system. On top of it all, heaven help the APZ held under the iron fist of a corrupt commander.

It was for this reason and others that, when the orders came for Maggie's area to be "concentrated," she had decided to take her son and escape if at all possible. Not that she had any experience in living off the land. Her idea of camping was a well appointed motor home with running water and electricity. But the idea of raising Mark in the increasingly hostile and dangerous environment of an APZ, especially without the help of Mike, her husband, dead for the past three months from the modern version of the plague, had been too much for her to take.

The cows reached the bottom of the canyon and began running and shoving each other to be the first to reach the water that ran along the surface of the stream bed at that point. Maggie's horse, Hank, picked up his pace as well. It had been a long, hot day on the plateau above, and water had been in short supply. Maggie was jerked back to the present; a present where she'd been living for a month in a primitive ranch camp, miles from anywhere.

For the next few minutes Maggie had her hands and mind busy ensuring that, once everyone had their fill of water, the cows headed in the direction she wanted; which was, as always, opposite the direction that the cattle wanted to go.

Why was it, she thought irritably, *that anytime a cow had two choices in a path, it always took the wrong one?* She gripped her saddle horn and bumped her horse in the sides, hustling up and around the animals to keep them from heading down the canyon instead of up stream as she wanted. Pulling Hank to a stop, she hooted and hollered, slapping her leg with her hat, trying to convince her four-legged adversaries that they really didn't want to go that way. The black and white cows and their young calves jerked to a stop and spent several minutes pondering the best way to circumvent the yelling human in their way. Then, with some shaking of heads and bovine curses, they turned and headed in the other direction.

For a brief instant Maggie's heart thumped into her throat as it looked as though the cattle would take the narrow trail back out of the canyon and return to the pasture where they'd started the day. The lead cow, a huge black specimen with a white face and one horn that curled down toward her right ear, reminding Maggie of a extra large Blue Tooth set, hesitated, took several steps in that direction, then suddenly changed her mind again and decided to play along. She turned and headed upstream with the remainder of the herd following her along the canyon bottom trail, aiming straight for Hideaway.

Maggie felt a wave of relief wash through her body with a burst of adrenaline. Her learning curve had been a steep one after moving to the camp, but she still didn't feel comfortable if it came to real all out cowboy style riding. If the cows had headed back up out of the canyon she would have had to go off trail at a run, scrambling through the rocks and brush in an attempt to head the cattle off before they got too far. While Maggie was pretty sure that Hank would make the scrambling run in good shape, she wasn't at all confident that he would arrive with her still on board. She was equally convinced that if she *were* to perform an unplanned dismount, the mother of all prickly pear cacti would just happen to be rooted right where she landed.

Now that they were heading in the right direction, Hideaway was only a half hour's ride away. *Good,* she thought. She hadn't wanted to leave Mark by himself at the camp, but she didn't have much choice. She had to gather a group of cattle into a pasture that was unlikely to be patrolled by seekers. These cattle would be providing them with food - *if* she could figure out how to butcher and preserve the meat without inducing lethal levels of botulism, salmonella, or any other nasty little bugs.

Ten-year-old Mark was a tough customer, but this past year had been hell on him, and the past five months had been especially rough. With his father dead from influenza, then catching it himself and the long illness that followed, the last thing he needed was to be subjected to his mother's incompetence in food preservation.

The Center for Disease Control in Atlanta said that the flu ravaging the country was the H5N1 strain that people had been dreading for years. Its virulence, however, turned out to be even more severe than the most sensational of the doomsayers had predicted. Some said that this was because the failing economy put so many people out on the streets, or caused them to put off health care until things became desperate. Others, more suspicious, thought that the severity of the bug was courtesy of a bioengineering lab somewhere in the middle east (or Korea, or north Africa, or, for all she knew, right here in the good old US of A, hidden behind the local Starbucks) that souped up the virus to maximum strength. Still others said that it was the result of the drastically changed climate having unsuspected effects on all life forms, including viruses and bacteria.

Whatever the cause, influenza spread across the planet in a tsunami, infecting ninety-nine out of every hundred people it encountered, and killing eighty-seven out of every hundred infected. Then came a wave of secondary infections, turning the morbidity to nearly one hundred percent. Less than one percent of the population didn't contract the illness at all. Maggie had been one of the lucky ones. For whatever reason, her immune system was able to block the virus before it replicated. Mike, her college sweetheart, and husband of nearly fifteen years, had not been so lucky.

As a paramedic, Mike had found himself on the front lines when people started getting sick. He and his teammates had repeatedly been called out to people with deadly fevers and floundering respiratory distress. He moved in and out of the hospitals, delivering those who couldn't make it on their own, and in the end, had been enlisted to help the shorthanded doctors and nurses when the disease began eating away at their numbers like a ravenous lion tearing into a tender gazelle. Finally, in spite of all the precautions he'd taken, he was infected. Within four days he was dead.

Their son, Mark, had also been infected, but he apparently had inherited a little bit of his mother's immune strength, and had been able to fight off the influenza and the multitude of secondary infections that plagued him even after the virus ran its course. His luck was even more extraordinary considering that by the time he contracted the illness, most of the hospitals were over run and the majority of health care workers were gone, in spite of rigorous quarantine and antiseptic procedures.

Once having decided on a direction, the cattle meandered steadily up the canyon, pausing here and there to grab a mouthful of the green grass growing on the banks of the stream. There were four cows, either black or black with white faces, and three calves ranging from a tiny little thing with big knobby knees and a squeaky bawl, to a strapping big bull calf nearly half the size of its mother. One of the cows, a tiny little black individual, was hugely pregnant, and when she walked her butt jiggled as though it had been given extensive plastic surgery by the makers of Jell-O.

Funny, Maggie thought, she'd never been a connoisseur of cows' butts before. In fact, the only thing she knew about cows' butts before her exile was how to fix them: rare, medium rare, medium and well done. When she stopped to consider things, looking at a cow's butt and seeing a walking steak was disconcerting. What happened to the gal who got queasy when picking a lobster to throw in the boiling water. Watching your steaks wander about added a whole new dimension to your dietary choices.

The air in the canyon was warm and small gnats swirled in the stifling air. Hank's tail swished in a steady metronome and the only sound was the buzzing of the insect life, the swishing of the tails and the soft thud of the horse's and cows' hooves as they trod the bare earth trail. Occasionally one of the cows would turn back and let out a low bawl as she checked up on her offspring. Maggie had been up since well before dawn, and gradually the warm, still air lulled her back into her memories.

She remembered vividly the day she came home from town to find a pair of Enforcers on the front porch facing a frightened looking Mark through the front door. As she walked up the steps to the redwood deck, the taller of the two men turned around, addressing her by name.

"Mrs. Margaret Langton?"

"Yes," Maggie replied, "I'm Margaret Langton. Can I help you?"

The Enforcer looked stiff and stern in his navy blue uniform, starched to the point that she wondered how he could move. His face was so immobile that she questioned whether the same person who cared for his clothes had added extra starch to his face as well. His black hair was ruthlessly cut to within a quarter inch of his skin and his blue eyes were cold, devoid of emotion.

In contrast, the smaller man with him looked uncomfortable with the situation. His uniform wasn't as pristine, the creases less razor sharp. His face also looked softer and more worn, as though he'd seen too much and was unbelievably tired. Softer look aside, however, she had no doubt that if she resisted he would be more than willing to slap on the handcuffs and put her in the waiting car.

"Your area is assigned for concentration," the tall man stated, handing her a sheaf of papers. "You have been assigned to the Phoenix Authorized Population Zone. You have two days to pack your property and report to the administrator."

In a fog of unreality Maggie looked at the papers in her hand with her name, her son's name and their address printed across the top. She had just gotten back from town in an attempt to purchase supplies. Luck hadn't been with her that day, though, and all she had to show for her journey to the stores were two ten pound bags of rice.

One of the reasons the government gave for concentrating the people was so that they could more fairly and evenly distribute food, medicine and clothing. It made sense, but Maggie had heard from a few journalistic contacts that life in the APZs wasn't easy, and that food and medicines were still in short supply and getting shorter considering that most of the farms were shut down until workers could be found and moved to the necessary areas. Her contacts told her about the gangs, and the crime waves. People were assigned jobs based on their skill levels and refusal to participate could result in cuts in rations or worse.

None of this information appeared in what news was available, of course. Freedom of the press was apparently in abeyance until such time that the government felt comfortable letting the people know what was happening.

9

That night, watching Mark sleep, his damp blond hair tousled on the pillow, she determined that she wouldn't have him exposed to that type of life. She remembered a story she'd done several years before about one of the oldest ranches in northwestern Arizona, the S Lazy V. While interviewing the owner at his home, he showed her a number of pictures and maps from around the ranch. One of these was of an isolated camp that they called Hideaway.

The rancher, Bob Tompkins, laughed when he talked about it. "That is one of the loneliest places in all of Arizona," he stated. "It's on a piece of deeded land that's in what we call a checkerboarded area; public and private lands all mixed up together. Somehow, it got mostly surrounded by a designated wilderness area, which meant that most of the roads, as bad as they were, couldn't be used any longer for motor vehicles. The one road left is barely passable by a goat in good weather. You can take a helicopter in, but the wind shears pretty badly down that canyon, so you have to hit it on just the right day.

"The camp itself is in the middle of Adobe Canyon, in an area that widens out. The geologists say it was probably a lake at some time, but now it's the prettiest little meadow you ever saw, a mile or so long, and a bit more than a mile across at the widest spot," Mr. Tompkins went on. "The house was originally built by miners who were prospecting Adobe Creek; then cowboys upgraded it a bit, added a barn and a windmill, and made it into a camp.

Mr. Tompkins showed Maggie where Adobe Canyon lay on the map, a long jagged slash, starting in the Juniper Mountains in the north and running down toward the headwaters of the Verde River. "Another problem is that in bad weather it can become sealed off for weeks, sometimes more. Snow and rain, as well as the winds can make it impossible to get in or out, other than on horseback and not always even then."

According to Tompkins, on the western edge of this meadow under an overhanging sweep of deep red sandstone was a house, built into the natural shelter of the cliff using the rocks found in the area, much as the ancient shelters of the Anasazi and Sinagua had been built into these types of declivities centuries earlier. In fact, a little further up the canyon were the ruins left by some of the earlier native inhabitants of the canyon. The floor of the house had many ancient pot sherds and arrowheads left by these people, concreted in alongside the sandstone and shale slabs, as well as a few mule and horse shoes for good measure.

"You just can't keep that camp manned, though, these days," Tompkins continued. "That place is so damned isolated. It was hard to find many single cowboys who wanted to live that far from anywhere for long, especially after the roads got shut down. And just forget it if there was a wife involved," he laughed. "There weren't many women who wanted to raise their kids that far from medical help, or any other kind of help, for that matter. So, we eventually just shut the camp down, leaving it provisioned for emergencies, but otherwise not using it."

It became much easier to work the pastures from camps on the outside edges of the wilderness area. A cowboy could easily work from the outside in, instead of the inside out, so for the past thirty years the small, hidden camp called Hideaway had become a legend, not forgotten, but its existence not completely believed by those who hadn't seen it, either.

During the research for her article the rancher gave Maggie copies of maps and pictures. However, he requested that she not make much mention of Hideaway since he didn't want a herd of recreational hikers, riders and ATV drivers swarming his ranch looking for the place. Of course, he said, being a wilderness area, the ATVs weren't allowed to cross, but that had never stopped them before and it was usually the rancher who incurred the expense of repairing the fences and waters that these people destroyed. Maggie respected his request and only made a brief mention of the various camps and the cowboys and families that manned them, leaving out the abandoned camp all together.

Gradually during the night the idea came to her that Hideaway was exactly the type of place where she and Mark could go. Even before the Enforcers began concentrating the population, Hideaway was a long way from any form of civilization. The only people who knew about it were the ranch owners, and the cowboys who worked the ranch. Considering the percentages, the odds were that either they'd died in the plague or been concentrated into one of the APZs.

Maggie figured that there was a chance she would run into someone at the camp, or one of the other nearby camps, but hopefully the independent, rebellious spirit of the cowboy would lead them to offer shelter and assistance until she could figure out where else she could go.

The next morning Maggie put her plan into motion. With Mark's help she packed four suitcases and placed them in the middle of the living room to make it look as though they were prepared to head for the APZ. The papers she'd received gave them permission to bring two suitcases per person. The rest of their property was to be left in their locked home, waiting for their eventual return. The papers stated that since the population would be living within the APZs, there would be no problem with looters, and any that did manage to escape the net would be easily detectable.

In another part of the house she also packed all the portable foodstuff they had, as well as water, outdoor clothing, some tools and her small laptop with its solar charger into various bags and bundles.

Overcoming qualms of guilt, she broke into her neighbor's house. These people were avid campers and she was able to gather many essential articles, such as warm sleeping bags, lanterns, and freeze dried foods, as well as many other helpful items such as a folding shovel, cooking utensils, a radio and two flashlights that worked by cranking or shaking.

Maggie also wanted to find a gun and ammunition. She hesitated before taking this last item, since she and Mike had always resisted getting a gun, especially since her husband saw so many gunshot wounds on his job. But, she thought, finally wrapping the rifle in a blanket, a gun could be the difference between life and death out in the wilderness. She tried not to think about what she'd do when the ammo ran out. Hopefully there would be abandoned ranches and camps not too far away where she could renew the supply. Actually, she thought, if they were lucky, the crisis would be over by then, and they would have returned home.

Finally, she and Mark went through their own house opening cabinets and drawers, throwing the contents on the ground in order to make it look as though someone had gone through the house looking for things to steal.

Ten years before, Maggie and Mike had bought an attractive redwood and granite home on the northern outskirts of Prescott, Arizona, only a short distance from public lands where they could hike on the weekends. Because their subdivision was in a semi-rural area, at least one of their neighbors, the Johnsons, kept horses. Maggie had been feeding them as well as the Johnsons' two Australian shepherds since the family died from the influenza. Now she was glad she hadn't just turned the animals out, as had so many others. Those four horses would be their passport to freedom.

Maggie figured she had a day, maybe two before the authorities realized that she and Mark were not going to show up at the shuttle to the APZ. Then hopefully, when officers checked the house, they would see the pile of suitcases as well as the disordered belongings and believe that looters had attacked while they were packing and either killed or kidnaped them. She hoped that the Enforcers wouldn't spend too much time looking for the two of them, and that even if a search were instigated, the two or three day head start would be enough to erase the hoof prints that would indicate in which direction she and Mark had headed.

That night, under the soft light of the crescent moon, Maggie and Mark slipped over to the Johnson's barn, caught and saddled the horses. The two dogs, Jack and Gypsy, danced around the humans, excited to go on what seemed to be a moonlight trail ride. Neither Maggie nor Mark had much experience with horses other than the few times they had been invited to go for a ride with the Johnson family. Each of those times, their mounts had been prepared for them and all they had to do was get on and steer. Saddling the creatures themselves was not as easy as it appeared, but with some fumbling and false starts they finally managed to get all four horses saddled, and their bundles distributed neatly.

With a final regretful look back at the house sitting silently in the shadows of the tall ponderosa pines, the small group eased quietly down the road heading for the gate into the forest on the west side of the subdivision.

Over the next five days, using maps, a compass and making liberal use of wire cutters, Maggie and Mark made their way out through the empty rangeland to where Maggie thought Adobe Canyon was located. A book on wilderness survival which she'd found at the neighbor's became their bible, and time and time again Maggie proved that she was not a nature girl. Especially when she discovered that a small, golden-brown bull snake had curled up in her boot one night while they slept.

Much to Mark's shock, and then amusement, Maggie promptly screamed, threw the boot into a cactus and climbed on top of a nearby rock. It took five minutes of concentrated effort on the boy's part to convince his parent that the inhabitant of the boot wasn't the Mojave green rattlesnake that had been prominent in the news lately, and that bull snakes were harmless.

Watching the growing expression of glee on her son's face, Maggie climbed carefully down from her rock, a growing suspicion entering her mind. Was it possible that the small reptile had been given a hand climbing into her boot? She wasn't positive, but just in case, she made sure that her boots were secure every night thereafter.

After nearly forty miles, five days of riding and three false starts down the wrong canyons, Maggie, Mark, their four horses and two dogs finally made their way between the towering red, yellow and white layered walls of Adobe Canyon and into the emerald green meadow of Hideaway. They were home.

Maggie and her small group of cows made their way into the home meadow, the name she and Mark had given the area around Hideaway, and she remembered her first sight only four short weeks ago. The brilliant green of the grass contrasted against the vibrant reds and aged yellows of the sandstone cliffs and the bright blue of the sky. It seemed too bright, too intense to be real. Upon first seeing the meadow a month ago, she was reminded of nothing so much as a painting touched by the brush of an artist with no taste for subtlety.

On that day, for the first time in five months, ever since the influenza stole her husband, Maggie felt a rush of relief cascade through her. For the first time the twanging tight strings of fear loosened their hold.

Maggie's body remembered that feeling of release and echoed it today. Again, she was home.

3

After waiting until the woman was well out of sight, heading deeper into the canyon toward Hideaway, the man followed her, picking his way through the thick oak brush and catclaw. He was wary of getting too close lest the horses give away his location through a hoof banging on a loose rock, or an ill timed whinny.

Pondering the question of the woman, he decided his best move would be to head down Adobe Canyon, away from Hideaway, to another small meadow he knew about. He could leave his four horses there, then make his way on foot to a concealed overlook that would give him a good view of the home pasture around the camp. He *needed* to know exactly what he was dealing with. The last thing he wanted was to walk into the middle of a group of armed ghosts, the name the Enforcers gave to those people who'd avoided concentration and were trying to live free of government "assistance." He thought it darkly humorous that he, one of those who had been assigned to conjure and "exorcise" the ghosts, was now one himself.

He'd first spotted the woman two days ago, as he was making for Hideaway. Not sure of the situation, and unwilling to jump into deep water without backup, he began watching her from a distance. Questions loomed in his mind and he considered briefly heading off in another direction, avoiding confrontation all together. The security of Hideaway was too big of a prize to give up uncontested, however.

As he observed the woman riding through the pastures adjacent to Adobe Canyon, he came to the conclusion that, if she wasn't alone, she also couldn't be with a very well organized or skilled group of ghosts. He spotted the telltale signs of a person not familiar with riding the range. No rope, spurs or chaps, even in the thickest brush. Her horse, while it seemed a good type, didn't strike him as being one used to the rough land in which it was working. The woman's hesitation and fumbling to complete even the simple maneuvers needed to gather a small group of cows showed that she didn't have that sense of what cows think that ranch kids learned from their earliest days.

Why on Earth, he thought, *would someone with so little experience be alone out here?* It didn't make sense. This wasn't some dude ranch adventure. Making a mistake out here, especially with the way things were these days, could get you killed.

This was rough land, slashed and torn by washes and canyons, covered with coarse grasses, juniper thickets, pinion pine, oak brush, catclaw and numerous other plants that were as tough as the land they grew on. Even cowboys who spent their lives in the saddle, with rears as tough as leather, occasionally got lost or killed if new to this unforgiving corner of the high desert. You couldn't spit without hitting a cactus or a rock, and the cattle had to be as agile as mountain goats to get around and make a living.

This was the land and the life he was born to, although it seemed he'd forgotten that for awhile. His father had been a cowboy on the S Lazy V Ranch and had been assigned to the Eagle Camp. His mother, a teacher, had been a rancher's daughter and had expected to marry a cowboy from the moment she was old enough to dream about such things. Many people would have considered their family's life at camp isolated and lonely, but he and his brother couldn't imagine a better one.

Because of their distance from town for much of his childhood, his mother had home schooled her two children. Much of their days, when they weren't doing their lessons, involved helping their father work the land he'd been assigned. Both he and his older brother, Jason, could hardly wait until they were old enough to go on the wagon, the two times of year when all the cowboys gathered, the chuck wagon was provisioned and they and the remuda - the ranch's string of cow horses - traveled around the vast ranch, branding and working the calves and their mothers. When the wagon rolled out, it was like the old west had come back to make a home in the 21st century and for two kids brought up on the stories of the cowboy life, even Christmas was second best.

He thought back to the picture that his mother had on their mantle for as long as he could remember. He and Jason, wearing their chaps and spurs, carrying their ropes and sitting tall in the saddles, even though their stirrups barely hit halfway down their horses' sides. A real pair of cowpunchers in the making.

His mind flashed to another picture his mother had, one he begged her to destroy. She'd always refused, though, threatening to bring it out and display it for the world whenever she heard he was dating someone new. She never did, and he knew she was joking. At least he hoped she was. It was a picture of him as a two-year-old. His father had just ridden into the yard, and he was so excited that he went tearing out the door to meet him. The problem was, he was wearing nothing but his boots and spurs, his hat and his rope.

When he was a kid, his mother kept that picture locked up so that he couldn't get to it. He'd lived in fear that on his wedding day his mother would bring it out and display it to all the guests.

She hadn't, but you just never knew with her. After all, there was that time when he opened a large, ornately wrapped birthday gift only to find a box filled to the brim with dried horse poop. It wasn't until he dug through the powdery manure that he found the small box encasing a coveted pocket knife. Things like that made birthdays and Christmases interesting at home, but they also sometimes made you wonder exactly how far she would go.

He'd grown up planning to become a cowboy just like his father, his grandfather, and his great grandfather before him. It wasn't until he was fifteen, during that terrible fall wagon, that the idea of becoming a law enforcement officer entered his mind. Then, during the next five years, while living in town, the idea blossomed and grew until that was all he wanted to be.

That's what he'd become too, for the next sixteen years. He probably still would be living that life if the flu and the reorganization hadn't intervened. Now he found himself at the age of thirty-six horseback again and about to reenter the cowboy life, only in a way that no cowboy had lived for well over a century, if ever. Maybe it was more the life of the legendary mountain men who left the world, went off and lived in isolation for the majority of every year, only contacting civilization when they needed something that couldn't be made off the land.

The man made his way down the canyon, listening to the soft tinkle and chuckle of the water running across the smooth black, pink and yellow stones lining the stream. The unusually abundant spring rains had caused the water to run on the surface of the creek for further than normal. For most of the year the water had a tendency to flow above ground for a hundred yards or so, sink out of sight, then suddenly

17

reappear as if out of nowhere. It all depended on the type of land it was traveling through.

He remembered his high school science teacher talking about the porosity, or some such thing, of different minerals and rocks, but all it meant to him was that some years Adobe Creek would be in sight most of the way to the Verde River, and some years it would play coy, like some of the girls he'd admired in school. Only putting in an appearance occasionally, then disappearing again out of reach.

Nearly a mile down the canyon, a second wash carved its way down through the land to join the main canyon, creating a slightly larger gap between the vertical multicolored walls. Some long ago rancher had built a small catch pen at the opening to this wash using juniper staves and wire. He'd stretched it across the wash and the canyon, building easily replaceable sections at the water gaps for when the flood waters ran high and debris tore out everything in its path.

Gates opened in all three directions and were left open most of the time so that cattle traveling down the trail that followed the wash from the plateau could move through to get to water or travel through to other areas of the pasture. At other times, though, when a cowboy wanted to gather a small group of cows without taking them all the way back to the camp, he would close the main canyon gates, go gather his herd and push them down the wash and into the catch pen.

Now the man led his horses inside and closed all three gates. He pulled the saddle off his stocky buckskin gelding first, then turned to the other three horses, unloading the packs and setting the supplies outside the fence, then returned to remove the pack saddles themselves. With all the horses freed of their tack they began to wander the pen, heads down, looking for the ideal sandy spot to roll and scratch their sweaty, itchy backs. Then, having comforted the body, they began to fill their stomachs, grazing on grass that had sprouted inside the pen since it was last used, and that had grown to lushness unusual in this harsh land thanks to the creek's abundant water.

The man leaned on the fence a few minutes watching the horses, then in a voice, scratchy with disuse, he bid them stay put, and he'd be back in a bit. The sound of his own voice startled him. Never what one would call a talkative man, over the days since he'd left the Laughlin Authorized Population Zone, he'd spoken less and less often, until he might go an entire day without uttering a sound. His ears had become accustomed to the quiet sounds of nature - the susurration of the ceaseless wind, the quail's chip-churring, the eagle's cry, the coyote at night, the occasional low of a cow, and the answering bawl of a calf - and the sound of his voice seemed harsh and out of place.

It amused him to think that most women mentioned the quality of his voice as one of the things that attracted them. He knew it was deeper, softer and huskier than average, but out here it just seemed loud and grating, and he felt the urge to look around and see where the strange sound had come from.

After leaving the horses in the catch pen, he made his way quietly back up stream, heading for the overlook that he and his brother discovered many years ago. It tickled the two boys that they could sit up on the cliff side, watching all the action in the pasture, yet no one knew they were there. They'd first found the overlook when they came to Hideaway with their father while checking the waters for the pasture. Even though the luck of the draw had surrounded this piece of deeded land with a designated wilderness, making the manning of the camp a thing of the past, the cows still had to be checked, and the waters maintained. His father, as the resident of Eagle Camp, held this pasture as part of his duties. Cowboying isn't just a job, however, it's a lifestyle and often when his father checked this remote pasture his wife and kids came along, especially if it was going to be a several day trip.

As the man drew near Hideaway, he moved slower, his scuffed brown leather boots making little sound on the hard packed dirt as he looked for the boulder that marked the narrow, water-eroded crack in the rock that led upward to a narrow trail. Finally, just as he'd begun to believe that past twenty-one years of weather and floods had rearranged the landscape to such a degree that the overlook was gone, he spotted the familiar rock formation on the left side of the canyon.

Squeezing between the boulder and the cliff side, he was surprised at how much smaller the cleft had become. Surely he couldn't have grown so much since leaving the ranch to live in town. He began to worry that he would either become stuck, or emerge on the other side sans buttons. The horrifying image of having to call for help, then having to explain himself to the woman gave extra impetus to his squirming, and he emerged on the far side of the boulder on a trail carved between a chunk of sandstone that had split off from the main body, and the cliff wall itself.

Now, he thought, *all he had to do was to get back through on the way out. At least he'd have gravity on his side in that direction.* He hoped that the trail was still intact after all these years. It didn't bear thinking about that he would make it all the way up here, only to be faced with a blocked trail.

After a few minutes of slithering, scooting and crawling - *Damn, how the hell did this trail get so much smaller, and the wall become so much shorter* - he arrived at the low opening of a small cave eroded into the sandstone wall. These cliffs were filled with caves, some that meandered miles underground through the sandstone and limestone layers. There was actually a rumor that if you found the right connections, you could make it all the way to the Grand Canyon, just like the cave network that included the Grand Canyon Caverns. Tour guides told how smoke from a fire set in the Caverns could be seen emerging from caves in the Canyon itself. No one had actually tested *these* caves, but he and his brother had explored occasionally when staying at the camp, and had never come close to covering all the possible twists and turns.

His destination in this case was only a small, singular cave, not part of any interconnected labyrinth. It was roughly ten feet by six feet, and about ten feet high at the peak with a crack that extended upward even further, possibly even to the top of the plateau, and which channeled in the water that had formed the natural enclosure and the trail he'd just followed. It was a dead end, except that at the far side a triangular crack opened, allowing visual access to the pasture beyond. The man slid into the cave and made his way across the sandy floor to the gap where he crouched, looking out.

The view was just as he remembered it at least. He could see nearly all of the pasture, with the exception of the area just below, to the right and left of his position. He could make out the northern opening of the canyon, the gray, weathered barn and corrals, and a portion of the camp's yellow and red granite and sandstone house with its nearby windmill. There was the woman's horse, tied at the hitching rail outside the barn with its saddle off. In the pasture was the small group of cows she'd been pushing, as well as four or five others. A short distance from the cattle grazed three more horses.

The man's gaze was pulled back to the barn's opening when a small blond boy, about ten or twelve from the looks of him, came running out, followed by two dogs and a young calf.

"Mark," came a voice from within the barn, faint but discernible.

The boy skidded to a stop, only to be run into by the closely following calf, knocking him to the ground. He got up, pushing the calf's nose away from his face and called back, "Yeah, Mom?"

"Would you brush Hank then take him back to the pasture, please?" the voice called. "I've got to milk Lizzie if we're going to feed Jenny and have some milk for supper."

"Sure, okay," answered the boy, Mark.

He walked to the hitching rail followed by his small entourage, and bent to pick something - a brush - from the ground near the base of the post and proceeded to brush off the horse's back. Once finished, he untied the gelding and headed for the pasture gate, putting the animal inside and removing the halter. The horse turned, nuzzling the boy and apparently received a treat for his efforts, then ambled off to rejoin the other three horses in the band. The boy returned to his original trajectory, heading for the creek where it widened into a small pond. There he picked up a fishing pole, planted himself on a boulder and cast his line into the water. The dogs and the calf who had accompanied the boy down to the creek, settled in to await the outcome, the dogs curled up in the shade of some nearby willows, and the calf grazing in the lush grass.

He saw the woman head out into the pasture toward the small group of cows, returning shortly with a small brown model and disappearing into the gloomy interior of the barn. Not long following this vanishing act, the sounds of banging and clanking and the occasional indecipherable exclamation wafted out of the structure, resulting in a soft chuckle from the observer. After about twenty minutes the woman emerged, looking slightly the worse for wear and carrying a bucket of what the man assumed to be milk. Toting her hard fought for treasure she headed toward the house, passing out of his sight as she made for the door.

The man saw no one else, nor any indication that anyone but these two were at Hideaway. As he worked his way back down the trail to the canyon bottom he deliberated his next move. It was time, he decided, to make his presence known. Regardless of where it went after that, it had to start somewhere.

4

Maggie, unaware that she was being followed, drove her small group of cattle down toward the barn. She was trying to steer them toward the pasture instead of the garden when Mark came running up from the creek, followed by Jack, Gypsy and Jenny, the small orphaned calf Maggie found next to its mother's dead body two weeks ago. She waved to him, and received his wave in return.

"Mark, run down and open the gate to the pasture," Maggie called out as the boy approached. "Then stand off to the right so that the cows don't turn the wrong way. And keep those dogs from spooking the cows, got it?"

"Okay, Mom." Mark turned and headed for the large gate next to the barn. The dogs hesitated, but responded when the boy let out a loud whistle. Jenny, the calf, started to head toward the cows, then suddenly cranked her tail high into the air, let out a strangled bawl and tore off after the threesome.

The gate Maggie had indicated opened into a large pasture that ran down to the stream and across to the far wall of the canyon and all the way down to the northern end of the pasture. Another gate at the far end opened into the canyon where it narrowed again. That trail followed the creek to where a spring burst out of the canyon face several miles further on, then up a wash to the pasture that bordered the canyon on its eastern edge.

Three cows, two calves and a bull were already in residence in the large meadow, as were the other three horses. The grass, fed by creek and spring rains, was deep and green, and the new cows headed gladly into the pasture through the open gate where they immediately began grazing on the unaccustomed abundance.

Maggie turned Hank and rode back to the barn where she

dismounted, tying him to the hitching rail outside. Having shut the gate, Mark ran over, followed by his animal bodyguards.

"What were you up to today?" Maggie asked Mark as she started unsaddling Hank "Did you get your school work done?"

"Yes, Mom. I finished all of it except I had some problem on the fractions in the math," Mark answered, looking up from the kneeling position he'd taken while playing with the dogs. "Then I watered the garden and I took Jack and Gypsy out into the pasture to try some of that stuff they talked about in that dog training book. You know," he said, face animated, "if we can train Jack and Gypsy like that book says, then they can gather the cows and horses, and you won't have to work so hard."

"Yeah, that would sure be great," answered Maggie, smiling into the saddle where Mark wouldn't see. "So, how did it go?"

"Well, not so good, I guess. I think I need to read some more in that book. Jack went out like they said, but he only got the calf." Mark paused looking down at the dog's ruff gripped tightly in his right hand. Then he glanced up with a hopeful look on his face, his green eyes flashing with excitement.

"But he did bring it back to me. It's just that Gertrude, the mom, got angry when the calf bawled, and took out after him full blast."

Maggie stopped what she was doing and turned to look at Mark. "What did you do?"

"Well, Jack wouldn't stop when I yelled at him, so I ran for the fence. Gertrude caught Jack and rolled him over, then took her calf back." Mark ducked his head again, sure what was coming.

Maggie took a deep breath and counted to ten. "I think from now on we'll wait until we're both here before we do any more dog training, okay?" Maggie stated, looking at Mark's bent head, the dark blond hair floating lightly on the breeze. "I do not want you taking those dogs into the pasture without me. Understand?"

Mark blew out a sigh of relief, glad that his chewing out was relatively mild. "Yeah, okay," he agreed, "but I really think we can get the dogs trained so that they can help us. That book talks about cool things and Jack and Gypsy are awful smart. They just get so excited sometimes, see, and they just can't help it." The excitement started to light his face again.

"Alright, alright, we'll try," Maggie said. "Just remember, not without me. And would you get this blasted calf away from me before I turn it into a pair of calfskin boots and a plate of veal fettuccine!"

While Maggie had been unsaddling Hank and talking to Mark, Jenny, apparently feeling that dinner was entirely too late in coming, began butting hard into Maggie, searching for milk and striking any available body parts, which unfortunately were all at rear end and crotch level. Maggie kept swatting it away, whereupon it turned its quest to Hank, who pinned his ears and stomped his feet in an irritated manner, apparently unappreciative of being butted in the stomach by the determined calf.

Mark laughed, and grabbed the small black and white calf by its rope halter and dragged it off toward the barn. Maggie followed with her arms full of saddle, pad and bridle, heading for the tack room. The cavernous area was cool and dark, the only residents being a flock of blue-gray pigeons. The air smelled of dust, hay and old manure. Maggie set the saddle down with a thump just as Mark came up.

"Mom, I left my fishing pole down by the pond. Can I go get it?"

"Go ahead, kiddo, see if you can get us something for dinner while you're at it," Maggie agreed and watched smiling as Mark took off running out the barn door, followed by his posse. Then, as a second thought, she called out after him, asking him to brush Hank and put him away first so that she could get on with the milking, a chore she hated.

Before finding Lizzie at an abandoned farm on the way to Hideaway, Maggie had never milked anything before, and she wasn't sure that Lizzie appreciated her newly developing technique. Milking usually devolved quickly into a wrestling match. Over the past few weeks Maggie had improved so that now the milk was only kicked over two or three times during a session, but she still put off the activity as long as possible.

Oh, well, she thought, heading for the pasture where Lizzie grazed with the other cows, *I'd better get on with it. If I don't do it, no one else will and waiting won't make it any better. Besides, if I don't get it done soon that damned calf will probably show up again and then I won't be able to get anything done.*

Later that evening, after a meal of bread, butter - made with her own little hands, thank you very much - and fresh baked trout, only slightly burned in the huge wood range, Maggie settled down at the table with Mark to deal with the dreaded fractions. The two dogs were stretched out on the cool stone floor after dining on the bits of bread and fish that were too charred to be eaten by the humans, their paws twitching occasionally as they relived the excitements of the day.

It's amazing how well Mark's adapted to life at Hideaway, Maggie thought. *Better than me, I think. I still miss the stores, and the restaurants, and the people. Mark's content with his animals. At least for now.* Maggie looked at Mark's tousled blond head, bent over a math problem, a slight frown creasing his face as he chewed on the end of his pencil.

The dogs were Mark's constant companions since coming out to Hideaway, with Jack filling the post of special guardian. Their presence calmed Maggie's worries when she left him for short periods of time while looking for cows. When Maggie brought the orphaned calf back one day, she'd joined right in with Mark's animal posse, doing everything with them.

It didn't matter how hard Mark begged, though, Maggie drew the line at Jenny moving into the house with the dogs and the people. When night fell, Jenny was turned out into the pasture with her other bovine compatriots. Maggie refused to cave in to Mark's sorrowful green eyes and his protestations that Jenny would be lonely in the cow herd without him. The house, no matter how bizarrely constructed, was not the place for a calf, especially one that was not housebroken, nor likely to become so anytime in the near future.

The only thing we're missing now, other than a regular bathroom, a proper kitchen, and a clue as to what we're doing, Maggie thought, *is chickens.*

Maggie had wanted to pick up some chickens at the ranch where she and Mark found Lizzie, but there was a limit to what they could carry on the already overloaded horses. *Soon,* she thought, *I need to get back to the nearest ranch, before all the chickens are killed off by hawks and coyotes. It would be wonderful to have chicken for dinner again, and we need the eggs.*

But she was faced with a problem. While she could leave Mark for relatively short periods of time, the nearest ranch that she knew of was a full day's ride away, and then it would take time to round up any birds left alive. She would be gone at least two full days if not longer, and if she took Mark, who would feed Jenny and milk Lizzie. Yet the chickens were necessary and she needed more seeds for the garden. Next week at the latest she'd need to make a decision and the dilemma was keeping her awake at nights.

As the pair bent over the math problems in the glow from an oil lamp, Maggie dimly registered a thump outside the door. Gypsy lifted her head and rolled to her chest, ears alert, and let out a soft growl. Immediately Jack scrambled to his feet, and stood, facing the door. Just as Maggie pushed back her chair and started to rise, the door slammed open and in stepped a tall, muscular man wearing the navy blue uniform shirt of an Enforcer, carrying a rifle at the ready with a handgun snugged into the holster at his belt.

"Mom, who...," Mark started to say, but stopped when Maggie put her hand on his shoulder and sank slowly back into her chair, wide green eyes, the match to her son's, fixed on the terrifying image in the doorway.

A thousand thoughts rushed through her mind, crashing off each other and causing roadblocks to action. *How could they have found us? What do we do? I won't go down without fighting,! I won't. How do I protect Mark? What... what... what...*

Maggie finally found her voice and asked in tremulous tones, "Who are you?"

5

This sucks, thought fourteen-year-old Christina Craigson as she sat on a bed in the tiny windowless room on the subterranean level of the converted hotel. *This totally, completely and fully sucks!*

The "this" she was referring to was the entire situation she found herself in. Parents dead; mother of the disease and father at the hands of the Enforcers. Separated from her brothers and now locked in this little cell. THEY may call it a "time away" to rethink her choices, and say it was for her own good, but she knew what it really was: a way to keep her from questioning what they were doing, and what they wanted her to do.

THEY didn't know Christina well at all, though, if they thought locking her away would shut her up, she thought. Uh uh, no way. Questioning how things worked was what Christina did best. Her mom and dad are - were scientists and taught her the value of questioning her senses and not accepting things at face value. God, she missed them, she thought as unshed tears stung her eyes. She was sure they had cameras in here, and she refused to give them the satisfaction of seeing her cry. They would take it as a sign of weakness and no one was allowed to think of Christina Craigson, daughter of William and Elizabeth Craigson as weak.

Christina had been at the Laughlin, Nevada, APZ for nearly six weeks. Before that she and her brothers had been staying at the shelter in Ash Springs, Nevada, where they'd been taken after their father's death.

"Poor little mites," the smelly old lady in charge of the shelter said in treacly, over concerned tones. Her hair, died an unnatural shade of red, bobbed as she shook her head in sympathy. "So hard to lose your parents at this age. Just you trust your Aunt Sue, honey, I'll make sure you're okay." Christina was afraid she was in imminent danger of falling into a diabetic coma if Sue continued in this sugary style.

"You'll be fine," said the harried looking social worker assigned to them. There weren't many social workers left alive, and those who were found themselves overwhelmed with the number of orphans left as the influenza swept over the country.

Then, in the manner of most clueless adults who tended to view kids as a lower form of life that didn't rank especially high on the intellectual scale, the social worker, "call me Jeannie," walked over to "Aunt" Sue and began talking quietly. Apparently she was unaware that Christina could hear and understand every word as she stood there, flanked by her two eight-year-old brothers, Ryan and Nick. Unaware, or just didn't care.

"It's such a sad story," Jeannie said in her high, nasal voice, "mother dead of the influenza and the poor children left with just their father. Then he commits treason. Actually stands up in front of a crowd and stirs them up against the authorities with some made up stories about how the government is working on some conspiracy and using this terrible disease to gain control over the people. As if our elected officials would do something like that," she huffed, looking out of the corner of her eye at Christina and her brothers.

Christina wanted to march up to the two busy bodies, kick them in the shins and yell, "Hey, I'm right here! I'm not deaf!" but she kept in her place.

"Then," Jeannie continued breathlessly, with Sue shaking her head and clucking her tongue against the roof of her mouth, "when the Enforcers were brought in to get things under control, Craigson tried to incite the crowd against them. Of course they had to do something. It's such a shame that the little ones had to see their father die that way, especially so soon after losing their mother."

"Did they have to shoot him?" Sue asked avidly, leaning forward to catch every word, mouth hanging open like a baby bird waiting for a juicy worm, her watery blue eyes eager behind half moon glasses.

"Yes," Jeannie verified. She nodded vigorously, her frizzy, streaked-blond hair writhing around her head like Medusa's snakes. "They say Dr. Craigson pointed the Enforcers out as agents of the government which was trying to deprive them of health care and food and everything. The crowd rose up and charged the Enforcers. The officers opened fire to protect themselves. Fifteen were killed, and one of those was Dr. Craigson, shot down right in front of his children." Jeannie shook her head as if despairing over this terrible situation that had fathers being shot down in front of their kids, but her voice betrayed the degree to which she savored the image of the dramatic scene. "It's shocking for the little ones, but what end do you expect for a traitor."

Finally, Christina couldn't take it anymore. "He wasn't!" She yelled, fists balled at her sides as if ready to fight, dark blue eyes blazing in a white face framed by dark brown hair. "Take it back! My dad wasn't a traitor! He was a great scientist and he knew more about what was going on than any of you stupid bitches, so you take it back!"

Christina paused, breathless, chest heaving and struggling to contain her sobs. Her brothers shrank behind her, scared brown eyes looking back and forth between their sister and the two shocked women.

Christina turned her back to the two women. *They didn't know. They didn't care.* Christina had been the one standing next to her dad when the Enforcers arrived. She was the one who was next to her father as he tried to reason with them, who saw the angry crowd turn on the uniformed men carrying the guns. She was the one who was splashed with her father's blood when the Enforcers opened fire with their assault rifles.

"Well, I'll..." Jeannie stumbled to a stop, protuberant brown eyes regarding the girl with amazement.

Aunt Sue was made of sterner stuff, though. "Young lady, I know you've been through a lot, but I'll thank you to keep a civil tongue in your head," she snapped, glaring at Christina's back, double chins wobbling in sympathetic outrage.

Christina turned back around and clapped her lips tightly together, staring defiantly at the pair of women.

As though frozen to the spot by the power of Christina's glare, Aunt Sue hesitated for a moment, looking at the three on the rug in front of her. When it was clear that Christina wasn't going to say anything more, she muttered, "good," turned back to the social worker and finished the transfer. Occasionally, though, she looked back over her shoulder, as if puzzled at this force of nature standing on the rug in the shelter's entry way.

Christina and her brothers remained at the Ash Creek shelter for just under three weeks, during which time Christina made a name for herself as a "defiant" child. She really didn't care what the adults thought, but the constant turmoil that surrounded her began to affect her younger brothers, already badly traumatized by the death of both parents. Nick and Ryan began to retreat into their own little world, using their own "twin language" for the first time in at least four years. It pained Christina to see the distance grow between them, but she was so caught up into her grief and sense of injustice that she couldn't bring herself to meekly acquiesce to the demands of the grownups.

At the end of the three weeks, Christina, her brothers, and all the other children at the shelter, as well as all the adults in the town were gathered and moved to the Laughlin Authorized Population Zone, one of the first APZs in the state. There the children all found themselves housed in a converted hotel, the boys in one wing and the girls in another. With them were other children from all over the state of Nevada and western Arizona up to the age of sixteen.

Once settled in the hotel, Christina continued asking her questions and spreading the information that had gotten her father killed. The caretakers in charge of this new shelter told her that until she began to follow directions and stopped stirring up trouble by spreading false information she wouldn't be allowed to visit with her brothers. When she still didn't fall in line, the adults told her that she would have to be removed from the program for awhile. That was how she found herself sitting in the little concrete cell.

Actually, Christina thought, it wasn't all that bad down here, without people yammering at her all the time, telling her that her dad was a liar and didn't know what he was talking about. The only people she saw were the people who brought her food and the occasional 'counselor' trying to talk sense into her. She had her books, and her thoughts, and was content for the time being until she could figure out a way to get free from here and take her brothers with her.

The other good thing about being here was that she'd met Him. He was the officer who'd brought her down here, and who came with the shelter staff when they showed up to try and convince her to drop her ideas. This Enforcer had nice eyes, though she thought they looked sort of sad and haunted.

Then, one afternoon, about three days after she'd been put in the cell, he came by himself. He told her he was in charge of the security station that afternoon, the one where the camera in her cell was monitored. He wasn't there about that, though. He wanted to ask her about the information her dad knew. Over and over again he asked her to repeat what her dad taught her and his eyes became more and more haunted with every telling.

This went on for several days; her talking, him listening. She wanted to know more about the APZ, and what was happening in the world outside, but he resisted her questions, always posing another of his own. Then, one day out of the blue, he began telling her about a place where one wasn't punished for telling the truth. It sounded truly fantastical, this place he described, as though it was in another dimension. He said it was a "camp" which seemed to mean a place where cowboys lived out closer to the cows. He said he'd been a cowboy. She studied him, trying to see the cowboy in the Enforcer. He was tall, with short-cropped wavy hair the color of the newly husked chestnuts she and her brothers used to collect every fall from the tree in their backyard; a sort of dark red-brown. His eyes were dark brown, almost black, and seemed so deep that you could fall into them if you weren't careful. She guessed that maybe he looked like a cowboy, but she wasn't sure.

He said that this camp was in a place that no seekers could find, and that if you hid there, you would be safe. Many of the things he described were hard to grasp. Christina had lived all her life in the city, seldom going camping or even spending days in the country, but as the man built upon his description of the camp, it began to take root in her mind.

Then one afternoon he didn't show up. When her meal was brought that evening, it was a different Enforcer escorting the shelter staff. The next day again he wasn't there. She wanted to ask about him, but was afraid of causing trouble. Besides, he'd never even told her his first name. All she knew was that the tag on his navy blue uniform said "O'Reilly."

As the week went on, and O'Reilly didn't come, Christina continued to think about the things he'd told her. She didn't know if he'd been killed in an uprising. He'd said there were some in the APZs when the residents protested the rules imposed upon them. She was afraid that maybe he'd been a late victim of the disease that had taken her mother.

But the thoughts that occupied her mind the most were those of the camp he'd told her about. The place where someone could live without worrying about this new government and this new rule where truth didn't count for much. It sounded lonely, and Christina wasn't sure if she could find it, let alone stay alive there, but it haunted her dreams more and more until she finally decided that, live or die, she had to try and get to it. She and her brothers.

The first thing, though, would be to get out of this isolation cell. And to do that, she would have to play along with the adults in charge of the shelter. With her mind filled with O'Reilly's descriptions, Christina waited for the shelter staff to arrive at the cell with dinner. As soon as the server got there, Christina would ask her to tell the administrator that she was ready to be a productive member of the APZ. Once she was out of here, she'd find her brothers and she would make a run for it; the camp he called Hideaway.

6

Two sets of wide, terrified green eyes met his as he stood in the doorway surveying the room. The woman's oval face, leached of all color under her summer tan, took on a grayish tint, as though she'd aged twenty years in twenty seconds. The boy beside her flushed, his mouth open as if to protest. The woman's hand rested on his shoulder, halting his movement and voice.

For one second... two... a thousand, there was silence, then in a soft voice robbed of all color she asked, "Who are you?"

When he didn't answer her immediately, but stood in the doorway as still as a statue, watching them, gun in hand, she spoke again, this time in a stronger voice, though with no less fear.

"How did you find us?"

"Are you the only two here?" the man asked, even though he was sure he knew the answer. He was curious to see if she would lie and try and convince him that help was only a short distance away, and would be home at any time.

The two plates on the side of the sink, the two glasses beside them, the two coats hanging on nails beside the door, and the two pairs of boots sitting underneath them all spoke of only two people being in residence. There was no indication anywhere in the front room that anyone else was living there.

The woman watched his eyes roam around the room, resting here and there. Her gaze followed his, and apparently she realized that it would be useless to try and prevaricate.

"Yes, there's just my son and me. What are you going to do with us?"

"Where are your guns?" He'd already seen one rifle on a rack near the door, but surely the woman couldn't be such a greenhorn that she only had one gun. He saw her drop her head slightly and knew that it was true. Only one gun, and she didn't even keep it nearby. Unbelievable.

"That's the only one. There by the door."

The man relaxed marginally, but didn't let his guard down completely. Just because she didn't have a gun didn't mean she wasn't dangerous. The proverbs of a mother bear protecting her young were accurate. There was nothing more cunning or more dangerous.

He stepped further into the room and closed the door behind him, shutting out the soft night sounds of crickets and frogs. Again he surveyed the room. Keeping the pair in sight he moved around the living space, turning as he went so that they were never behind his back. As he reached each of the four doors at the back of the main room, he opened them, and using a small pocket flashlight, quickly surveyed the interiors.

These rooms, closer to the actual wall of the canyon and tucked further back underneath the overhang, were windowless, side walls made of the same material as the outer wall of the house, but with a solid rock back wall and ceiling. The first three rooms were bedrooms, two evidently occupied and one used as a storage room, with bundles piled on the two double bunk beds. The fourth door hid a pantry which was pitifully empty, testifying to the hard work the pair was required to go through just to keep themselves fed.

As he moved around the room, the woman and her son swivelled in their seats, keeping him in sight, but they remained silent, the woman's hand still resting on her son's shoulder. Finally he returned to his original position near the door and looked directly at them again.

In the wordless stretch while he explored the house the woman had evidently regained some measure of her composure. Her body was still tense, but she met his stare directly. Her face was still ghostly pale but her gaze held a degree of challenge which surprised him. Her hand moved down from her son's shoulder to the table in front of her. Beside her the boy still looked terrified, his face so much like his mother's. The same honey gold hair, the same wide bottle green eyes, the same smooth, tanned skin. But where the mother had an oval face, and a long thin neck, the boy showed evidence of a more masculine structure to come with age. His chin was more squarely shaped, neck stockier, his shoulders already beginning to take on the broadness that would come with his future growth.

The pair sat still while the man studied them, tolerating his examination without protest though he could see a rising anger in the woman's eyes. He was impressed at how quickly she regained command of herself after the surprise of his entrance. She must have thought she was well beyond the reach of the Enforcers, and to have him show up on her doorstep had to have rocked her carefully tended belief that they had escaped.

Finally, when the suspense, fed to ripeness by the silence and menacing appearance of the man, was no longer bearable, the woman spoke.

"I asked who you are." Soft voice, a little husky. Tremors of fear under control.

"O'Reilly," said the man, "James O'Reilly," and he felt an unexpected frisson run though his body at the sound of his own name on his lips. It had been many weeks since he'd thought of himself as "O'Reilly" and even longer since he'd thought of himself by his full name. In many ways his journey to Hideaway had been much more than physical.

He'd thought that Jim O'Reilly had died with Sarah and Kay-Tee, back before the influenza, before the APZs and the secret. *That* O'Reilly had died in a car crash one night in January, four years ago, when a drunk driver lost control of his car and ran the silver Toyota Camry off the road where it plunged over a cliff to explode in flames at the bottom. *That* O'Reilly hadn't stood a chance, although he'd been sixty miles away at the time of the accident.

At least he'd thought that Jim O'Reilly died. But then there was that band of ghosts up by Oatman.

He'd believed in the governmental line that ghosts were traitors and they needed to be rounded up or terminated. But *that* band of ghosts was just a couple of families, trying to make it on their own. One was a little girl of ten or so. The squad destroyed them nonetheless. That night haunted him.

Then, before he had a chance to repair the cracks in his emotional fortress, he met that girl, Christina, at the Laughlin APZ, where he'd been assigned after balking and defying orders on the night of the "exorcism," the term the Enforcers gave their anti-ghost operations.

This girl was so smart, so brave. Even though she had brown hair and blue eyes, he saw in her his flame haired, green eyed ten-year-old Kay-Tee, questioning everything, wanting to know how everything worked, and carrying an undying faith in the invincibility of her father.

In meeting Christina, the Jim O'Reilly he'd thought dead and buried, and whom he really didn't want to reincarnate, started to reemerge anyway. Now, back in Hideaway, in the land where he grew up, *that* Jim O'Reilly was ready to take back his life.

"Okay, Mr. O'Reilly," said the woman, now completely in control of herself. Afraid, yes, but unbelievably in control. A flush stained her cheek and her green eyes glittered in defiance, head held rigidly upright on her slender neck. "It's obvious that you're an Enforcer, unless you attacked one and stole his shirt and weapon. Are you here to take us in to the APZ? I warn you, we worked too hard to get here. Unless you have a lot more help out there than it appears, you'll have trouble getting us to leave with you.

"Really," the woman continued, "It would make much more sense to leave us here. After all, the APZs are crowded, supplies are short, and we're not interfering with anyone out here. What does it matter if we're living here on our own." Her words began to speed up as if to fill in the vacuum left by his silence.

Suddenly, he made his decision, set his rifle on the table next to the door, walked over and pulled out a chair at the table across from the pair. Seated, he placed both hands on the table and looked both the woman, who'd grown silent when he made his move, and the boy in the eyes, one at a time.

"You have nothing to worry about. I don't intend to do anything with you."

"Oh, yeah?" replied the woman, looking quickly at her son then back at O'Reilly, eyes narrowed. "Then may I ask why you were standing in my doorway a moment ago, holding a gun and looking as though you were about to call the wrath of the so-called government down upon our heads?"

"No, I know how it looks, but I'm not an Enforcer any longer. I've left that life and I want nothing more than to be left in peace."

"Well, don't let us stop you," she replied acerbically. "Enjoy your trip to wherever it was you were heading. It was a pleasure meeting you... and your gun." There was a snort of strangled laughter from the boy, which earned him a glare from his mother. The man took his eyes from the woman's face for a second and glanced at the boy whose features had taken on a redder hue. He'd clapped his hand over his mouth as though trying to hold in either more laughter, or an additional comment.

"Actually," O'Reilly said, attempting a smile that felt foreign to his face, "this was where I was heading. Hideaway Camp. What I'd like to know is who are you and how did you and your son find this place? It's not exactly in the guidebooks of five star resorts in Arizona."

There was a brief silence as the woman pondered the wisdom of revealing their names, which was interrupted by the boy.

"I'm Mark Langton."

"Mark ...," the woman started.

"And this is my mother Maggie Langton. She writes stories for magazines and stuff and learned..."

"Mark!"

"What, Mom?"

"I'm not sure how much I trust Mr. O'Reilly, or how much we should be telling him about ourselves," the woman, whose name was apparently Maggie, stated, looking over O'Reilly again, obviously appraising the expression she found on his face and trying to decide whether or not he was telling the truth.

"I can assure you that I'm being honest to you when I say that I'm not here to cause you any trouble. But I'm not just passing through," he asserted quietly, in that soft gravely voice that drew so much attention.

"Wait just a minute...," Maggie started to bluster.

"I was brought up around here. I spent a great deal of time in this camp as a child, and I headed here with the intention of making it my home." He smiled again at her and the boy.

"When I saw that someone was already here, I had to rethink my plan a bit, since I figured I'd be out here on my own, but I'd guess that there's room for three. It might even make things easier, sharing the work and all."

He could see Maggie gritting her teeth, as though the taste of what he said was bitter beyond belief. He waited for her next shot, figuring that she wouldn't give in that easily.

"Mark," the woman finally said, "Would you please go out and check on Jenny and Lizzie."

"But..."

"Mark, I need to talk to Mr. O'Reilly alone for awhile and I'd like you to go out and make sure that Jenny and Lizzie are okay. Just hang out in the barn until I call you."

"Alright, I guess," Mark hesitated, then started to get up from his seat and head for the door.

"Mark," O'Reilly said.

Mark turned back, "Yeah?"

"My horses are over behind the barn, tied to the hitching rail. Would you be so good as to take them in, unsaddle them and turn them into that side pen with water while you're out there?" Then a "Wait" to the woman as she started to interrupt.

Mark hesitated, looked at his mother, and then as she subsided into her seat, face grim, he nodded. "Okay, Mr. O'Reilly. Wha... what should I do with your stuff?"

"Just leave it in the barn, I'll come out and get it later."

With another look at his mother, and a whistle to the dogs, Mark opened the door and headed out into the moonlit night.

Once Mark was gone, and the door was shut behind him, O'Reilly turned back to the woman. "What was it that you wanted to say without the boy?"

"I'm going to be straight with you," Maggie said, eyes unflinching and chin uplifted, giving her whole face a defiant demeanor. "It has been hard here. Mark and I don't have a lot of experience in this 'living off the land' thing, but if you think you're going to move in here and take advantage of the work we've done, and collect some fringe benefits on the side, you've got another thing coming."

"The fact is, lady..." he could see her start to rise again to the bait of his sarcastic use of the word "lady."

"The fact is, lady, it's perfectly obvious, even in the short time I've been watching, that you and the boy don't have the foggiest idea how to make a living out here." He paused, looking on as Maggie struggled with her temper.

"Your animals are fed adequately for now, but you're putting too many cows in a pasture that won't hold them for long. The horses' feet are in desperate need of attention. You can't just put shoes on a horse and leave them, so I'm guessing that you took those animals from someone who was dead, and brought them out here, not realizing that the shoes aren't a permanent addition.

"I've watched you ride for several days, now, and how you've managed to avoid being killed, I'll never know. Hell, I figure even if you make it through the summer down here, the winter will put an end to that. You've got very little food in your pantry..."

"We'll have the beef from the cows! And the milk! And the garden!" she interrupted sharply.

"Yeah, there's the garden, and you actually might be one of those women who knows how to put up food without creating a botulism farm. And, you've got the beef, if you actually know how to use that gun, and to dress out the meat. But as far as milk goes, were you aware that cow of yours needs to be bred again and have a calf to keep milking? No? I didn't think so," he said seeing the look of surprise on her face.

"The thing is this. Three can make it here probably as easily as two, especially since only one of those three, me, knows exactly what's involved with living on a camp in the middle of nowhere. And, as far as 'fringe benefits' are concerned, I don't take nothing from a woman that she don't want to give." He held up his hand as he saw Maggie start to interrupt again. "I'll take the third room, and I'll teach you and your boy what's involved in making a living out here. If it doesn't work out, then we'll figure out how else things can be arranged." His voice grew deeper and more serious. "But, I warn you, I don't intend to leave, and considering how things are going out in the 'civilized' world, I think making things work here with me is your best option."

He stopped talking, and watched Maggie evaluate her options. He could tell from the expressions that flitted across her face that she didn't like the corner she found herself in, but that she also didn't see an easy way out. Finally she took a deep breath, and looked at him again.

"Fine," she said in a cold sarcastic voice. "We accept your most gracious offer..."

He choked on a surprise burst of laughter, a sound he hadn't heard from his throat in, what, years? God, she had guts this one.

"As I said," she continued, bestowing on him a glare fit to char the meat off an elephant, "We accept your offer, on the condition that we're equal partners in this undertaking, and all decisions are made between the two of us. Mark and I are not your slaves to boss about."

He frowned, "There are a lot of things you don't know about life out here, things may need to be done and you wouldn't realize the importance of them..."

"Equal partners," she maintained firmly. "You seem like an intelligent, well spoken man, even if you are impressed with yourself a bit much." Again he felt the uprush of that unexpected laughter.

"I figure you can explain to me the importance of any actions that need to be taken. And I, being a moderately well educated woman, even if, as you say, completely lacking in survival skills, a point I'll debate with you later, will listen to you and make my judgement.

Dazed by this last convoluted argument, O'Reilly agreed to the partnership, wondering at the same time how he'd lost control of the situation. He wasn't used to losing his position of power when dealing with others. Sarah had been the only one who could run circles around him that thoroughly, and this woman certainly wasn't his sweet, quiet Sarah.

After agreeing to the formation of the new partnership, O'Reilly excused himself from the table, stating his intention of gathering his belongings and letting Mark know that he could come back to the house. On his way out to the barn he smiled to himself suddenly. Judging from tonight's encounter, the first battle of wits might, in some lights, be considered a draw, though he wasn't quite positive about that. It seemed the next few months would get more interesting than he'd originally figured.

7

The next morning the loud banging of pots and pans startled Maggie from a deep, troubled sleep, where navy uniformed Enforcers were marching her into a cell and interrogating her while holding a chicken over her head. Dragging herself from bed she opened the door of her room to find O'Reilly pouring milk though a clean piece of cheesecloth into several large containers. Mark was at the kitchen table stirring what appeared to be batter of some type, and Jack and Gypsy, the two dogs, appeared to be in a quandary over which human could be the most expected to produce spills needing to be cleaned up.

Upon hearing her door open, O'Reilly glanced in her direction, looking her up and down as she stood framed in the doorway, wearing the old Minnie Mouse pajamas that Mike had bought her as a joke the last time they went to Disney Land. "I've just got this thing about mice, I guess" he'd laughed when he'd presented them to her. "Squeak, squeak," she'd answered him.

When she and Mark had packed to run away, she just couldn't stand to leave the silly things behind. She had to leave so many other mementoes. Though, when she thought about it, Mark was the best memento of her husband that she could possibly have.

Pulling herself back to the here and now, she returned O'Reilly's look, seeing him for the first time dressed in boots, jeans, and a blue work shirt covering a white t-shirt. He'd found a bunch of worn clothes in storage in the empty bunk room last night and helped himself. He told Maggie that frequently cowboys would leave things like this at the camp so that if someone got stuck here in a storm they would have dry clothes to wear. The pantry was also left provisioned with a week's or month's worth of dry goods for the same reason.

Yawning and rubbing her hands over her sleep tousled hair to cover her discomfort at O'Reilly's scrutiny, Maggie asked, "What time is it?"

O'Reilly looked back down at the bucket in his hands. "5:30 or thereabouts, as if it makes a difference," he replied. "The cow's milked, calf's fed. Mark here is getting breakfast ready so you've got around fifteen minutes to get dressed before food's on the table."

Maggie bristled at his offhand approach, but she caught his meaning. He didn't intend to give orders as though she worked for him, but he made it clear that a cowboy's life started early in the day. It probably irked him that he had to restrain his comments since he was obviously a man accustomed to giving orders.

She nodded her understanding and stepped back into her room, closing the door behind her. Searching for jeans and a shirt, Maggie thought ruefully that she and Mark had been under the belief that they'd been working hard, but apparently they'd been slacking off by rancher's standards, rising late, dawdling through the chores without a set schedule. Apparently they were about to be indoctrinated into the agricultural lifestyle good and proper, and she wasn't quite sure how she felt about it.

Less than ten minutes later Maggie reemerged from her room, clothed and brushed, to find Mark at the stove while O'Reilly instructed him with moderate success how to flip the pancakes without throwing them on the floor or into the fire.

Mark looked back at his mother as she passed through the room on the way to the outer door, heading for the outhouse. The ten-year-old grinned and waved his spatula at her.

"Breakfast in five minutes. If you're late I'll feed it to the dogs," he called. The two dogs sitting at a respectful distance with tongues lolling and eyes avid indicated that the threat might be more than idle.

"No worries, kiddo, unless I fall in, in which case I don't care about the pancakes, just bring a rope," Maggie joked back as she opened the front door and stepped out into the fresh morning air.

Later, after enjoying a breakfast of pancakes with fresh butter and drizzled in honey that O'Reilly fished out of one of his packs, Maggie and O'Reilly headed outside to begin the day's labor, while Mark settled in to work on his school assignments. When O'Reilly heard about the morning's plans for Mark, he looked curiously at Maggie, but chose not to make any comments regarding the issue. Maggie caught the look, but refused to justify herself at that time.

On the way to the barn O'Reilly insisted that one of the first things that needed to be taken care of was to trim the feet of Maggie's four horses. "I'm stuck in a bit of a dilemma here," O'Reilly confided. "These horses have never had to make it out in the rocks, so their feet are soft. They depend on their shoes. The problem is that we don't have a supply of shoes any longer, so these horses are going to have to get used to going barefoot."

"What's wrong with that?" questioned Maggie.

"Well, there's nothing wrong with that," O'Reilly said, matter of factly, "It's just that they're going to be awfully sore footed for awhile. Think about when you were a kid and it finally warmed up in the spring so that you could go without shoes. How did it feel?"

Maggie winced at the memory. "Does that mean they can't be ridden?" she questioned.

"They can be ridden, but at the beginning they won't be able to be ridden much." At Maggie's worried look O'Reilly went on to assure her, "It's okay, their feet will toughen up just like yours did, but it will take awhile; months or more, before they're really rock footed." O'Reilly nodded to emphasize what he was saying. "Also, we'll be able to save the shoes we do have, so that if there's an emergency and we have to take them out for longer, I can slap a set of shoes on for the trip, then pull them off again when we're done. We'll get more use out of them that way."

"Okay," agreed Maggie, still not sure. "But what about your horses?"

"I caught these horses up off a ranch near Laughlin after I left the APZ. They'd been running out on the range and weren't shod already. Their feet will be fine as long as I keep knocking off any long bits. They're used to making it in the rocks out here. Not like your horses. They're city horses and have never had to make a living in a spot where the feed isn't brought to them." He looked out of the corner of his eye at Maggie, "Sort of like some people I know."

"Alright, enough of the city slicker comments," she growled. "Show me what needs to be done."

For the remainder of the morning O'Reilly worked on the horses' feet, carefully trimming away the excess growth and returning the hooves to the proper balance using tools found stashed in the barn. Fortunately, he said, it appeared that the horses had been trimmed not too long before the disease struck and their owners died. Their feet were long, but they weren't nearly as bad as they could have been.

Maggie was nervous about having her primary means of transportation, and more importantly escape, put in an 'out of commission' status. However, she realized that if the horses weren't cared for properly, they wouldn't be available if and when the proverbial cow poop hit the fan. She watched carefully all the moves O'Reilly made, asking questions the entire time. Her journalistic background made her a voracious seeker of information, and in this case the information could be vitally important to her survival. By the fourth horse, she demanded to try it for herself.

"You're sure?" O'Reilly asked dubiously, sweat beaded his arms and matted his dark red hair to his head. He wiped his face on the sleeve of his t-shirt. "It's not an easy job for a city sli... uh, I mean, novice." He grinned. The smile looked more natural than those that came before, and less like someone with a face full of botox or the victim of abnormal muscle contractions.

"Yes, I'm sure," Maggie stated with a determined set to her face, and a stubborn tone to her voice. "You were right when you said Mark and I didn't have the skills we needed to live out here for an extended period. Hopefully it won't be that long," O'Reilly gave her a puzzled look, "but we need to be prepared for anything."

Two long hours later Maggie had finally completed her horse's front feet to O'Reilly's demanding standards and was dripping with enough sweat to raise the ocean's level at least two inches. O'Reilly was taking it easy on a nearby boulder in the shade, *enjoying the view,* she thought sarcastically. She slowly straightened to a standing position, flexing her blistered hands and rolling her shoulders. Breathing heavily, she wiped her sweaty face with the back of one dirty forearm, then massaged her sore back. Her hair, darkened with sweat, felt as though it was glued to her head.

"People actually do this for a living?" she asked in incredulous tones. "What *are* they, masochists?"

"Don't worry," O'Reilly said, hiding a smile. "You only have two more feet to go. At this rate you'll be done by midnight."

"You, my friend, are a sadist," Maggie stated with conviction. "And I am a complete fool for asking to be subjected to this torture. When all of this is over, I will never look at a horse's foot again. They can look elsewhere for their pedicures."

"You're thinking that this situation won't last long?" O'Reilly asked in an offhand manner, causing Maggie to glance quickly in his direction. He was still sitting on his boulder, but he no longer appeared relaxed. Instead of looking at her, he seemed busy studying the lines and creases of his darkly tanned hands.

"Well, how long can it last?" she replied, studying his bent form. "Sooner or later the government will get their act back together. People aren't going to put up with this concentration and APZ crap for long. They're going to want to get back to their lives. At the most a year, maybe a year and a half."

"Mmmm," he gave a non-committal answer and continued to examine his cuticles.

Maggie tilted her head, looking at him intently. "I don't get you. You left the APZ and left the Enforcers, and you haven't given me a reason. What are you hiding?"

Every muscle in O'Reilly's body telegraphed his discomfort at this interrogation and Maggie began to wonder if their newly formed partnership would stand the strain of the tension without ripping asunder.

Finally, after a long silence O'Reilly looked up and met Maggie's eyes. "I had my reasons for leaving the APZ and the Enforcers, and those reasons are something that we're going to have to talk about sooner or later. I realize that. It's just that right now I'm trying to make sense of them in my own mind, and I don't know how to explain them to someone else so that they seem rational."

"You've got to understand how much trouble I have accepting that," Maggie countered.

"Yeah, I know it sounds shaky," he sighed. His dark brown eyes took on a distant expression. "It's just the way it is. The thing is this, though. I want you to think about what direction the government, and the world as a whole, has been heading for the past twenty or thirty years, and do you really think that now that the authorities have total control over a completely demoralized population, they're going to willingly give up that control any time soon?"

Maggie's look sharpened, her brow furrowed as she considered the scenario he presented and her journalistic sixth sense began to send out a clamourous ringing of warning bells. "You're saying that they're going to try and... what, develop a world where people only live in designated areas, under supervision and control? I can't see how that would ever work," Maggie stated adamantly, though even as she said it, a small voice in her mind spoke to the truth of the plan.

O'Reilly looked up at her, studying her intently.

"Global warming has been a concern of all the world's governments for quite awhile now, even though many say it isn't true. What's one of the chief causes of global warming? People. People and all the things that people make and drive and are probably unwilling to give up. People and their wasteful habits and their refusal to take the environment seriously.

"Now answer this question, what would be the best thing to happen to the environment? Reduce the number of people. Well, mother nature took care of that problem." A fleeting look crossed O'Reilly's face, more a flicker in his eyes, so quick that Maggie almost missed it. "Now our administration, with it's loudly proclaimed green agenda, is considering taking up where mother nature left off." O'Reilly's agitation was growing extreme. He rose from his boulder as if pulled upright by an electric current.

"Oh, come on." It was Maggie's turn to become agitated. "Do you really think that people are going to let the government get away with this? You can't be serious." Yet still the warning bells rang in the back of her mind.

The pressure was finally too much for O'Reilly. "Who do you think has been running this country for the past couple of decades, lady? Politicians and lawyers, that's who. People have been giving up their responsibility for a long time now, and if you think that those politicians and lawyers wouldn't make this type of decision, will give up the control they have now, think again. They've been making these type of decisions on smaller scale for a long time now." O'Reilly spun on his heel and stalked away toward the creek.

Maggie was left sanding there, stunned, with no company but a half trimmed horse that was beginning to look impatient, a small black and white calf, and two sleeping dogs. Her mind was a whirl of ideas.

Part of her kept denying O'Reilly's statement, but there was a small niggling part of her that said there was truth in his words.

She stood on the bare, dusty ground, looking at the stream where O'Reilly stood facing the running water, head bowed. After a few minutes of hesitation Maggie began to walk over toward him, wondering what she would say when she got there. As she approached him, he turned and the torment in his eyes was as obvious as a slap in the face. She faltered and stopped.

He looked at her, his face and body under iron control, even if his eyes betrayed him.

"There are a lot of things we are going to have to discuss, though not now. Needless to say, as an Enforcer, I was introduced to a number of things that I didn't want to see, and that I'm not proud of participating in. I know you have questions, and you'll get the answers, though you may not like them. The only thing I can assure you now, though, is that I'm no danger to you and your boy. I may be the one thing that will keep you from dying in the next few months. And, the secrets I hold do not require immediate attention. Our first goal should be to get this place set for survival. I can tell you that it will probably be a very long time, if ever, before you get the chance to go home again."

Nodding her head slowly, and ruthlessly squashing all the questions that her journalistic instincts threw up in her mind, Maggie turned back toward the barn and the waiting horse, then turning her head, looked at O'Reilly and simply said, "Okay, come on. I've got two more feet to finish."

8

There was a sharp rap on the outside of the office door, followed by an equally sharp "enter" from the dark haired man sitting behind the large wooden desk covered with papers and maps.

The door swung open with a bang, admitting a sandy haired young deputy. He came to a stop in front of the desk, snapping the large, barrel chested man sitting there a salute.

Great, thought Captain Seth Rickards, *it's one of the military ones,* his expression sour. With the recent devastation of the country's population, the government had been forced to cobble together a new type of law enforcement agency from the remnants of the many different military and law enforcement agencies in place before everything went to hell. Because the members of this new agency came from so many diverse backgrounds, the ranks had become intermingled, as had the rituals and procedures.

Rickards had served the Laughlin Police Department for the past thirty years, since joining the force at twenty-five upon his graduation from the academy. Now he found himself in the position of having to integrate and streamline this branch of the newly formed, quasi military group aptly named the Enforcers. He took his job seriously, and worked hard to bring his team together, but he still hated dealing with the salutes and sirs that the military group brought to the table.

Fixing the deputy with an intense stare, designed to turn a subordinate's bowels to water, Rickards snapped, "What's the report?"

Deputy Knox seemed oblivious to the intensity being directed at him from the brown eyes. "Sir, the northwest annihilation team reports the areas of Preston, Lund and Hiko have been erased."

Rickards cringed inwardly at the matter of fact way that Knox reported the eradication of hundreds of homes and businesses. Most

48

of the owners of these buildings were dead; some in the fire storms that had ravaged the Southwest for the past ten years, but many more from the disease that put the exclamation point to the end of an era. A few of these places, however, still had owners who where housed here in the Laughlin APZ, or in the Elko APZ to the north. Owners who came here expecting their properties to be waiting for them when they were allowed to return. In spite of his belief that what he and the other Enforcers had done was necessary for the community's good, he still felt a wave a guilt over the wanton destruction, and over the lies that had been told to the people they were sworn to protect.

The government gave a plausible excuse for the destruction. First they said there were so many buildings that had been damaged during the last few years of monster wild fires and violent weather, that they needed to be removed to prevent danger to the people when they returned.

In addition, the government line was that many of these buildings were incubators for the disease. The authorities said that bedding and other belongings harbored the virus, and just as in the middle ages up through the 19th century it was accepted practice to burn the belongings of plague victims, the government now had to make similar decisions to prevent any more deaths from the influenza..

Maybe, thought Rickards. His wife had been a nurse, and while he'd learned from her that animals could frequently become reservoirs for disease for long periods of time, and in fact the common held belief was that birds had been the original purveyors of this virus that had so devastated the world's population, he couldn't remember her ever telling him about viruses that lived for longer than a few weeks or months on inanimate objects. Maybe the authorities meant that there was a possibility that animals would get into the buildings and become infected and thereby become reservoirs, but somehow he doubted it. The Enforcers weren't the only ones twisting the truth to make it more appetizing.

Finally, the government claimed that these abandoned buildings provided the perfect hiding place for ghosts, those people who had avoided concentration, refused the authority of the restructured government, and were now considered dead for all intents and purposes.

Rickards felt a wave of nausea roil through his stomach at the thought of these cutesy little names that were being handed out right, left and center. This post apocalypse era seemed to be filled with new meanings for old terms: ghost, exorcism, concentration, APZ. *Why the hell do we always have to try and pretty things up?* Rickards thought. *It's not as if it makes the situation any more palatable. We're still destroying buildings, lives and changing futures, even if it is for the people's own good.*

As much as it disgusted him, though, he knew these acronyms and other forms of shortened terms had been around for probably as long as there had been governments and other bureaucratic agencies. He didn't have to like it, though.

The problem of ghosts plagued him every day. The government considered these malcontents to be nothing short of terrorists, committing treason by refusing the concentration order, avoiding the APZs, and stealing from the communities' already short supplies in order to survive. The governmental stance on ghosts was simple. Concentrate those possible of being converted to the community way of mind, and exorcize, or eradicate, those groups too entrenched and violent to be converted.

Fortunately for him, and for the other Enforcers, the majority of people were so demoralized by the devastation wrought by the virulent disease that they were more than willing to let anyone who acted as though he knew what he was doing take charge. The concentration of the population of southern Nevada and the adjoining areas of California and northwestern Arizona had gone much easier than Rickards had ever imagined possible. Nevertheless, a few holdouts remained and now he asked impatiently for the deputy's report on the most recent excursion of the exorcism team.

"Team A surprised a small group of ghosts northwest of here about ten miles," Knox reported. "They were well armed, with weapons apparently taken from abandoned homes and businesses in the area. There were five adult males and two adult females, as well as three children, two of them infants."

Knox paused. "What was the result?" Rickards rapped out.

"The adults put up a fight, and all seven were terminated. The three young children were brought in and taken to the Nursery. After the fight it was discovered that this was the group that intercepted the supply shipment from the Elko APZ two weeks ago. They had the truck with all the food hidden in a large barn on the property. It has been recovered and brought in."

"Good," said Rickards. That was the worst thing about the ghosts.

Until the government was able to get the farms and factories back up and into production with a limited task force, APZs were forced to be extremely careful with the food and other goods that had been on the shelves prior to the climax of the disease when all production and importation halted. These ghosts had probably stolen enough food to last them six months to a year, while others here in the APZ went without.

Deputy Knox stood at attention, waiting for a dismissal from the captain.

"One last thing before you go, Knox," said Rickards, "Has there been any word of O'Reilly?"

"From what we can tell, O'Reilly made it out of the APZ, probably through the northwest entrance. We think from there he headed north, but it's not certain." A slight note of amazement crept into the deputy's voice. "He's done an impressive job of hiding his tracks, sir. He just seems to have disappeared into the back country. There have been no suspicious sightings on the seekers, nor have any of the patrols caught wind of him."

Rickards' stomach soured again at the thought of O'Reilly, gone without a trace. With the information the man possessed, he was a danger that the authorities could not afford to leave at liberty. The odds were, with his taciturn nature, O'Reilly might easily head somewhere remote by himself and never encounter another human. However, recently he'd seemed different, less the self contained hermit, although he didn't interact any more with his fellow Enforcers. But there was that girl in isolation at the nursery. He left her there, though, when he disappeared. *He couldn't have been that invested*, Rickards thought.

It had always been hard to understand what was revolving in O'Reilly's mind. There were rumors of a tragedy not long ago in his past that changed him. Hard to say if those rumors were true, since no one here knew him before the creation of the Enforcers and the concentration.

Hell, he thought, *no one knew anyone here before the concentration. Survivors were too few and far between for it to be anything more than chance that someone might know another person in his unit.*

Considering his options, Rickards said, "Have someone see if they can do some research into O'Reilly's past. There might be something in the personnel file that would help us understand him and where he's headed. Go back as far as possible. There's got to be some clue about where he would go."

Deputy Knox nodded and, saluting again, turned to leave.

"Knox, tell them to make this a priority. We have to find him and either bring him back in for questioning, or eliminate him all together. Am I understood?"

"Yes, sir," Knox stated, standing again at attention. "I will relay the message," and he turned swiftly and left the room.

Rickards rose from his desk and began to pace the room, finally coming to a stop before the window looking out toward the Colorado River. *He's got to be found. O'Reilly's got to be found and removed before he spreads dissension, before he causes an upheaval that will break down this whole shaky new system of doing things.*

9

Maggie was ripped out of a deep sleep to find herself lying on the lumpy, thin mattress that was her bed, drenched in an adrenaline induced sweat, heart beating so hard it felt as though it was going to burst from her chest..

She lay there, staring at the ceiling, or where the ceiling would be if she could see it. These back rooms, built snugly into the overhanging cliff, received no light from outside unless the door was open. Most people, brought up to take the electronic glow of the alarm clock and other electronic indicators for granted, had never experienced the utter darkness that can occur when those things were no longer available. In the past few weeks, however, Maggie had grown to appreciate the soft, quiet darkness that fell with night.

Now, however, as she lay there wondering what had woken her so abruptly, the darkness took on a menacing quality, as though monsters crouched in the corners, ready to spring at her slightest movement.

Then she heard it again. The hoarse shout, indecipherable, from somewhere else in the stone house. Rising from her bed, she fumbled for the flashlight that she kept within reach at night, shook it a few times to regenerate the batteries and turned it on. Following its soft yellow glow, she walked out into the main room of the house and paused. Everything was as she'd left it when she went to bed that night, exhausted from a day spent learning those things that O'Reilly felt necessary to their survival. *Damned slave driver.*

Again she heard the voice, clearer this time, though no more intelligible, and she moved toward the other two rooms. She paused briefly at Mark's door, turned the knob and listened at the crack, hearing nothing but his soft breathing, slow and deep. *That kid could sleep through a tornado*, she thought, smiling to herself. Hearing the voice raised again in anger she quietly closed Mark's door and moved on toward the third room, which O'Reilly had taken as his.

Halting outside the door, she could hear clearly the voice from inside.

"No, no, no. Stop! Stop I said! It isn't right! You can't! NO, STOP!" The soul crushing pain that permeated the words froze her to the spot, her hand outstretched for the door knob, but unable to turn it. Then the voice retreated from its roar, to an agitated murmur and she found the courage to knock lightly, then turned the knob and pushed the door ajar.

Playing the beam from the flashlight around the interior of the room, it illuminated one of the bunks, blankets tangled at the foot. O'Reilly, apparently waking when she knocked, pushed himself up on one elbow, rubbing his eyes with his free hand.

"What is it?" he asked. "What's wrong?"

"I heard some yelling. Actually it woke me," Maggie answered, taking in his dark, sweat soaked hair, his dampened arms and torso and the knotted blankets

"You must have been dreaming," he growled, looking up at her and squinting in the beam of the flashlight. "Everything's fine in here. Go back to sleep." He threw himself down onto his side, facing away from the door, giving her a view of nothing but his muscular back.

Fine, just damned fine, Maggie thought as she pulled back through the door, angry at the brusk way he'd brushed off her concern. *Just keep your nightmares to yourself from now on.*

Closing the door, she made her way back down to her room and returned to her bed.

She lay awake for a long time thinking, however. Wondering what James O'Reilly, ex-cowboy, ex-enforcer, and current ghost, had gone through to cause such a well of pain to exist. And what would that mental torment mean to all of them in the upcoming months.

10

It had taken Christina a week to convince the caregivers at the nursery that she was ready to play along, and to allow her to rejoin the rest of the children on the upper level of the converted hotel. Her abrupt change of heart was met with suspicion by those who'd decided to lock her away. Finally, however, they decided that she'd seen the light, and brought her back upstairs.

Being released from isolation, however, seemed to be the limit of her progress. A week after coming above ground she was no closer to getting on with her plan than she had been when locked in the cell in the basement. At least it felt that way.

While sitting in the small subterranean room, Christina put a lot of thought into what she needed to make good her escape. At the top of the list were her brothers. There was absolutely no way she was leaving without them. The problem was, however, that the boys and girls were housed in different wings of the hotel, which they had, unoriginally in Christina's mind, decided to call the "Nursery." Geez, the Nursery. Like they were some little babies or something! Granted, there were about thirty or forty little kids on the lower floors, but still, it was insulting.

She sighed as she put away her clothes in the dresser drawers allotted to her. She had been assigned a room with a fourteen-year-old named Alysa Thalman, a pretty girl with a round face, huge, dark brown, almond shaped eyes, straight black hair and skin the color of an aged penny. Unfortunately, Christina thought, Alysa also had the curiosity and ambition of a snail. Several times during the past week Christina had carefully ventured to broach the subject of the APZs, and the people's imprisonment there, but each time Alysa had looked at Christina as though she had suddenly grown a few extra heads, and possibly an arm or two.

If pushed too hard, Alysa would say that the APZs were the only way that the government could make sure that everyone was cared for, and that it was important that all of them work together to make sure that all members of the community had what they needed. Her words so exactly mimicked those of the teachers at the Nursery that Christina began to wonder if she'd been programed just like a computer.

Her dad had told her how loss and sadness could affect some people; make them more malleable, a word dad had taught her to mean flexible, or easily molded. Christina loved learning new words and ideas from her dad and constantly pestered him to teach her more, more, more... A sudden spike of pain slashed through her middle. She missed him so much.

Based on the other things her father taught her, and the things she'd seen since coming to the APZ, she figured that brainwashing wasn't out of the question. When the Nursery was formed, the caregivers had apparently felt that it was important to get back to a semblance of normalcy as quickly as possible.

And for the kids, that meant school.

The problem was the most of the teachers had died, along with everyone else, in the influenza outbreak that swept across the country. When she thought about it, though, that might have worked in the government's favor since they could then handpick the people they wanted teaching the children. They could handpick the curriculum as well, she thought, because from what she could see from the classes she'd attended this week, lessons had changed radically from when she was last in school a few months ago.

Sure, there was still reading and writing and math. You couldn't get away from those things if you tried. But now there was an emphasis on the environment, reducing the "footprint" of the humans on the planet, and organizing communities so that everyone was taken care of, while the planet was also left in a healthier condition.

It was interesting, Christina thought, that while her mother was an environmental scientist, and had frequently talked about the damage of greenhouse gases and that type of thing, the lessons being taught at the Nursery school seemed to be taking her ideas to such an extreme that Christina almost didn't recognize them. It scared her. Badly.

To distract herself from the chilling thought that the people in the APZ were being programmed, Christina turned her mind once again to her escape plan.

Several times during the week she'd asked to see her brothers, but so far had been denied. She figured that the powers that be still didn't fully trust her, and they wanted to watch her for awhile. *So be it,* she thought. She'd be the best little robot they'd ever seen if it meant that she'd get some freedom and be allowed to visit Nick and Ryan.

The rest of her plan required her to stockpile some food and other supplies, find a map of northern Arizona, and find a weakness in the defenses surrounding the APZ so that when they did make a break for it, they wouldn't be immediately spotted and brought back. She guessed that she wouldn't get a second chance if she were caught.

None of these things had been easy so far. Christina's assigned chores were in cleaning, so she didn't have access to any easily portable and storable food supplies. The ideal situation, she thought, would be to be assigned to the kitchen detail. She had to be careful, however, because if she pushed for a change of assignment, people might become suspicious. So far, she'd merely dropped hints about enjoying cooking and liking to help in her mom's kitchen. She hoped that someone would catch on and consider moving her soon.

Christina had also been assigned a counselor, as had all the children in the Nursery, to help her deal with the loss of family and home. Shandra was a young woman with black hair and skin the color of a toasted almond, who admitted to Christina that she'd been a third year psychology student prior to the outbreak of the virus, and based on that limited experience had been assigned to the Nursery. Shandra was nice, but Christina felt that she had to be extra careful with what she said, since she was pretty sure that any suspicious actions or remarks would be relayed directly to the Enforcers in charge of the Nursery. Still, Christina didn't think it would hurt to 'reminisce' wistfully about her imaginary kitchen expertise.

She was having a bit more luck with the rest of her plan, though she still hadn't been able to secure a map, which could be a deal breaker. She'd managed to secret away several warm blankets, hiding them in a small utility closet near her room. She'd also managed to get her hands on a couple of canteens that some of the Enforcers had left sitting in the dining room after a meal. She still had a long way to go, but there were no doubts in her mind that she would manage, just given time and patience. That's what dad had always said about science; that it just needed time, patience and imagination.

Christina was standing at the window of her room looking out over the city, toward the Colorado River and Arizona on the far side, daydreaming about the deep canyon with its running stream and green meadow. In her mind she could see everything just as O'Reilly had described it; house built back beneath the undercut of the cliff, blending so perfectly that you couldn't see it at first unless you knew where to look. Large front windows facing out onto the pasture with its barn and windmill. Just as she was losing herself in the image of the rising cliff walls, enfolding her and protecting her, she was startled back into the here and now by the banging of the room door being opened suddenly by Alysa.

"Christina, grab your shorts and a t-shirt and hurry. They're taking us on an outing to the river to go swimming."

"What do you mean?" Christina asked, turning from the window. "We've got the pool."

"Yeah, but the caretakers thought we'd like to get out and see the river. A lot of us have never been there since we're not from this city. We're all going. Come *on*," Alysa urged with more animation than Christina had seen in her during the entire the week she'd lived there. She remembered that when Alysa had shared a little about her life before being concentrated she'd mentioned living in a small town in the country where she could go out and wander in the desert near her home whenever she felt like it. Maybe the *"it's for our own good"* line that Alysa had been repeating wasn't as ingrained as it seemed.

As Christina rummaged through her drawers looking for a pair of shorts and a shirt she could wear to the river, she glanced back over her shoulder at the excited Alysa, "What do you mean that we're all going? All the girls?" She felt a tremor of hope spark inside her.

"No, all of us. At least all of us old enough to go. I don't think they're taking the little babies. But everyone over, say, seven or eight? Boys and girls. We're going to have lunch down there and not come back until this afternoon."

Christina felt the spark of hope grow. *Please, please, please let them take Nick and Ryan. Please let them be old enough. Please, please let me be able to talk with them.* She hurriedly grabbed her clothes, threw them on and, stuffing a towel into a small day pack, rushed out the door, followed closely by Alysa.

11

Maggie groaned as she fell into bed, every muscle in her body protesting at the unaccustomed work she'd been demanding of them. The last two weeks had passed in a blur, with O'Reilly unrelenting in his demands that she and Mark master the skills required to live at the camp. Sure, there were down times, fun times, but even those were filled with activity instead of sitting quietly in an easy chair, reading a book.

That first night Maggie had been sure she was going to die. That all her muscles were going to rise in revolt leaving her flopping on the ground like a fish out of water.

The second night she thought that she might actually survive, although as a permanent cripple, requiring assistance to do simple things like use the outhouse.

The third and fourth nights, survival became a sure thing, and although she wasn't convinced that she was looking forward to it, she was pretty sure that she didn't prefer it to a swift and painless death.

Now finally, when she slipped between the blankets, she ached, but she knew that she was becoming stronger, and that in the morning she would be ready for whatever new tortures O'Reilly had cooked up.

Several times during the week she had again been awakened by the sounds of O'Reilly's nightmares. Twice she had gone to stand by the door, listening as he thrashed and cried out. After his recent abrupt dismissal of her concern, however, she chose not to open the door again. Every time she stood there she heard anew the pain, the frustration and the torment that he worked so hard conceal during the day. Her curiosity, always a driving force in her life, ate away at her, but she decided that a subtle approach would gain her more than a direct assault. To that end, she watched and waited, taking note when his defenses seemed to be the weakest, when he was the most likely to share his inner thoughts and let his guard down.

She had plenty of opportunities to observe him during the last few days. Since she still insisted that Mark put in part of every day in school work, she became O'Reilly's primary pupil and they spent a great deal of time together. As much as she hated admitting it, he had much more experience in this type of life than did she, and she found herself relying on him more and more to decide what needed to be done around the camp.

During the past two weeks the garden had been put in, one much bigger than the one that she and Mark started. O'Reilly asserted that they didn't have any idea how much would be required to get them through the winter, and that what they'd planted would barely get them through the summer. To water the garden, she and O'Reilly dug several irrigation ditches, which Maggie insisted rivaled the depth of the Grand Canyon. They had also rejuvenated the irrigation system that served a small orchard at the far end of the meadow. All the horses had pedicures, she could now milk the cow in under thirty minutes, and she and Mark together were learning to rope.

Okay, Maggie grudgingly admitted to herself while mentally cataloging the progress of the past two weeks, *Mark is learning to rope. I'm learning the best way to tangle a rope, and how to make steam erupt from O'Reilly's ears and potentially induce a fatal stroke, should it become necessary in the future.* She sighed and turned over, trying to find a comfortable position on the old mattress.

O'Reilly took Mark out one day on horseback, moving Maggie's hard won cows up to a nearby pasture, further from the possible prying camera eyes of any seekers. Maggie was sad to see them go, but O'Reilly'd made a point when he said that the pasture needed to be kept fresh as possible, since they would be unable to provide hay in the winter and the horses would have to fend for themselves. He also said that most of the horses would have to be turned up in the other pasture which made Maggie uncomfortable, but she had to admit he had more knowledge of livestock, and the feeding of such, than she did.

That evening when they came home, they were packing a large buck, which O'Reilly proceeded to butcher out, cut into strips and demonstrate the correct way to make venison jerky. He explained that in the warm weather, jerky would be about all they could do with larger animals they killed.

Feeling her stomach rise into her throat at the sight of Bambi being reduced to strips of meat, Maggie merely nodded. The sight of Maggie's pale face brought a slightly sarcastic grin to O'Reilly's.

"Where did you think the meat on your dinner table came from? This is it."

"Is it too late to become a vegetarian?"

Later that evening, however, as she savored a venison steak, prepared by Mark and O'Reilly, the designated cooks for the evening, she reconsidered her planned dietary change. She claimed it was the best steak she'd had in a long time, and silently tried to get the sight of the deer's lifeless eyes out of her mind

One of the most important projects that O'Reilly insisted on, and that Maggie had the greatest difficulty in accepting, was that they develop an escape plan. When she questioned him about the need for something that drastic, he looked at her, then up at the yellow, red and pink water-stain-streaked canyon walls that towered above them.

"What do you think will happen if they find us holing up in here?"

"What makes you think that they will find us?" She bristled at the implication that she'd never paid attention to her surroundings. "Surely we're far enough out that they won't bother to send seekers or search parties. They can't *want* to waste their resources in that manner, can they?"

"Think what you want," he retorted sharply. "But for me, I want a place to go if they should show up, and while this canyon is a great place to hide out, it can also be a great trap. I want a fall back plan."

Eventually Maggie gave in, acknowledging that having a hideout within the hideout wouldn't hurt anything. That afternoon O'Reilly took Mark and Maggie and headed for the caves at the northern end of the pasture.

When Maggie and Mark first arrived at Hideaway, Mark had been excited by the caves peppering the sides of the canyon. Some were high with no visible way of reaching them, but others were near ground level and Mark was eager to begin exploring. Maggie, however, had laid down the law in regards to possible subterranean exploration. First and foremost, he was never, ever, on pain of death and fear of a furious mother, to enter any of the caves without her. Maggie had no idea what might be in a cave, but those that went further back than could be easily viewed from the entrance stirred in her an ill defined fear that curdled her stomach. She had visions of bears and mountain lions (*foolish* she told herself), snakes and bats (*maybe not so foolish*), and dead prospectors whose ghosts were determined to protect their claims (*totally, absolutely and unequivocally nutso, cause for immediate commitment to a mental hospital*).

Dead prospectors' ghosts or not, so far Mark had respected his mother's commands and hadn't ventured into any of the caves. At least she hoped not. It helped that they'd been so busy just staying alive and fed that free time to go exploring was hard to come by. Now, however, regardless of her fears, the caves were exactly where they were heading and she felt a sudden burning desire for a clove of garlic, a cross, or anything else that might drive the ghosts away.

O'Reilly knew exactly where he was going, apparently, and aimed straight for a small inconsequential hole, near the northern end on the western side of the meadow behind the old orchard. It was about ten feet above ground level, though a steep scree made access possible, if not easy. Near the mouth of the small cave grew a large juniper, roots entwined among several large boulders, all but obscuring the opening unless you knew where to look.

Having scrambled up the loose, rocky slope, the three stood at the entrance, peering into the dusky gloom beyond. Mark was almost jumping out of his skin in excitement, ready to rush into the lead but O'Reilly put out an arm, halting him.

"Slow down, buddy, you don't want to go ramming around in these caves. They're filled with side turns, drop offs as well as rock falls." Maggie's nervousness ratcheted up a few more notches. "You also need to always know where you're putting your feet and your hands," O'Reilly warned. "Rattlesnakes love these places during the hot weather. It keeps them cool during the day time and there are usually a fair number of rodents who wander in here, making for good eating."

"Maybe we should reconsider," Maggie started.

"*Mom.*"

"Well, maybe there's somewhere safer," she continued, over Mark's protest, "and not so... well... so creepy."

A snort of laughter met her ears, though when O'Reilly turned back to look at her, his face was perfectly straight, dark brown eyes serious.

"Listen, yeah, there are dangers in here, but there's no where else in this canyon that you have any hope of eluding people who really want to find you."

"What good does eluding them do if you fall down a shaft and wind up sitting in the middle of a pile of rattlesnakes?" Maggie shot back.

"Well, I don't know, I guess you could throw snakes at them if they came after you. Either that or make a really nice hatband while you're waiting to be captured and hauled off to an APZ. *If* they let you get that far," he answered sarcastically.

Mark's head swivelled on his neck as he looked back and forth between the two of them arguing. "Mom, it's okay. I trust Mr. O'Reilly. He said he and his brother spent a lot of time in these caves when he was a kid. He knows where we're going." Mark looked pleadingly at his mother, obviously eager to proceed in spite of the mention of snakes and armed pursuit.

Maggie relented, grudgingly, acknowledging to herself how large a place O'Reilly had already taken in Mark's life.

Mark's father had been a hero in his life, and for several months following Mike's death Mark had spoken of him often, holding up what he thought his father would do in certain situations as proof that they were heading in the right or wrong direction. Over this past week Mike's name had come up less frequently, and simultaneously "What Would O'Reilly Do?" became Mark's mantra.

Maggie felt a pang at this change. She understood it. Mike was dead. He could no longer be there to protect them, and in these days of fear and uncertainty Mark needed someone to look to for strength and as a role model. She just missed Mike so much and regretted any thinning of the connection between them.

"Okay, I'm going first," O'Reilly stated. "Mark you're second and Maggie, you're bringing up the rear. Do not go past me. Do not go anywhere I do not go, even if you see something you think is cool. No taking side trips, understand?"

"Yes, sir," Mark snapped O'Reilly a mock salute that made him smile.

"I spent a lot of time in these caves, but that was over twenty years ago, and there likely have been changes since then, so we're going to go carefully this first time."

"How do we keep from getting lost?" Maggie queried.

"Every time we change directions we'll use loose rocks to make an arrow pointing back in the direction we came from. We'll have time later to make the markers less obvious once we find where we want to set up camp." Maggie and Mark nodded in concert and the three ventured into the cool gloom of the cave.

Once past the entrance, it seemed that the ambient temperature dropped at least twenty degrees and Maggie suppressed a slight shiver. O'Reilly proceeded deeper into the cave, heading for the back wall which appeared solid in the dim light. He didn't hesitate though, and moved to the left around a large rock, and bending down, moved into a small opening which appeared like magic.

The thought passed through Maggie's mind that anyone giving the cave a cursory inspection might not even venture in as far as the back wall since you could see it from the entrance, and therefore might miss this second opening all together, hidden as it was behind this boulder.

O'Reilly kept a running commentary going while walking. "We need to get a pine or juniper bough here to mask our footprints in the dust and sand. It would need to be kept at the opening and once used, stashed in the inner cave here.

Once past the second opening, the cave abruptly hooked to the left, and seemed to lead back down toward the southern end of the canyon, though exact directions were difficult to determine underground. Although she'd never before been prone to claustrophobia, Maggie began to feel all the tons of earth overhead and her nervousness increased with the darkness. The air was damp, cool and musty with an odor, difficult to describe, but nonetheless unpleasant.

The three of them walked single file for several minutes, moving between small caves and the occasional short tunnel. Gradually all talking ceased, except for the occasional question posed by Mark who seemed to be avidly enjoying this experience. Several times O'Reilly glanced over his shoulder to assure himself that they were all right, and Maggie saw in the soft glow from her flashlight a small smile play around his lips when he looked at Mark's excited face.

They were just passing through a small cavern replete with fanciful limestone sculptures from the mineral rich water that had formed this underground riverbed, when suddenly from in front of Maggie came a sharp *ch-ch-ch-chchchhchch*. Mentally flashing on the rattlesnake (not the ghosts, she assured herself afterward) Maggie let out a brief shriek, tried to grab for Mark and jump backward at the same time.

Proving once again, as she thought later, that she was not cut out to be a dancer, the only part she got right was the shriek, which came out as loud and as high as a train whistle, reverberating off the walls of the small cave. The rest of her moves were closer to those choreographed by the Three Stooges than by any ballroom dancer. She missed her grab at Mark's shirt, tangled her legs and wound up flat on the floor of the cave, looking up at the startled face of O'Reilly, and listening to the hysterical laughter of her beloved first born.

Sitting up she saw Mark doubled over laughing, and a growing suspicion began to invade her mind. Eyes narrowing, she looked at O'Reilly, and saw that his surprise was giving way to amusement, though he wasn't convulsed as was his young companion.

"Mark." Teeth gritted, glaring at her son, Maggie growled his name with a warning tone that should have sent him running in fear of his life.

The tone and the glare had no noticeable affect on him, and Mark continued to snort and sputter with laughter at the spectacle of his mother sitting on the floor.

The sight of Mark laughing freely began to melt the anger she'd felt after such a scare, though she didn't lessen the intensity of her stare one iota. "Mark, if you want to live to your next birthday, you are going to come over here right now and help me up. Do you understand?" Maggie spoke in a low voice, full of menace.

"Yes, ma'am," Mark said in a mock contrite manner, still choking on the laughter that kept bubbling to the surface. He walked over to his mother and held out his hand to assist her to her feet. Maggie reached up her hand, and just as Mark took it, she jerked backward, yanking him off balance and down into her lap. Into his ear she growled, "If you ever, *ever* scare me that way again, sir, I will personally rub hamburger into your hair and stake you out in front of a mountain lion's den. Got it?"

The laughter flooded over again, but Mark managed to spit out a second, "Yes, ma'am," before clambering to his feet and offering her his hand a second time. Maggie accepted and rose to her feet where she faced O'Reilly, who seemingly had enjoyed the interaction between mother and son immensely.

Cheryl Taylor

She shot him another glare from slitted eyes, whereupon he struggled to wipe the smile off his face, turned and started walking toward the far entrance of the cave, calling back in gruff tones, "Enough of this goofing around, we've got to get going."

Falling into line behind him, Mark, followed by Maggie, headed out. Every once in a while, however, Maggie swore she could hear a strangled burst of laughter, quickly smothered, and she couldn't tell if it came from Mark or from O'Reilly.

The pathway they took seemed to be slanting slightly upward, higher into the cliff's face, and when Maggie questioned him, O'Reilly affirmed that yes, they were moving up toward the plateau. The smooth floor was primarily composed of the solid rock of the mountain, as well as dirt and various stones, from pebbles to large boulders, that had fallen from the roof. Here and there patches of sand glimmered in the yellowish light from the flashlight.

Several times they came upon openings to other caves on the right, or tunnels that led deeper into the ground, but each time they passed by, stopping briefly to make an arrow with some of the small loose rocks scattered along the floor. Finally, after it seemed they had walked for a hundred miles at least, O'Reilly began carefully examining the walls along the left hand side of the cave they were in, obviously looking for something. At one point he shut off his flashlight, bidding the others to do the same. Maggie, expecting that absolute darkness that one finds in caves and mines, was surprised to see a soft glow from somewhere ahead near floor level.

Moving slowly, O'Reilly scanned the floor of the cave, stopping suddenly at a crack in the sandstone next to the wall.

"This is it," he said triumphantly.

"This is what?" Maggie asked doubtfully.

"Do we go down that hole?" chimed in an excited Mark.

O'Reilly nodded, knelt down on the cave's floor and began to wriggle into the small opening feet first.

"Wait just a minute, here."

O'Reilly stopped and looked up at an agitated Maggie. "Yeah, it's fine. Trust me." He grinned and proceeded to worm his way into the small opening.

Mark, looking ready to burst from excitement, looked back at

66

his mother with a imploring expression. Maggie hesitated, then, as O'Reilly's head disappeared into the hole, she released a breath she didn't realize she'd been holding, and nodded for Mark to follow.

Mark wasn't about to wait for his mother to change her mind and practically dove into the hole head first, slithering on his stomach as though he were the snake he'd imitated so successfully earlier. Watching her son's feet disappear into the hole, Maggie paused, then shook her head, got down to her hands and knees and proceeded to inch her way into the roughly triangular gap.

The passageway was straight and approximately ten feet long. Once Mark exited in front of her, Maggie could see a soft light, strong enough to make her flashlight unnecessary. At the end of the crack, she found herself in a horizontal cleft in the wall of a cave, about three feet above ground level. The cave itself was relatively small, about fifteen feet by twenty-five or so, and she could see the source of the light coming from a small opening in the wall directly opposite her.

O'Reilly was standing in the middle of the cave, next to Mark who was turning around taking in his surroundings with an astonished look on his face. Looking around herself as she clambered down from the ledge, she felt she had to agree with Mark, the cave was a source of amazement.

The sunlight admitted through the opening lit the cave with a soft glow that was reflected off millions of tiny crystals in the sand on the floor and throughout the walls, creating a shimmery effect. O'Reilly was telling Mark something about ancient waterways wearing down the sandstone and other soft rocks, while leaving a large vein of granite complete with quartz crystals to create the walls of the cavern. Whatever it was, the effect was stunning, she thought.

Maggie started to walk around the cave, when something caught her eye. Walking across the sandy floor, Maggie approached the far wall, reaching up to touch the shapes carved into it.

Mark, noticing his mother's reaction started to hurry over, calling out, "What is it, Mom? Are they Indian petroglyphs? We learned about those in school. That would be so awesome. Do you think this was some sort of sacred spot or something?"

A smile crossed her face as she ran her hand gently over the rough wall. "No, it's not Indian petroglyphs," she said. She looked back at her approaching son and saw O'Reilly watching her with a smile on his face. "And I don't think it's a sacred spot to anyone, unless it's to two young boys." she said, meeting O'Reilly's eyes and resting her hand on the characters carved into the walls, characters that made out the words, *Jimmy O'Reilly* and *Jason O'Reilly.*

"Terrible what kids will do," O'Reilly said ruefully, nodding toward the words.

"This is where your brother and you would come?" Mark asked excitedly.

"Yeah, this was a favorite place. Got us in a bit of trouble though. Want to see why?"

Mark eagerly turned away from the carved words and headed back over to where O'Reilly was standing, followed more slowly by Maggie. O'Reilly turned and, beckoning to them, moved toward the opening that let in the sunlight.

The crack was roughly triangular, three feet high and four feet across at the base, and about five feet off the ground. Underneath several rocks had been piled to allow a shorter observer to climb up and look out the opening.

Mark scrambled excitedly up on the rocks and leaned out the gap, exclaiming as he did so. "Mom, we're right above the house. I can't see it, but I can see the barn and the animals and all the rest of the pasture. This is so cool!"

Maggie stepped up beside Mark and looked out onto the meadow, noting the view this secluded spot gave them. She acknowledged to herself that O'Reilly had been right on the money thinking that this would give them the perfect hideout within a hideout. She'd never really noticed this little opening far up in the cliff before, and she was sure that if they were careful, no intruders would be able to see them from the floor of the valley. At the same time they would be able to spy on anyone who entered the pasture area.

Looking back at O'Reilly with a quizzical expression on her face she asked, "What got you into trouble in this place? Was it because you weren't supposed to go into the caves?"

"No, we were allowed to explore a little, as long as we used obvious markers to indicate where we were going, took plenty of batteries for our flashlights, and weren't gone over a half hour at a time. No, we got in trouble for something a little different than that." There was a half embarrassed look on his face.

"Okay, give," Maggie commanded. "What were the sins of the O'Reilly brothers? What do I have to watch out for?" A huge grin split her face.

"Well, you see Jason and I found this place on one of our visits to Hideaway with our dad. He was working this pasture and he brought us with him for a sort of a treat. We spent several days headquartering in the house. We thought it was pretty neat that we could see the people and they didn't see us, and that's where the idea came from." He hesitated.

"The next time we came, we brought a package of water balloons we'd picked up on a trip into town, and several canteens."

"Somehow I think I know what's coming," Maggie said in failing tones while Mark watched O'Reilly, avidly listening.

"Yeah, well, we got up here and filled the balloons. It wasn't easy without a hose and some real water pressure, but we managed."

"How?" asked Mark, excitement growing. "Those balloons are tough. I've tried to fill them without a tap or hose and haven't been able to do it."

Maggie put her head in her hands, shaking it in despair, and slumped in a sign of defeat. With a glance at her, O'Reilly continued in contrite tones belied by the smile on his face .

"I guess it's sort of gross, but we would fill our mouths with the water, then blow it into the balloons."

"Awesome!"

Maggie just groaned at the image of mayhem to come as a result of Mark's new education.

"Well, it took awhile, but we eventually got several balloons filled enough. Then it was just a matter of waiting." O'Reilly laughed at his recollections. "Mom had come with us that time, and she was a horrible practical joker. So, we waited until she came out of the house and was headed for the clothes line with some stuff she'd washed. Then 'bomb's away.' Unfortunately for us, our aim was pretty good, and Mom and the blankets got splattered with mud and dirt." He shook his head. "Mom liked a good joke, but not when it meant destroying all the work she'd done trying to wash those blankets by hand. When we got up the courage to come out of the caves, we ended up being assigned to do the camp's laundry for the next two weeks, and Dad made sure that the laundry was plenty dirty."

During the story Maggie had started laughing, and by the end she had tears trickling out of her eyes at the vivid mental image of O'Reilly's mother dodging when the balloons started falling. Regaining control of herself, she fixed Mark with a look, knowing the signs of a ten-year-old making plans.

"You, my friend, had better think twice before you throw anything out this hole," she said, nodding toward the crack in the wall. "If I find anything falling on my head, I won't just rub hamburger in your hair and stake you out in front of a mountain lion's den. I will douse it in A-1 and hand the lion an engraved invitation."

"Okay, Mom," Mark sighed exaggeratedly with head bowed, then looked up at her from the corner of his eye. "You know, you're no fun at all."

"Yeah, and just you remember that, lion bait."

"Okay, okay, I got it!" Mark laughed, throwing his hands up in mock surrender.

Turning back toward O'Reilly, Maggie said, "Now let me get this right. You think we ought to provision this cave, and use it as a fall back should the Enforcers find the valley and try to capture us."

"This cave is really an ideal place," O'Reilly averred. "These cave networks go on for miles and it would be easy for someone to get lost, but this chamber isn't very far from the opening, meaning that we wouldn't have far to carry things. Or, we could hoist supplies up using a rope and save even more time. Most of the floors are rock so footprints won't be an issue, and the opening to this cave pretty small."

"Tell me about it."

"It would be easy to defend if necessary, though it could also be easy to lay siege to. I'll have to think about how to handle that possibility. In addition, we would be able to keep an eye out for what is happening in the pasture below, and to know when they leave."

Feeling a sense of deflation over the scenario that O'Reilly described, Maggie nodded. "Okay, you're right. I guess we'd better start getting the things up here that we'd need should the worst happen."

"Well, I'd say the first thing that needs to happen is for me to take the horses, head out to the nearest ranch and gather whatever supplies I can carry. The horses' feet are taken care of and most of the other urgent issues have been dealt with. Lets say I head out the day after tomorrow."

Maggie nodded, "Sounds good," but all the way back to the opening of the cave Maggie had the feeling that O'Reilly had been leaving something out. Something about why he felt this hideaway within a hideaway was so important, and she determined to question him more thoroughly before he left.

Maggie sighed, turning over again, wishing for her soft euro top mattress sitting presumably unoccupied at home in Prescott. She'd worked all day yesterday to pry out the secret she knew O'Reilly was keeping. He would be leaving in the morning. Whatever it took, she thought, he would have to tell her before he left tomorrow. With that thought circling through her mind, she finally drifted off to sleep.

12

*D*amn it, Captain Rickards thought as he stood in the street surveying the burning buildings in front of him. *Damn it all to hell!*

Rickards spun on his heel looking for the man in charge of responding to this fire. He spied his target over by one of the large engines, talking on a radio to his crew. Barely controlling his temper Rickards stalked over to the vehicle.

"What the hell is going on here," he demanded.

The man on the radio, fully dressed in turn out gear, didn't pause his conversation. He simply turned away from the Rickards and thrust out his arm, palm facing back toward the captain, in a well known but little liked signal. Rickards stood there, fury building as he waited for the fire chief to get off the radio.

Finally, after several minutes, and just when Rickards was ready to grab the man and spin him back in his direction, snatch the radio, throw it on the ground and stomp it into many tiny pieces, the man said "over" and turned to face Rickards.

"What can I do for you, captain," snapped the man, eyeing him up and down, taking in his Enforcers' uniform and obviously not swooning from an overload of respect. The name penned in black permanent marker on his turn out coat said F. Stevens.

"I asked what was going on here," Rickards barked back, gesturing at the line of burning homes behind him.

"Central Control labeled these buildings for annihilation."

"So close to the APZ? Why? What the hell is Central Control thinking?"

"Apparently it was reported that these homes were being used to hoard food, clothes and other items needed by the community. Orders

72

came through from Central Control that each of these neighborhoods were to be cleared then torched. All recovered goods are over there waiting for transport into the APZ."

Rickards looked in the direction Stevens indicated, noting for the first time the tractor trailers being loaded with food and other goods needed desperately by the community. It appeared that the fire department had made quite a haul.

"Why wasn't our annihilation team notified if the buildings were going to be fired?" Rickards demanded, looking back to Stevens.

"I don't know why Central Control made the decisions they did," Stevens snapped. "They didn't call and ask my opinion. They probably chose us because the annihilation teams are being used for areas further outside the APZ, and controlling spread isn't as important there as it is here. I'm sorry if your team wasn't notified, but we're just following orders." Rickards thought he didn't sound very sorry.

The radio trilled and a voice broke through the static asking Stevens a question. He turned away from Rickards as he addressed the issue raised by the anonymous speaker on the other end. After signing off he turned back to Rickards.

"If there isn't anything else, I've got to get back to work here."

"What am I supposed to tell the people in the APZ? These buildings were supposed to be the last to go, after all the other areas were demolished. Now people are going to start getting suspicious. I've already got people asking when they're going to be allowed to return to their homes. I'll have an uprising on my hands."

"You follow protocol as laid down by Central Control. That's what you do. If people ask about smoke from annihilation sites in the distance, you use the wildfire explanation, right? Here you've got the choice between wanton destruction by ghosts, electrical malfunction, disease reservoir, whatever." Exasperated at Rickards' angry expression and obvious disapproval, Stevens snapped, "It doesn't really matter, does it. All of these buildings will eventually be destroyed back to the boundaries. The government of this country and all the others are committed to maintaining a smaller footprint. Eminent domain had been happening for quite a while now for other purposes, this is just a new one. With this move, it's just developed a different focus.

"Now, if that's all, I've got work to do." With that Stevens turned away and holding the radio to his mouth began calling his team and asking for updates.

Furious over the abrupt dismissal from Stevens, and the rapid turn of events, Rickards stormed back to his vehicle, one of the few gasoline powered trucks still allowed on the roads. With the refineries shut down, and oil imports at a halt, the only people allowed to use combustion engines were the ones approved by Central Control as necessary to the forward movement of the government's agenda. Even then electric vehicles were preferred, since they could be powered by renewable resources such as solar, wind and hydroelectric. The problem was there were still too few of those vehicles available. Gradually, as the remaining population began to accept this radical shift in lifestyle, people would be retrained, the factories would be retooled and reopened, and more vehicles would be produced that met the government's standards. For now, though they were stuck with the older technology.

Central Control had told all the Enforcers and other agencies in power positions to expect resistance, and to police their own forces diligently. The official stance was that people had become entrenched in the wasteful lifestyles of the past seven or eight decades, and they were not going to embrace a more frugal existence with open arms. However, the recent radical reduction in the world population, combined with the growing evidence of drastic world climate changes, and the subsequent disasters that were resulting from it, gave the governments of the world the rare opportunity to take the reins and make changes with less upheaval and backlash than might normally occur in more settled times.

Less upheaval, Rickards snorted at the thought. *It wasn't that there was less upheaval, it was that there was so much upheaval, from a natural source, clearly identifiable, that a little extra thrown in on top by the world's governments was hardly noticeable.*

Traveling back to his office in the APZ, Rickards considered this change, and how people were handling it. At the time of the final disaster, the population of the United States had been somewhere over 330 million, and the population of the world well over six billion. Center of Disease Control estimates said that, over all, only about ten percent of the pre disaster population remained, leaving the population of the United States only about thirty-three million, which in anyone's book was still a hell of a lot of people.

The funny thing, if anything in this situation could be funny, was that some states had been hit much harder than other states. The flooding in the south and east had apparently created a perfect reservoir for disease spread, and the heavily populated cities, with people living in close contact with one another, facilitated contagion, in spite of quarantine.

The rural areas were not immune, however, especially once people started trying to escape the disease by avoiding quarantine barriers and heading out into the country, carrying the virus with them as they went. *The damn black death all over again,* he thought, remembering what he'd learned in school about how people tried to outrun the plague in the 1300s, often carrying it with them and infecting new villages and populations along the way.

His APZ was one of the smaller ones, housing only about eight thousand people, gathered from the surrounding areas of Nevada, California and Arizona. Central Control had chosen many of the larger cities, such as Phoenix and Laughlin for formation of the APZs with the idea that these areas sported more apartment style housing and had a greater stockpile of goods necessary to maintain the people until production could be restarted.

A grim smile crossed his lips. At least unemployment wouldn't be a problem for awhile. Everyone would be needed to get this new enterprise off the ground.

Another interesting thing, he thought, was how some countries had adapted more easily to concentration. Some people in the world were already accustomed to a stronger governmental role in their lives. This tended to work for them, since the citizens were more likely to look toward the government to tell them what to do in times of emergency.

However, in the United States, home of so many independent minds, but which had also dealt with so few natural or man made disasters on its own soil until recently, the demoralization and confusion had been especially severe. That allowed the authorities to step in and present a plan with few people questioning them. Problem was that now some were starting to emerge from that swamp of confusion and seem interested in taking their lives back. The government had other plans for that, ones developed in highest secrecy with other governments across the planet. Even people like Rickards weren't sure about the extent of the plans; were only informed of the roles they needed to play at that time, and warned that confidentiality must be maintained at all costs.

God, he wished he knew where O'Reilly was. There was a loose cannon if ever there was one. Much of the information O'Reilly had put into his file, when he'd bothered to fill in the spaces at all, was of no help. Rickards' men had been diligently searching out O'Reilly's history, trying to determine where he might go. Unfortunately, a crippled network system that was only gradually returning to normal meant they weren't having much luck tracking him down.

He's got to be found, thought Rickards, *He's got to be found, brought in and kept silent. Whatever happens, he can't be allowed to tell what he knows.*

13

The sun was high on the western cliff wall, still leaving the rest of the canyon pasture in shade when O'Reilly finished saddling his string of horses for his foray to the nearest ranch in search of supplies. He'd considered waiting until evening to head out, in hopes of avoiding any seekers that might be around, but he decided that Maggie was right, and the odds of encountering seekers or Enforcers out here on these little ranch roads was not high. Still, the exposure made him nervous.

Nonsense he shook his head *If they've figured out where I've gone, and have sent out the seekers, they'll find me whether I'm in the canyon or not.* Once again he hoped he'd hidden his tracks well enough when he left the APZ. If he was extremely lucky, he thought, the authorities believed that he'd headed for the wilderness in the Sierra Nevadas, or up into the remote areas of Wyoming and Montana. He'd thought about it. A person could stay lost a long time in those rugged mountains and deep forests, but the winters would be brutal, and besides, Hideaway was home territory. He smiled. *Home field advantage.* He sure hoped so.

He heard the creak of the house door opening and turned to see Maggie heading toward him carrying a saddlebag and a canteen. That was another thing, he thought. Now he had two other people dependent on him. He turned back to his horse, shaking his head as a grimace crossed his face. That wasn't in the plan, though he'd grudgingly changed the plan when he found Maggie and Mark already in residence. Now they were tied together, and there was no getting around it.

He figured in the short term they could live on food they harvested themselves, as well as those staples they were able to gather from the ranches and camps in the area. The problem was that those things wouldn't last forever and eventually they would either have to be able to learn to do without, or they would have to take the same action most ghosts were driven to; that is stealing from the APZs.

Well, he thought, *We'll deal with that when it's time. Hopefully the nearest ranches and camps will be fully provisioned, and hopefully the annihilation teams will ignore these small, out of the way places for a while longer since they're so far, and since there are no clear maps indicating where they are.*

O'Reilly knew the annihilation teams were ordered to go to small towns and subdivisions and destroy the buildings in those areas, after taking all useable goods. So many places were left empty, however, that at least the teams he was familiar with were concentrating on larger groups of houses. Most were not actively looking for small homesteads far away from civilization, unless they got word that a group of ghosts were holed up there. That didn't happen often, either, since the majority of the ghosts made their livings off the APZ supply trains, and didn't want to move too far away from where they could get their groceries.

He heard Maggie's footsteps as she approached, and he turned to watch her, this tall, slender, golden blond woman. She wasn't beautiful, he guessed, not like the models you see in the magazines, but she caught the eye. Even out here, completely out of her element, she walked with a subconscious aura of confidence.

No, he thought, *not beautiful, but she sure stuck in your mind, haunting you when she wasn't there to torment you in person. Those huge green eyes looking deep inside and seeing all your secrets.* Not that he'd ever be attracted to someone like that, no way, no how. She was about as prickly as a porcupine, without the cuddly personality, though watching her with Mark was a joy. It was like looking though a window and seeing a whole new person inside.

"Hey," Maggie called out, while still about ten feet away, breaking him out of his reverie. "I brought you some of that venison jerky for the trip. And here, the last of the coffee in this canteen. I hope you appreciate the sacrifice since I figure I might go into caffeine withdrawal before you return and Mark will be forced to check me into rehab." She grinned up at him as she approached closer and he smiled in return. "You ready to head out?"

"Yeah, everything's all set," he affirmed. "Now don't forget what we talked about last night. I'll be gone today and tomorrow, maybe the next day depending on what I find."

"I remember," Maggie nodded. She paused, then, unable to resist, added sarcastically, "And if you don't get back within three days, I'm to take Mark and everything we can carry and head for the caves and stay there for at least a week until we're sure no one has back tracked you. I still don't think that's necessary. I figure it's more likely that you'll get lost and I'll need to come out looking for you."

"Just do it, Maggie, okay? Humor me." *Why did she always get so edgy when talking about this stuff?*

"Okay, we'll do it. I just think you're worrying a bit too much."

"Fine, I'm worrying, just don't forget." O'Reilly untied his lead horse, turned him away from the hitching rail, and swung on board. "Hand me that rope will you?" He gestured toward the lead rope on the first of his pack horses. He was taking his original three, plus the two strongest of Maggie's four. He figured with five horses, even with her two still sore footed and probably unable to carry as much as the others, he should be able to bring back enough supplies to last them for awhile. Assuming he found any.

Maggie untied the pack horse, and handed the rope up to O'Reilly who then dallied it around his saddle horn. He nudged his horse in the sides with his spurs, and his small pack train started off, heading for the two-rut trail leading down the canyon and calling back over his should, "I'll see you in a couple of days."

"Drive careful," came Maggie's reply, surprising a laugh out of him and lightening his mood as he headed away from Hideaway.

It took five hours of hot, sweaty riding, but finally O'Reilly began to see increasing signs of habitation. He'd headed for the S Lazy V headquarters, instead of the remote ranch house Maggie had in mind when she came up with the chicken collecting idea. That house was easily a day and a half's ride with a pack train. The S Lazy V was closer, though not as close as Eagle Camp, and he was familiar with the route. He'd go to Eagle Camp another day, he decided. Just now he didn't feel he could deal with any more visitations from the past.

The journey to the caves had stirred up many memories he'd have preferred to leave buried, but it couldn't be helped. Yesterday, with Mark's and Maggie's assistance, he'd shifted as many supplies as they could spare into the small cave in preparation for its possible use, even though Maggie obviously still wasn't totally sold on the idea. Mark, on the other hand, was all for creating a secret hideaway.

The land out of the canyon varied between dried grasses, clumps of yucca and the occasional thick standing of shaggy bark and alligator juniper. At times the land rolled gently, then suddenly, without warning, a rock escarpment would thrust it way out of the surrounding hills. As he drew closer to the S Lazy V headquarters, the two-rut track he'd been following joined another track and then another, each appearing more and more like a real road. In the distance he could see the tops of the large elms that grew around the barns and outbuildings of the ranch, and then the top of the barn itself. There were no signs of human activity and he breathed a sigh of relief, tempered by a pang of sorrow. As much as he didn't want to try to explain his presence on the ranch, he also felt grief that Tompkins, the man who'd given his dad a job, his parents a place to live, and he and his brother the best place to grow up he could imagine, was gone. This ranch had been in Tompkins' family for five generations, and the odds of that continuing on to the sixth were slim indeed.

As O'Reilly drew closer to the cluster of buildings, a small herd of horses ran up out of a pasture on his right, their tails high in the air, snorting. Sun glinted off their red, brown and yellow coats, white markings flashing brightly. This band was made up of about ten mares, their foals, and one of the ranch's stallions. If he remembered right, there would be at least one more group in another pasture, further to the east.

Looking toward the barn he dreaded seeing other horses, and maybe cattle, lying dead in the pens that surrounded the compound. When he didn't see any sign of carcasses, or the buzzards that would feed off of them, he felt a knot of tension loosen. He hadn't realized how much apprehension he'd built up knowing that any animals that had been left in the pens and corrals would have long since run out of food and water if they hadn't been able to escape. Apparently whoever had been living here at the headquarters had freed the horses and any cattle before either dying or heading into the APZs. He didn't know which to hope for, though he knew which was most likely.

He glanced up toward a small hill a short distance from the compound. That was the family's cemetery. It was there that Tompkins' ancestors were laid to rest, and it was there that Tompkins would want to be if he had died. O'Reilly didn't think he wanted to go up to see if there was a new headstone, or several. He was tired of dealing with death.

Riding into the barnyard he was met with silence, broken only by the sounds of birds and the gentle rustle of the wind in the elms. No horses nickered, no cattle lowed, no dogs barked. Dismounting, he tied Ace, his gelding, to the nearby hitching post, then proceeded to disconnect his pack train, tying each of these horses in their turn to the long log rail. He figured if necessary, he could collect some of the other horses from the pasture to act as pack animals for the trip home, that is if he could find saddles, or pack saddles for them. Any extra horses brought back could then be turned out in the upper pastures and caught and used as needed.

He unsaddled Ace first, then removed pack saddles from three of the other five horses, two horses having come equipped with only halters. Finally, he turned the animals out one at a time into the large turn-out attached to the barn. Checking the water tank and finding it low, he turned the faucet, hoping that it was still connected to the windmill system as it was when he was a kid. When the fresh water gushed out, splashing into the tank, he blew out a relieved breath. At least he wouldn't have to haul water.

The eerie silence played on his mind and he determined to get what he needed and get out of this place as quickly as possible. Silence was much easier to take out in the middle of the rangeland, where silence was expected. Here it was like a sliver in your hand, a constant irritation, never completely leaving you alone.

He walked into the large open barn, noticing the alfalfa hay stacked inside.

Plenty of feed, he thought, *No way to get it to the animals unless we move up here and that's not going to happen any time soon.* He shook his head. The abundance was something to keep in mind for the future, though, should next winter become severe enough to drive them out of the canyon.

Using his pocket knife, he opened a bale of hay and tossed several green leafy flakes over the half wall of the run in connected to the pen where his horses were milling around. After drinking their fill, they wandered into the barn at the sound of the hay thumping into the feeder. There was some jockeying for position as they determined who was the boss, then they settled down to eat. Leaning on the half wall, O'Reilly watched them a few minutes, loath to begin what he was here to do. He found himself wishing that Maggie and Mark were with him and wondered what they were up to back in Hideaway.

Cheryl Taylor

Damn, he thought, *not two months ago in the APZ I was wishing I could get away from people. I wanted to be done with them, their bickering and complaining, and the scheming of those people in charge. Now here I am, missing one of the most irritating women I've ever met and a know nothing kid. There is something seriously wrong with me. Got to be.*

Finally, taking a deep breath and shoring up his resolve he turned away from the quietly eating horses and into the dark, dusty shadows of the barn. Walking into the tack room he found saddles, bridles and pack saddles. Again good. He'd brought several of the horses with only halters, hoping to find proper pack saddles and panniers in the barn. He was glad he wouldn't wind up improvising packs on the way home. Coming without the proper equipment was a gamble, but one that had paid off. Hopefully the rest of his bets would pay off as well.

Once he determined that all the tack he needed was in the tack room, he walked back out into the sunlit barnyard and headed for the chicken coop on the far side of the hard packed dirt yard, near some small outbuildings. He could see that the door was open allowing the birds free run. Luckily for him, however, some of the chickens had stayed close to home, pecking around in the dust, clucking and squawking to themselves. It was a miracle, he thought, that the entire flock hadn't fallen prey to coyotes and hawks.

A sobering thought flitted though his mind, reminding him that maybe the reason the chickens had survived was because there was so much abundant food elsewhere; horses and cattle trapped without water, humans who didn't make it to medical help in time. These predators weren't picky. Quickly quashing those mental images, he turned his mind toward the problem of conducting a chicken roundup.

If he could find some grain and scatter it back in the coop, he thought, he would be able to capture enough of the stupid birds to take back to the Hideaway. He grimaced at the thought of the five hour ride with a basket of complaining chickens tied to a horse behind him and briefly considered telling Maggie that there hadn't been any fowl in sight, not a one. He didn't like chickens much, but Maggie was right when she said that the eggs and meat would be a welcomed and valuable addition to their diet.

Of course, he figured, *probably after the ride home I'll never want to eat a chicken or touch an egg again.* Actually, he thought, he might get fed up and feed them all to the coyotes before he ever got home. Maybe he should look for ear plugs when he was in one of the houses. That, or spices for fixing roast chicken.

Luck was shining on O'Reilly's head, because inside the door to the coop, he found a fifty-five gallon drum half filled with chicken feed which he scooped out and scattered on the dirt floor of the enclosure. From all corners of the barnyard chickens came at a run, kicking up dust and squawking like a bunch of school kids, reminding him all over again why he didn't like the noisy things. Then he laughed. Twenty minutes ago he had been fussing over the silence, now he was fussing over the noise. Guess there was no pleasing him, just as his mother sometimes said.

Waiting until every visible chicken entered the coop, he shut and latched the door. Looking in, he was able to count somewhere around ten hens and three roosters. The damn things wouldn't hold still long enough for a good count, but however many there were, it should make Maggie happy *if* he managed to get them back to her without either ringing their necks, or killing himself.

Finally, with all outside chores done, and having procrastinated as long as possible, O'Reilly turned to face the nearest of the three ranch houses, one of the two meant for the families of the hired hands. The owner's house, a larger redwood and granite affair, was further away, just visible on the side of a nearby hill.

The best plan of action, he thought, was to head for the closest house, go through it from top to bottom and collect all the items needed near the front. Maggie had given him a "shopping list" of things she felt she needed. *Like I'm running out to the grocery store*, he snorted. But he'd better keep an eye out for those things to keep her happy.

After one house had been thoroughly scoured, he'd move to the next, then the next. Once he was finished with all three, he'd know how many horses he'd need to carry all the supplies, or whether he'd have to cache some things to retrieve later. If he could complete clearing all the houses that afternoon, he planned to saddle the horses, load the provisions, gather the chickens, throw them on the last horse in line, as far away from him as possible, and head back home. The abandoned ranch filled him with an ill defined dread, and he didn't want to spend the night there if at all possible.

He felt a little start at the thought of Hideaway as "home." No place had been "home" for an awful long time, and he wasn't sure if he liked thinking that way now. Home implied a place where you had roots, where you wanted to stay. In this case, though, home was a primitive building at the bottom of a canyon. Hidden, but still vulnerable to attack, and housing an exceptionally stubborn woman and her son.

Home is where the heart is, indeed, he snorted.

The back door to the first house was weathered brown wood, blending well with the graying green paint. When he tried the knob, it opened easily. He wasn't surprised that the door was unlocked. Often this far out in the country people left their doors unlocked much of the time. You never knew when someone might need shelter from bad weather, and the next time it might be you needing to shelter somewhere else. When he was a kid, his parents had never locked their doors. However, with the encroachment of city people further and further into the rural landscape, some of their city habits, good and bad, were bound to come with them.

Years ago he'd nearly died laughing when a friend of Sarah's came to visit at their home far out in the country. After getting out of her car, the woman had flicked the electronic lock button on her key ring. The *whoop-whoop* of the car's locking and alarm system was so out of place in the country that it seemed to come from another planet. He'd badly wanted to ask her if she was concerned that a jackrabbit with a submachine gun was considering stealing her Camero, but one look from Sarah had squashed that question in his throat.

Of course, the city people did bring more crime with them, and looking back at how things had turned out, maybe that woman wasn't too far off the mark when she'd engaged her car's security system.

Opening the door, O'Reilly stepped into a mud room that opened into a small kitchen. Green and white linoleum covered the floors, spotted here and there with colorful hand braided throw rugs. The sun shone through bright yellow curtains hanging in the windows, giving the kitchen a warm golden glow. A wooden table with two chairs was tucked into one corner, while on the sideboard sat two coffee mugs, waiting to be washed. The entire atmosphere gave him the eerie feeling that the residents of the house were merely out of the room and would be back momentarily. A closer look, however, revealed a layer of dust had coated everything with at least two month's worth of accumulation. No one had been in this room for quite awhile.

O'Reilly headed for the pantry and began gathering the goods that he would need to take back to Hideaway with him. Fortunately for him, it appeared that the residents had made a trip into town shortly before being forced, either by disease or authority, to leave the home. He found a twenty pound bag of flour, and one of sugar, both unopened. A ten pound bag of cornmeal, as well as a container of a generic brand of shortening; some yeast; a large, mostly full sack of rice; and two five pound bags of potatoes, beginning to go to seed, were also added to his stash.

In a plastic grocery bag he found under the sink he placed bottles of spices, salt and pepper, as well as any other small items he thought might be useful. He didn't bother to look in the refrigerator. Since the power had been out, anything in there would have turned long ago.

Coffee, he said to himself. *Where do these people keep the damned coffee.* He figured his life wouldn't be worth spit if he didn't come back with at least some form of caffeine, so he felt a huge sense of relief when he finally located two plastic containers of ground coffee under the sink and reverently added them to growing heap, along with a box of tea, a bottle of dish soap and another of laundry detergent that he found nearby.

Leaving the kitchen, he headed for one of several closed doors on the far side of the living room. Opening the first door he reached, he found himself in a bathroom where he helped himself to the towels in the linen cabinet, as well as those hanging on the towel holders. He also picked up the soap and toothpaste. Eventually they would have to make due with homemade, but there was no sense in letting this go to waste.

After taking these items back to his pile in the kitchen, he returned to the next door in line, finding himself in a bedroom. He gathered the blankets from the bed, as well as some that were folded neatly onto a shelf in the closet. These he also took back to the kitchen and his growing stash.

As quickly as possible he finished going through the last bedroom, managing to find some jeans and shirts that would fit him, as well as more blankets and sheets. Then he returned to the kitchen for the final time and carried his treasure trove out into the yard to await loading onto the horses.

Glancing at the sun, he realized that there was no way he was going to gather everything, pack and head back before dark. The feeling of dread intensified and he briefly considered heading out into one of the nearby pastures and camping there for the night. The thought was discarded quickly, since the time wasted going out, setting up camp, then returning in the morning could be used more wisely.

I'm not staying in one of those empty houses, though, he thought. *I'll just bunk down in the barn with the horses. These buildings give me the creeps.*

Hurrying to get done before dark, he moved on to the second house. As before, he headed for the back door, walking into a mud room and kitchen that was a twin to the first. This house was also neat and well cared for, though there was an undefinable odor permeating the building, reminding him of a septic tank that needed pumping. It was similar though not quite the same; faint but irritating nonetheless.

Duplicating his search pattern from the first house, he moved through the kitchen, gathering supplies, then ventured out into the living room.

As he stood, hand on the door knob to the bathroom, he heard it. *Thump, whump.* Followed by a high thin cry from the bedroom furthest from the bath.

What was that?

Turning toward the distant bedroom, hand reaching for the gun at his hip, he called out.

"Hello? Is anyone there?"

Receiving no answer, O'Reilly began to walk toward the far door, drawing his weapon as he went. Quietly he approached the door, holding the pistol in his right hand, he reached out with his left and turned the knob. In an abrupt movement designed to take any attacker off guard, he quickly swung the door open, bringing the gun to bear on the room, quickly scanning for any assailants.

The smell struck him first, like a solid wall; a putrid stench of human waste and illness. A split second later his eyes registered the sight of a form lying on the bed underneath a thin sheet, other blankets tangled and kicked into a pile at the foot of the bed and on the floor.

She might have been pretty once, but it was hard to tell. Her facial bones jutted out under her skin, reminding him of a piece of paper mache where someone had laid tissue paper over a sharp frame. Her brown hair was matted with sweat and tangled on the pillow.

Her eyes were closed and at first he thought she was dead, until he heard her deep raspy breathing, slow and irregular. Holstering his weapon, he softly approached the bed, watching the still form as he came closer.

Apparently this was a late victim of the flu that had ravaged the world's population. Most people who had fallen victim, had done so early on in the onslaught. However, the disease moved in waves, and some who had managed to avoid contagion during the first or second wave, fell victim later on. It appeared this woman was one of those. Either she had been able to remain isolated here on the ranch, or more likely, she was a ghost who had run when the order for concentration came, carrying the disease with her. From her appearance, he would never know. Most people who made it to this stage of the illness never recovered, even with extensive medical intervention, none of which was available here. Unfortunately he had seen an uncountable number of people in this condition during his last months as a sheriff's deputy, prior to the reorganization and his rebirth as an Enforcer.

Hoping against hope, he leaned over the still form, and gently touched her shoulder. He wasn't concerned about his own health. Apparently he was one of those for whom the flu virus held no danger. Surely if he were going to catch the disease he would have done it long since. From what Maggie said, she was in the same boat; immune to the bug. Mark had already caught and developed an immunity to the virus as well, so although he felt a high level of reluctance in approaching the still form, he didn't think he was taking a risk.

"Ma'am," he said quietly, softly shaking her shoulder. Her breathing caught, paused, then started again with a bubbly cough, but she didn't open her eyes. He tried again, louder and more insistent. "Ma'am, can you hear me? Open your eyes if you can hear me." He shook her more urgently.

A low moan issued from her throat and O'Reilly found himself looking down into a pair of dark brown eyes, foggy with illness. The woman began to cough violently, the force of the paroxysm doubling her over and squeezing tears from her eyes. Kneeling on the edge of the bed, he tried to support her and help her through the attack, though he knew ultimately it would do no good.

Finally, collapsing back on the bed, the woman closed her eyes, her breath becoming more labored and irregular with each passing moment. O'Reilly knelt there, hand on her shoulder, wondering what he could do, knowing that there was no saving her, but loath to walk off and leave her to die alone.

After a few minutes passed, the woman again opened her eyes and looked up at O'Reilly. Fighting to draw breath, she managed to choke out a single word "Lindy."

"Your name is Lindy?" O'Reilly asked.

She shook her head slightly and again struggled to take in a breath of air. She lifted a right arm that shook like a leaf in a strong wind and pointed toward the pile of discarded blankets on the floor, repeating in the weak voice, "Take care... Lindy..." her voice so quiet at the end that he could barely understand her. Another coughing spell, worse than the first, grabbed her. It twisted and wrung her like a dishcloth until she fell back on the bed showing no spark of life except for the occasional, irregular bubbling respiration which was growing weaker by the second.

Rising from the bed, O'Reilly walked toward the pile of blankets with a feeling of trepidation. A brief hopeful thought passed through his mind that maybe "Lindy" was the lady's little pocket pooch. One of those yapping little dogs that women these days liked to dress up in bows and carry in little shoulder bags; in which case he could stick it in with the chickens, take it back to the Hideaway and leave it for Maggie to take care of. He had a feeling, though, that he wasn't going to be that lucky.

Taking a deep breath, which he instantly regretted, he looked down into the pile of blankets and saw a small girl, about two years old, curled up asleep with her thumb in her mouth. How she'd ever slept though the noise that he'd made upon his entrance, and that created by her mother's coughing spells, he'd never know, but there she lay, breathing the deep, slow, quiet breaths of sleep.

Quietly he knelt down beside her, reaching out to brush a soft reddish-blond curl from her cheek. The little girl opened her large brown eyes and looked up at him. He expected her to react with fright upon seeing a strange man hovering above her, but instead she simply lifted her arms to him in the universal sign of small children wanting to be picked up and held.

He reached out and gathered her into his arms, and instantly regretted the move. She was undoubtedly the filthiest child he'd ever encountered. It appeared her mother had been too ill to attend to basic hygiene for longer than he wanted to think about, and much of the odor in the room emanated from the child's food smeared clothes and overflowing diaper. The little girl didn't seem to notice, though, and simply put her arms around his neck and looked at him.

"Lindy?" he asked.

The child didn't answer, but tucked her small head under his chin, keeping her arms tight around his neck. Looking back at the bed O'Reilly suddenly realized that the low raspy breathing had ceased sometime in the past few minutes. Rising carefully to his feet, he looked upon the still form under the blanket and realized that Lindy's mother had finally lost the fight for life.

He shook his head, *How long had she hung on for her child? You hear about things like this, but you don't usually believe them.*

Turning, he headed for the door, closing it quietly behind him. Once in the living room he paused, head bowed, feeling the weight of the warm, smelly bundle in his arms, and thinking about the woman who gave it life, and possibly gave her life for it.

A soft squeak and a wriggle under his chin brought him back to the here and now, and he was again made aware of the various odors given off by the child, none of them good.

Craning his head back and looking at his new companion, he smiled down at her. "First things first, little one. You are going to have a bath, and the sooner the better." Deciding not to remain in the house with the dead woman, O'Reilly headed back down to the barnyard where there was fresh water, stopping by the first house to pick up some of the soap and towels he had placed outside.

Thank God it's summer, and warm enough to do this outside with well water, he thought, carrying his burdens to the barnyard. Sticking his head into various stalls in the barn, he eventually came upon a black plastic feeder that would do nicely as a bathtub and carried it back out into the waning sunshine where he filled it with water from the hose that he'd used to fill the horses' water trough.

The little girl, *I must start thinking of her as Lindy,* toddled around after him, silent as a real ghost. He remembered Kay-Tee at this age, always laughing, never quiet for a second, and wondered about Lindy's lack of speech. Was it the result of what she'd been through, or had she been mute before her mother's illness? He sighed. He might never know, he realized.

This was definitely not on Maggie's shopping list, he thought ruefully as he plopped Lindy into the cool water and began to soap her down, pausing several times to pour water from a small bucket over her head. Even those actions elicited no verbal response from the girl. She merely kept her eyes glued on O'Reilly, as if afraid he would disappear if she turned her attention away from him. *Another slave to fortune,* he thought. *Heaven knows what Maggie's going to make of this.*

A pang of regret twanged though his guts. How many more would he collect before everything fell down around his ears? How many would get hurt if he didn't gauge things right? He shook his head. Not that it mattered, he thought. There was nothing he could do about it, but damn, he didn't know if he could handle any more deaths at his doorstep.

14

Christina lay in her bed, listening to Alysa's soft breathing from across the room, the breeze flirting with the curtains at the window. Jumbled thoughts of the events of the past two weeks filled her mind.

She felt an increasing rush of frustration that was keeping her from falling into the sleep her body craved. It was as though her mind was on autopilot, spiraling around and around, rehashing the past two weeks since the Colorado River outing.

Christina had been overjoyed at seeing Nick and Ryan at the river, but it quickly became obvious that the caregivers were deliberately trying to keep the boys away from her. Whenever she began to move in that direction, they stepped in, either drawing her or them away to another activity. It wasn't until the end of the day, during the chaos of the trip back to the Nursery, that Christina managed to speak with her brothers privately for a few minutes.

She was disappointed to find that both boys seemed to have accepted life in the Nursery as the way it was going to be, repeating rules they'd been taught, and some of the things they'd been learning in school. When Christina tried to remind them of their father, their eyes dropped and they started to turn away.

Then Nick, always the bolder of the two, turned back to Christina, looked her in the eyes and said, "Tommy says that Dad did some bad things," referring to Nick and Ryan's counselor. "He said that Dad made some mistakes, but that now things are all straightened out and we're going to live here because that's what's right." Then he turned and began to walk after Ryan.

"Wait, Nick," Christina started after her brothers, arm outstretched. Nick and Ryan stopped and looked back at her. "You don't believe that about Dad, do you? You know he didn't make any mistakes. He was right about what was happening with the weather and the people and everything. You know that don't you?"

Ryan walked back toward Christina, stopped in front of her and looked up into her face, his dark brown eyes bottomless. In a soft voice he said, "We don't like it here, Christy, not at all." Nick and Ryan had always tended to talk of themselves as a single unit. "We don't like living in this place, but what are we going to do? They tell us this is the way it's going to be, that everyone will be living in places like this, that Dad wasn't right. We got to live somewhere, you know." He started to turn away again but stopped when Christina put her hand on his shoulder and looked up to face her again.

"Ryan, it doesn't have to be this way," she pleaded. She glanced back over her shoulder, spotting some caregivers heading their way. Voice dropping low, she continued hurriedly, "I know about a place out in the country. In the empty lands in Arizona." Her voice dropped even lower. "Just have patience. Tell Nick. This place I've heard about is so isolated that no one can find it. We can make it, I know it."

The caregivers were almost upon them and Christina's voice dropped to just above a whisper, while her hand tightened on Ryan's shoulder. "Give me a chance, guys. Don't give up. I'll get us out of here. Just give me a chance. Promise?"

Ryan and Nick fixed her with identical deep brown stares and identical serious faces. They looked quickly at each other and a wordless communication passed between them. They nodded then turned to face Christina again. Ryan uttered one word. "Promise!"

Then he and Nick turned away and walked toward another group of boys, while Christina turned to face the caregivers, Andrea and Robert. Plastering a smile on her face she greeted them and went willing when she was asked to join the other girls on the way back to the Nursery.

Since that day she'd only seen her brothers at a distance, walking with other young boys to their classes, and playing out in the Nursery's play area. She wasn't given the chance to talk with them, but when she was able to catch their attention, she would give them the interlinked pinky sign that had always indicated a promise kept in their family,

92

and they would give her the sign back, lightening the load on her heart a little.

Finally, a week ago she'd achieved her goal of working closer to the kitchens. She was rotated to the dining room, bussing the tables, wiping them down once everyone had finished eating. In this new position, not only did she have a greater chance to interact with her brothers while they were eating, but she also found opportunities to hide small amounts of food in her pockets, taking it back to her room where she hid it in a backpack under her bed.

The opportunities were plentiful enough that she began wearing oversized shirts, and a large smock type apron so that she could hide more food, always choosing those things that would stay relatively fresh for a long period of time; boxes of raisins, granola bars, small bags of cereal. Her stash grew slowly, but it was growing, and Christina was becoming more and more confident that she would be able to gather enough to last her and her brothers several days until they were able to reach the canyon O'Reilly spoke about.

Then today he came. That Enforcer... Captain Richards or Rickards or something like that. He tried to be nice at first, acting sugary sweet like some adults, not accustomed to kids, will when faced with one of the beasts. Generally treating her as though she had nothing between her ears but feathers. Humph!

What surprised her the most, though, was not the visit by the Enforcer captain, but what he wanted.

When she saw the big, broad uniformed man walk into the dining room she felt a rush of adrenaline and a flood of panic as though he could see through her smock to the six granola bars hidden under her shirt.

He came while she was busy with her chores, cleaning tables and disposing of the post meal debris, either into the compost bins, or into her pockets if no one was looking. When she saw the tall, dark-haired man approaching, she ducked her head, trying to avoid notice although his direct stare made it obvious that it was she for whom he was heading.

"Hello, Miss Craigson," the man began with an ingratiating smile. "My name is Captain Seth Rickards of the Laughlin Enforcer Division. May I take some of your time?"

Christina raised her head to look at the captain, unsure as to how to answer his question. *Hell no, get away from me you murdering son of a bitch* seemed a little extreme, though she desperately wanted to use that phrase. After a hesitation that seemed to last forever, she settled on "Uh... yeah, I guess. But I've got a lot of work to do here," stammering embarrassingly in confusion and kicking herself mentally for not having a quick comeback that would cause the captain to leave with a bee in his bonnet, whatever that old saying meant. She bent her head back to her work.

"I understand," he smiled that greasy smile again. "I checked with your supervisor," nodding toward the woman standing in the kitchen doorway, watching them, "and she assured me that it would be fine if I spoke briefly with you about a friend we have in common." Again, Rickards attempted a smile which made Christina think of a shark watching a school of tuna.

"Here, have a seat." He pulled out one of the table's chairs for her, then one for himself, taking a seat and looking up expectantly at her.

Hesitating for a moment, then moving slowly, she sat in the offered chair and faced him, a look of puzzlement on her face. What "friend" could he be talking about?

After what seemed like an interminable silence, Rickards finally spoke, keeping his voice soft and nonthreatening. *Or at least as nonthreatening as a shark's voice could get. If, of course, sharks could talk. And, if you could get past the sight of all those teeth and actually listen to him,* she thought.

"Several weeks ago one of my officers, James O'Reilly, started visiting you while you were in isolation."

Christina felt a jolt pass through her at this opening. She didn't really know what she expected, but it wasn't this. Surprised as she was, though, she kept quiet, waiting for Rickards to get to the point.

Apparently surprised by Christina's silence, Rickards paused, then resumed speaking, trying to make his voice even friendlier than before.

"I understand you and he spent quite a bit of time talking with each other." Again he paused, waiting for her to volunteer information about their conversations. Again he was disappointed as Christina merely watched him, not uttering a sound.

Finally he began again. "We'd like to speak to Officer O'Reilly, but he seems to be missing."

Christina knew this time the shock was visible on her face. She'd thought O'Reilly had stopped coming because he'd been reassigned. She never dreamed that he'd disappeared.

Rickards was watching her and she knew he could see her surprise.

A look of mingled satisfaction at shaking her, and disappointment that she couldn't place, crossed his face and Christina wondered at it.

After another brief pause, Rickards continued once again. "We were thinking that since you and he spent so much time together that he might have said where he would go, or told you a little about his past that might help us find him."

This time remaining mute wasn't really an option. Rickards was obviously looking for a response and Christina was at a loss as to what to say to him that wouldn't endanger her future plans for escape. Stalling for time, Christina posed her own question, curious to see how Rickards would answer.

"What do you want to talk to him about?"

"While Officer O'Reilly was stationed here in Laughlin, he was involved in bringing in a number of people from outside the APZ; people who were trapped in the small communities, without resources. The last group that he escorted here contained several young children, and we've been having trouble determining if they have any relatives still alive." Rickards tried his smarmy smile again, apparently counting on his story of orphaned children to strike a resonant chord in Christina. "We need to talk to Officer O'Reilly to determine exactly where he rescued the children so that we can run a search now that the Internet is functioning reliably again. These poor children are so young that they can't tell us their addresses. But if there's anyway to reunite them with loved ones, we'd like to accomplish that."

As Rickards had been spinning his tale of orphaned children, Christina's mind was racing, trying to decide on a plausible story that Rickards would believe. Christina was sure that the captain's story was bogus, since O'Reilly himself had told her that he'd been assigned to bring in what he called "ghosts" before being assigned to security on the Nursery, and he'd told her that he'd been assigned there because he'd gotten in a little bit of trouble for not following orders. O'Reilly's story didn't sound much like Rickards version of altruism, and she was sure who she believed, even though she knew O'Reilly had probably left a great deal out.

Thinking fast, Christina came up with a tale of her own. One that would pull the Enforcer's attention away from northern Arizona if she had any luck whatsoever.

"Officer O'Reilly talked about spending time in the mountains, up around Wyoming and Montana, maybe as far as Canada. He said he liked going fishing and hunting there because it was so lonely." Christina tried a smile of her own, and hoped it didn't come off as fake as Rickards'. "He said that when all this was over, and we were allowed to go home, he was going to buy a place up there and move to the mountains permanently."

When she began her story, Rickards had a satisfied look, as though what she said confirmed something he already suspected. However, at her mention of buying a home following things returning to normal, a look of doubt flickered across the captain's face, telling Christina that she needed to do a better job of selling her narrative. Then another thought crossed her mind. Rickards would have maps. All kinds of maps, and she needed a map to get herself and her brothers to Hideaway. Maybe, just maybe...

"He told me once where he'd like to go, but I can't remember the name exactly. I think maybe it started with an 's' or 'c' or something like that. Maybe if I could see a map, I'd remember where it is and you could find him there." Christina peeked up at the captain, trying to make her face look as innocent as possible and hoping that Rickards would run true to form and underestimate her simply because she was a young girl. Besides, there surely had to be someplace in one of those states that began with that sound.

Just as she hoped he would, he rose to the bait. "I don't have any maps available here, but in the office I have many. I'll arrange for you to come down to my office tomorrow and we'll see what we can find."

Christina nodded, eager to appear helpful, and once again a brief look of doubt crossed Rickards' face, quickly brought under control. Christina realized she had to tone it down a bit, since her rapid shift from silent and distrustful, to eagerly helpful had apparently set off warning bells in Rickards' mind. She didn't want to do anything to jeopardize her chances of gaining access to the maps she desperately needed.

Hesitating for another minute, studying her intently, Rickards finally rose to his feet, and held out his hand to Christina as she stood. She took it quickly, disliking the dry rough texture.

"Very well, Miss Craigson," Rickards nodded, smiling a more natural smile this time. "I will speak with the caregivers here and arrange for someone to bring you down to the central office tomorrow sometime. We certainly appreciate any assistance you are willing to give us."

With another brief nod, the captain turned away and strode quickly across the dining room, stopping momentarily to speak with her supervisor, then leaving the dining room by the main exit.

Blowing out a deep breath, and contemplating the meaning of the visit, and the implications of her intended trip to the central office, Christina returned to wiping down the table where they'd been sitting, pushing in the chairs as she went. Hopefully tomorrow she would get her chance to find the best way out of town, and a map to Hideaway.

Lying in bed that night her mind hashed out all the possible scenarios that could materialize at the Enforcers office. That evening she'd been told that Ty, one of the younger male caregivers, would be escorting her downtown tomorrow morning around ten. She just had to pray that she would have a chance to find and take the map she needed. It would be a risky move, but even if it didn't work out, she could always go back again as long as she didn't get caught. Now she had an in. All she would have to tell them was that she remembered something else that O'Reilly had said.

Eventually, mentally and physically exhausted, Christina fell into a deep sleep, filled with fanciful dreams of a green valley deep within a canyon filled with buffalo and Indians, where she rode a white unicorn and was accompanied by an enormous white owl, who spoke to her, telling her the secret to living in the valley.

In her sleep, Christina smiled.

15

"**B**last it Mark, get that calf out of this garden before she tramples all the plants!" Maggie used her makeshift hoe to prod at the wayward animal as she ventured down a row of carrots, pausing here and there to sample the green tops that had begun to poke out of the dark, rich soil.

"But, Mom, Jenny just wants to help, don't you girl?" Mark said giggling. The calf stopped, hunched, and deposited a large pile of green poop squarely on top of a tomato plant in the neighboring row.

"Mark!"

"Mom, it's just fertilizer, that's what you said." Mark moved toward the rapidly growing calf, intending to take her halter and lead her out of danger.

"Mark," tone much more menacing.

"She's just saving us the time of carrying it to the garden, you know." Mark was laughing freely now.

"If you want to eat something more than veal...," an evil look was thrown at Jenny at the word veal, "this winter, you're going get that calf out of this garden and put her into the pasture where she can learn to be a real cow."

"Okay, okay. Geez, come on Jenny before Mom starts carving you up for supper." Mark glanced back at his mother as he led the calf from the garden, a wicked grin on his face. "Don't hold it against her, girl. She hasn't had any caffeine in two days and she's going though the DTs."

"That's it, buster," Maggie said in mock anger, starting toward the pair as they picked up speed to avoid her. "I'll show you the DTs. Where the heck did you hear that term anyway?"

Mark hauled on the calf's halter, pulling her into a trot heading out of the garden. At the edge of the worked land, he stopped and turned to look at her, pulling the calf around with him. "It was in that movie, the one where the uncle was drunk all the time. What was it's name? What are the "DTs" anyway?"

Maggie was saved from an answer by the sound of hooves on rock coming from the southern opening to the canyon. Turning, she shaded her eyes with her right hand against glare from the lowering western sun and made out O'Reilly leading his string of horses out of the gap on the two rut trail that ran beside the stream.

As he emerged from the canyon she was able to count a total of eight horses, the six he'd originally taken plus two that he'd apparently picked up at the ranch. Each horse was packed high, and O'Reilly even had another bundle in front of him on his own horse.

Maggie was surprised at the feeling of relief that washed through her at the sight of him. The past two days she had been plagued by a vague, unspecified disquiet. It haunted her nights, shivered down her back while she was doing the chores and tightened her neck muscles as she watched Mark doing his school work. Now, seeing O'Reilly riding into the barnyard, she recognized this feeling for what it was. She had missed O'Reilly's presence. She hadn't realized how greatly his being there added to her feeling of security; her feeling that she could handle this life that was so completely different from any that she'd ever imagined.

Her recognition of her dependence on him was a disquieting thought in its own right. Maggie had always thought of herself as independent, and since Mike's death, she had strongly resisted any temptation to rely on someone else. Now, without her being aware of it, she had become dependent on a virtual stranger. She didn't like that idea at all. No way. No how. Not one little bit.

Maggie joined Mark and the calf on the edge of the garden, watching as O'Reilly and his pack train moved closer. She was thrilled to see how many supplies he'd been able to collect from the ranch, and was especially excited to hear squawking from the last horse in line, indicating that the egg train was on its way.

In the middle of Maggie's blissful contemplation of all the things she would be able to do with the eggs, the mysterious large bundle in front of O'Reilly erupted into an earth shattering scream that threw everything into chaos.

O'Reilly's horse pinned its ears and tried to bolt forward. Foiled of that plan by the reins, and the rope attaching it to the pack train, the buckskin gelding bogged its head and began to buck. O'Reilly, hands full with reins and the squirming, screeching bundle in his arms, didn't possess the third arm necessary to release the pack horses from his saddle horn.

Spooked by the caterwauling whirling dervish at their head, the pack horses decided to leave town the way they came; running backward, sideways and around in circles, hauling on their leads, eyes rolling in panic.

Their own eyes wide in amazement, Maggie, Mark and the calf stood, slack jawed, watching the equine fireworks and wondering who would win. Finally, after what seemed like ten minutes, but was more than likely less than one, the entire train wreck came to an uneasy stand still. O'Reilly's horse stood, spraddle legged, nostrils wide and blowing, ears twitching back and forth nervously and eyes rolling white at the continuous noise.

The pack horses likewise came to a stop, pulled back to the far ends of their ropes, also blowing and trembling.

The screaming from the writhing bundle in O'Reilly's lap gradually resolved into one word, repeated over and over.

"Mommy, Mommy, Mommmmmmy!"

"Maggie!" yelled a frazzled O'Reilly, barely maintaining control over his horse. "Get over here and take this thing!"

Shocked into movement, Maggie began walking cautiously toward the horses, then began to move a bit faster as she saw O'Reilly fighting to hold both his mount and what appeared to be a small child. At about ten feet, she slowed again and approached more carefully until she was nearly within touching distance. Without warning the creature in O'Reilly's arms launched itself at Maggie, eliciting a shout from O'Reilly that nearly put his horse over the edge again.

Maggie, taken completely off guard, put out her arms by reflex and found herself clutching a little girl of about two, who abruptly became quiet, snuggling into Maggie's chest and popping her thumb into her mouth. Maggie took several steps backward, staring up at O'Reilly, open-mouthed in astonishment. Relieved of his noisy burden, O'Reilly slumped in the saddle, catching his breath, then slowly swung off his horse, patting him on his neck.

Mark came running up to his mother, followed closely by Jenny, the calf. Stopping in front of her, he stood on tiptoe to peer at the little girl in his mother's arms, craning his head to look into her face and shooting questions back at O'Reilly.

"Who is she?"

Sighing, O'Reilly slowly led his horses over toward the hitching rail. "Her name is Lindy. I don't know her last name."

"Where did you get her? Where's her family?"

Looking back over his shoulder in irritation, O'Reilly snapped, "I got her at the corner Circle K, now would you get over here and help me unload these horses."

Looking crushed, Mark walked over to the pack horses and began untying them from each other and fastening their ropes to the hitching rail, side by side. The crushed look was of short duration, however, as he thought of another question. "Is she going to stay with us. I mean like forever, like a sister? I always sorta wanted a sister."

Maggie, finally recovering from her shock at finding herself in possession of a small, warm lump of humanity, walked over to where Mark and O'Reilly were untying bundles from the pack saddles and piling them off to the side. "Mark, can the questions for now. It appears that O'Reilly has had about all he can take. We'll get him to fill us in later, okay."

"Yeah, sure, Mom. But where..."

"Mark, enough."

"I was just going to ask where you wanted all this stuff."

"Just start carrying it into the house, will you. We can sort it out there."

"Okay, I..." Mark's next question was drowned out by a raucous crow from a pack on the last animal in line, which caused all the horses to twitch and fidget. A pained look crossed O'Reilly's features and he turned to face the boy.

"Before you take anything to the house," he said through gritted teeth, "Would you please," he emphasized the word please, "*please* find a place to put these damn chickens."

Maggie buried her face in the little girl's hair to hide her laugh.

Later that evening, when all the goods from the packs were stowed away in the pantry, or closets, or wherever else they might belong, O'Reilly, Maggie and Mark sat around the table, enjoying bottles of cola cooled in the nearby stream, and a bag of chips. Taking a sip, Maggie closed her eyes in enjoyment, savoring the bite of the acid, the tickle of the bubbles, and the unforgettable taste of the drink, following it with the rich grease and salt goodness of the chip.

O'Reilly, having just told them about his finding Lindy, though leaving out many of the more disturbing details in consideration of Mark's young age, grinned at the expression of decadent bliss on Maggie's face at the taste of the junk food. Lindy, exhausted from the day's ride, was curled up on the sofa under the window, clutching her blanket and occasionally twitching in her sleep like a puppy.

"So," Maggie said, opening her eyes and facing O'Reilly again. "You mean she hasn't made a sound since you found her?"

"Not a peep, even when I doused her in the water trough. I'd begun to think she was deaf or mute or something."

"Why do you think she started screaming when she saw you, Mom?" Mark asked, enjoying his own bottle and trying to make it last as long as possible, since heaven knew when he'd see soda again.

"I don't know, bud, unless it's because, in her mind, I've taken the place of her mother who died. I wonder how long she'd been shut in that room with the sick woman." Maggie shuddered at the thought of what the little girl had gone through.

"There's no knowing, really." O'Reilly's face became somber at the memory of the fetid room and the dying woman. "It had been a little while at least, although it couldn't have been too long or she would have been in worse shape. But even several hours could seem like a lifetime to such a young child." He looked over at the sleeping child, face softening.

Not for the first time Maggie wondered about O'Reilly's past. He'd never volunteered much information, other than stories about when he was about Mark's age and living in the camp. At one point he'd said that his family left the camp and moved to town so that his mother could work as a teacher when he was fifteen and his father died unexpectedly. Past that time, O'Reilly's life was a void that Maggie had not yet been able to breach, but her journalistic instincts told her that something drastic had occurred to form the man that was before her today. The look on his face as he watched the small, strawberry blond girl sleeping resonated within her, making her wonder if somewhere in the past he'd lost a daughter or wife.

Several minutes of silence passed as O'Reilly watched Lindy, Maggie watched O'Reilly, and Mark happily munched his way though the family sized bag of chips that made it to Hideaway only moderately crushed. Finally, taking a deep breath, and hauling her attention away from the man sitting across from her, Maggie turned to Mark.

"Okay, kiddo, time to finish that drink and head off to bed. It's getting late and we have plenty of work to do tomorrow."

"Alright, Mom." Mark upended his bottle, draining the last drops, and set it back on the table, looking at it longingly. Pushing his chair back, he rose to his feet and walked to the sink, where he washed his face and brushed his teeth, the house lacking a regular bathroom. Finished with his nightly preparations, Mark crossed to Maggie and gave her a hug.

"Night Mom, night O'Reilly."

"Night kiddo," Maggie returned his hug.

"Night Mark," O'Reilly nodded at him.

Mark walked over to the couch and looked at the new member of his family. "Night little Lindy," he whispered. "I'll see you tomorrow morning."

Then with a yawn wide enough to crack his face apart, he turned and headed for his room.

Silence reigned again once the door closed behind Mark, and Maggie and O'Reilly were left alone in the front room. A soft breeze entered through the front windows bringing with it the sounds of the night; the soft burbling of the distant stream, the quiet calls of the night birds, the peaceful song of the frogs and crickets.

Maggie and O'Reilly sat quietly at the table, each lost in thoughts all his or her own. Several minutes passed without a word while the flame of the oil lamp flickered in its chimney, casting a warm yellow haze over everything in the room. Lindy murmured in her sleep, her legs twitching, then she relaxed again and fell quiet. The silence was a tangible entity, soothing everything around it with a gentle hand.

Finally, O'Reilly drew a deep breath, and seemed to shake himself, as if coming out of a dream. He appeared to inwardly reach a difficult decision and looked up at Maggie, only to find her watching him closely.

"There are some things we need to talk about, I guess," he said.

"Yeah, I would say there probably are." Maggie nodded carefully. "Like what exactly is this situation we're in? Obviously there's something I'm not aware of. Ever since you arrived you've acted as though you're being hunted."

As he started to open his mouth, she held up her hand. "Oh, it's not readily apparent. Mark hasn't seen it. You've hidden it well, but it's there, nonetheless. A watchfulness. A wariness. That business with the caves and creating a stronghold that would be difficult to penetrate. Those all indicate someone who is feeling less secure than he would like us to believe." Maggie continued to study O'Reilly's countenance as she talked, watching a myriad of expressions flicker across its surface, trying to attribute meaning to all of them, not always successfully.

A contrite look finally settling on his face, O'Reilly met her gaze with one of his own, and posed a question that she never expected.

"What do you think is happening at your house right now."

"I don't know, the mice are throwing the mother of all parties?" Confused, Maggie bent her head, considering for a minute before answering more seriously. "Just sitting there, I guess. When the orders came to report to the APZ, we were told to empty our refrigerators, set our plants outdoors if we weren't taking them, shut off the water and to lock our doors. They said the power would be off, but that everything would be fine until our return."

"Why didn't you choose to go to the APZ where there would be food and water and medical care?"

"What is this, twenty questions?" Maggie felt frustration temper her voice and struggled to quell it. After a moment she continued more calmly. "I had some business friends that went into the APZ before my area was concentrated. They sent me a few text messages before the cell towers went down, and they told me that a lot of things were going on in the APZs that they didn't trust. They didn't think it was a safe place, and I had to agree from what I was hearing. Why, what do you know?"

"Well, for one thing, I know your house is likely no longer standing, or if it is, it won't be for long."

"What do you mean!" Maggie felt a deep tearing pain at the thought of her beautiful redwood and stone house tucked back unobtrusively into the ponderosa pines north of Prescott. All the memories left there, all the pictures and other items left from her marriage.

"Ever since the survivors were brought into the Authorized Population Zones, teams of hand picked men, they called them annihilation teams, have been going out and razing the buildings left behind. They collect any items that can be reused or recycled, and the rest is bulldozed or burned or both."

"You can't be serious." Maggie's frustration began to boil over anew. "Those are people's homes, they own them. I know you said before it would be a long time before we could go home, but they can't actually be destroying them.

"Have you heard of eminent domain?"

"Yes, that's been in the news a lot lately. But there's no way they can be claiming the right of eminent domain in this situation, is there? This is unbelievable." Maggie could feel her anger reaching critical mass at all these questions and reminded herself to keep her voice low so that she didn't wake Lindy or Mark.

"It's like this, Maggie. Shortly after the disease swept through this country, the administration found itself faced with some interesting choices. So many people died in the illness, or shortly afterward, and the hardest hit groups were many of the higher educated ones, the ones in healthcare, emergency services and education. The administration found themselves in a position where they could handpick the replacements, giving those replacements the information the administration wanted them to have."

Maggie nodded, aware that Mike had died because he wouldn't leave his post and abandon the people in his care.

"I'm guessing that you are well aware of the buzz that global warming has been making lately."

"Yes, you spoke of this earlier, when we were trimming the horses' feet."

"There's been a lot of pressure on the governments of the world to begin to reduce greenhouse gasses, carbon emissions and all the other things that have been contributing to the change in the climate. Many of the bigger countries have resisted making sweeping reforms, however, because it would possibly damage their economies, and more importantly, at least here in the United States, the people would strongly resist giving up any of their toys."

O'Reilly stopped to take a sip of his soda, swishing it around in his mouth and savoring the taste. After a couple of seconds, during which Maggie waited patiently, he continued. "Then this last administration was elected, and one of the platforms on which they campaigned was a 'green agenda.'"

Maggie nodded again. O'Reilly had touched briefly on this when they'd had their explosive conversation while working on the horse.

"The problem still was, though, that the American people want to reduce greenhouse gasses without giving up any of the things they've come to see as their birth rights: The ATVs, the big cars, the energy consuming gadgets in their homes. Not only are they willing to continue lavishing energy upon the running of these things, but they don't even take into consideration all the pollution released in their manufacture.

"It was thought for awhile that if gas prices went up significantly, it might start people moving in the right direction, but even that really had little effect. Sure, the sales of large SUVs dropped for awhile, until auto manufacturers managed to come out with more fuel efficient models, but you still saw people on four wheelers and modified golf carts ripping up the forest trails. Just for the thrill of speed I guess. Heaven forbid they actually see nature on foot and get to know it. They would rather race through it, spewing as much noise and fumes as possible on the way."

"Okay, nature boy, I take it you really don't like ATVs. I don't care for them much myself, though Mark's always wanted one. Let's get on with the story. I want to know why my beautiful house is toast."

Too deep into his narrative to be hauled out by Maggie's quip, he continued, expression becoming darker and stormier. "Funny thing is that, while there were some suspicions, no one actually realized that the real reason for the price increases wasn't trouble in the Middle East, or storms in the gulf. It was actually manipulation right here under our noses."

Maggie started to object, but O'Reilly ignored her and continued on without stopping.

"In addition to all of woes over the economy, the weather patterns began to change. It wasn't really all that recently, starting what, nearly twenty years ago. Storms became more violent. Then drought took over places that had been used to provide a lot of food for our nation and others. People who previously thought of themselves as safe began dying in floods, tornadoes and hurricanes and then looking to the government for assistance once their communities were leveled or washed away. Then this flu bug hit and it was way more dangerous than anything that had been predicted, and the vaccine didn't work. In fact, many of those vaccinated seemed to get the sickest."

Maggie started to attention at that. "What do you mean the

vaccinated ones seemed to get the sickest?" He was right, though. It had been all over the news that the vaccine, which was made only at two or three labs around the world, hadn't worked. The United States and Canada had been two of the last countries afflicted with the disease, and it had been thought that they had plenty of time to make sure that enough of the high risk population was vaccinated to limit its spread. That hadn't happened, though. Something was wrong with the vaccine, and those vaccinated seemed to succumb the quickest.

Mike, as a paramedic with frequent exposure, was vaccinated early on through his job. Maggie and Mark should have been on the list as well, as members of his family, but car troubles had caused them to miss their appointment at the doctor's office. Then the vaccine supply ran dry and they were waiting on a new shipment, which never seemed to come. Finally the flu was upon them, and it seemed pointless to use a vaccine that was in short supply when they'd already been exposed. At the time Mike had gotten ill, Maggie had cursed herself for missing the appointment and putting Mark in harm's way. But now, after hearing O'Reilly's story, she began to wonder if missing that appointment had saved their lives.

"Are you saying that someone tampered with the vaccine?" Her temper started to boil over.

"I'm not saying anything like that. I don't know if the vaccine was tampered with, whether it was contaminated, or if it was cow piss in a bottle made to look like a vaccine. I just don't know. What I do know is that it didn't work, and that we suffered devastating losses of professional personnel possibly due to either it, or to the people's mistaken belief that the vaccine rendered them safe and thereby they weren't as careful in their exposure as they should have been.

"The disease came in waves, catching the people off guard the second and third times it came around, and that, combined with secondary infections, wiped out much of the population of the planet, hitting some countries harder than others. Follow that with a population that has been completely demoralized, especially in a country such as ours where we have always pretty much believed in our invulnerability, and you wind up with a high number of depressions and mental breakdowns that resulted in deaths and outright suicides.

"Now in steps our administration, who has been living in relative safety in some bunker somewhere, and they realize that an opportunity has presented itself. Meeting with the governments from around the world they come upon a strategy that will both care for the people left alive, and possibly begin to restore balance to the planet that has been disrupted by the wasteful consumption of the people living on it."

Maggie stared at her nearly empty bottle of soda, suddenly losing her taste for the sugary sweet liquid. "I think I need something stronger to drink," she said. Looking up at O'Reilly, catching him watching her intently, she said, "Let me guess. They didn't decide to call everyone to a peace circle and a 'Global Lights Out Night' to demonstrate the conservation of energy."

"No, it was actually a fairly simple plan. Concentrate the people into designated population zones, claiming that it was the only way to make sure that there was an even distribution of food, fresh water, and medical services. Then, using eminent domain, take all the remaining land and destroy all signs of human habitation, claiming that either criminals were using the buildings as command centers, or that testing had identified them as reservoirs of the virus. After all, there had already been three waves of the disease and they had to come from somewhere. It was likely that the people would believe that viruses, those sneaky little creatures, could hide in abandoned homes, waiting for an unsuspecting host to walk back in.

"People who resisted concentration were to be either forcibly brought into the APZs, where 'persuasion' could be used to convince them of the necessity of the action, or they were to be eradicated as 'terrorists.'"

O'Reilly's face grew, if anything, even more stormy, his eyes flooded with pain at unvoiced memories. "These people, they were called ghosts, and some ass with a sick sense of humor called the teams sent out to deal with them exorcism teams. After the first month or so, the orders changed. The only ones to be brought back were children young enough to be converted to this new way of life. Anyone else was to be killed."

A look of horror coursed across Maggie's face as she looked at O'Reilly and realized that he had been part of this. No wonder his sleep was filled with nightmares. No wonder he had been so reluctant to confide in her what his life had been like prior to coming to Hideaway. Imagined images of mothers begging for their children's lives, only to be cut down in front of those same children flickered though her mind and she wondered how she would be able to sleep tonight. Then another thought leaped into her mind.

"How... how could you be a part of that, and how did you get away?"

Pained by the look of revulsion on Maggie's face, the clenched hands on the table, O'Reilly looked down at his own hands, unable to stand the sight of his haggard, haunted face reflected in her eyes.

"You've got to understand, Maggie, when we were recruited, or assigned is more like it, to the Enforcers, we were given the same story as everyone else. That the APZs were the only way to make sure that all people were cared for. Most of us had served in some form of law enforcement or military, and we were used to following orders, even if we weren't sure about them. And, hell, they were convincing. There's no arguing that.

"Then, when the annihilation teams began going out, we were again told it was because of the virus, or the crime. It was unfortunate, but there it was. Eminent domain. The government taking private property for the good of the people. If someone in the APZ happened to see the smoke, we were to either tell them that a hotbed of the virus had been discovered, or more likely that ghosts had set a wildfire in order to try and get hold of a supply train. Since those things were happening on a regular basis, we were never entirely sure when the story was the truth.

"The people were shell shocked, devastated, demoralized. They were looking for anyone to take charge, and we were the ones who were put in that position. For the most part, we believed in our jobs wholeheartedly."

"The first few exorcisms I went on, the targets were groups of men, bent on raiding our supply trucks. I didn't enjoy killing them, but I couldn't let the people in my charge go hungry. It was necessary, just as my using my service weapon was occasionally necessary when I was a sheriff's deputy. Then one night my team was sent to an encampment of ghosts just outside of Oatman, Arizona, north of Kingman. We took them at dawn, when they were all asleep. They hadn't even posted sentries."

O'Reilly abruptly rose to his feet and began stalking around the room, hands clenched at his sides. The pain in his voice became more pronounced, if anything, and he spoke more quietly as if fighting to control his emotions. Then, as he was passing the couch where Lindy was sleeping, he stopped, and stood, looking down at her.

"This band of ghosts wasn't a criminal group. They were only trying to make it on their own. They weren't asking or taking anything from anyone." His voice became even softer and he reached out to smooth the hair off Lindy's sweaty cheek. "There were a couple families, including children, and the team wiped them out." He closed his eyes at the memory, apparently unable to erase the sight from his mind.

Opening his eyes again, he looked back at Maggie still seated at the table. "I tried to stop them. I grabbed the gun from the man nearest me, but it made no difference. And I just couldn't bring myself to open fire on my comrades myself. When it was all said and done, nine people died, including five children, and I was reassigned to a job at a security post in the APZ for my refusal to follow orders.

"They couldn't just let me go, see. I knew too much. So I was kept under close surveillance but also given a job to do while they waited to see how badly I was broken." He took a deep breath before he continued, and Maggie realized again how much recounting this story was costing him emotionally.

"While I was working there, in a place they called the Nursery, where all the orphaned children were kept and taught the new green gospel, I met a young girl named Christina. Her father had been a sociologist before he was killed for 'inciting a riot.' Since I was the only one manning the security station, I was often able to visit her while she was being kept in isolation for talking about what she'd learned from her father. It was there that I started to realize how far the governmental conspiracy to control us really went.

"You see, I had believed the story that people needed to be gathered together in order to make sure that everything was distributed fairly. That the social order would break down quickly in the face of a disaster of such magnitude. After all, there have been stories of other disasters and the looting and crime that followed. It seems, however that some of that has been blown out of proportion. Back at the beginning of the 21st century, the government took on a 'command and control policy' toward disaster management, actually making FEMA part of Homeland Security. This action turned disaster response into a more militaristic operation than it had ever been before, even when the disaster had nothing to do with the military, terrorists or anything of that type."

Maggie was watching him carefully now. She remembered 9/11 and Hurricane Katrina, and all the other weather related disasters that followed. She also remembered studying in school how following 9/11 the community of New York had organized evacuations and searches, but how during Hurricane Katrina many people had died due to the failure of the social structure.

"The president at the time said that the results of research following Hurricane Katrina indicated that the command and control method was the optimum way to handle a disaster of this scale. According to Christina's father, though, many sociologists thought that the administration at the time had reached the wrong conclusion from the research: Had interpreted it incorrectly. Christina said that her father and others believed that it was better to provide outside assistance to the small communities, because they felt the research showed that these communities could help and heal themselves much more effectively than if the government came in and took over. Sure, it would have been difficult to reach everyone considering how widely spread this disaster was, but in many scientists' opinions that would have been preferable to the APZs. Her father was talking out against concentration when he was gunned down." O'Reilly stopped, head bowed, then looked up at Maggie again, obviously almost at the breaking point.

"She was such a brave little girl. She reminded me so much of my daughter." He stopped, unable to go on.

Maggie's eyes opened wide in shock and she wanted to ask him a thousand questions, but knew it wasn't the time. Soon, but not now with the wounds on his spirit so freshly torn open. So instead she simply asked, "What happened to Christina?"

"She's still at the APZ. It was a miracle I got out without being captured, and who knew what I would find when I got here. I couldn't expose her to that. At least at the APZ she's fed and clothed and has a roof over her head. Medical care if she needs it. She's smart. She'll learn to play the game."

"Was it what Christina told you that made you decide to run?"

"No, though that was part of it. I started to realize that much of what we'd been doing was wrong, though I still believed that the administration had just simply deluded itself into believing that this was the only way to handle things. Government agencies are good at that you know; putting on blinkers and not evaluating other ideas. Only moving forward on the one in front of them.

"No, what really pushed me into moving was a shear accident. I received an interdepartmental envelope one day, originating from Central Control. It should have been a census of children staying at the APZ, but somehow a copy of a set of memos from the Chinese government, the British government, and several others had become mixed in with the census pages. Somebody in the Central Control office screwed up royally. These memos all outlined the progress their countries were making with consolidating their populations and returning land to its original condition.

"These memos made it clear that the APZs were here to stay. That the governments never considered them temporary. They only used that line to convince the people to go. Anyone who tried to rise up against the new control was to be disposed of discreetly."

Maggie was shaking her head, wondering what was wrong with her. Why hadn't she seen this coming?

"See, the authorities felt that with the population drastically reduced and demoralized, it would be easier to convince them of the necessity of sacrifice, just for survival's sake. Of course no one is complaining that they don't have their ATVs, their TVs, their SUVs. Hell, they're just happy to be alive, fed and sheltered. History's filled with accounts of people doing things they normally wouldn't consider doing when faced with survival challenges. Think of the Donner party, or that plane crash in the Andes when people ate their companions in order to survive.

"Then there are the children. For some reason the bad vaccine wasn't as dangerous for the children, though many still died. Not as many as the adults, though. So many were orphaned and these children will be taught the way the government wants them taught. One might even say brainwashed. They're so much more vulnerable to that because of the emotional trauma they've suffered. The government estimates that within a couple of generations no one will even consider living outside the APZ as a desirable goal. Hell, within a hundred years or so, they might even have the population convinced that living outside the APZ is tantamount to suicide.

"But what about elections?" Maggie asked, frustrated at the image that O'Reilly painted of a world so drastically altered. "We have a democracy. They won't have a hundred years, or even several generations in order to make this happen. The next election should start to bring balance back to the government if they go overboard."

"They have plans for that too. Don't think they forgot that. I don't know everything, but I do know they wouldn't be foiled by something as simple as an election and a change in administration. They'll get around that, I'm sure. Just the judicious use of the correct type of propaganda in the right places might be all it takes. Much of Hitler's ability to stir Germany into the atrocities it carried out during World War II was simply due to propaganda applied at the right time in the right places."

"So, that was it? That was what made you decide to risk running?" Maggie asked finally after contemplating O'Reilly's last statement.

"Yeah. I realized that this thing was so big, there was nothing I could do about it. But I wouldn't be a part of it any more, so I made a plan and escaped. The problem is that they know I know what's going on, and they may not want to take the chance of my spreading the information and trying to instigate a revolution among the ghosts."

"You're not, though." Maggie said, confused. "You came here by yourself, not to spread anything."

"I came here to think, probably to stay, but they can't know that. I only hope that I hid my tracks well enough on my escape that they're currently looking for me anywhere between Laughlin and Alaska.

O'Reilly stopped, bowed his head and sank down on the end of the couch. Maggie, mind whirling from all the information he'd given her, rose to her feet and walked over toward him. She placed her hand gently on his shoulder.

Looking up into her eyes, he said, "I don't think they'll be able to trace me here. It's too remote. No one in Laughlin knew me, or anything about my past, but I know they'll want to find me. That's why I insisted on the caves. If things get bad, you are to take Mark and Lindy and go to the caves. I'll turn myself in. They won't suspect that you're here."

"No, O'Reilly, I don't..."

"Maggie stop and think. They won't just take you back. Lindy and Mark maybe, depending on what they see, but not you. I didn't plan on ever having anyone depend on me again. I don't want anyone to depend on me." The raw pain in his voice tore at Maggie's heart. "But here we are, and you've got to think about both the kids. Give me your promise that if they come, you'll protect them."

Maggie considered for a moment, then said, "I'll promise if you'll promise me one thing."

"What?"

"If they come, you won't give yourself up right away. You'll come to the caves with us and we'll hope that they believe that we heard them coming and escaped before they got there. Only if they stay, or come toward the caves will you give yourself up."

"Maggie..."

"That's the only way I'll give you my promise."

"Okay."

"Okay what, buster."

The knot of his features loosened slightly and a ghost of a smile played around his lips at her pugnacious tone. "Okay, I promise that surrender won't be my first action and I'll only do it if it appears our hideout will be found."

"It's a deal then," Maggie stated with a false level of confidence in her voice. "And it won't matter anyway because no one is going to come out here into the middle of nowhere looking for you. Now, me and the little lady here need to hit the hay. We've got a slave driver for a partner and he doesn't let us sleep in."

The ghost of a smile became more pronounced.

Maggie bent to pick up the little girl who immediately snuggled into her chest and tucked her head under Maggie's chin without waking. Turning, Maggie began to walk toward her room. "Go to bed O'Reilly. No nightmares tonight."

"Maggie?" the note of pleading in his voice was so unexpected that she jerked to a stop and turned to face him. He looked at her, his dark, haunted eyes drawing her in like a whirlpool.

"Do you hate me for what I did? I'd understand, but I was only doing what I thought was right at the time."

"Go to bed Jim." Maggie said softly, gently. "I understand that you were misled. I don't hate you, I only wish I had your courage."

Maggie turned back and entered her room, closing the door behind her.

Silence once again laid claim to the main room of the house. The gentle susurration of the nighttime breezes, the frogs, the crickets. In the distance, on the plateau, he heard a coyote yip-howl, only to be answered by several more seconds later. All the sounds that O'Reilly had grown up with and thought of as normal. All those same sounds that seemed so alien and terrifying to so many people born and raised in the middle of the big cities.

If the governments of the world had their way, in a generation, maybe two or three, nearly everyone on the planet would find these sounds strange and fear inspiring. The idea of a world full of people who didn't know or understand nature, whose idea of getting to know the wilderness was a form of reverse zoo, where the spectators were kept safe in cages while the rest of the world went on around them, terrified him.

O'Reilly remained seated on the couch, staring at Maggie's closed door. Thinking. *You have more courage than I'll ever possess, Maggie Langton.*

16

Rickards was talking with Deputy Knox in his office when a rap on the door announced the arrival of Christina Craigson. Dismissing Knox, Rickards rose to greet the young girl, inviting her to sit in the large chair opposite the desk.

"Well, young lady, I appreciate your coming down this morning to help us out." Rickards smiled at her. "Can I get you anything? Water? Tea?"

"No thank you, Captain, but I'd be happy to look at those maps now."

Rickards studied Christina unobtrusively. She was dressed neatly, her brown hair brushed tightly back into a pony tail and her face free of the makeup that used to mark the teenagers of world just prior to the disease and reorganization. She appeared nervous, but that was to be expected, being called down to his office and all. Most kids would be uncomfortable spending time at the Enforcers' headquarters, even though she had volunteered.

She'd made big advances since coming to the APZ. When she'd been brought into the Nursery she'd been an angry, argumentative little thing, spouting off about her father and what he'd taught her. *Those weeks in the isolation chamber have certainly done her good*, he thought, nodding to himself.

The only sour note from his interview yesterday was her story of O'Reilly telling her that he planned on moving to the mountains once everything was over. O'Reilly knew this wasn't a temporary situation. He wasn't supposed to know, but he did. Why would he tell her that he might be moving after everyone was released from the APZs. Unless, of course, it was just a story that you told children to help them feel more comfortable. That was probably it.

Rickards had reread the reports on Christina Craigson last night, noting her refusal to follow the program and buy in to the new order of things when first brought to the APZ. She'd been isolated from other residents, as well as her brothers, since it was deemed that the information she kept repeating was of a sensitive and possibly inflammatory nature, and it was necessary to first disabuse her of the validity of that knowledge. It had apparently worked, since there had been no reports of anything other than behavior worthy of a model citizen since her release from isolation.

He remembered a line in the file stating that she was making frequent requests to spend time with her brothers. Twins, six years younger than her. Neither had caused a problem during their stay at the Nursery. *Well, we'll see how she does today, and maybe that request can be granted.*

"I'm sure you'd like to get out of here, Miss Craigson, so we'll get moving as quickly as possible. Lets get some maps out here on the table that you can look at. You said north of here?"

"Yes, sir. He talked about places like Wyoming, Montana, sometimes Canada, and once even as far as Alaska. He said he liked wild lonely places with lakes and lots of trees." Christina looked up at him, wide-eyed and helpful. "He talked about the place he'd like to buy and said that it was near a small town so he could get groceries and such. I'm sure the name he said started with the 's' sound. I'm sure I'll remember the name when I see it in writing."

Christina started to rise and walk over toward the table that Rickards had indicated. From a cabinet under the large bank of windows, Rickards hoisted a large box of maps and scattered them on the flat surface so that Christina could look them over.

The girl started flipping through the different maps, looking for ones depicting Montana, Wyoming, Idaho, Alaska and the western Canadian provinces. When she found one of those, she set it to the right side of the table. Other maps she carelessly set on the left side, out of the way. Once she had examined all of the available maps, she went back to her right hand stack and started opening them one at a time, and looked through the indexes cross referencing with the locator coordinates.

Finally, on the third map she was looking at she exclaimed, "Here it is. It's name is Shelby" Christina pointed excitedly to a small spot on a Montana map.

"You're sure that's it?" Rickards said, looking puzzled.

"Yes, I'm completely sure. That's the place he talked about." Christina was so excited at being able to find the correct location that she began to spin about, hugging herself. Rickards stepped back, watching the girl, smiling ironically at her joy, thinking how easy it had been to get her to give up her hero. If, of course the place she indicated was really where O'Reilly headed. There was something about that spot. He wasn't sure what, but as soon as she left, he'd have to find someone who knew Montana and ask him to look at Christina's pick.

Suddenly, in a flood of exuberance, Christina flung out her arms, accidentally knocking all the maps from the left side of the table, the ones she'd discarded, onto the floor, scattering them everywhere. Christina stopped abruptly and looked guiltily at Rickards.

"Oh, I'm so sorry! I'll pick them up right away. Please don't be mad." Christina knelt to the floor and began gathering all the maps into a pile, crawling under the table, and into the space between a large chair and the wall. As Rickards stooped to help her she became even more agitated.

"Please sir, don't help me. I can do it myself. It was my fault. Please, please let me do it!" she stammered, gathering the maps even more quickly. Rickards, stood up, and took a step back, watching her as she scrambled to gather all the pieces of paper and pack them into the box.

"It's fine, Miss Craigson. Don't worry yourself. Accidents happen." Rickards spoke in as calming a tone as possible. *Girls are such mercurial things,* he thought to himself. *All excited and giddy one moment and half in tears the next. God save me from too many more teenage girls. I may not survive. Or they won't.* Rickards turned his back on Christina, grimacing to himself as he walked back to his desk.

Sitting, he waited as Christina picked up the last of the maps from the floor, placed them in the cardboard box and set it on the table. Then she turned toward him, a question on her face.

"Is there anything else you want me to do, Captain Rickards?" Meek voice, apparently shattered by her accident.

"No, Christina, just come and sit down here a moment." As Christina moved to obey, Rickards opened a desk drawer and withdrew a chocolate bar, a valuable commodity in a community where candy was hard to come by.

"Here you go, young lady. I certainly appreciate your help in this matter. Finding Officer O'Reilly is immensely important as I told you."

Christina accepted the candy bar, thanking Rickards politely, then tucking it into one of her many pockets. Rickards was surprised, expecting her to eat it immediately. *Maybe she's taking it to share with her friends in the Nursery, though. She seems like such a nice, polite child.*

"Christina, I see in your file that you've been asking to spend more time with your brothers." At the mention of her brothers, Christina snapped to attention, fathomless blue eyes fixing intently on Rickards. For a moment he had the disquieting feeling that the child had changed into another person right before his eyes. Before he could evaluate the change, however, Christina softened again, a glimmer of unshed tears shining in her lower eye lashes.

Momentarily taken aback, Rickards nonetheless persisted with his intention. "I'm thinking that you deserve a reward for the excellent progress you've been making these past few weeks. I will speak with the caregivers at the Nursery and arrange for you to spend at least an hour a day with your brothers. Would that make you happy?"

"Oh, yes sir! Nick and Ryan are the only family I have in the whole world, and I want to see them so bad." One of the tears escaped her eye and trickled down her face where she dashed it away with the back of her right hand. "I can't thank you enough, really I can't." She bounced up from her seat and ran around the desk where she bestowed a huge hug on the captain.

Taken completely by surprise, Rickards patted her hesitantly on the back. "Well then, uh... That's good... That's fine then."

Christina, releasing her hug, returned to her seat, face shining.

"I'll make the call this afternoon, Miss Craigson." Rising from his seat, he walked to the office door, beckoning her to follow him. Opening the door he summoned the young caregiver who had escorted Christina to the headquarters. Turning back to the girl, Rickards again reached out with his hand, taking Christina's and shaking it.

"Again, I thank you for all your help. You've made things much easier for us."

He watched as Christina, escorted by the caregiver, crossed the floor, leaving by the main double doors at the front of the building. Returning to his office he took the map that Christina had chosen, spread it on his desk, then sat and studied the area that the girl had indicated. Something continued to tickle the back of his mind. He just couldn't put his finger on it. Just something not right.

He was sure, though the Christina had done her best to help them.

No, if there was something wrong in all of this it wasn't her fault. She had definitely done her best.

17

Nighttime again.

Christina lay in her bed, unable to sleep. She was too excited; so totally wound up that she wanted to jump up and down, not lie quietly on her bed. But that wouldn't be acceptable behavior and she didn't dare draw attention to herself again. Not after today and the progress she'd made.

That captain was such a moron it was unbelievable. He completely underestimated Christina, although, even if she did say so herself, she'd put on a masterful performance. What an ass! She couldn't believe that he actually fell for her map sorting, and the 'accidental' knocking of the maps to the floor. She'd had a moment's concern when he'd started to help her pick them up; worried that he'd find the one she wanted. But no, he'd been dissuaded easily by her protestations. She was sure he never suspected that she'd slipped the Arizona map into her shirt. Then on top of it all, to offer her the only other thing missing from her plan. Access to her brothers.

Christina had been able to spend time with Nick and Ryan that afternoon during free time. There hadn't even been extra supervision, proving to her that she'd convinced Rickards of her total change of heart.

Out on the play area Christina, Nick and Ryan retreated immediately to the sand pit, a convoluted depression filled with white sparkling sand. Apparently the hotel designers thought that the irregular borders made it look more high class than the average sand box.

Once there the three children began diligently constructing an enormous sand castle complete with turrets, draw bridge and moat.

While they molded and patted the sand, Christina quietly filled the boys in on what had been happening with the escape plan, while they told her all about life on the boys' side of the hotel.

Adding sand to a battlement worthy of any European palace, Christina spoke quickly in a soft voice, keeping an eye out for anyone who might be close enough to listen.

"I got the map this morning, guys. I haven't gotten a chance to look at it yet, but I'm sure I'll be able to find the canyon on it. It can't be that far. I've been collecting food, and blankets and almost everything else we'll need.

Ryan, head bowed over the tower he was shaping, glanced up at Christina out of the corner of his eye. "How far do you think it is, Christy? Will we be able to walk that far?"

"It'll be a long walk, no doubt about it, Ry, about seventy or eighty miles. But we can do it, I know we can. It's got to be better than staying here for the rest of our lives."

"We've never walked that far, Christy," said Nick, molding a bucket of sand to the top of another tower. "Where would we get water? How will be eat when we get there?"

"It'll be okay, honest, Nick." Christina assured her brother. "There'll be houses and farms and such for part of the way, and we'll carry canteens. Maybe we'll even find bikes or something so we can move faster."

The boys looked at each other and nodded. Nick looked at Christina, "Fine, we're ready when you are, Christy. What else do we need?"

"Well, can you guys get some backpacks like the ones we carried at school? I've got one to carry my books in that the caregivers gave me when we got here."

"Yeah," Ryan said, nodding again more vigorously. "They gave us each a pack, too. We can use those to carry food."

"We can tie our blankets on the bottom of them with shoelaces. Do you have hats? Boots or walking shoes?" The boys nodded assent to each of Christina's list of items needed to go on the lam.

"I still need to gather some more food, and find some things like flashlights and such, but I think I know where to get those." Christina said, using a stick to etch a stone pattern into the sides and floors of the castle. "I also need to find the best way out of town, so that we don't get caught, but I've got an idea on how to do that. We could maybe be ready in a week or two at the most."

"Good," said Ryan, Nick nodding in agreement.

"We meet here every afternoon, okay? And see how we're doing?" The boys both nodded.

"Christina! Christina Craigson!" One of the caregivers was standing in the doorway, hand shielding her eyes, looking around the play area.

"Yes, I'm here!" Christina called, waving toward the woman.

"It's time to come in and get ready for the dinner service."

"Coming," Christina turned back to the boys. "I'll see you tomorrow afternoon during free time. Remember, don't tell anyone. Got it?"

"Got it." Ryan said.

"Aye Aye, Chief." Nick chimed in.

The three rose to their feet and the boys, looking at each other and grinning from ear to ear gleefully destroyed the castle, kicking it to pieces, laughing like loons the entire time. Christina looked on for a moment, shaking her head, but smiling, then turned and headed back into the hotel where she was scheduled to help at the dinner service.

That night in bed, Christina thought back over the day and contemplated her future. *Two weeks at the most,* she thought. It had to be soon. The rainy season was coming, and while that would make it easier getting water, it would definitely make it more difficult in other ways. The most important thing though, was that they would be out of here.

Two weeks at the most.

18

The next two weeks passed in a whirl of activity. Maggie and Mark worked hard to get the extra seeds O'Reilly brought back from the ranch into the ground. Seeds already planted were growing nicely, and the chickens had only broken into the garden once, decimating a row of potatoes and one of beans. However, because they were also decimating the grasshopper population, and producing nine to ten eggs every day, Maggie was inclined to forgive them.

O'Reilly went hunting and brought in several more deer and a large bull elk, efficiently rendering them into jerky and storing much of it in the cave hideout. Following a recipe he found in one of the books discovered in the camp's house, he also began to tan the hides. As he explained it, a few hides would make valuable additions when winter came blowing down the canyon. The skins might also be the only thing that stood between them and nudity when they were no longer able to get material.

Several times O'Reilly took Mark or Maggie and rode up in the eastern pasture, checking on the cows they had turned out there. By his count, they had approximately twenty cows, fifteen calves, and three bulls. In talking over things with Maggie, he said that he felt that pasture could maintain that number nearly indefinitely as long as they didn't just let the calves keep building up and either butchered them out in the fall, or turned them out into other pastures.

Lindy had been absorbed into camp life as though she'd always been there. She toddled around following one of the others and chattering non-stop about subjects of vital importance to a two-year-old, but largely unintelligible to everyone else. Which was fine since her conversations didn't seem to require a second participant.

Strangely enough Lindy persisted in calling Maggie "mommy" even though O'Reilly said Maggie bore little resemblance to the dead woman. They didn't know if at some point in the future Lindy would be able to tell them why, or if for the remainder of her life Maggie would replace her mother in her mind and memories.

It didn't really matter, Maggie thought, since Lindy had taken root in her heart as thoroughly as any natural daughter would have done. She would give her life for either of her children, though she certainly hoped that this ultimate demonstration of maternal love wouldn't be required of her any time soon.

Mark had fully embraced his new role as big brother, taking Lindy around the home yard, introducing her to all the animals. Gypsy fell immediately and deeply in love and would follow the little girl everywhere, much to Lindy's delight. Jack was not quite as convinced, but even he would put up with Lindy grabbing his neck ruff and pulling his ears without protest. Especially if the fingers she was shoving in his mouth happened to be covered with something tasty.

Such was Gypsy's devotion, that every night she began sleeping immediately outside Maggie's door, trying to sneak in when Maggie wasn't looking. If she did manage to gain entrance without being spotted, she would immediately go to the side of Lindy's makeshift crib and curl up, remaining there the entire night, or until her trespass had been discovered and she was forcibly ejected.

Her position outside the door caused problems on more than one occasion when Maggie, leaving the room in the dark, tripped over her. After four or five nights of this, Maggie finally decided that it was better to have dog hair in the bedroom, than crack her skull falling over the pooch in the mornings. From that point on, Maggie would let Gypsy into the room every night when they went to bed, letting her out in the morning when they got up.

Throughout this time period, O'Reilly, Mark and Maggie worked diligently to provision the cave for possible use. Now that Maggie was acquainted with the conditions of O'Reilly's escape from the Laughlin APZ, she understood and embraced his sense of urgency. However, to Mark she continued to act as though the cave hideout was a bit of a joke. Mark had lived with enough fear and anxiety these past few months. She didn't want to increase it for no reason, and she still believed in the bottom of her heart, that the Enforcers would never find this hidden canyon.

The most difficult and worrisome aspect of hiding out in the caves was the difficulty in obtaining fresh water. Jerky, prepared correctly, could last an extremely long time. Likewise, once Maggie deciphered the instructions in the home canning manual O'Reilly brought from the ranch, and once the garden started producing, preserved vegetables and fruits would also last a long time.

And if not, Maggie thought, *We can always leave the jars available for the attackers, and inflict a deadly level of food poisoning. We have to seize all the possible advantages here.* The image of Alice in *Alice in Wonderland* flitted through her mind, finding a jar marked "eat me." Maybe if she left a loaf of fresh bread and a lethal jar of preserves on the table, she could take care of all their problems without firing a shot. They'd simply be able to capture the invaders as they squatted in the bushes, groaning from the cramps.

Water was a problem, though. It wasn't as if it wouldn't last. It might taste funny after a couple of days, but it would last, especially if they boiled it before putting it into the containers. It was those containers that were the problem. O'Reilly had brought back all the bottles and jars he could carry from the ranch. The collection was varied without a doubt, and many had to be saved for canning, but after sterilizing and filling all that remained and carrying them to the cave, they still only had about 10 to 15 gallons of water laid by for emergencies. For four people, two of them adults, that translated into less than a week, even if they rationed it carefully. If you added in the dogs - and Maggie was pretty sure that Gypsy would be more of a liability left outside, pointing out their location, than brought in - the only conclusion Maggie could reach was that they needed a lot more bottles and they needed them fast.

A belligerent crow tore Maggie out of a blissful dream filled with hot baths, scented with sweet smelling bath salts.

A familiar mantra began to run through her mind, *chicken pot pie, roast chicken, fried chicken, chicken fajitas, chicken nuggets, chicken cordon bleu.* Another crow split the predawn air. *Chicken salad, sweet and sour chicken.* Yet another crow pealed forth eliciting other answering crows from the distant chicken coop. *The hell with it! I'm throwing the damned thing in the river to see if it can swim!* One more crow. Maggie groaned, gritting her teeth and clenching her hands. This was only the most recent of her plans to dispose of this particular rooster in a mental activity that had become a morning ritual during the past two weeks.

For some reason, Houdini, as Mark had named the rooster, simply would not stay in the chicken coop. They had hunted for all the holes, patching them diligently. Every evening they made sure that he was tucked up safe and sound when they shut the chicken coop door. Every morning, however, found him perched on the windowsill of the house, crowing to wake the dead, and anything else within a five mile radius.

They'd tried closing the windows at night, but the hot summer air and increasing humidity as they neared monsoon season, made sleeping uncomfortable. They simply had to leave the windows open during the night, ridding the house of any warm air built up during the day time, then close them tightly against the heat of the day. It was just their bad luck that Houdini had chosen that location to make his morning announcements.

They spent several days debating on what to do with the cocky black and white rooster. Maggie's suggestion of inviting him to dinner as the main course was turned down flatly by O'Reilly, much to her surprise since he tended to dislike the chickens.

"If we kill off the rooster, the hens won't be producing chicks, and eventually your flock will die out. How much sense does that make?" was O'Reilly's reasonable explanation.

"We've got three roosters. How many do we need to produce chicks?" Maggie demanded. Thoughts of chickenacide ran through her mind in a wide variety of forms after the fourth morning of Houdini's self-appointed alarm clock act.

"Yeah, we've got three roosters," O'Reilly admitted. "But what if next week a hawk gets one, and a coyote gets the other. If you've already killed Houdini, then you're out of luck unless we can find another abandoned chicken flock to raid."

"But we've got a hen sitting on some eggs right now," argued Maggie, refusing to give up her dreams of gory dismemberment. "There's got to be a rooster in that batch."

"You've heard of counting your chickens before they hatched, haven't you?" O'Reilly countered, looking at her out of the corner of his eye. "I know that rooster is as annoying as hell, but it would be just plumb foolish to kill him off before you have a guaranteed replacement or two or three. I didn't bring those damn things all the way on horseback just to have them die out because one rooster doesn't know when to shut his beak."

Maggie's stormy face, and grumbled replay apparently amused O'Reilly because a huge smile flashed out from his deeply tanned face.

"Just every time he annoys you, think of all the things you'll eventually be able to make when we have enough extra chickens to butcher. The roast chicken dinners, the fried chicken, the chicken sandwiches. If we don't get a self-renewing supply of chickens, all of those things will be out of the question."

Every morning since that discussion, when Houdini mounted his perch and greeted the morning, Maggie ran through a litany of her favorite chicken dishes, trying to convince herself that putting up with the rooster was worth it. It was a hard sell, though.

Lindy stirred in her bed, causing Gypsy to get up and check on her charge. Suddenly from another part of the house, Maggie heard a door slam open with a muffled curse, the sound of something hard flung hitting the window frame, and a strangled squawk. Getting out of bed, Maggie opened her door to find a half dressed O'Reilly pulling on the boot he'd apparently pitched at the rooster, muttering the entire time. Smiling, Maggie withdrew behind her door and got dressed, ready to start the new day.

That evening, after Mark and Lindy went to bed, Maggie and O'Reilly sat at the table, looking over the progress that they'd made in the recent weeks and discussing what still needed to be done in order to be ready for the upcoming winter. Maggie had difficulty thinking about cold and snow when they were sitting there in hundred degree temperatures, but O'Reilly assured her that the canyon could become bitterly cold in the winter, the result of cold air sinking. *Blasted laws of physics. Never work for you when you want them to and always do when you don't!*

For the past few days something had been nagging at the back of Maggie's mind, but she hadn't been able to put her finger on it. As they ran over their preparations, the food stored, or soon to be stored, the clothing, the animals and feed, she continued to be frustrated by that elusive feeling. Positive that it was something of vital importance, but also unable to identify exactly what it was.

"What are we missing, O'Reilly?"

"Things are actually looking pretty good, Maggie. If the garden and that old orchard keep going the way they are, and you actually manage to master canning, we should have a plentiful supply of vegetables and fruit to get by," O'Reilly said, looking at the list in front of him. Maggie noticed how the lamp caught the deep red of his hair as he bent over the records, then was surprised that she had noticed something like that.

O'Reilly, apparently unaware that he, rather than their supply situation had become the focus of her attention continued. "Deer hunting has been good. We've still got quite a bit of ammo, though I'd like to have more. When the weather cools sufficiently, we'll be able to butcher a calf. Hopefully the rains will be good this summer. Last winter's moisture left us with plenty of grass, but this hot weather is starting to dry it out. A good monsoon will keep things going well enough to keep the calves fat. The chickens are producing well, although they'll probably stop laying in the winter, especially since they have to pretty much find their own feed. We might try our hand at pickling eggs for the winter."

"We need more jars, both for canning and for water."

"Yeah. Things are pretty quiet right now. You don't need me here as much since you've gotten pretty good at the chores that need to be done." He grinned at her. "It's probably time for me to head off to another ranch or camp and see what I can find." O'Reilly's mood shifted. He sighed and Maggie knew he really didn't want to leave the relative safety of the Hideaway.

"Is there another ranch nearby?" she queried.

"Eagle Camp is off to the southwest about a day's ride." An indecipherable looked crossed his face and Maggie remembered him talking about Eagle Camp. It was where he grew up. A small camp on Eagle Creek, he'd said. Something had happened there that had killed his father and caused his mother to take him and his brother and sisters and move into town.

Since the night when O'Reilly had unburdened himself to her about his reasons for leaving the APZ, he had never again spoken of his previous life and before that it had only been funny stories about growing up in a camp. Countless times she wanted to ask him about the daughter he'd briefly mentioned, and about the mother of that daughter, the wife he never spoke about. Something about the character of the sorrow he'd expressed that night forbid her from probing where she wasn't invited. This evening, however, she felt, if not an openness, at least less density to his reluctance to reveal himself.

"What happened at Eagle Camp? You mentioned that your father died. Was it an accident with a horse or something like that?"

Her question was met with silence, and Maggie thought that he would shut her out and refuse to answer her. After a pause, however, he began to speak, quietly, head bent, as though he were talking to the dog lying at their feet on the cool stone floor.

"It was time for the fall wagon to go out. When we gather and work the cows and wean the calves?" Maggie nodded, understanding his terms. He'd talked before of the wagons when the cowboys went out as they had for over a hundred years, and performed those tasks needed to keep the cattle healthy and producing for another year.

"That year the wagon boss and the jigger boss had decided that Jason and I could go along, at least when they were nearby the camp. It was the first year we were allowed to go and we were so excited, it's hard to describe. The wagons hold a lot of tradition. This ranch actually still had the old chuck wagon that was used to carry the food, pots and pans, as well as bedrolls and teepees back before automobiles. Our wagon had been on the ranch for nearly a hundred years and kept in perfect condition. We didn't use it as an actual chuck wagon anymore. Pickups are handier." O'Reilly smiled at the memory.

"That first morning we got up with the rest of the crew and helped hold the ropes around the remuda. You know, the horses? See, there aren't a lot of small corrals in some of those places, and most of the ranch horses aren't exactly walk out and catch types. So the cowboys stretch out their ropes and make a temporary pen to hold the horses in. Then each cowboy calls out his mount for the day and the jigger boss ropes it and brings it out to him.

"Neither Jason nor I had more than one horse. We were going to only be there for the day or two it took them to work our pastures, but we still got to participate and our Dad was watching, proud as all get out, though he was treating us like he would any other cowboy and giving us the rough side of his tongue if we screwed up."

Maggie sat patiently, listening quietly to the story, nodding occasionally. There had been times in the past where O'Reilly talked about life on the ranch, so she was familiar with some of the terms he was using. Her mind, always ready to take in more information and file it away for future use on articles, painted a picture of cowboys, holding ropes around a milling group of horses, while one man, dressed in spurs, chaps and hat swung a loop out and over a horse's neck.

"The cowboss had hired a couple of new cowboys, most of them good, experienced men. But one of these guys was a real gunsel, no experience or sense whatsoever, Tompkins, the owner, wanted him because he was some cousin of a cousin, going through some rough times. Tompkins thought it would be good for him."

"A gunsel is like a city slicker?" Maggie asked, clarifying the new term in her mind.

"Yeah, someone with no experience. You might call him a 'dude,' or a 'greenhorn.' It's usually not a good term to be slapped with, sort of used in derision."

"So, Mark and I are gunsels?"

O'Reilly laughed, the lowering storm cloud of expressions that had settled on his face as he told this story suddenly lightening. "Oh, yeah. You two couldn't go much farther in that direction. But, like I said, it was usually not a polite term. Though, of course, most died-in-the-wool cowboys tended to look down on anyone who wasn't born in spurs, with a rope in his hands."

"Anyway, my dad and this gunsel crossed paths several times during the day. This idiot wasn't much at taking direction from anyone, including Dad, the jigger or the cowboss. Only reason he wasn't fired on the spot was because the owner wanted him there. Me, I wish they'd taken his horse and sent him walking back to headquarters the first time he'd crossed with the jigger."

"That night, while everyone was around the fire, eating dinner, the talk turned to this gunsel, and some of the stupid things he'd done during the day. The cowboys gave him a pretty bad time, and I guess my dad was one of the worst, ripping the guy for being a danger to horses, cattle, and cowboys alike, and how he should turn in his saddle and get himself a desk job so as he wouldn't get anyone killed. This guy just sat there, steaming. Staring into his plate of stew and not even looking up at the rest of us laughing at him.

"That night, after everyone turned in, the calves we'd weaned during the day panicked. We'd left them in a small water trap, intending to drive them to a new pasture the next morning. All weaned calves spend some time yelling for their mothers, but this was different. We could hear them bellowing and milling around, and it sounded as if they were about to break through the fence. Everyone headed out to help get things under control. It didn't take long, but when all was said and done we couldn't find my dad anywhere. In fact, it didn't appear he'd ever been in his bedroll."

Maggie felt a growing sense of horror, sensing what was coming next.

"Finally we found his body, trampled into the dust and manure. Looked like he'd been run over by the cattle in the panic, though what he'd been doing there no one could figure, until they turned him over and found the knife sticking out of his chest. Got looking more, and realized that the gunsel was also nowhere to be found."

Maggie was watching O'Reilly intently, seeing how much this memory was costing him, and appreciating his willingness to share. She was surprised at how far they had come in such a short time.

"That was really my first experience with the law enforcement, and seeing how they handled the investigation, talked with my mother and my brother and me, made me think I might like to be like them some day. When they caught the guy and he ended up standing trial and going to prison for murder, I was sure of it. Mom had to move into town to support Jason and me. I graduated high school and became a sheriff's deputy and Jason went back to cowboying. Now they're both gone with the flu.

"You haven't been back to Eagle Camp since you moved into town after your father's death?" Maggie asked

"No. Another family was assigned to it. I don't remember their name. I suppose it doesn't really matter, anyway. There's stuff there that we need, and a few bad memories won't kill me. Besides there are more good memories of living there than bad"

"Thank you for telling me about your dad. I know it wasn't easy. I appreciate it," Maggie said, reaching out toward O'Reilly's arm where it rested on the table in front of him.

O'Reilly reached out and took her hand briefly, giving it a little shake. "Yeah, well, if we keep on like this, pretty soon you'll know all the dirty little secrets that I've worked so hard to hide." He gave her a rueful smile and released her hand, and rose from his chair. "It's late, and Houdini will be waking us early in the morning so we'd better hit the sack. I'll plan on heading out day after tomorrow if everything goes well. Maybe Mark can come with me. It'd be good for him to see some more of the country."

Maggie looked up in surprise at O'Reilly's suggestion, and a little flower of fear bloomed in her chest at the thought of letting Mark out of her sight. But she nodded, recognizing the wisdom of Mark becoming more familiar with the land around the canyon. If anything should happen to her and O'Reilly, it could be left to him to get Lindy and himself to safety.

O'Reilly looked down at her and grinned. "He'll be safe. *I* won't feed him to a mountain lion, no matter what he does, unlike some people I know," referring back to the threat Maggie had made in the caves. Then he turned and headed for his room, leaving Maggie sitting at the table in the wavering light of the oil lamp, thinking.

Mark was burning with fever, thrashing and moaning, calling for Maggie. She reached for him, trying to calm his cries. She tried to lower his temperature by draping his body with wet towels with little luck. She didn't know how long he could take this punishment. If she couldn't lower his temperature soon, he wouldn't make it. She needed antibiotics, aspirin, something more than wet towels. What was she thinking bringing him out here. If they were in an APZ he would have medical attention. He'd be in a hospital or a clinic or something. It was all her fault. All her fault. His rising cries meshed with her own, reaching a crescendo of tortured voices.

Maggie jerked awake, sitting up in bed, bathed in sweat. Her breath came in gasps and her throat ached as though she'd been screaming. There was no sound in the room, except for the soft breathing of Lindy and Gypsy.

Rising carefully from her bed, she walked out of her room and over to Mark's door. She gently eased it open and listened. Nothing except his quiet breathing. No cries. No fever driven thrashing. It was a dream, she told herself. Only a dream.

She knew, though what they'd been forgetting in all of their plans. When she and Mark had escaped to the Hideaway, Maggie had brought a simple first aide kit. Bandages, antibiotic ointment, aspirin, those types of things. O'Reilly had also had a few medical supplies when he'd come, and had picked up a few more things at the ranch. But life at the camp was a bit hard on the fingers and knees and other body parts, and they'd gone through many of those supplies in the couple of months they'd been there. And there was no friendly neighborhood pharmacy at which to restock.

If they were going to be here as long as O'Reilly said they were, then they needed some serious medical supplies. Ones that would keep as long as possible. And they needed books, or some other type of information on how to treat basic illnesses.

O'Reilly wouldn't find those things at Eagle Camp. They were going to have to get to some type of store before they all fell to those annihilation teams O'Reilly had spoken about. It would be dangerous. It would mean going back toward one or another of the APZs, but she didn't see a choice.

Maggie shivered in spite of the warm night air. She refused to believe that the dream was a premonition, but it was so real. They had to get prepared. Wrapping her arms around herself, she stood outside Mark's door, head bowed, contemplating their options.

A sudden flutter at the window announced the arrival of their feathered alarm clock. Before she could react, a crow split the dark predawn sky, heralding a new day.

19

The monsoons were coming. Christina could feel it in the air; the growing heaviness as the humidity built, day by day. In the afternoons she could see clouds building over the distant mountains, hear rumbling from far away and see flashes of light, but no drops of rain speckled the dust on the balcony outside Christina's window.

The heat and humidity were oppressive and as the week progressed she began to feel a growing agitation. She wondered if she was making the right decision, or if she would be placing her brothers in danger for no reason. *No,* she kept telling herself, *we can't stay here. Dad wouldn't want us here.*

In fact, the ease with which her plans were coming together almost seemed to argue that there was a higher power watching over them. In the past week Christina had been afforded several choice opportunities to explore the kitchens on her own after her cleaning chores in the dining room were completed. On these occasions she'd managed to secure several large bags of jerky, boxes of granola bars, several boxes of raisins, and, miracle of miracles, fifteen packets of freeze dried entrees, the type people took camping. These must have been part of a stash brought in when teams cleared out area houses, since there weren't many, but they were perfect for Christina's needs.

Ryan and Nick had also been busy, getting lucky enough to find an unattended maintenance cart with flashlights, duct tape and several tarps. They'd quickly helped themselves, stashing the items under their beds in their room.

Every afternoon the three met at the far side of the sand pit and reviewed their progress over a wide variety of sand sculptures. The caregivers were so impressed with the children's structures that they started hanging around while the Christina and her brothers were in the sand, making it difficult to continue their planning. In a way, thought Christina, it was funny. They were building the sand castles to avoid suspicion and wound up attracting even more attention than they might have if they'd snuck off into a back corner and spent the entire time whispering among themselves.

Regardless of the interest their castles generated, however, they still managed to find enough time to compare notes.

The only thing the three were missing was a solid plan on how to make it out of the Nursery, through the streets of the APZ, past the barriers and into the open land. The most difficult part, as far as Christina could see, being the escape from the Nursery with all the supplies they'd collected.

The entry way for the hotel wasn't guarded. Who would need to guard a nursery for children? But there were cameras, as O'Reilly had told her, and there were always caregivers about.

On one visit while Christina was in isolation and when O'Reilly had been in an especially talkative mood, he'd told her that all the adult members of the APZ were given jobs upon entry and registration. The disaster scientists like her dad had said that standing around feeling helpless was a sure moral buster. That's one thing the government had gotten right. Giving the people a meaningful occupation helped them focus on the positive aspects of helping others, and aided in the survival of the social structure.

Because of this policy, however, Christina had a higher number of adults to deal with than might normally be found in an orphanage facility and figuring out a way to avoid these well meaning individuals was a challenge that she had not yet conquered. She was positive it could be done, but no amount of brainstorming with Nick and Ryan had struck upon a feasible plan.

The biggest challenge in getting out of the Nursery was the need to get the backpacks, blankets and other supplies out as well. She was pretty sure that if they waited for times when the caregivers were exceptionally busy, the children could get themselves out, but they wouldn't get far if they didn't have the things they'd collected.

After talking more with her brothers Christina decided that the only way to handle the problem was to somehow get their packs out and hidden within easy access. Then later, the three could grab opportunities to sneak out, retrieve the packs and make good their escape.

If the children tried to walk out with the packs, they would draw much more attention than if they took the packs out one by one, and secreted them in some nearby spot. Of course, they would probably draw a lot of attention even with just one pack, and if a caregiver stopped them and searched the bag their whole plan would be discovered. She couldn't think of any reasonable excuse to give someone as to why she had a backpack filled with food and clothes and with a bedroll tied on the bottom. She had a pretty good opinion of her ability to come up with stories, but she was sure that one was beyond even her.

Christina and her brothers talked whenever possible, but none of the three could come up with a solution to the problem until an unexpected ally emerged one afternoon about a week after she'd secured the map and begun meeting with her brothers.

Christina completed her dinner chores and headed back to her room in the Nursery with the problem of how to sneak their backpacks out of the hotel dancing through her mind. She was positive that once they'd gotten outside with their supplies they could make it through Laughlin. It would probably have to be done at night, but she was convinced that it could be accomplished.

She was deep into this distracted state when she opened the door to her room and entered to find a scene so unexpected that it took her a moment to realize what she was looking at, and what it could mean to her and her plans.

Alysa, Christina's roommate, was standing next to Christina's bed, vacuum humming nearby. On the bed in front of her was Christina's backpack, unzipped, clothing and food packets overflowing onto the eye-searing blue, gold and purple bedspread.

At the sound of the opening door, Alysa jerked upright and her head snapped around so that she was looking at Christina's surprised face.

"Wh... wha... what are you doing with my pack?" Christina stammered, then more demanding, "Who said you could get into my stuff?"

Simultaneously Alysa blurted out, "You're running away, aren't you? Where are you going?"

Both girls ground to a halt and stood, staring at one another; intense blue eyes meeting dark brown. Belatedly Christina realized that the door into the hallway was still open, and anyone passing would have an excellent view of her backpack, complete with stolen food items cascading out of it. If that didn't advertise her intention of making a run for it, nothing would.

Quickly she stepped further into the room and closed the door behind her. She then turned to face Alysa again, a storm of confused thoughts whirling around in her mind. *What do I do now? How do I convince her not to turn us in? Oh, my god, I don't want to go back into isolation. I can't!* Christina started to open her mouth to say something, anything, but the look in Alysa's eyes stole the words before they were uttered.

Alysa's bottomless dark brown eyes were wide and intense with shock, but also with an emotion that Christina couldn't identify. Keeping her voice low, so that no one passing in the hall could hear, Alysa repeated her last question.

"Where are you going with all these things? You *must* be running away, but where to?"

Christina's tongue thawed, and she asked a question of her own, softly, vehemently. "What were you doing under my bed?"

Alysa ducked her head briefly, as though embarrassed, but then lifted it again, and that same intense emotion in her eyes grabbed Christina, holding her captive. "I'm on room cleaning duty. You know that. I was vacuuming our room and when I was sweeping under the edge of your bed the vacuum caught the shoulder strap of your pack. When I pulled, it hauled the backpack out with it." She continued to watch Christina intently.

"I'm sorry I snooped. I know I shouldn't have. But, where are you going and... and... *can I come*?"

Christina was taken aback at Alysa's question. It was so unexpected. She'd considered Alysa completely indoctrinated into the dogma being taught at the APZ's school. In fact, Christina had decided a while ago that they'd made Alysa her roommate because she so religiously quoted the lessons being programmed into the children of the Nursery. That it was "dangerous outside the APZ." That the "only way to stay safe and healthy was to live within these new confines." That the "virus and the weather related disasters were a result of man's tampering and their disregard for the balance of nature."

True, a few times, as on the river outing, Christina had caught a glimpse of another Alysa. But it was elusive and Christina had learned little about the dark skinned, dark haired girl's life before the flu and the deaths of her parents resulted in her being brought to the APZ.

Now Christina found herself faced with a dilemma. Trust Alysa and take her with them, or try to pawn her off with a story and hope she didn't tell the authorities before Christina and her brothers could make good their escape.

The undefined expression burning in Alysa's eyes decided Christina.

"I'm taking my brothers and getting out of this place. I know about a hideaway, quite a ways from here. It's out in the country and no one can find us. We'd be safe. You can come with us if you promise not to tell."

It may have been late afternoon, but it was as if the sun had come up a second time in one day within Alysa's face. She seemed to glow from inside, her eyes radiating her joy.

"I don't get it, though," Christina added. "You always acted as though you wanted to be here in the APZ. You talked like you believed in the stuff they were telling us. I figured that you'd been assigned to be my roommate because you so totally believed in what they're doing that you wouldn't be ruined by someone like me."

Alysa ducked her head again, not meeting Christina's eyes for a moment, then looked up and Christina saw an expression of pain on her face. "I saw what they were doing to people who didn't go along with the things they were teaching us. I saw what they did to you. I couldn't do that. I would have gone nuts if I'd been treated the way you were and I figured that the best way to make sure that I didn't get put into isolation, or treated how you, or some of the others were, was to be the best damned convert I could be."

"But when I tried to talk to you about things - about what was happening here - you blew me off." Christina said, confused. "I wouldn't have turned you in. Why wouldn't you talk with me, here in our room?"

"I *had* to make myself believe, don't you see? I couldn't take a chance that someone would walk in. Or that I might slip up outside the room and let them see. I just couldn't. I'm so sorry, but I couldn't take that chance."

It was Christina's turn to drop her head, and she contemplated the mottled blue and brown carpet at her feet for a minute before looking up to see Alysa studying her intently, waiting for what she would say next.

"Okay. I guess it doesn't really matter," Christina admitted. "What matters is that we understand each other now." She smiled at Alysa tentatively and walked over to the bed, sat down next to her pack and started putting the supplies back where they belonged.

Alysa plopped on the bed on the other side of the pack, bouncing a little. "What's your plan? When and how are we getting out of here?"

"I want to leave within the next week, but we're having a bit of a problem figuring out how to get out of the Nursery without anyone catching us."

Alysa nodded attentively.

"Our biggest problem," Christina continued, "is getting the packs out of here. Ryan, Nick and I have gone over it again and again, but can't come up with an idea. We need to get the packs out and hide them where we can get to them easily when we make our escape. But if we walk out the door with the packs, we'll be stopped and the caregivers will figure out what we're doing."

"Maybe I know a way," Alysa spoke up diffidently, as though afraid to tender her suggestion. "What if we take the packs out in the recycling bins, one at a time, and hide them near the big collection bins outside. I'm on the cleaning team. No one will question if I take a bag of garbage out."

A frisson of excitement jolted through Christina. Alysa was right. She could walk right out with the packs hidden in the large wheeled recycling bins. The APZ worked hard to make sure that everything that could possibly be recycled was. Recycling was no longer an option used by only a few. It was now a way of life in the community. Food waste was put into a composting bin which was then collected and used by the agriculturalists, those people who'd been assigned to grow fresh food for the APZ. All other garbage was sorted into various recycling bins that were kept out behind the hotel. As a member of the cleaning team, Alysa wouldn't be questioned if she was taking out a container of garbage for the composting bin, or recycling bins. Once behind the hotel she could remove the pack and secret it nearby, empty the bin and return to the hotel unquestioned. She could even go into the boys section and retrieve their packs without arousing suspicion since she was assigned to clean throughout the Nursery.

The girls' eyes met and the level of excitement could no longer be contained. Christina threw herself across the backpack, hugging Alysa. Drawing back, Christina's blue eyes sparkled. A huge grin split her face.

"That will work, I know it will. Oh, my god, we're going to get out of here. We really are!" The words tumbled out of Christina's mouth as she felt the huge weight of the dilemma fall away from her. "When can we start? I don't want to wait much longer. The monsoons are coming and that will make traveling way more difficult."

Alysa pondered the question for a moment. "Well, I can take your pack out now, today. After all, I'm supposed to be cleaning this room. It would be easy to get a bin. We need to wrap your pack in a tarp or bag or something, though, so that it doesn't get wet if it rains."

"I hadn't thought of that. I don't have a tarp. The boys do, though. They managed to grab some off a maintenance cart that was left in the hall, but they're in the boys' room." A sudden thought struck Christina. "We may not have enough food yet for a third person. We may have to wait a bit longer. Damn!" Christina hated delaying their escape yet again, but she saw no other option.

"You have plenty of food here to get started, especially if your brothers have any at all," Alysa said, thinking hard, face serious. "You don't really need enough for the whole trip, you know. There will be houses along the way, no matter where we're going, We'll be able to break into them and gather more food."

Christina realized Alysa was right. She'd become so focused on gathering food, she hadn't considered that they would be able to raid homes along the way. She'd thought of the abandoned houses as a source of water, using outside spigots, but had never contemplated actually breaking into the buildings and raiding the pantries. The idea of breaking in and stealing someone else's property left a queasy feeling in her stomach, but it wasn't as if the owners had any use for the items any longer.

The place they were heading was remote, however, according to O'Reilly, and she wasn't really sure how many houses there would be. She'd considered waiting to tell Alysa exactly where they were going just in case she turned out to be setting them up, but maybe it would be better to get her ideas up front.

"Do you know anything about Arizona? I mean, have you ever been over there?" Christina asked, studying the other girl.

"Yeah, my grandparents, I mean my mother's parents, live in Tuba City, on the Navajo Reservation in the four corners. I spend... I used to spend part of my summers with them every year." Alysa's voice started to choke up and her eyes began to glisten with tears unshed.

"You're Navajo," Christina exclaimed, surprised. She realized how little she actually knew about her roommate. Other than the fact that Alysa had mentioned enjoying walking in the desert, and that she'd come from a small town, Christina realized she knew almost nothing about this girl she'd just hitched her and her brother's fates to.

"I'm half Navajo. Actually we call ourselves the Diné. My Dad is... was half Apache. He worked on a lot of farms and ranches around here and in northern Arizona. Mom and I traveled with him. Sometimes I'd get to go out with him and help on the ranches, like if we lived at a camp or something. We were living in a small town northwest of here while he was working in a feedyard when the flu hit and both my parents died. That's when I was brought here."

"Wow. I've never lived in the country before," Christina was impressed in spite of herself. It appeared that Alysa might be more help than Christina had originally realized if they were to make their home in the middle of nowhere.

"Why did you ask about Arizona?"

"The place I told you about, the one where we're going, it's in a canyon in northern Arizona."

Alysa grew more attentive, "Where at?"

"I was told it was between highways 93 and 89, and south of I-40. I got a map and have sort of pinpointed where it might be, but it might take a while to find it. We've got to have enough food and water to make it out there."

Alysa considered the information Christina had given her. "That's a lot of empty land in that part of Arizona. We lived up by Peach Springs for awhile. That's north of that spot, but I sort of know what it's like." Alysa thought a while longer as Christina looked on. "We'd need to head over toward Kingman. It's around thirty miles from here."

Christina nodded. She'd seen Kingman on the map, but wasn't sure how large a town it was. There was another concern as well. "You said that it was empty in that direction. Do you think we will find any houses that we can raid?"

"I'm sure there will be some. We'll have to move carefully if there are ghosts. We don't want any part of them. The caregivers say they're like outlaws in the Old West and it wouldn't be safe. But there can't be that many so we should be able to avoid them."

"I was thinking we could find bikes to make the trip faster, we..." Christina stopped as Alysa began shaking her head violently, her black ponytail swishing over her shoulders.

"No, not bikes. We'd have to stick to trails and roads if we were on bikes. It's too dangerous. Once they realize we're gone, they'll be looking for us all over the place. There will be seekers for sure. We need to look for horses. That way we can go wherever we need to go without worrying about roads." Alysa stopped at the appalled look on Christina's face.

"Don't tell me you've never been on a horse before. How were you expecting to live out there?" Alysa appeared amused by Christina's naivete.

"Hey, I was raised in the city. We either drove, or rode our bikes to wherever we were going. We didn't use a form of transportation that left piles of green poop in the middle of the road!"

"No, you used transportation that left clouds of black smoke in the sky. I may not like living here in the APZ, and think these guys are totally nuts, but some things they say do make sense. People have done a pretty good job lately at messing up the planet, and something had to give sooner or later."

Christina shivered at the thought of spending days upon days sitting on a horse. It wasn't that she hadn't been on a horse before. She had. Years ago and the experience had been less than enjoyable. She'd decided that she and horses were not meant for each other and that the closest she ever wanted to get to the smelly things again was watching them in the parades. She remembered an old comedy routine where a guy had said that all he knew about horses was that one end kicked and the other end bit. She was more than willing to let her knowledge of horses end right there, but Alysa had a point.

"Okay, I'll ride a damned horse, but you'd better find me a nice gentle one that doesn't eat kids for lunch," Christina grumbled, noting sourly that Alysa seemed to be gaining a great deal of amusement at her expense.

"It shouldn't be a problem," Alysa said, nodding happily. "This is horse country. Even if they turned all the horses out when the flu hit and people were moved to the APZ, it shouldn't be hard to find some that are willing to help us."

Great, Christina thought crossly to herself, *now I'm going on the run horseback. Get out the six shooters. Jesse James here I come.*

Four days later the backpacks had been moved. Alysa had a ridiculously easy time slipping them out of the Nursery and hiding them near the recycling dumpsters. All they needed now was the perfect opportunity to leave themselves, gather their belongings and work their way out of the APZ.

Christina felt the growing tension. It seemed as though there were eyes everywhere, watching her and waiting for her to make a move. She continued to meet with Nick and Ryan every afternoon during free time. However, she and Alysa were afraid that having Alysa start joining them might draw attention, so Christina acted as liaison, setting up things such as the backpack switch. Much to Christina's disgust the boys were excited about the idea of moving on horseback.

"It'll be so much better, Christy," Ryan said excitedly while Nick nodded behind him.

"Yeah," added Nick. "We'll be like real cowboys. It will be so cool!"

"I simply *cannot* be related to you two," Christina said in revulsion while the boys cracked up with laughter at the look on her face. "Mom and Dad must have made a mistake and picked up the wrong set of kids from the hospital."

That afternoon following her dinner chores Christina stood again at the window of her room, looking toward the Arizona border and the building storms over the mountains that lit the sky with flashes of lightning. They seemed closer this afternoon. Maybe even close enough to hit Laughlin. She was convinced she could smell the rain and the sharp tang of the ozone. They needed to get out of there. The rains would make things so much more difficult.

Suddenly there was a knock from behind her. Christina turned and started for the doorway, but before she could reach it, the white panel was thrown open and Ms. Drew, the head caregiver, quickly strode through the opening.

"Christina, I just received a message from Captain Rickards at the Enforcer headquarters. He's concerned that you were not truthful when you went down to his office the other day and he wants to see you tomorrow."

Christina's face blanched. "I... uh, I don't understand Ms. Drew." Her mind raced, trying to find an explanation for Rickards' call. There was no way that he could know she'd just picked Shelby, Montana, simply because it had an "s" name. "I did my best for Captain Rickards. I don't know what else I can tell him."

"I don't know, young lady, but I'm to have a caregiver escort you to his office tomorrow morning, bright and early. And, I can tell you, miss, he will not be happy, nor will I, if it turns out you've been misleading him." Ms. Drew's pinched face grew, if anything more sour looking, as though she'd bitten into a massive lemon. She glared at Christina accusingly.

A movement behind Ms. Drew attracted Christina's attention. Alysa, done with her afternoon chores was standing in the doorway, looking from Ms. Drew to Christina, a frown of worry creasing her face. Christina stared hard at her, trying to telepathically send her the message to run. Apparently her telepathic skills were on the fritz that evening, however, because Alysa only appeared more confused, and stayed rooted to the spot.

Seeing Christina's attention focused behind her, Ms. Drew turned and saw Alysa standing uneasily at the door.

"Miss Thalman, is there a reason you're eavesdropping at the door?" Ms. Drew bestowed a sharp look on Alysa that caused her to drop her head in embarrassment. Turning back to Christina, Ms. Drew gave her an equally frigid glare. "Tomorrow morning, Miss Craigson. Don't make us come find you."

As though in response to Ms. Drew's tone, the sky outside the window split apart in a brilliant flash of light, followed almost immediately by a crash of thunder that made the windows rattle and caused Christina to clap her hands over her ears, ducking her head into her chest. While Ms. Drew had been talking, the clouds over the nearby mountains had built into towering pillars that then collapsed and spread over the town, stirring up the wind. The air outside the building was filled with a choking, thick dust churned up before the rain front.

Another flash of light, and another clap of thunder; almost simultaneous. Christina, Alysa and Ms. Drew moved toward the window, drawn by the building fury outside. The view began to clear slightly as speckles of rain began to pepper the dust covered window and wash the dust from the air.

The sky had taken on a swollen purple blue color, tinged with an acid yellow. Lightning flashed and thunder grumbled steadily.

Without warning the sky was rent with another sizzling burst of light that was indistinguishable from the roar of thunder that followed. The air seemed to contract, then suddenly expand around the observers, causing Christina and Alysa to throw their arms over their heads and drop to the floor.

Again the lightning blazed and thunder cracked, sounding as if the fabric of the world was being torn apart by giants with sledge hammers. The lights flickered and went out, then an alarm sounded stridently, insistently. Ms. Drew grabbed the girls' arms and pulled them to their feet, away from the window and toward the door.

In the hallway other children were running out of their rooms and heading toward the exits.

"Hurry girls, that last bolt of lightning must have hit the roof. There must be a fire." Ms. Drew pushed them into the chaotic hall to join the stream of hurrying children. "Go down the stairs and to the far side of the square, just as we practiced."

Christina seized Alysa's arm and pulled her down the hall. *Saved by the bell,* she thought, struggling to keep her footing in the crush of girls heading down the stairs. Pushing close to Alysa, counting on the growing clamor of scared voices in the stairwell to cover her words, she whispered urgently into Alysa's ear.

"Alysa... Alysa!"

Alysa turned her head toward Christina, looking dazed by all the commotion.

"We've got to get out of here. I mean run. Tonight. We can't wait."

"You can't mean in this storm," Alysa hissed back, worried eyes glancing around her to see if anyone was paying attention.

"Yes, tonight," Christina insisted. "That Enforcer captain has figured out that I told him a lie about where my friend went and he wants to see me tomorrow morning. If we wait, I might get locked into isolation again. We've got to go now while everything is confused."

Alysa nodded, continuing to hurry down the stairs. "If we're lucky, the power is out all over the APZ. If there's a fire here, then most of the Enforcers and anyone else in charge will also be here. Maybe we can get through the barriers without being caught."

"Right," Christina agreed. "When we get to the square help me find the boys, then we go for the backpacks. Everyone is gathered on the square at the front of the building. We should be able to get around to

146

the side without being caught. We'll just have to watch for firemen and Enforcers."

Alysa nodded again, and continued to hurry forward until the two girls made it to the lobby of the hotel. From there they hustled out the front door and through the pelting rain, across the square, past the still fountain. They joined the large group of children and caregivers in the shelter offered by a neighboring building, and looked back toward the Nursery. Nothing could be seen, though Christina wasn't sure if it would even be possible to see a fire through the murk and rain.

Many of the children, especially the younger ones, were crying. So much had happened to them in the past months that the stress of possibly losing the one home they'd found was too much. Christina and Alysa started weaving their way through the throng, looking for Nick and Ryan. In spite of the chill wind, and her soaked clothes, Christina broke out in a sweat, fearing that the fire alarm would be called off before she could find the boys and the four could sneak away. In the distance sirens wailed, drawing closer, announcing the arrival of the APZ's fire brigade.

Just as Christina was sure she would never find her brothers, a hand pulled at her sopping shirt from the left. Looking back and down she saw Nick, with Ryan close behind. An explosive breath she hadn't realized she was holding blew out of her lungs. She grabbed Nick by the arm, and, with Alysa and Ryan close behind, headed for the northernmost flank of the crowd.

Once they broke free of the majority of the onlookers, Christina stopped, Alysa, Nick and Ryan all crowding around her.

"What's up Christy?" Nick asked, looking up into Christina's face, his brown hair plastered to his head. Drops of water fell from his chin and nose. The rain, however, already seemed to be letting up and the celestial pyrotechnics were moving off to the east.

"We're getting out of here now, guys." Christina watched the looks of surprise cross the boys' faces. They looked at each other and that indefinable communication passed between them. Then they looked back at Christina, expressions of trust shining from their faces.

"It makes sense," Ryan said. "Where do we go from here?"

"We've got to get our packs, then head north, toward the barrier. It's getting darker, and if the power is out all over we should be able to get past the sentries without being seen."

Alysa suddenly chimed in. "Four is too many to head toward the dumpsters where the packs are. I'll tell you what. You take the boys up this street. Stick to the shadows where you can. I'll go with you for a block, then circle back and get the backpacks and meet you with them."

"Are you sure?" Christina asked, looking dubiously toward the building where the firemen were busily moving around like a colony of ants. "Four packs are a lot to carry. I think I should come with you. That way we can each carry two. The boys can wait for us somewhere hidden a few blocks away."

Alysa pondered Christina's statement for a moment, then nodded assent, recognizing the wisdom of having two people to carry the loaded packs.

"Fine, but lets get going. They're going to start counting heads soon, if they haven't already, and we need to be out of sight before they start looking for us."

The four children slowly slipped further away from the crowd, waiting until the growing dusk masked them from view, then turned and ran steadily northward, toward the boundary of the APZ, and freedom.

20

In the end it took O'Reilly four days before he was ready to head out on his next scavenging foray. The morning following his telling Maggie about his father's death she came to him and told him about her nightmare and her concern that they were not prepared for any type of medical emergency. He had to admit she was right.

He also had to point out that neither of them was exactly trained as a doctor, so being prepared might be the least of their worries. But Maggie was adamant. They needed medical supplies, antibiotics, other medicines. As far as he was concerned, too many medical supplies in the hands of untrained novices could be as dangerous as the diseases and injuries themselves. Maybe more so. He might have experience in sewing up injuries on cattle and horses, as well as diagnosing and treating many bovine illnesses, but the idea of trying to jab one of those needles into Maggie or Lindy made his stomach clench.

Nonetheless Maggie was right in one aspect. If something happened, an injury or infection, antibiotics could be the difference between life and death. And, the only place to get antibiotics, or any other medications they might need, was a pharmacy. Maggie and O'Reilly discussed their options, O'Reilly hating the necessity that would drive him back into danger.

"The way I see it there are three, no four, options," O'Reilly stated as he was working beside Maggie in the garden the next morning while Mark was doing his schoolwork. "I could head south to Prescott or Chino Valley, west to Wikieup or Kingman, or north to Ashfork, Williams, or maybe Seligman."

"What's the fourth option?" Maggie asked as she attacked a particularly stubborn weed.

"I could just make the rounds of all the camps and ranches in the area and collect whatever I can find in the medicine cabinets." O'Reilly stood up and stretched his back, then leaned on his digging stick and watched Maggie aggressively assail the large horehound that had begun to grow among the tomatoes.

He caught himself admiring how the muscles of her back and arms moved under the t-shirt and how her golden, honey blond hair stuck to the nape of her neck. Mentally shaking himself he bent his head back to his row in the garden before Maggie caught him looking at her. He was relatively certain that she wouldn't appreciate being scrutinized. Lately there seemed to be a definite softening in their relationship. She wasn't quite as ready with a quick comeback when he showed too much authority for her taste. He didn't want to damage this strengthening friendship just for the sake of a momentary look, nice as that look might be.

"I know going to town would be more dangerous than the camps, but I'm not sure you'd find what we need just by going through houses," Maggie said, breathing hard after her exertions while pulling up the stubborn plant. "Who the heck invented horehound anyway? Whoever it was had a real sick sense of humor." She tossed the plant off to the side of the garden.

"Actually, there are some benefits to horehound," O'Reilly answered, preferring a discussion about the noxious weed to continued talk about venturing into town.

"Nuh, uh. There's no way that smelly, prickly thing could be used, except as a torture device for obsessive compulsive gardeners." Maggie shook her head, thick braid flapping back and forth, from shoulder to shoulder.

"Really," O'Reilly grinned at her disgusted expression. "It can be made into a tea or syrup for sore throats. Supposed to be real soothing too." He paused for a second, thinking. "You know we actually might do better if we found information on natural remedies. Things we can make using plants and minerals found right around here. After all, even if we score big at a pharmacy, that stuff'll eventually all go out of date and we'll be stuck either having to go into the APZ, or trying to hit a supply train."

"Oh, come on. You mean treating diseases with weeds? Give me some penicillin any day," Maggie looked at him in disbelief.

"And exactly where do you think penicillin came from? Moldy bread, that's where." O'Reilly's grin became even more pronounced.

"No honestly, some of those old remedies really worked. Sure some were a bunch of hooey. I'm not suggesting we tie garlic to Mark's feet to treat the whooping cough, though some people swear by it, but other remedies were unquestionably effective," O'Reilly said thoughtfully as he finagled some errant bunch grass shoots out from under a squash plant. "I'm not saying we shouldn't get some more modern medicines, but we need to find a book or something on herbal stuff as well. It can't hurt."

Maggie looked askance at another horehound pushing it's way up between two zucchini plants and then looked back at O'Reilly. "If I get sick and you try and dose me with that damned plant, you'll see what hurts."

"Come on, city girl, we need to explore all our options. This is a new world, but some of the old remedies may be the way to go. The fact is we can't afford to ignore anything that may help us survive out here." O'Reilly grew serious. "We're not far off from the original pioneers, moving out into unpopulated land, too far away from help to be able to count on it. I'll go into Wikieup, and gather what I can, but we also need to actively cultivate our other options."

"Okay, I'll take the damned weeds. Find me a book when you go into Wikieup or one of the camps," Maggie gave in. "Or, maybe the Internet is back up and I'll check some things out there."

"Wait, Internet? What do you mean Internet?" The change in O'Reilly from easy going and joking around, to intense, focused Enforcer was sudden and obviously disturbed Maggie. She turned to look at him, a slight puzzled frown creasing the skin between her eyebrows.

"I have my laptop here. I haven't been using it much, only for journaling when we first got here, that type of thing. Writing down my thoughts. I tried to go on line shortly after getting here, through my satellite broadband card, but I couldn't get logged on. Probably because no one was manning the servers or power was down. I probably haven't had it out since you got here. You might not have noticed, but you do keep the days pretty busy." Maggie smiled up at O'Reilly. "Maybe some things are working again, though. I'll try tomorrow. I'll..."

"No!" O'Reilly's voice snapped out, surprising Maggie, her face registering her shock at his abruptness.

"What...?"

"Maggie, promise me that you won't try and access the web with your computer! Not from here. It's important. Promise me!"

151

"Okay, but what gives?" Maggie was growing more confused and suspicious at O'Reilly's insistence.

"You know that all computers have their own IP addresses and the authorities have been able to track those for quite a few years. Well, when I left they were setting up a system by which all computers were registered, and any unregistered computers or IP addresses attempting to access the net would trigger an immediate alert and GPS tracer. They've got it set up so no one can jump onto someone else's wireless connection and get by unnoticed.

"Remember, they currently want to monitor the information getting out to the public. They also want to make sure that ghosts don't manage to hack into information about supply trains. The best way to do this is to make sure that the only people with net access are using registered items, and that any unregistered items immediately trigger alarms." Every muscle in O'Reilly's body was vibrating with tension. "If you attempt to access the net, they'll immediately start trying to get a fix on your location and we'll have them on our doorstep before you know it."

The enormity of the mistake that she'd nearly made clearly rocked Maggie. Her eyes went blank and a tremor seemed to pass through her body, as though the ninety degree day had suddenly turned frigid. O'Reilly saw her legs begin to buckle and grabbed her arms, pulling her closer, holding her upright.

"I didn't know. I didn't... I could have gotten us all killed. I could have..." her voice quivered in a way that he'd never heard, not even when he'd surprised them at the table that first night. Her oval face had taken on a grayish tinge under her summer tan.

"You didn't, though. You know now and we're safe. Mark and Lindy are safe." His voice was gentle, consoling. He was surprised at how much her distress affected him. He'd grown to think of Maggie as strong, indomitable, and to see her so visibly shaken rocked him to the core.

"Oh, God. If you hadn't said something I'd have tried to log on one of these days just to see if the web was back running again. I'd have given us all away."

"I didn't realize you had a computer or I would have told you long ago. I didn't think about it. I'm sorry. There's so many things going on in the world. I just didn't think that was important."

Suddenly O'Reilly realized he was still holding Maggie and at the same time, Maggie apparently realized that she was being held. They abruptly stepped back from each other. A red flush washed across Maggie's face and O'Reilly suddenly became obsessed with rooting out every last little bit of bear grass from under his row of plants.

Studying the ground as though he could find all the answers in the shape of the emerging squash leaves - a modern day sooth sayer - he remained silent, letting Maggie regain control of herself. Laying down her stick, Maggie went to the edge of the garden and took a long drink out of the canteen she'd left sitting in the shade there. She stood a few minutes, watching the chickens poking around in the barnyard. Then, having apparently regained her composure, she set the canteen down and returned to O'Reilly in the middle of the garden, picked up her digging stick and resumed work on her row.

"I guess that means there's little choice in the matter. We have to get the things we need from town." Maggie started, voice controlled. O'Reilly was impressed all over again how quickly she could come back after such a shock. A minute ago she looked to be on the verge of complete collapse, and now she was talking as calmly as if they were discussing a simple run into town before the virus struck.

"You're right." O'Reilly said, resigned. "If it's ever going to happen it needs to be now, before the towns are all destroyed. Wikieup was quite a way down the list of priorities, but who knows what's changed since I left. It will take a few days to get everything ready. Eagle Camp is on the way to Wikieup, so I think I'll take the pack train that far, leave them in the corrals there, and only take one or two horses the rest of the way. If there are any Enforcers or seekers being used, they'll be closer to the town and a large group of horses would be easier to spot."

"Okay, just tell me what you need us to do before you go."

"Make a list of things you want me to look for. We'll have to let Mark know he won't be able go with me on this trip. It would be too dangerous to take him that close into town."

"I agree. He'll be disappointed, but that's the way it is." Maggie's cool reserve stabbed O'Reillly to the bone. He wanted to ask her what they could do to bring their relationship back to the way it was, but didn't know how. Finally, he decided to just leave it alone and hope that things would mend themselves in their own time.

"Fine, I'll plan on leaving in three days. I should be able to get everything ready by then. I figure that the trip itself should take four or five days to get there and back."

Maggie simply nodded and continued to work down her row of vegetables, steadfastly refusing to look at O'Reilly. Sighing to himself, he bent back to his work and in silence the two finished weeding the garden.

21

The night air was hot and humid. The monsoons were coming and the last few days had been increasingly uncomfortable. Maggie caught herself being more sensitive, more likely to snap at Mark for minor irritations, less able to laugh off mistakes. Mark had asked her finally what was wrong, and she'd passed it off as a result of the humid air and the growing heat, but alone at night, trying to find a comfortable spot on her old lumpy mattress, she had to admit the truth to herself.

Damn, she thought, *denial is a so much more enjoyable state to live in. No responsibilities, no changes, no dangers.* The truth was that her mistake with the computer had shook her world to the roots. She found doubts of herself flooding in, making her question her ability to keep Mark and herself safe in this strange place, but if that was the only shock she would have quickly regained her assurance.

No, the greatest blow to her confidence was how she felt when O'Reilly had taken her arms and held her while she was reeling from the news. It was less than a year since Mike's death. She didn't want to feel anything for another man. But there was no denying that while O'Reilly was holding her arms, supporting her, she badly wanted him to pull her to his chest and shield her from the world. When he released her, she felt lost, and then she hated herself for feeling that way.

During the intervening three days the two of them had been able to reestablish some of their previous easy relationship, but it had been strained, as though they were both trying too hard. Mark and Lindy had both picked up on the increased tension. Mark was quiet, but looked back and forth between the two of them with a confused expression. Lindy made her dissatisfaction more obvious by becoming clingy and whiny, crying if Maggie left her sight, and wearing Maggie's already frayed nerves to a state of disintegration.

When O'Reilly left for Eagle Camp and Wikieup this morning, Maggie thought that she'd be able to put him out of her mind and regain some of her composure. However, she'd found herself even more on edge. Repeatedly during the day she'd caught herself on the verge of tears, but being the only adult left with two children she didn't have time to break down. When evening came, she was more than ready to send the kids to bed and have some time to herself.

The small house felt claustrophobic, so she wandered out into the small flat area in front, tilting her face up hoping to catch some sort of breeze to cool her overheated skin. She could hear thunder nearby again, for the second night in a row, and from where she stood, she could see lightning backlighting the edges of the canyon. The green smell of rain wafted down on the breeze and she hoped that they would finally get the moisture that the pastures were craving.

More thunder and more flashes of light. A drop of rain pelted her upturned face, running down her right cheek, leaving a trail that felt like a tear. The breeze picked up, carrying with it more raindrops that bathed her face in coolness. She thought about O'Reilly and wondered if he'd made it to Eagle Camp, or if he was camping out in the pastures, watching the rain coming closer. He hadn't taken a tent - they didn't have one - so things could get uncomfortable if the storm was a violent one. He'd know what to do, though. He always knew what to do out here. She envied that assurance and wondered if she would ever be able to fit into this life she'd chosen as well as he did. Probably not, but hopefully she'd adapt to the point that she wouldn't get them killed.

Thunder sounded even closer, and the lightning that flashed this time wasn't just backlighting the cliffs, it was over the canyon itself. The rain began to fall harder, wetting her shirt and jeans. The wind sharpened, causing a chill when it touched the damp material. Looking reluctantly at the pasture where the wind whipped the grass, she finally turned and went back inside the house and to bed.

She was exhausted and wanted to sleep, but sleep eluded her. The old mattress seemed lumpier than ever tonight and she briefly thought she should have asked O'Reilly if there was any way to bring a better one back from one of the camps.

Damn, there he is again. Why the heck can't he leave me alone. But she knew why, although she didn't like it. *I have to get control of this. I have to get him out of my mind.* He wouldn't go, however. She tried all of the mind blanking techniques she'd ever known, but every time she relaxed her guard his face floated into her memory. The way he'd looked out in the garden, sun glinting off the deep chestnut hair. The way his hands felt as he held her.

She threw herself over onto her right side and punched her pillow. She lay there a few moments, but an overwhelming feeling of restlessness caused her to flip back onto her back again and stare toward the dark ceiling, listening to Lindy's soft breathing. Through the open bedroom door she could hear the thunder grumbling through the canyon and the quicksilver patter of rain blown against the windows in the main room of the house.

A knot tightened inside her and she turned over again, lying on her left side, staring toward the back of the room. She was furious with herself. She'd always been so in control, and now she felt so out of control. She hated this feeling. Again she twitched onto her back, kicking the light sheet to the foot of the bed. The knot tightened, then tightened again. She twisted to her right again, and, unable to relax, Maggie finally gave into the knot, buried her face in her pillow and cried herself to sleep.

22

"*What the hell do you mean she's gone?*" Captain Rickards roared at Deputy Knox who stood in front of the him, looking uncomfortable. Rickards' voice dropped to a menacing growl, "Where is she?"

"Sir, we think that she slipped away last night during the storm, taking three other children with her; Alysa Thalman, Nicholas Craigson and Ryan Craigson." Knox swallowed audibly, his prominent adams apple bobbing agitatedly. "A bolt of lightning struck the Nursery, causing a fire and all the children were evacuated until the flames were brought under control. When the children returned to the building it wasn't noticed right away that these four were missing. Things were exceedingly confused, they say, with kids having to stay in different rooms due to fire, water and smoke damage and no one realized that four children were gone until this morning."

"Incompetence," Rickards spat, turning and beginning to pace the room. "Could they have made it out of the APZ? The barriers are secure, aren't they? Did the seekers pick up anything last night heading away from the Laughlin?"

"The thing is, the storm was bad, and the fire department was calling for reinforcements, so the sentries on duty felt it would be safe." Knox paled even more, his light blue eyes seeming to bulge out of his bony face. He nervously wet his lips with the tip of his tongue before continuing. "They left one man on duty, but the rain was exceptionally heavy, and, well he thought no one would be out in that weather. He didn't say so, but I got the impression that he might not have been as... as diligent as he might have been. He didn't see anyone, though, and surely four kids couldn't have gotten that far. The seekers didn't pick up anything but animals - cattle and horses and wildlife - as usual. We've got men going over the records again, but there was nothing, they're sure of it." He looked hopefully at the captain, then his face fell again.

"What about the chip," Rickards asked, referring to the micro identification chip that was implanted in every resident upon check in. Refugees were told that they were receiving the micro identification chips to ensure an equitable distribution of food, medical supplies and other items being rationed. A central computer would keep track to make sure no one was taking more than his fair share.

They hadn't been told that the chip was also a GPS tracer. In the recent years there had been a movement to have these chips implanted in autistic children or adults with alzheimers to make it easier to find them should they wander away from their care givers. However, since many people had reservations about marking people as though they were pets, and since there were simpler devices, such as bracelets, that would perform the same job, micro chipping people had never really taken off. Until now.

"Well, sir, about the chip... some problems have arisen with the software. The techs say it might be solar flares, or something with the storm last night. Lightning hit the main dish and seems to have scrambled some of the computers." Knox continued to stand at attention, though it was obvious he'd rather be just about anywhere else. "We're having trouble getting a fix on anything, but the techs are convinced that they'll have the problem solved very soon."

"*Damn it, Knox. How the hell could we have lost four little kids!*" Rickards' face was growing red. The chips were the fail safe. It was the way the authorities could make sure anyone becoming dissatisfied with the new system couldn't just take off and try to make it on his own. If someone left the APZ without authorization, he could be tracked down and either returned or eliminated.

This was supposed to be a fool proof system, he thought sarcastically. *Other than the shortage of chips, glitches in the software, and an underlying incompetence, everything has been going so well with the identification process.*

In the past ten years the rice-grain sized micro identification chips had progressed from being encoded with simple numbers that would help owners identify lost pets, to being encrypted with entire medical records and other important information that a person felt necessary to keep available at all times. Some financial institutions had even been pushing to expand the chips' use as banking tools, eliminating the need for debit and credit cards.

The premise was simple: Implant a micro chip in someone's wrist or hand, where it could be easily scanned when that person made a purchase. Money could be added to the account simply by passing the person's wrist over a scanner in the bank or through a home computer interface. At least that was what the micro tech gurus envisioned.

They even suggested that the home computers could be equipped with scanners that would require a micro chip scan in conjunction with a finger print or iris scan in order for the account to be accessed, thereby making identity theft nearly impossible, since no would-be thief would have access to a victim's prints or eyes, even if they did manage to clone the chips themselves.

It all sounded pretty big brotherish to Rickards, though he sure liked the idea that no one would be calling on the phone any longer, trying to sell him things. No way to scan or verify identity through that medium. Too bad for the telemarketers. He wasn't crying.

Following the disaster, when the remaining population was concentrated into the APZs, the government thought of a new use for the micro chips. Implant all of the survivors. Use an explanation that they wouldn't question, allowing the people in charge the freedom to monitor the whereabouts of any APZ resident at any time.

Records showed that Christina Craigson, Alysa Thalman, Ryan Craigson and Nicholas Craigson had all been implanted upon their entry in the APZ. The chips had registered with the scanners, and the children had been using them for the past several months to scan in when receiving food, clothing and other supplies. There was no reason to suppose that they knew the chips would be traceable, so finding the runaways should be easy.

Apparently it wasn't going to be that simple, however. The chips were no good unless the satellites could get a fix on them, and thanks to the incompetence of the tech department, that's exactly what wasn't happening. *Damn!*

Deputy Knox continued to stand uneasily in front of Rickard's desk, waiting for orders. Rickards considered the paperwork in front of him for a moment; a report on a series of violent rapes in apartment building F. Coming to a decision he looked up at the deputy, standing uneasily at attention.

"Give the order that door to door searches be conducted throughout the APZ. The odds are that these kids haven't made it out of the perimeter, but are lying low in some abandoned building or have found some bleeding heart to take them in. If so they'll run out of food soon, and they can only claim more if they have their chips scanned. We can't wait for that, however." Rickard's frowned over the manpower that would be required for a search of this type. "Make sure that no building, or spot within a building is left unexamined."

"What if people question us sir? They're not going to like us invading their homes in that manner. They'll want to see warrants."

"Warrants don't apply in this matter. Tell them that one of these children is in eminent danger if she doesn't receive her medication. No. Better yet, tell them that the two older girls have taken the younger boys hostage, that they're terrorists intending to bomb parts of the APZ. That way the laws passed back at the beginning of the century, the ones that put homeland security above citizens' expectations of privacy will come into play." Rickards nodded, liking the cover story. "Hell, if you tell them that, and also tell them that if they're harboring these children they will also be considered terrorists, anyone giving these kids shelter will turn them in immediately."

"Won't it seem strange, saying that kids are terrorists? Will anyone believe us?"

"Show pictures of the girls. They look older in those photographs, and there's no age limit on terrorists anyway. Anyone who's heard stories of eight-year-olds luring GIs into mine fields during that war in Iraq knows that."

"Yes, sir. Will there be anything else?"

"No. You're dismissed. Go get this search underway. I want an update every hour on the progress. We need these kids!"

Saluting again, making Rickards teeth clench, Knox turned on his heel and left the room, closing the door behind him.

Rickards stood and began pacing the room, concentrating on the problem of the missing children. How could this have happened right now of all times? Yesterday morning he'd found an Enforcer, a young sergeant who'd grown up in Montana. He hadn't lived in Shelby, but was familiar with that area. When asked about the mountains and forests around the town, he'd laughed.

"Well, I suppose you wouldn't have to go too far to the west to get to the mountains and forests, but the area around Shelby is mostly farm land. Pretty flat. There's trees, sure, but it's not really a place someone would go to get lost in the Rockies or anything like that."

She tricked me! That girl played me like a fiddle. I don't believe it, Rickards thought furiously. The difficulty was that O'Reilly still could have headed in that direction. His information source had said it wasn't too far from the mountains, but it seemed much less likely than it had before. He needed to interrogate the girl. He needed to find out why she lied. Did she know where O'Reilly was headed? Was she going to meet him? That seemed unlikely. What man would leave a fourteen-year-old girl to escape on her own, unless... Unless he'd come back in and taken her and her brothers and friend.

Was that it? Had he stealthily slipped back through the perimeter of the APZ, to the Nursery and happened to get lucky enough to arrive there on the night of a major storm, find them and sneak back away with them? Rickards still had trouble believing that four kids had the intelligence and skills to make an escape like this by themselves. It seemed much more likely that an adult had assisted them. That had to be it.

That brought up another question, however. They'd always assumed that O'Reilly had left the APZ. Maybe that was a false assumption. Maybe he never left. Maybe he'd simply laid down a trail of "breadcrumbs" to make them think he'd taken off, when he actually had a hideout somewhere here in the APZ, and had only been biding his time until he could break the Craigson girl out too. That made more sense, and if it was what actually happened, then his door to door search should turn them up quickly.

As an Enforcer, O'Reilly had known about the GPS tracers, and had apparently removed his shortly after leaving his post in the Nursery and making good his escape. It wouldn't have been hard, but it would have taken some guts. He would have had to make an incision in his wrist and remove the small chip, then destroy it, probably by fire. They hadn't been able to pick up a signal from O'Reilly's chip since the first day following the escape, about ten miles away to the north. When the crews got there they'd found nothing but the remains of a campfire. No tracks. Nothing indicating which direction he'd headed.

It would have taken some real cojones to come back to the APZ after that. He had to know that he would be executed if he was found. Rickards felt himself developing a headache trying to out think the crafty bastard. If O'Reilly were meeting the kids, he would have already removed their chips. There was no way he'd overlook that. Which brought him back to the original question; were the kids going to meet O'Reilly or was it just a coincidence?

Rickards' brought his fist down on his desk, causing the pens and papers to jump in place. His team hadn't had much luck unearthing information about O'Reilly's past. He'd kept too much to himself. All they'd been able to find, from DMV records, was that for the past three years a James R. O'Reilly had lived in Mohave County, Arizona with a mailing address in Kingman. If he knew that area well, he might have headed in that direction; but he just as easily could have headed in any other. Arizona was filled with empty land, as was much of the southwest. One of the blessings and curses of having so much public land. In this case it meant that there was a lot of space for someone to disappear.

But did he go that way? Back at that question again. He could continue to go around in mental circles for hours and still never come anywhere near the solution. Rickards took a deep breath. He might not like it, but the only answer was to wait. Wait until they got the computers up and running again and were able to get a fix on the kids' GPS tracers. Wait until the door to door search had either turned up or ruled out the kids' and O'Reilly's presence in the APZ.

Wait.

23

*F*east or famine around here, thought O'Reilly as he made his way across the drowned pasture, trying to pick a path that would coat his horses with the least amount of sticky, red-clay mud. He wasn't having much luck and in some places clods of thick red sludge were flung out from the horses' feet, splattering the bottom of his boots and jeans and the faces of all the horses in line, except the one he was riding, making them look like the victims of some vile disease.

The promised rain finally materialized last night making traveling much more difficult than O'Reilly had anticipated. Twice he'd had to stop at larger washes and smaller canyons to wait until the water flow dropped to a safe level.

When he'd left Hideaway the day before, the rain was still a unfulfilled promise. Black clouds had been gathering over the mountains west, north and east of there, and for several afternoons and nights the vague rumble of thunder had wormed its way in between the canyon walls, although the accompanying flash of lightning had not yet made an appearance.

Yesterday morning, when he'd headed out from the camp, the pasture had been dry, coarse golden grass crisping in the early July sun. However, dampness in several of the deeper washes made it clear that the monsoon was happening somewhere, even if it wasn't right above his head. Rain falling in the mountains had far reaching effects and it was clear that at some point water had made its way through this dry land, either in the form of a slow muddy roil, spending its energy further upstream, or in a wild flash flood that took everything in its path.

He'd planned to make his way to Eagle Camp that day, and spend the night there, gathering everything that he needed. He intended to leave all but two horses in the small home pasture where they would have access to food and water. Then, the next morning he would strike out for Wikieup, which he figured to be around twenty miles as the crow flies. Of course, he wasn't a crow, and he was likely to go further in an effort to avoid the worst of the rugged terrain. Say a day and a half or two days to get to the small town.

When he got close, he would have to move more carefully, keeping an eye out for the silvery, orb-like seekers, or Enforcers that usually followed them. There was no knowing how far the annihilation teams had progressed since he'd left, and he wasn't sure whose jurisdiction Wikieup was in anyway; but the last thing he wanted to do was to walk into their hands.

Now he wasn't sure how long it would take him.

He'd made it to Eagle Camp late that first day, rolling in around four in the afternoon. *Just in time* he thought as he watched the bloated black thunder heads rising into an anvil shaped formation off to the north. *The rain won't hold off much longer, and it looks as if it could be a gully washer.* He could see flashes of lightning, followed after a long interval by the deep rumbles of thunder. For fifteen years he'd watched monsoon storms build this way, and the sight of this one twanged the strings of his memory. Storms that built the way this one was building usually rushed down hill, straight over the camp, deluging it with rain and sometimes hail, turning this peaceful little valley into a raging maelstrom for the short time it lasted. Unless he was very much mistaken, this storm was headed straight at him. He looked around the home yard. *At least I'll be sleeping warm in a bed tonight, not out in the middle of it. Hopefully they kept the roof in good repair.*

The camp was just as he remembered it. He grimaced. It would have been easier if the new residents had totally redone everything after his family left, but no such luck. The small two story house, painted a dusty green with a cream colored trim still sat back under huge elm and ash trees, benefitting from their shade during the summer; keeping the house cool even without the benefit of an air conditioner. Rough yellow and pink granite stones, gathered in the area, had been used to make a fence about three feet tall, separating the house's front yard from the parking area and barnyard. Across the shaded driveway and barnyard, about seventy-five yards from the front of the house, stood the main barn, faded red with a breeze way running back between two lines of stalls and run ins for horses and cattle kept nearby. Behind the barn stood a tall windmill, responsible for pumping all the water for the barn and the house.

In the parking area in front of the house stood two trucks; an older, beat up model, and a newer, shiny one, making him wonder if he would find anyone at home. He didn't think so. Surely if someone was living this close to Hideaway, he or she'd have ventured in that direction sometime in the past few months. No. More likely these two trucks had been left behind when the family went into town, either to the APZ, or because someone was sick. Probability said they'd never returned.

O'Reilly shook his head, grinning ruefully to himself as he acknowledged a reluctance to enter this house after his experience at the ranch headquarters. God only knew what Maggie would do to him if he came home with another kid.

Unfortunately that thought opened the door to other thoughts of Maggie, Mark and Lindy; his new family whether he wanted them or not. Damn, he'd been doing so well at keeping them out of his thoughts on this trip. He needed to clear his mind to figure out exactly what he was feeling since he couldn't seem to control it.

He rode over to the barn, dismounted and tied his horses to the hitching rail. One by one, his thoughts miles away, he unsaddled and led the horses to the run in shed on the right side of the breeze way; the one with the largest of the pens. Automatically, as though his body remembered all the chores of his childhood, he checked the automatic water float in the tank and stored his gear in the tack room immediately to the left upon entering the barn. The sight of all the saddles, pads and bridles awaiting service sent a pang through him much deeper than that he'd experienced when at the headquarters. He saw the rack his father had constructed to hold the young Jim O'Reilly's saddle. Looking up he saw the tin cans that he and his brother had mounted to the walls on which to hang the bridles and halters. Everything much as they'd left it.

After throwing hay to the horses, he finally turned and faced the small house, both drawn to, and reluctant to face the memories that would be lying in wait within that structure. Out of the blue a picture flashed through his mind of Maggie sitting on the front steps, waving, while Lindy and Mark played in the front yard. *God dammit, will you let me face my ghosts on my own!* he thought in annoyance. However, the picture was so alluring that he couldn't help playing it a few more moments before banishing it from his thoughts.

Girding up his loins, metaphorically speaking, he stepped out across the barnyard toward the green gate that had been set into the rock wall, spurs ringing softly against the hard packed dirt. It was time to face his past.

The next morning, after spending a night disturbed by memories and storms, O'Reilly fixed himself a cup of coffee in the kitchen that used to be his mother's. The people who'd lived here had left the house well stocked and he had started collecting all the items that he would need to take back to Hideaway.

Yesterday he'd considered taking one of the trucks into town, but the rain last night would have turned the roads into an impassible mud slick in many places, and he could see more clouds on the horizon already. The truck would have shortened the trip drastically, but he'd grown up on these roads, and he knew it would take a day or two until they'd dried out enough for even a four-wheel drive vehicle to pass.

He'd weighed his options. Wait and see if the roads dried enough to get out before the rain hit again, or take the horses and leave this morning? Finally he decided that the horses were the wisest move since one couldn't trust the weather this time of year and the worst thing he could imagine would be to get stuck in town, or trapped and unable to escape from the Enforcers. It might take longer, but horses were the way to go.

Later that afternoon, he was regretting that decision as he slogged his way across the saturated pasture. To the north and west he could see the clouds building, and resignedly prepared himself for a wet afternoon and evening if things progressed the way they looked. *Feast or famine indeed,* he thought, *it's more like dehydration or drowning.*

He'd ended up deciding to take the entire seven animal pack train with him and secret them closer to Wikieup, just in case he found more items than he'd originally planned on. In scouting around Eagle Camp, he'd found three horses turned out in the home pasture, and figured that he could always use them to haul the things from the camp itself. Of course, sooner or later he needed to stop bringing horses home. Horses and kids; he seemed to be a magnet for them lately, and he didn't really need any more of either. He had enough mouths to feed already.

The wind started to pick up, bringing a refreshing coolness that had been lacking in the stifling air that morning and most of the afternoon. Unfortunately, that cool breeze had a price. It usually meant that rain was getting closer. He briefly debated stopping and setting up camp, pitching the teepee he'd found in the barn, unrolling his bedroll and hunkering down for the night. The pull of Hideaway, and Maggie, Mark and Lindy won out, however and he kept riding. Camping out here in the open wouldn't be very comfortable anyway. He knew of a sheltered bluff where trees grew large from the water seeping from a spring in the cliff's face. He would have more shelter from the storm there, the animals would be more comfortable in the small catch pen than they would be picketed out. At the rate he was going, he figured, he should be able to reach it in another couple of hours. He'd camp there for the night, push on at first light, and should arrive in the town by noon at the latest.

The first spatters of rain pelted him from the right, sounding hollowly on his gray felt hat. Reaching behind him he untied his yellow slicker from the back of the saddle and pulled it on, pulling up the black corduroy collar. The rain became more intense and he tucked his chin into his chest and rode on, saying a quick prayer that he wouldn't get struck by lightning. He sighed. The next few hours would be slightly less than pleasant.

24

I am so tired of seeing horses' butts, thought Christina irritably, letting her horse pick its way down the narrow mountain trail after Alysa's, Ryan's and Nick's mounts. Even the beautiful Hulalapai Mountain scenery failed to lift her spirits, wearied after four days of riding. The unaccustomed activity left her muscles sore and her confidence severely dented.

She watched her brothers riding ahead of her. They seemed to be having the time of their lives, doing things like "real pioneers," like "real cowboys." *Yeah, right. What on Earth was I thinking, heading out here.*

The rain and mud didn't daunt the boys in the slightest, and they'd developed quite a case of hero worship for Alysa, who, in their eyes, knew everything about living in the wild.

Christina had to grudgingly admit that they were very lucky to have teamed up with Alysa. As much as she hated it, she had to concede that they probably wouldn't have made it without her. At the very least the trip would have taken much longer, and been much, much more uncomfortable than it had been. Not that the trip had been a piece of cake, heading over the mountains as they had, camping out at night in the rain.

Christina had always been taught by her parents that there was nothing she couldn't accomplish if she only tried hard enough. They said that a healthy self-esteem was very important and worked hard to praise their children's successes and encourage them to try new things. The last four days, however, also taught her that she simply didn't have the skills to live out here.

Not that she couldn't learn, she assured herself quickly before the sense of despondency had a chance to grow. It was just that for some reason any tent she erected was the last to stand, and the first to blow down in the wind. Her fires barely smouldered long after Alysa's and her brothers' blazes took off, and her horse, that conniving spotted fiend that gave her the evil eye whenever she was near, was the last to get saddled, and the first to wander off the trail.

Christina wasn't used to having to struggle to master a skill. She was always the one in school who barely had to study for the tests, to whom the assignments came easily, who made friends quickly and effortlessly. Out here, though, she couldn't seem to do anything right.

That first night, as the four ran through the darkened streets of the Laughlin APZ, Christina had felt completely in control. She had organized this escape. It was she who knew where they were going. She'd been faced with an imminent threat and seized the opportunity to make a break for freedom.

As they made their way toward the perimeter, Christina led her small group through the sheeting rain. Lightning continued to flash, followed by long rolls of thunder. The storm seemed to be stalled out over the APZ, but Christina was glad of the foul weather in spite of her wet shoes and clothing. The rain would provide cover. Hopefully no one would realize the children were missing, and if they did, they would assume that the kids were taking shelter from the storm somewhere else nearby.

The four splashed their way through the puddles, trying to stay close to the buildings, and keeping and eye out for anyone who might turn them in. Several times they heard the low hum of a vehicle approaching and they quickly ducked into doorways or behind large oleander hedges.

They'd been moving steadily through the deserted streets, leaving the scream of the sirens far behind when they turned a corner and suddenly found themselves facing the perimeter.

The wet street continued on, but at either side a line of buildings had been demolished in a line perpendicular to the road. The rubble had then been used to erect a ten-foot-high barrier wall that extended into the growing rain filled dusk to the east and west until it vanished into the murk. A small shed had been constructed in the center of the pavement, presumably as a sentry post. Tinted glass windows looked out upon the thoroughfare.

Christina and the other three stopped abruptly upon seeing the sentry station. They retreated quickly to the shelter of a large hedge, well out of sight of anyone who might be standing guard.

"Stay here," Christina whispered to Alysa, Nick and Ryan, motioning them to stay secreted behind the wind torn green leaves. Carefully she stuck her head out from behind the hedge and gave the shed a long look. There was no movement. It was certain that no one was standing at the windows. The question was, did a sentry stand deeper inside the shed, seeing but unseen?

Moving cautiously, Christina stepped out from behind her shelter. She took several crouching steps toward the shed, body tense, ready to turn and run at the first sign of movement. Glancing over her shoulder she saw Alysa peering out from behind the hedge, watching her. She made a palm up "wait" gesture with her right hand, and continued to creep toward the sentry post.

Hugging the left side of the street, she finally made it to the tan building. She prayed that if someone was inside, that the rain and darkness would keep her hidden. Slowly she raised to her full height and peered in the window. Inside she saw a man dressed in the navy blue uniform that many of the Enforcers had adopted. He was standing in the middle of the shed, staring out in the direction of the river which was invisible in the current weather.

Christina ducked back down and looked toward the hedge where Alysa and her brothers were hiding. She beckoned for Alysa to bring the boys and the three children scurried out from behind the greenery and down the street toward the perimeter.

The four children reunited at the side of the shed. Slowly Christina peeked again over the edge of the window and saw the sentry continuing to stare off into the ever deepening gloom. It was almost completely dark at this point; even the spot lights mounted on the shed failing to push their light through the thick air. Crouching and moving as quickly as possible the four children ran from the side of the shed toward freedom, stopping only when they reached the safety of the next set of buildings.

"Is everyone okay?" Christina asked once she caught her breath. She looked at the other three children, rain coursing off of them in rivers. So far the evening's activity and the naturally warm Nevada desert climate, had kept the four of them relatively comfortable, but Christina knew that would change rapidly if they didn't get into dry clothes soon. It was unusual that a monsoon storm would last for as long as it already had. They usually blew in and out quickly but violently. She wasn't complaining. It had provided the cover the children needed to make good their escape. Now they needed to get dry.

"We're fine," assented Nick, answering for the other three. "What do we do now?"

"I guess we should find a place to hole up." Christina said, making her decision.

"We need to get across the bridge tonight," spoke up Alysa, referring to the Highway 68 bridge across the Colorado River. "That road is watched by the sentries at the APZ. There's no way we could get across in the daytime. If we stay on this side of the river, you'd better believe that they'll have Enforcers and seekers out looking for us. Right now they don't know we're missing, so hopefully they won't have beefed up the security. We might not get another chance." Alysa looked serious.

"But we're soaked," Christina said, growing frustrated. "We'll get sick if we continue on like this."

"Rain won't kill us. It's a warm night. We need to get out of here now before they start their search."

Christina paused, studying Alysa's face, and seeing her determination, felt her own begin to falter. She looked at her brothers beginning to shiver as the warmth generated by their run to the perimeter was leached away by the continuing rain.

"What do you guys think?" she asked.

Nick and Ryan looked at each other for a moment before they nodded their heads. Looking back at Christina, Ryan spoke.

"Alysa's right, Christy. We don't want to waste everything we've done. We'll be warm enough if we keep moving. We can find some place across the bridge to hole up for the night."

Christina hesitated a moment longer, then realizing that the others had a point, sighed and nodded her head. "Okay, guys, lets go for the bridge. I think the rain is beginning to let up. We'll try and get across before we lose the cover. Keep an ear out for the seekers. There might be more out here on the outside of the wall."

Quickly the four children shouldered their packs and headed for the bridge.

The rest of the night passed in a blur of mud and exhaustion. Moving between buildings, they made it to the bridge in short order. Full night had fallen, and the blackness was only relieved by the occasional flashes of the lightning that had moved off to the east. Watching for vehicles, and keeping their ears open for the high pitched whine of a seeker passing overhead, the children scurried across the bridge, hearing the roar of the Colorado River flowing below them in the darkness.

Once across, they moved off to the side of the road, planning on staying in the brush for cover. However, the rain had made much of the ground slippery with mud and clay and finally, after an exhausting half hour where they seemed to make no progress whatsoever, they moved back to the side of the highway. It wasn't an ideal situation, and the stress of constantly listening for seekers and vehicles stretched their nerves to the limit.

Twice they heard the high pitched keen of a seeker and scrambled to take cover. The seekers worked through infrared detection, and would be sure to focus on their body heat if caught. The first time they heard one approaching, they scrambled down the bank and climbed into a foul smelling culvert ankle high with fast moving muddy water. The four huddled together, hoping that the seeker's scan wasn't strong enough to read through the asphalt of the highway, and the dirt of the embankment.

The second time there was no culvert handy, so the children ran as quickly as they could into the desert and crawled together under a large bush. Christina hoped that if they lay still, gathered together, that the seeker would only pick up a large blob of heat and that whomever was watching the scans would identify it as an animal - a cow or a deer or some other four-legged creature - and pass over without investigating. After all, there so many animals out in these deserts that they couldn't be expected to investigate every time a seeker picked up a heat signature. She also prayed that since they were under a large clump of scrub oak that the seeker's night vision camera wouldn't be of any help.

Luck smiled upon them as they huddled together in the mud trying hard to look like a cow, because the whine of the seeker paused briefly over their section of desert, then passed away to the west. Waiting until the seeker was gone from hearing while the heat was sucked out of their bodies into the cold, wet ground, Christina felt herself begin to drift off. She couldn't imagine what the boys were going through. They'd all been up since six that morning, and it had to be after ten at night, with hours and miles yet to go. She had to fight off the feeling of despair that tried to creep in, telling herself over and over again that they were doing the right thing, that they would make it.

Finally, after all evidence of the seeker had passed, the four crawled out from under the covering brush and made their way back to the side of the highway, turned to the east and continued on.

They were silently walking down the verge of the road as the night was graying toward dawn when suddenly Alysa, who was leading the band, nodded off to the right, pulling the others out of their exhausted stupor.

"Look, over there. A windmill. A house and barn." Alysa indicated the roof tops barely visible in the predawn light about a mile south of the highway, down in a small valley.

Alysa seemed to have weathered the long night better than had Christina, Nick or Ryan. Christina wondered about it, finally deciding that Alysa had the benefit of one less concern than had the other three. All four children were tested by the wind and rain, by the fear of being caught again and having to keep an ear and eye out for pursuers. Christina and her brothers had one additional source of anxiety, however, that Alysa seemed to lack. None of the three of them had ever spent much time outside the environs of a city. They were used to buildings and cars and scores of people, not cacti, rocks and wildlife. All the noises out here were new and they didn't know what was dangerous and what wasn't. The call of coyotes in the distance triggered fear in the three of them, but barely affected Alysa. The consequence being that sometime during the night Alysa had taken over as their leader, and the other three were taking their cues from her, rather than from Christina.

Christina wasn't sure exactly how she felt about that. Earlier in the planning she'd been mortified to realize she felt a few twinges of jealousy when the boys seemed to take to Alysa so quickly and accept the things she said so readily. She'd squashed those feelings, but now the familiar twinges rose again as she watched her brothers, and even herself, turn to Alysa time and time again during the night when some strange noise sounded in the distance. Now it was Alysa who'd found shelter, offering the promise of cleanliness, dryness and warmth.

Get over it, she thought to herself, *Alysa's familiar with living like this. I should be grateful that she's along.* Christina recognized the irrationality

174

of her jealousy and instantly began trying to banish those feelings as she looked toward the distant roofs that indicated habitation.

"We must be getting near Kingman, Arizona," said Christina as she noted other growing signs of human habitation. "It's starting to get light. We need to find somewhere to hide before the sun comes up."

The boys stood close together, quieter than Christina had ever seen them.

Alysa nodded toward the house and barn she'd first indicated. "We should go there. Check it out. There won't be anyone living there. Not this close to an APZ, so we should be able to stay there for the day."

"Are you sure," Christina asked dubiously. "Aren't we too close to the APZ. Surely they'll check all the places nearest to the city first."

Alysa looked over at Christina and the boys. "They probably haven't even realized we're gone yet, and even if they have they'll check out the abandoned buildings in the city first; especially since we were able to duck the seekers last night. We can't be out in the day, though. It will be harder to fool the daytime cameras than the infrared and night vision ones." Alysa gave Christina a tired grin, pushing her heavy black hair back from her face with a grubby hand. "Face it, they're not going to want to believe that four kids could fool all of them and escape. We need to go to that ranch. We need to get dry, clean, get some sleep and above all, we need horses."

Christina pondered Alysa's statement for a moment then sighed. "You're right. Let's go. We need to get out of sight of the highway as quickly as possible."

The four children climbed down the embankment, Alysa and Christina assisting the two younger boys who seemed to be nearly at the end of their reserves, then headed across the open desert land toward the winding dirt road that led to the ranch house. The sunlight gradually became stronger and they picked up their pace, aware that the light exposed them more and more as every minute passed.

It wasn't long before the road wound down into the small valley, through a large stone gateway and into the yard between a stone ranch house and a red painted barn. The windmill in the pasture rose into the sky where it was silhouetted against a brilliant orange sunrise.

The children paused in the yard for a moment, then Christina turned and headed for the house. There were several trucks in front of the building, but no sign of anyone living there. Christina walked up to the front door and banged loudly. No one answered. She turned back and looked at her companions. The boys continued to huddle together, shivering. Alysa stood next to them looking up at Christina.

"If anyone was living here, they'd have been up already, feeding the animals." Alysa gestured back toward the barn where loose chickens scratched around in the dirt. Behind the barn stretched two huge green pastures, apparently irrigated by the windmill. Several horses and cows grazed in the deep grass, apparently surviving quite nicely in spite of the absence of their owners.

The sight of a few partially stripped carcasses in smaller pens on the north side of the barn spoke of other livestock that hadn't been quite so lucky. These animals had either run out of food, water, or both, and hadn't been able to escape to the green abundance on the other side of the fence. Dry weather and scavengers had turned their dead bodies into partially mummified monuments to the devastation of the disease and human stupidity.

Christina tried the door and found it locked. Feeling guilty, even though she knew that the owners were probably gone for good, she went back down the steps to the walkway which was lined with smooth river stones. Picking a large, dark red one, she returned to the front door and used the rock to smash a pane of glass in a side window. She pulled her sweatshirt sleeve over her hand and used it to push the glass out of the frame, then reached through to unlock the door.

"Come on guys," she turned and beckoned to the other three. They followed her into the house, moving quietly and cautiously. Stopping just inside the door way Christina couldn't shake the feeling that they were trespassing. She looked around at the large front room, decorated in ranch and cowboy memorabilia. A cup sat on the coffee table, a magazine lay open next to it. The leaves of dead plants littered the sill of the large bay window. The entire house had an unsettling air, both of abandonment, and of owners simply away for a few moments about to return.

The children wandered throughout the dusty house noting the signs of habitation long gone. Christina tried the switches in several rooms without success. Apparently the power had been shut off at some time in the past months. Likewise there was no water when they turned the taps in the kitchen and bathrooms.

So much for a hot shower, Christina thought regretfully, looking at her dirty hands and feeling the prickle of drying mud in her hair. She realized that the water in the house must rely on an electric pump, while the water for the animals, at least those grazing in the pasture, must rely on the windmill they saw in the distance. There must be water out there or the livestock wouldn't be alive, but she decided that she was too tired to go looking for it right now.

Afraid to leave each other's sight for very long, the children gravitated back to the large, open living room of the ranch house. Exhaustion finally had its way as the four sprawled out on the overstuffed furniture and quickly fell deeply asleep.

The sun was beginning to sink toward the western horizon when Christina finally stirred, shifting on the brown suede couch which had been her bed for the day. A ray of the lowering sun slanted in through the window, splashing light across her face. Briefly she raised her arm, laying it across her eyes to block the light, but she was awake now, and sleep could not be recaptured.

Sitting up, she looked around the room. Her brothers were still asleep, curled together in a large leather recliner. Nick murmured in his dreams, answered by an equally indecipherable sound from Ryan. Then, as if in a choreographed dance, both boys shifted in their sleep and then subsided into new positions; deep breathing unchanged.

Christina had often envied the twins' closeness and the effortless communication they shared. They always seemed to know what each other was thinking, and where the other one was. As Christina sat and watched her brothers sleeping she wondered once again what it would be like to have someone know her as well as they knew each other.

Sighing, she finally pushed herself up off the couch and went in search of Alysa.

Alysa was found sitting on the back porch of the house, looking out to the east. She was so intent that she didn't even look around as Christina pushed open the screen door and walked out to join her.

"What's up?" Christina asked as she moved over to stand next to Alysa.

Alysa answered Christina's question with one of her own. Gesturing with her chin she said, "What do you think's going on over there?"

Christina looked in the direction Alysa indicated, shading her eyes with her hand. In the distance she saw towering columns of smoke.

According to the map that she'd liberated from Captain Rickards' office, the only thing in that direction was Kingman, Arizona. From the amount of smoke billowing into the sky, it appeared that the entire town was on fire.

Christina turned to look at Alysa. "O'Reilly said that there were teams out destroying buildings that were no longer going to be used. Recycling things that could be recycled, but eliminating everything else. He said that they were concentrating on towns first, moving out in concentric circles from the APZs." She considered their position so close to the town.

"They must not have wanted to bother with small places like this until they had the towns taken care of, I guess. We shouldn't stay here long, though."

Alysa nodded. "We need to get out of here tonight. We should get the boys up, get food, gather anything else we might need. There are six horses out there. We ride four and use the other two to carry food, water, and anything else we can use."

"We can't ride at night can we?" asked Christina, appalled. She had accepted that in order to make it to the canyon O'Reilly had spoken of, they would have to use horses, but she'd never thought they'd have to ride in the dark.

"We're too close to the town. There will be Enforcers. Seekers." Alysa said, calmly. Even if we head south, we're too close for it to be safe to move in the daylight. Once we're well past Kingman, we can start riding in the daytime, but for now we need to move at night.

Christina tried to find fault with Alysa's reasoning, but couldn't. "I'll get the boys," she said resignedly, turning and heading back for the house. "We'll start gathering the things we want to take. Then when the sun is a bit lower we can go out to that big water trough next to the windmill and clean up. We'll leave as soon as the sun goes down."

Alysa nodded, turning for a final look at the smoke as it rose to join the monsoon clouds building over the mountains, brown eyes worried.

The remainder of the late afternoon was spent ransacking the house for anything they could take that would help them on their journey. The pantry offered up a bounty of foods such as rice and flour that stored easily, kept for long periods of time and were easy to prepare. Christina fought down some qualms as she considered how naive she'd been when planning their escape. Granola bars and cheese sticks. How long would they have survived on those alone?

Christina was raised in a world where you simply ran down to the store if you ran out of something. While in the APZ, she'd been fully focused on escaping and hadn't allowed herself to wonder how they'd survive out in the wilderness. Last night, in the chaos of the storm and escape, she'd been too absorbed in the moment to consider the difficulties ahead of them. Here in the ranch house, however, she began to wonder whether she'd made a huge mistake and whether they'd be able to learn fast enough to keep themselves alive.

Looking over the books on the shelves, she found several wilderness survival guides, and carried them to the kitchen where they were making a pile of the provisions they wanted to take. *If I don't know it, I can certainly learn it*, she thought with determination. *We will make this work. We have to.*

The storms seemed to be holding off for the day, apparently having spent much of their energy in yesterday's downpours. Clouds were building over the high country, but they lacked the authority of the evening before and Christina held tight to the hope that they'd have this night to make good their escape without the complication of rain. Riding the horses at night would be bad enough, but having to do it in the rain would be beyond imagining.

After examining the skies for seekers, the children hurried out to the green pasture, where they quickly stripped down to their underwear and bathed in the large water tank, Christina only cringing slightly at the wispy green algae growing along the sides and the water bugs skittering across the surface. Ryan and Nick treated the whole episode as an adventure, teasing Christina mercilessly when she shrieked as a salamander brushed past her bare leg.

While the four children were busy bathing, the six horses residing in the pasture came wandering up, apparently curious to see who was causing such a commotion in their drinking water. Christina paused to watch the animals approach, realizing with misgiving that in a few short hours she would be sitting on one of their backs and be entirely at its mercy.

Christina had enjoyed watching horses when she was younger, and had even begged her father to get her a pony for years, just like nearly every other young girl. For a long time she'd dreamed of herself racing across the desert, swift as the wind, on her bright golden palomino stallion.

Then reality struck one summer at Girl Scout Camp, when she'd gotten up close and personal with Fred.

Fred was an older gelding who'd recently been donated to the camp, and unfortunately who didn't have much use for kids in spite of what his previous owners had said when they signed over the papers. At the start of camp, Christina drew Fred's name, and for the next two weeks it was her job to care for him, and it was on him that she took riding lessons. During those days at camp, Christina had quickly come to the realization that horses were much different than the pretty pictures in the movies. Fred bit, kicked, stepped on her feet when she wasn't paying attention, and the day he deposited her into the middle of a cactus, Christina swore off horses forever.

As the pasture residents milled around the water tank, Christina studied them intently, trying to determine if they were of the kid eating variety, but with no luck. The horses' ears were pricked as they watched the four children splashing around in livestock's drinking water, *probably trying to figure out if we're the horse eating variety,* Christina thought sourly.

There were two red horses, a darker red brown horse, that if Christina remembered correctly was called a bay, a gray horse, a yellow horse with a black mane and tail, and a black and white spotted horse that she was pretty sure was called a paint. If it wasn't, she thought, it should be since it looked as though someone had thrown buckets of black and white paint at the horse, letting it run down the sides.

Baths over, the kids pulled themselves out of the water and redressed, pulling jeans on over sticky wet skin, and slipping into their sneakers. Alysa had been poking around in the barn and brought six halters with her when the children headed out for their bath. She used these to quickly capture the horses. Handing a lead rope to each of the other children, and taking three herself, they led their new mounts back toward the barn where Alysa had saddles waiting.

As the sun started dropping behind the western horizon Alysa saddled four of the six horses, putting pack saddles on the other two. They brought their treasure trove out from the kitchen and Alysa directed the distribution of the goods. Darkness was falling as the small group headed out of the ranch yard, heading southeast into the Hulalapai Mountains.

That was four days ago, and the intervening hours had tested the four children to the limit. For the first two days, Alysa had insisted that they ride only in the dark. Using the map which Christina had taken from Rickards' office Alysa managed to guide them south of Kingman, avoiding the seekers and annihilation teams. She led them to a forest road leading up into the Hulalapai Mountains, and by some means unknown to Christina managed to keep them going approximately southeast. A one day break from the monsoon activity was all they were given, and several afternoons had found the children huddled in the sleeping bags inside the tent they'd found at the ranch house as wind and rain assailed their shelter as if determined to blow it to the next state.

Now, as the afternoon sun slid slowly down from its noon zenith toward the mountains behind them, Alysa's lead horse suddenly lifted its head and let loose with a shrill whinny, causing the other five horses to also lift their heads. The small group ground to a halt and Alysa rose in her stirrups, craning her head to try and see what had caught her mount's attention. Faintly in the distance Christina heard an answering neigh and her heartbeat ratcheted up a notch.

"Alysa, do you see horses up there?" Christina whispered loudly.

Alysa held out a hand behind her, palm facing the rest of the children, signaling them to be quiet. Her horse, originally the most troublesome of the six, had quieted over the last four days of steady riding, but now it grew restive again at the wait. Christina envied Alysa's easy manner in controlling the red gelding as he fidgeted in place, pawing in frustration. After a moment Alysa turned back toward the others.

"I don't see anything yet, but its probably just ranch horses, loose in this pasture. Maybe mustangs. Go careful. If it's wild horses, they may get our horses acting up.

"Cool, mustangs," said Nick in tones of awe as Ryan nodded in eager agreement. Both boys intently watched the brush and the thickets of mesquite and creosote that had replaced the junipers of the Hulalapais, trying to find where the elusive herd was hiding.

"We're coming up on a town or something," Alysa said. "See that narrow line over there? That's a highway or road. If the map is right, we should be just a bit above Wikieup. We can stop there for the night, if it hasn't been destroyed, then move on tomorrow morning."

The small group of horses moved on down the trail, weaving among boulders, joshua trees, creosote and countless other types of desert plants that Christina couldn't identify. Signs of human habitation became more evident as they crossed several trails left burned into the land by ATV riders, careless of what they were doing to the fragile ecosystem. Several times on the ride Alysa had broken her habitual silence to educate her three citified companions about the way of the land, and one of the things that had surprised Christina the most was how fragile it actually was. It was hard to think of something that was as big and solid as the ground, as fragile and easily damaged.

According to Alysa, a trail used by an ATV or other off road vehicle only a few times could leave an impression that would be visible for years or decades to come.

"My father told me that it was getting so bad nine or ten years ago that the National Forest people wanted to ban ATVs on all but developed roads on some of the public lands, and that if the riders couldn't follow those rules, then to ban the ATVs completely," Alysa told them.

"What happened?" asked Nick. He and Ryan had pestered Christina's parents a long time for ATVs after they went riding with friends one weekend. Her parents had refused on the basis of safety, but now Christina began to wonder if there were other reasons that they hadn't mentioned.

"Some forests banned them, but the ATV riders went up in arms. It's actually still, or I guess was still, being fought over. I suppose now that everyone is in the APZs, the argument is pointless."

Christina thought a long time about those trails after Alysa explained how they were made. Her father had told her that there was a huge dichotomy among people in regards to things like ATVs and not all of it made sense. You had some people singing the environmental song, conserving energy and working hard to live in a way they felt was responsible to the planet. In the past decade more and more ads on TV had jumped on the green bandwagon, touting their products as environmentally friendly, whether or not they actually were.

Then you had the others who lived to please themselves, using resources any way they wanted without regard to the future, or to anyone else using the same resources. These people screamed that the public lands were just that, public, and that they, as members of the public had a right to use them in any manner they saw fit. Their wants came first, and others using the public lands, whether it be for ranching or recreation, were seen as a nuisance. These people treated the land, and everything on it, including corrals and windmills as theirs to use, pollute or destroy as they wished.

Christina remembered her father laughing when he explained this schism to her. Sometimes, he said, you even had a split in the same person. He called these people "environmental schizophrenics." These were the people who used the compact florescent bulbs in their lights. Who always bought from the organic aisle in the grocery store. Who recycled all their paper, glass and aluminum, then spent the weekends ripping up the land with noisy ATVs or were careless when filling the tanks of their boats and figured that the gas and oil spilled into the waterways wouldn't matter. He even included those people who planted green lawns or installed flowing waterfalls in desert towns like Las Vegas and Phoenix.

The trail continued downward until it finally broke out of the thick scrub into an area of lower growth plants. Before Christina lay a two lane road leading into a cluster of houses, announcing the presence of the town of Wikieup. Alysa's horse pealed fourth with another ear splitting whinny, which was quickly answered. Everyone's head snapped in the direction from which the sound emanated. Before them, on the far side of the road were several more horses, only these ones weren't wild as Alysa had thought. These horses carried pack saddles and wore halters, and on the lead horse was a man, looking at them with surprise equal to their's, the sun glinting off the deep red of his hair as he raised his hand to shade his eyes from the early afternoon sun.

A man that Christina knew.

25

"You have *got* to be kidding!" Maggie stared in horror at the small black cow laying approximately twenty feet in front of her.

"Is she having the calf, Mom?" asked Mark as he stood beside Maggie, holding Lindy's hand as they watched the cow's sides heave and a pair of large white hooves bulge out from beneath her tail, only to disappear back inside when the contraction eased up. "O'Reilly said he was afraid she was too little and couldn't calve on her own."

"She darned well better be having that calf on her own," said Maggie, "cause her obstetrician happens to be MIA and I have no intention of acting as a substitute."

O'Reilly had been gone nearly four days, and Maggie was becoming worried. He'd said that he might be gone for up to a week or a week and a half, but Maggie had held onto an irrational conviction that he'd show up much sooner. Every day that she didn't hear his horses' hoofs echoing through the canyon her anxiety increased, as well as her annoyance with herself.

The thing that frustrated her the most was that, for the life of her, she couldn't decide whether her anxiety was for him, personally, or whether it was the fear that if he'd been captured, she, Mark and Lindy would soon be discovered. The not knowing was driving her mad, and now she was faced with this cow on top if it all.

"What's an obsta... and obstita... that thing you said, what is it?" Mark asked. He looked from the cow up to Maggie while Lindy pulled at his hand, trying to reach the prostrate bovine.

"An obstetrician is a doctor who delivers babies."

"Baby calves?"

"No, baby humans. A vet delivers calves. Actually cows deliver calves, unless they're like Miss Emily here who can't seem to manage it on her own. Then she needs a vet to help out."

"Cow, cow, cow. What wrong cow?" Lindy fought to get free of Mark and reach Emily, the name that Mark had given the small cow when Maggie first brought it to Hideaway.

"We don't have a vet. O'Reilly said he might have to help her have the calf. He's not a vet, but he said he could *pull* the calf?"

"I'm seeing a bit of a problem with that plan at the moment, kiddo."

"What?"

Maggie looked in exasperation at Mark as he watched the cow straining in front of him. "The problem is that O'Reilly isn't here. I am here. You are here. Lindy is here and Jack and Gypsy are here. None of us who are here, with the possible exception of Emily, have any *idea* how to deliver a calf. The one human we know who does have an idea of how to deliver a calf is conspicuous by his absence."

"Okay, okay... Geez. How hard can it be? Just grab on and pull, right? You can do it."

"If it were that easy, it would be hard to justify how expensive it is to get into vet school. For one thing, I'm not sure how much Emily is going to want me messing around with her rear end. From what I remember of child birth, it's not a time when you want well-meaning but inept help and advice." Maggie studied the groaning cow in front of her. Two feet. That had to be good, since you would think two would need to come through at once. Big feet, at least to her eyes. That might be bad since the calf attached to them would probably be big as well, and Emily was a small cow.

Maggie took a tentative step toward the animal. Then another, and another. The cow looked around toward her and shook her head, flinging cow snot through the air, but didn't try to get up. Another few steps and Maggie was at Emily's rear end, looking down at the wet, sticky mess. Another contraction wracked the heifer and the feet jutted out. Gritting her teeth, Maggie reached down and grabbed them before the contraction ended and they could be drawn back inside, grimacing at the slimy feeling.

The strength required to keep the calf's feet from disappearing back inside the cow surprised Maggie. She wrapped her hands around the legs above the hooves. The slime covering the limbs made getting a good grip nearly impossible, and her hands quickly began to ache with the effort. When she attempted to pull, she felt as though she was tugging on something permanently attached to the cow, not a presumably removable calf. Emily, deciding that she wasn't interested after all in having a novice midwife, chose that moment to lunge to her feet, pulling the calf's legs from Maggie's hands, whereupon they swiftly vanished back into the nether regions of the cow.

Emily lumbered off several yards before stopping. She pawed the ground, arched her back and emitted a strangled bellow as another contraction took control of her body. The large feet appeared once again, but seemed to make no more progress than before. When the contraction released its hold, they once again slipped back inside.

What do we do now? Maggie thought, as she stood watching Emily, hands liberally coated with slime hanging limply at her sides. She had to do something. She couldn't just let the cow die this way. She briefly considered going inside to get O'Reilly's gun. A swift bullet - assuming she could bring herself to pull the trigger - had to be better than this lingering agony. A look over her shoulder at Mark and Lindy, standing watching her with eyes full of trust put an end to that plan, however. She was going to have to deliver that calf, one way or another.

Closing her own eyes and taking a deep breath, Maggie reached a decision.

"Okay, guys," she said, turning back toward the children. "Mark, I need you to help me get Emily into those pens behind the barn. We'll run her up the alley then into that chute at the end. That way we'll be able to hold her still while I try and get the calf out." Maggie's stomach clenched at the thought of what would be coming.

"Then I want you to go back to the house, take Lindy with you, and look through that bunch of old books and magazines that were here when we came."

"Gotcha. What am I looking for?" Mark answered promptly.

"I think I saw some books about raising cattle. Maybe in one of those books, or in a magazine, there will be information on how to deliver a calf that doesn't want to be delivered. It looks like we're about to get a crash course in bovine midwifery."

Mark nodded avidly, obviously ready to turn and head out on his mission. "Okay, Mom. I look for an article or book and bring it back here. Anything else?

"I don't know. In all those old movies where the woman is having a baby they say to bring hot water, soap and towels or sheets. That ought to work for a cow as well, I guess."

"Got it." Mark turned and started to run toward the house.

"Hey!"

Mark stopped and turned back toward his mother, a questioning look on his face.

"You've got to help me get Emily in the chute first."

"Oh, that's right. Sorry." Mark turned back with a sheepish look on his face, towing Lindy behind him. "What should I do with Lindy?"

"Lord, I don't know. Uh... I know, put her in the big box stall in the barn with Gypsy and Jack. She won't be happy, but she should be safe for the few minutes it takes us to get Emily rounded up."

As it turned out, Emily wasn't overly excited about going into the pens and the few minutes turned into over twenty of hard work. By the time the heifer was safely ensconced in the interconnecting labyrinth of pens and alleys Maggie and Mark were both out of breath and sweating profusely and Maggie was seriously beginning to reconsider getting the gun, while at the same time wishing that she'd had that much energy when she'd delivered Mark.

From the barn Lindy was shrieking her discontent at her temporary imprisonment joined in a discordant harmony by howls and sharp barks from Gypsy and Jack, who apparently felt that they could do a better job of rounding up cattle than the humans could.

Maggie stood, hunched over, hands on her knees as she panted, the sweat dripping off her nose.

"Okay, Mark... now... get Lindy and go... to the house and find me a book."

Mark nodded and turned, heading for the barn where he liberated the toddler and the dogs, then headed for the house, urging Lindy to move faster.

As her heartbeat and respiration gradually returned to normal, Maggie stood up and watched the small black cow as she went through another contraction.

"I guess this is it, girl." She took a deep breath and stepped through the gate and began pushing the heifer through the alleyway to the chute.

26

The coolness of the thick-walled house was a welcome relief after the scorching day outside. Mark paused briefly to allow his eyes to adjust to the light before releasing Lindy's hand and making his way to the bookshelves that flanked the fireplace at the right side of the big room.

Lindy, still apparently insulted by her incarceration in the barn, plopped herself down on the cool stone floor where Mark left her and continued to snuffle and whine. Upset by Lindy's distress, Gypsy stood in front of her and vigorously began to wash the tears and snot from her face with a warm, wet tongue. Lindy began to giggle, and reached out to grab Gypsy's white ruff in both hands.

Glancing over his shoulder at the two sitting in front of the door, Mark assured himself that Gypsy had everything under control then turned back to the task at hand. When they'd arrived at Hideaway, they'd found a number of books and magazines left on the shelves, presumably for the entertainment of anyone who found himself spending time at the camp.

The selection had been eclectic, to say the least, ranging from ancient livestock manuals to a ten-year-old copy of *Modern Bride*. That last one had caused some puzzlement and laughter when it was unearthed amid several old copies of the *Stockman's Journal*. His mother maintained that some cowboy had kidnaped it from his girlfriend in the interest of self-defense, while Mark insisted that a cowgirl had brought it with her on a visit. O'Reilly had looked briefly at the magazine, then turned away with a slight smile and declined to voice an opinion as to how it came to be at the camp.

Mark yanked books off the shelves, looking quickly through anything that mentioned cattle, but quickly became frustrated. Many of the books were from the middle of the last century, and in none of the indexes could he find anything about calving. The magazines proved to be an even bigger challenge, since each had many articles, and none of them had indexes.

He looked out the window toward the barn, stamping his foot in impatience at his difficulties.

This is stupid, he thought. "I'm never going to find anything in all this mess."

He turned to throw several magazines on the table behind him, his agitation causing him to use more strength than he intended. The magazines cascaded across the table, fetching up against his mother's computer. She'd taken to writing every morning and evening, using the solar charger to replenish the batteries during the day.

"Too bad she doesn't have a program on cows. Then I could just do a s..." his sentence trailed off as an idea blasted into his mind, stunning him with the simplicity of it. *A search! Google calving problems!* "Yeah!"

Mark hit the table in excitement, causing Lindy, who was busy wrestling with Gypsy, to turn and look at him quizzically, uttering a confused string of sounds that probably meant "Excuse me, was there something you needed?"

Mark hurried around the table to the computer, raised its cover and pressed the power button. The computer hummed quietly to life, flashing up the screen with the picture of him and his dad taken at Christmas two years ago. Looking quickly over the icons, Mark clicked on the browser and waited for the familiar screen to pop to life.

NO CONNECTION DETECTED. CHECK INTERNET CONNECTION AND RETRY.

What the heck does that mean? Mark examined the computer. Maybe he couldn't get the Internet down here in this canyon. Then it struck him. The card. The satellite card his mother had shown him. He remembered how tickled she was when she'd gotten it.

"With this little card, I can get on the Web anywhere in the world. See, it just goes in this slot here," she demonstrated, "and hey presto, I'm ready to go. Way better than the old cellular technology."

Mark turned the computer around and looked at the slot in the side where the card was supposed to go. Nothing. She had to have it here somewhere. He ducked under the table where the computer bag sat, and began rifling through the pockets. There it was, in its little plastic case.

He was so excited that he nearly dropped it, scared to death that he would break it before he could get it installed. In fact, the first time he tried to slide it into the slot, it refused to budge. He pulled it back out again, and stared at it. There were little gold wires, and a notched corner. The wires had to be what went into the computer. Maybe he'd had it upside down.

Hands shaking with nervous tension, he turned the card over and tried it in the slot again. This time it slid in perfectly and the computer emitted a soft *ping* as it recognized the new hardware. Mark waited for it to say the hardware was installed and working, then clicked on the Internet browser icon again, holding his breath until the familiar window appeared on the screen.

"Oh, yeah, now we're getting somewhere," he said softly as he waited for the popular search engine to finish its download. His hands found the keyboard and he was ready to type in his search when a second window appeared in front of the familiar Google logo.

UNREGISTERED DEVICE DETECTED. PLEASE TYPE IN USER NAME AND AUTHORIZATION CODE.

Two small windows appeared below, one labeled user name and the other authorization code, followed by a small timer, counting down from 60. Puzzled, Mark tried typing his mother's name, and the password that she'd used on the computer at home; his and his father's names. Nothing. The clock continued counting down. Mark sat staring at the computer, feeling his stomach sink. He wouldn't be able to search for how to deliver a calf unless he knew the user name and password.

Sighing, he turned from the computer and headed for the front door. He'd have to waste the time going back down to the barn and ask his mother for her information before he could log in. Grabbing Lindy by the hand, he ran back out the door and hurried toward the barn.

He found his mother in the pens behind the barn, dirty and disheveled. A large smear of manure crossed her left cheekbone and there was a fresh tear in the knee of her jeans. The look on her face would have set fire to an ice cube, if such a thing had been present on this broiling day.

Emily, on the other hand, looked to be completely in control of herself, standing in the alleyway, facing his mother. Apparently she hadn't felt like cooperating with the chute plan. It took Mark a moment to realize that lying behind her was a large black and white calf, liberally smeared with manure, blood and other muck.

"She had the calf!"

"Yes, she certainly did." his mother replied, through gritted teeth. "I think that all the running and turning and twisting shook it out of her."

Emily turned to nuzzle the calf, licking it vigorously and emitting several low humming moans, then turned back toward the humans, pawed the ground and shook her head at them, making it clear that she wanted absolutely no more help from either of them.

"That's so great," Mark said, temporarily forgetting his mission. "The calf's so cute. Is it a boy or a girl." He struggled to keep his hold on Lindy who'd just noticed the calf and was determined to climb through the fence to see it.

"I haven't asked," his mother said, taking a deep breath and starting to back away from the pair. "Keep an eye on them for me will you? I'm going to open the gate and let Emily leave in her own sweet time. If she moves toward me, yell."

"Emily wouldn't do that, would you girl," Mark crooned to the cow, who continued to give the both of them the evil eye indiscriminately.

"Emily would grind me into the ground and tap dance on my skull given half a chance right now, and I'd probably do the same for her if the opportunity arose in the near future. We are not exactly seeing eye to eye on a few issues."

His mother limped to the gate and fiddled with the tangled chain for a few moments, casting uneasy looks back over her shoulder. Finally the tangle gave in and she was able to open the rusty green metal panel. Pushing it wide she used a piece of rope hanging on the fence to secure the gate so that it wouldn't swing shut again, and trap the cow and her calf. Finished, she made her way over to the main gate where Mark met her, Lindy in tow.

"I suppose it doesn't matter now, but were you able to find anything on delivering calves?" A tired smile drifted across her face. "I don't think 'run and yell' is an approved method."

"I couldn't find anything in any of the books, so I got on the computer but it wouldn't let me log onto the Internet. It says it wants your user name and password, so I was just coming to get them. I didn't know you'd put a protection on the Internet hookup? I..."

His mother came to an abrupt stop and was staring at him with a look of horror on her face.

"You tried to go on the Internet? With my laptop?"

"Yeah," Mark said, confused by his mother's sudden change in mood. "I was going to Google how to deliver..."

Mark found himself talking to thin air as his mother whirled and ran toward the house. Burdened by Lindy, who wanted to stay and see the baby calf, Mark hurried after her as quickly as possible. By the time he reached the house, his mother was already standing at the computer, typing on the keyboard agitatedly.

"It's frozen, I can't shut it down. Nothing is working." Maggie's voice was tinged with an emotion that Mark had never heard before, but which caused his stomach to clench in fear.

"I don't get it, Mom. What's wrong?"

"If they get a fix on the computer they can track us down using the satellite connection. We've got to shut down the computer now!"

"Who..."

"The people who want us in an APZ. The government. It doesn't matter who." She continued to try different keys to no avail.

"How about the card, Mom. The satellite card. Pull it out of the computer and it won't be..."

"Genius." his mother exclaimed before Mark had even completed his sentence. Reaching for the card where it projected from the side of the computer she pulled. It stuck for a second, then pulled free with a soft click. The computer emitted a soft two-tone *ping* and the screen reverted to its normal appearance.

She sat for a moment, staring at the image of Mark and his father. She seemed to be barely breathing and Mark felt his heart begin to race even faster. Something was wrong. Something was really, totally and completely wrong, and he'd caused it. Just when he thought he'd explode, his mother took a deep breath, and turned from the computer to face him where he stood in the doorway, holding Lindy's hand.

"We've got to talk, kiddo. There are some things that O'Reilly has told me that I didn't think important for you to know. I think now maybe they are." She indicated the chair next to her at the table.

Closing the door and releasing Lindy's hand, Mark moved to the chair she'd pointed at and took a seat facing her.

27

It had been a good day, O'Reilly thought as he finished tying the last pack on his horses, a really good day.

Just as he'd planned, he'd pulled into Wikieup early that morning. Tying the horses in a sheltered wash a short distance from town, he spent some time scouting the area, making sure that no one was in residence, either ghosts or an annihilation team. The town had the eerie, abandoned feeling of the old time ghost towns. Tumbleweeds had blown into the street and had not been cleared away. Mud, washed down from the previous week's rains, lay thick in the roadways, with no tire tracks to mar the surface. It was strange and sad to think of an entire world covered by these modern ghost towns, but that was the legacy of the disease.

After he satisfied himself that nothing inhabited Wikieup except for birds, rodents and coyotes, he made his way through the empty streets toward what passed as the commercial section of the small town. Several times on his solitary journey he turned away from pens that had once housed horses and cattle, but now only housed rotting carcasses. Carrion birds, never before so well fed were reluctant to fly off at the sight of a single human.

Dogs had also been left behind at some houses, as, he was sure, were cats. The difference was that the cats weren't to be seen. However, he caught sight of several dogs skulking between the houses, sharp ribbed. A couple approached him on his walk, but never came close enough for him to touch. He felt a pang at seeing these abandoned animals reduced to this level, but he knew there was nothing he could do for them. Either they would learn to hunt and join their wild cousins, the coyotes, or they would become food for others that were more able to adapt. It was the way of the wild. Those that were capable, would heed the call of their ancestors and would succeed. Those for whom a life lived on the coat tails of humans had become too completely ingrained, would fail.

Only one dog tempted him, making him smile, rather than frown. As he was passing a small, blue double wide trailer, surrounded by roses and bird baths, a loud, high pitched barking assaulted his ears. Turning he saw a small brown and tan long haired Chihuahua come tearing down the front walkway, apparently intent on tearing him limb from limb. This was one little dog that was giving no quarter in the fight to survive.

If, in time, the surviving dogs in communities such as this were to join packs of coyotes and wolves, then the resulting breed of wild canine was certainly going to take on some interesting features. The image of this little spitfire running through the desert in the company of a pack of coyotes was certainly one that made him smile. He figured that the coyotes would eat it first, but the little dog sure wasn't going to make it easy on them.

Wikieup hadn't been on his route while a deputy, but it fit the pattern of a number of other small western towns and he quickly found his way to what might generously be referred to as the center of commerce. He wasn't expecting much, and wasn't disappointed. People living in Wikieup who wanted to do some serious shopping obviously traveled the distance to Kingman to the north, or Wickenburg to the south. There were, however, several small stores catering to the people traveling from I-40 down to Phoenix who found themselves sitting in the middle of the desert, needing a few extra supplies.

Looking around at the empty buildings, he realized that this might be his last chance to visit this town. Surely the annihilation teams wouldn't bypass this place much longer. He'd planned to return and collect the horses as soon as he'd verified that the area was safe, but looking at the buildings, still snugly locked up and filled with goods, as though the owners would return the next morning, he recognized an opportunity that might not present itself again.

Returning the way he came, he quickly reached the outskirts of town where he'd noticed a large beat-up mud brown diesel pickup with a sleeper cab hooked to a rusty 32-foot gooseneck stock trailer. He checked the ignition, but found it empty. Thinking back to all his years on the ranch, he quickly checked under the seat, then under the floor mats. Sure enough, the key, hanging on a silver ring with a braided horse hair fob, was tucked under the back of the driver's side mat. Just where his father had always left his key.

The next few hours he hurriedly packed everything he thought they might be able to use into the stock trailer, the cab, and the back of the truck. He couldn't take the trailer back to Hideaway, of course, but he was sure he could drive it out to the sheltered wash where he'd left the horses and leave it there. With the rains coming frequently, his tire tracks should be washed away in a day or two, and it would be sheer bad luck if an annihilation team arrived before then. Several large mesquites growing along the undercut bank should shelter the vehicle from over head watchers, and the odds of anyone venturing out the rough forest road were small. The truck and trailer should be safe there.

His feeling was that even though the annihilation teams hadn't targeted Wikieup yet, it couldn't be long before this small town would be wiped off the face of the desert landscape. However, if he could gather enough supplies and get them some place away from town, he could bring the horses back as often as necessary, or even possibly bring Mark with him and drive the truck to the Eagle Camp, while Mark led his horse back.

Using plastic bins, found in one of the stores, he gathered dry goods such as flour, salt, sugar, and rice. He also gathered a number of spices that couldn't be grown at the camp. A gardening display in the feed store proved to be a treasure trove of seeds for corn, melons and squash, as well as many herbs. A small variety store provided several books on natural remedies, causing O'Reilly to smile at the thought of Maggie using "weeds" to treat illnesses. He double checked to be sure that the book included a recipe on how to prepare horehound.

By the time O'Reilly began loading articles of clothing such as jeans, shirts and jackets, the old gooseneck was filled to the roof bows, and the cab was overflowing. The afternoon was fading fast into evening, and the clouds were lowering. Deciding it was better to get the truck moved before rain made the roads impassable, he drove as quickly as possible out of town, heading the two miles northeast to the base of the steep ridge where he'd left the horses.

The night was spent in comfort in the sleeper cab of the truck, with the horses dozing in the catch pen nearby. The next morning he decided to help himself to one more truck and trailer, quickly finding an old pee-green pickup with the keys under the floor mats and a 16-foot bumper pull horse trailer nearby.

He hit a small hardware store and a tiny drugstore, making one pile to go into the trailer, and another pile that he would load onto the pack horses. By mid morning he'd moved his second truck out to the corrals and parked it next to the first, trusting that the trees would be thick enough to screen the vivid yellow-green truck from view. That was one vehicle you'd never lose in a parking lot.

Gathering the horses, he readied them for a last trip into town. If everything went the way he'd planned, he'd be headed home by afternoon, and within a few days he'd be back at Hideaway. Back with his family. If this trip had done nothing else, it had shown him that he was going to have to deal with his feelings for Maggie, Mark and Lindy.

The memory of Maggie confronting him about his intention to collect 'fringe benefits' flashed through his mind. Unfortunately, fringe benefits were exactly what he was wanting right now, but he'd been truthful when he'd told her he didn't take anything from a woman she didn't freely want to give. The question was, how to get her to see it his way. He didn't think she'd fall for the "it's our responsibility to repopulate the world" line. He didn't want something that shallow, anyway. He didn't just want 'fringe benefits.' He wanted her whole heart.

Lost in thought, he mounted his horse and led his pack train toward Wikieup.

It didn't take long to pack the horses, securing all the bundles tightly to the pack saddles. Since there was no way of knowing whether the trucks and trailers would be discovered, O'Reilly had saved the most important items for the horses. He loaded the medicines, most of the seeds, and a portion of the dry goods into the panniers, as well as tying bundles on top of the saddles.

He saved a special spot for three large bags of coffee, figuring that the way things had been going lately, he might need it as a peace offering at some time in the future. For Mark he packed a .22 rifle, as well as ten boxes of ammunition. He also found a large compound bow for himself, and a smaller compound bow and a number of arrows that would fit the boy well. The fact was that their ammunition would only last a limited amount of time. The bows would be what they would need for hunting in the future, and the sooner they learned, the better. It would be wise to save what ammunition they had for emergencies.

Wrapped in plastic and tucked safely into the saddle bag of his horse was a special gift O'Reilly had picked out for Lindy. In addition to medicines and cosmetics, the drugstore had also boasted a large selection of gift items, including many stuffed animals. One caught his eye in particular; a large buckskin horse. When he'd touched it, and felt how soft it was against his work worn hands, he knew that this was exactly the present for Lindy.

The girl had a special attraction to animals, and his big buckskin gelding, Ace, in particular. Ever since that day when he'd brought her home on the pack train, she'd laid claim to his horse. Whenever O'Reilly brought him out, Lindy would come running - or toddling, rather - followed closely by Gypsy, her self-appointed protector.

The toy horse would be a perfect gift for the little girl.

Securing the final bundle, O'Reilly swung up onto Ace, dallied the rope of the pack train around his saddle horn and headed north out of town. The wind was beginning to pick up, blowing from the southeast, and he could see the sullen gray clouds once again building on the horizon, over the mountains. If he pushed it, he might make it half way back to Eagle Camp before the rain caught up with him. He'd have to sleep out tonight, but tomorrow night he should be able to sleep warm in his childhood bedroom. Then, the next night he'd be back at Hideaway and put into motion his plan to capture Maggie's heart.

Yeah, right, he snorted. *As smooth as I am, it's more likely she'll decide to try her hand at castration. Gotta try, though.* He didn't want to think what would happen if he couldn't convince her. He couldn't leave her on her own. Especially not with two young children to take care of. But he wasn't sure he could continue living in the same house as though he was nothing more than a colleague or maybe a brother. Not the way he was beginning to feel. It would be too hard.

As the horses approached the edge of the town, Ace, threw up his head and let out a whinny, looking intently off to the north west. In the distance another whinny echoed back. O'Reilly pulled the gelding to a stop and looked in the direction the horse indicated.

Nothing.

After a minute the horse relaxed and moved on out of town.

Local horses running loose, O'Reilly thought to himself. *Pretty soon we're going to have mustang herds as big as anything that ran the plains in the 1800s. Of course, most ranchers preferred geldings, so when they die out there won't be any more. But any mares running loose will get bred to any loose stallions. It'll be survival of the fittest all over again.*

O'Reilly made his way out between the last few houses on the edge of town and headed for the forest service road that would lead him back to the trucks and trailers and from there to Eagle Camp and home. Just as he was moving off onto the two rut dirt road he heard another whinny. His horse again threw up its head, answering loudly. O'Reilly looked in the direction of the sound, shading his eyes against the afternoon sun, expecting to see a herd of loose horses.

To his astonishment he was confronted with several riders coming out of the thick desert scrub on the far side of the road. He squinted, trying to get a better look.

What the... They're kids! What the hell are kids doing out here by themselves?

The last horse, a black and white paint, moved out of the brush into view, the female rider sitting straighter and craning her neck to get a look at him, her brown hair blowing in the newly freshened breeze. O'Reilly began to ride slowly toward the children then stopped, surprise hitting him with the strength of a flash flood.

Christina. That's Christina!

He couldn't have been more surprised if the skies opened up and it started snowing in July, right then and there. What was Christina Craigson doing here and who were the other children with her? It wasn't possible. She couldn't be here. She was in the APZ, sitting in the Nursery, either following the rules, or still sitting in isolation. None of them could be here. They couldn't have escaped. The chips made sure of that. The chips...

The chips! His face blanched under his tan. He looked down at his right arm where the small white scar still showed where he'd dug the small grain-of-rice sized microchip from under the skin. Reflexively he looked up into the sky, as if expecting seekers to come from all coordinates, targeting the small group. *They can't be here without the Enforcers knowing and if they know the kids are here, they'll find out I'm here as well.*

"O'Reilly!" The brown-haired girl was waving her left arm wildly, causing her horse to jitter. Kicking him into a run, she shouldered past the other three children and tore toward O'Reilly, causing the other three horses to toss their heads and jig. In a matter of seconds Christina was rushing up, obviously out of control. The wide-eyed panicked look on her face betrayed her fear as the paint shouldered into Ace, causing him to stagger and the horses of the pack train to spook and run backwards.

He grabbed the paint's reins, bringing him under control and found himself face to face with Christina, the girl he'd left in the APZ. The girl he thought he'd never see again.

"Sorry, that was stupid," Christina said, chest heaving. "I lost control. I can't believe we found you. This is amazing." The paint horse continued to toss its head and fidget in place.

O'Reilly looked back over Christina's shoulder as the other three riders and their pack horses approached. The lead rider was a girl about Christina's age with heavy black hair pulled back into a braid and dark rose brown skin. Behind her were two boys, twins by the look of them.

They must be Christina's brothers, thought O'Reilly. He studied their faces. Christina had spoken of her brothers several times. They looked to be about Mark's age or a bit younger, but he could see the resemblance to their sister.

God, Mark... and Maggie and Lindy. He closed his eyes momentarily as his mind tried to wrap around the disaster that was looming over their heads. Were they all about to be tracked down and captured because these kids had escaped from the APZ and followed him out here? It would be on his head if it happened. That thought was beyond bearing.

"O'Reilly. O'Reilly? Is there something wrong?" He opened his eyes and looked down at Christina who was staring into his face with a worried expression. "What's going on?"

"I'm just surprised to see you. I thought you were safe and sound in Laughlin, not running around the country side."

"That's not it." Christina shook her head frowning then looked back at the other three children who were waiting a short distance away. "You don't have that 'gee, I'm surprised to see you' look on your face. You have an 'oh, shit' look on your face."

"Let me see your right arm."

"What?" Christina looked down at her right hand and arm in confusion. "What do you want to see my arm for?"

"Just let me see your right arm."

Christina transferred her reins to her left hand and held out her right hand and arm, palm down. O'Reilly took hold of her hand and turned it over, palm facing upward and ran his thumb over the upper edge of her wrist. There it was, the small bump made by the microchip.

Why hadn't they been picked up already? Was Rickards hoping that the children would lead him to O'Reilly? Was he really so desperate that he'd let a group of kids wander around in lion infested mountains just to catch a deserter?

Christina was watching O'Reilly with growing concern.

"What's wrong? That's where they put our identification chips. It lets us get food and stuff. I don't suppose we need it out here, but it hasn't caused any problems or gotten infected or anything. We all have them. Tagging us like dogs and cats." Christina frowned, apparently at the thought that they'd been treated like animals.

O'Reilly met Christina's worried eyes with an equally serious expression. "Christina, I'm going to need all of you to trust me. Our ability to stay free will depend on it. The chips need to be removed.

Fear blossomed in Christina's deep blue eyes, mirrored by the other girl's expression. The two boys drew closer to each other.

Taking a deep breath, O'Reilly tried smiling to reassure the four children. "It's going to be okay. We just need to get those chips out of your arms and destroy them before we go any further. Once they're gone, we can head to the canyon."

Damn, he thought suddenly. *What the heck was Maggie going to say when he showed up with four more children.* Deciding he wasn't brave enough to contemplate his future in that regard, he resolutely turned his mind away from Hideaway, and to the task at hand.

28

The young brown-haired girl stood in the hallway in front of Rickards. He could see the pleading look in her green eyes as she raised her arms to him, asking him to save her. Rickards stepped forward, reaching out his hand to take hers and pull her to safety. He could see the long dimly lighted hall behind her and knew, just knew, that some terrible danger lay beyond one of the many doors that populated the walls.

He reached further toward the girl, expecting to feel her warm hand in his, her weight against his arm, but nothing was there. Looking up, he saw her, ten feet away from him, still reaching toward him, fear flickering in her face.

A rumble told him that the train was approaching, which didn't make sense. There shouldn't have been a train here, in a hotel hallway. He looked to the right toward where the rumble seemed emanate and was surprised to see that what he'd thought was a hallway was actually a wide open platform, a train waiting on the far side. The area was crowded with people, all ages and genders, all lining up to enter the train. What surprised him even more was that no one seemed to want to go. The platform lacked the typical babble and noise that would be expected on a typical journey. Instead, all the people were quiet, shuffling heads down toward the doors.

Looking around again, he searched for the girl, but she was nowhere in sight. A feeling of dread washed over him and he began running down the hallway, now miraculously a train station platform, hunting through the crowds of people.

Nothing. No sight of her anywhere.

Then... There! There she was, in a line at the end of the platform, getting ready to board the train. She looked back over her shoulder at him as she put her hand on the rail and began to step onto the railway car.

"Stop! Wait!" Rickards shouted. He ran toward the doors desperately trying to reach them before the girl was completely on board.

Too late. The girl stepped onto the train and turned to face him as the doors of the car slid shut with a woosh, but instead of regular folding train doors, these doors were made of bars, reminding him of cages in a zoo.

The locomotive rumbled to life, preparing to leave the station. Rickards skidded to a stop outside the cage doors and looked at the girl as she looked back at him. The pain in her emerald eyes jolted through him, and a tear began to slide down her face as she reached through the bars. Starting forward he reached out to her again, but their fingers barely brushed as the train began to pull away.

"Captain Rickards," she said, her voice barely audible over the rumble of the train. "Please, Captain Rickards. Captain Rickards!" The voice was louder, more demanding.

"No, stop. What's going on? Where are you going?" Rickards yelled to be heard over the train. The terror he felt exploded in his chest and he began running along the platform, trying to catch the boxcar.

"Captain Rickards. Seth Rickards. Seth," the voice pleaded as the rumble became an explosion of sound, jolting him out of his nightmare and back to the real world. The rumble resolved itself into a cataclysmic thunderstorm, and the voice emanated not from a young brown-haired girl, but from the young, raven-haired deputy standing in the doorway of his room, looking at him with an expression of concern bordering on fear.

Rickards struggled to a sitting position, heart pounding as though it would explode out of his chest and fly away at any moment. He looked around his room, trying to reorient himself. He was laying on his bed. The dim light outside the window told him it was either late afternoon or early evening, with a thunderstorm raging outside. Taking a deep breath, his heartbeat beginning to return to normal, he looked back at the deputy standing just inside the door.

"What are you doing here, Deputy Kail?" he snapped at the young woman standing in front of him. "Haven't you heard of knocking? You have no business entering my rooms uninvited."

"Uh... sir... Well, sir I... um... I'm sorry sir, I... uh... I did knock sir, but you didn't answer, and I heard you yelling inside." Deputy Kail stumbled and stammered, then finished in a rush. "I thought you might be injured, sir, so I came in. You were in the middle of a nightmare; thrashing and yelling. I was worried." The deputy blushed, lowering her gaze away from Rickards' bare chest emerging above the thin, tangled blanket.

"Fine," Rickards growled, noticing for the first time his state of undress. He'd returned, exhausted, to his rooms early that afternoon after nearly forty-eight hours on duty. The last thing he remembered was undressing and falling into bed. Apparently he hadn't been asleep more than four or five hours, and now here he was, being disturbed again.

"I asked you before, what are you doing here? I'm sure you didn't just come all the way up here to see how I was."

Deputy Kail continued to look flustered but had started to regain some measure of self control. "We couldn't reach you on the radio, sir."

Rickards glanced at the radio on his bedside table. Sure enough, it was either off or the battery had died. He tried briefly to remember the last time he'd charged it, then gave up. It didn't really matter anyway.

"Why did you need to reach me?"

"The techs got the monitoring system working. They got a fix on the missing children, or at least a temporary fix. They seem to have lost the signal again, and..."

"They got a fix? On the missing children?" Rickards started to struggle out of the tangled blanket, then subsided after he realized that he hadn't taken the time to put on any form of sleeping garment before he'd fallen into oblivion.

"If you don't mind stepping outside, deputy, I'll be with you in a moment."

Deputy Kail blushed again and turned to step outside the bedroom door. As soon as her back was turned, Rickards finished untangling himself and reached for the dresser which held clean underwear.

Pulling a clean uniform from his closet, he called out over his shoulder, "Where did they get the fix? Are they still in the city? Have you dispatched a patrol to pick them up?"

"No sir, they're not in the city and we wanted to find out how you wanted to handle this. It seems the signal came from near a small town on Highway 93 in Arizona of all places. A place called Wikieup? We were only able to zero in on the signal for about fifteen minutes, then one at a time they blinked off, but the techs are sure it's them."

"What do you mean, they 'blinked off'?" Rickards questioned. He pulled on a fresh khaki uniform shirt over a clean t-shirt, hurriedly tucked it in, then began looking for where he'd kicked his boots earlier that afternoon.

"Well, sir, I don't completely understand, but they said that all four were there, then there were only three, then two, then one, then none. The techs said they didn't think it was a software malfunction again. Maybe the kids went into a cave or something that blocked the signal, but it hasn't come on again. Of course it's raining and there's a lot of lightning, but the computer gurus said that if there was a problem with the storm they should have lost everyone all together. So, it's much more likely that they simply went into some type of structure that's blocking the signal."

Or they've met up with someone who knows about the chips and who is removing and destroying them, Rickards thought grimly.

"Do we have a team in that area that we can send?"

"No, sir. The annihilation teams are working north and west of here, and there are no exorcism teams out at the moment. We tried to call the Phoenix APZ, but apparently the storms have disrupted communication and we can't get through to see if they have anyone out in that direction."

"What teams do we have available here?" Rickards asked, heading for the door with Deputy Kail trailing in his wake like the tail of a comet.

"Andrews' team is in, sir, but some of them were injured on the last mission. They cornered a well armed group of ghosts and..."

"I know, I know. Lister and Smith caught fire. Serious injuries, but recovering. How's the rest of the team doing?"

"Fine, as far as I know, sir. There's also Larson's team. They were pulled off ghosts and have been working with the fire squads, removing houses outside the APZ perimeter."

Rickards headed for the stairwell, walking quickly, not bothering to look back to see if the deputy was following. "Radio ahead, Kail, and tell dispatch to put a call in for Larson's team. We've got to get someone out to Arizona and pick up those kids before they disappear again."

"Yes, sir," said Kail, already reaching for her radio to make the call.

It took less than ten minutes for Rickards and Kail to reach headquarters, and most of that time was spent in silence as Rickards pondered the implications of the children's signal coming from a remote area in Arizona, as well as the implications of the signal's disappearance shortly after it was intercepted. It was impossible that the children would have removed the chips themselves. If they'd known the true nature of the chips, they would have removed them before ever leaving the APZ, certainly before heading east into Arizona.

Could they have met up with someone who knew about the chips? The most likely person on that list would be O'Reilly. That would mean that he'd headed north to throw searchers off track, removed his chip, then headed east. They'd already suspected something of the sort. What didn't make sense was that the children would meet up with him out in the middle of nowhere.

Knowing O'Reilly as he did, and the sense of honor that he possessed which caused him to throw away his career, Rickards was fairly certain that O'Reilly wouldn't have left the children to escape on their own. If he had planned on them escaping at all, he would have made sure that he was there to protect them, and he would have removed the chips immediately, rather than wait until they were nearly a sixty miles away into the Arizona wilderness.

Of course, it was possible that they were perpetrating yet another subterfuge, and O'Reilly was planning on taking the children in a completely different direction. Maybe he'd even stolen a vehicle, driven the chips down to this little town, then destroyed them, planning on backtracking. But how could he be sure that it would take them this long to get a fix on the chips? No, that couldn't be the answer.

In the midst of this stygian swamp of conjecture and confusion, the memory of the nightmare constantly intruded. He'd never been one to attribute meaning to dreams, but his wife had been a firm believer. A lesson in a high school social studies class floated, unbidden, into his mind. The one where they talked about the Jews being loaded onto trains to be sent to the concentration camps. It suddenly struck him that the looks on the faces of the people in the videos were the same as the expression he'd seen on that dream-world train platform. The connection was obvious, but Rickards couldn't figure for the life of him, why his subconscious would have pulled that visual image out of thirty year old memories.

Another memory rose to the surface. The ghettos in Europe, as well as the Japanese internment camps in the United States. People being forced to leave their homes and relocate to a governmentally approved location. Just as they were being forced to move now. The situations were eerily the same... or were they? Rickards shook his head, trying to banish this unwanted train of thought.

Rickards' mind was beginning to spin and he felt the onset of a headache by the time he and Kail finally walked through the door of the enforcer's headquarters. Walking into the large room used by the deputies he looked around, noting that the room was nearly empty on this stormy afternoon. As he paused in the large entryway, a young, sharp-featured deputy - *damn, why can't I remember his name?* - rushed over to him.

"Sir, dispatch has paged Larson and he will be here within a half hour. He's calling his team. He didn't seem too happy about having to switch assignments again so soon, and head back out."

"Well, deputy...," Rickards paused expectantly.

"Harlan, sir. New transfer from the Albuquerque APZ."

"Well, Deputy Harlan, Larson's just going to have to suck it up. We need to get those kids back here immediately and find out what's going on."

Rickards made as if to walk past Harlan, heading for his office when the deputy cleared his throat again.

"Well, what is it?"

"Sir, there's been another development over in the same direction as the runaways. An unregistered computer attempted to log on to the net yesterday morning. Not exactly in the same small town, but not more than fifty miles away to the northeast, either. What's even stranger is that it's out in the middle of nowhere."

"Why didn't I hear of this before?" Rickards snapped.

"It was a short lived signal; only a few minutes of access. Tech thought it must either be a bug or glitch in the new tracking software. There's no power out there, so it didn't make sense that a computer was trying to log on, though the techies did admit it could be a small satellite enabled handheld. It was noted on the day log, but since it couldn't be confirmed, and the connection couldn't be backtracked, they didn't think much of it. After all, that area of Arizona is a lot of nothing. I mean, empty, rough land with nothing but a few ranches and a lot of cows, rocks and cacti."

"What made them change their minds, then?" Rickards snapped, impatient with the entire conversation.

"They didn't, sir. It's just that... well, I know that land, sir. I grew up just west of Flagstaff, Arizona. If the children are in that area, and there's someone with computer access that close, well, I think it's more than a coincidence. If we don't find the children at Wikieup, then we need to consider sending seekers out into the ranch land and see what we can find."

Rickards stopped and studied Deputy Harlan, taking in the light brown hair, the sharp, almost hawk like features that made up his long face, the strange light brown, almost golden eyes. Here might be just what he had been asking for. Someone familiar with the empty lands who could possibly out think O'Reilly, because Rickards was positive that O'Reilly must be involved with this somewhere.

"Harlan," Rickards said, "How would you feel about taking a trip out to Wikieup?"

29

The daily showdown was underway and it was proving to be of epic proportions. Neither side would give an inch and the tension between the two adversaries was reaching the point of no return. Neither party moved. Narrow-eyed green glare met hostile yellow stare. The hot, humid breeze that lifted then died went ignored by both antagonists, so intent was their focus on each other. It seemed that the entire barnyard stood still, waiting for the next move in this battle of titans.

Maggie had the advantage in height and reach, as well apparently possessing the greater degree of intelligence. Her opponent, the advantage in speed and agility. Both knew how this conflict had ended on days past, but that didn't affect either's determination to be the victor on this occasion. Minutes passed as each sized the other up, waiting for him or her to lose focus just for a second.

Maggie shifted her weight subtly, moving her broom handle from left hand to right. Her stare narrowed even more as she studied the rooster in front of her, looking for an opening that would allow her to move past him, unassaulted, and gain admittance to the hen house. Houdini's focus was unwavering. If she could just manage to...

"Mom? Mom, where are you?" The call came from the house, distracting Maggie for just a second. A second was all it took, however. Houdini saw his opening and came flying at Maggie's legs, spurs outstretched, beating his wings against her shins and emitting strident shrieks the entire time.

"Dammit you animated Sunday dinner, get the hell away from me!" Maggie jumped back, tripped and flailed wildly with her broomstick catching the rooster along his left side and sending him flying five feet away in a cloud of dust. Before Maggie could regain her balance and

make a run for the hen house, however, Houdini recovered and once more entered the fray.

This contest ended the same way it had for most of the past week, with Maggie finally admitting defeat and retreating from Houdini's territory while the rooster strutted belligerently back and forth across the front of his yard, stopping here and there to scratch aggressively at the dirt. All the while he maintained a cold yellow-eyed stare on the woman against whom he'd declared war.

"Mom? Where are... Oh." Mark came around the corner of the barn, Lindy, Gypsy and Jack tailing along behind. "Do you want me to get the eggs? Houdini doesn't mind me going into the hen house."

Maggie shot Mark the narrow-eyed green glare that had so lately failed to impress Houdini. It had an equally unimpressive effect on her progeny since Mark started to laugh. It was true, though. Sometime during the past week Houdini had decided that Maggie was public enemy number one, while Mark could wander through the chicken yard without molestation. Even Lindy was able to toddle into the hen house and take eggs out from under the residents, while Houdini followed her about with a slavish devotion.

"Fine, you get the eggs." Maggie thrust out the bucket she'd been carrying over her right arm. "But if that rooster doesn't get his act together real quick, we're going to be meeting over the stew pot."

Houdini let out a cackle and ruffled his feathers, obviously disputing her statement.

Maggie headed across the open ground toward the house with the intention of getting something to drink and contemplating the joys of a chicken dinner. Just as she was walking up the slope toward the front door she heard the dogs begin to bark and a jolt of adrenaline shot through her body.

It had been over a week since O'Reilly left, and even though she tried to deny it to herself, she was becoming more and more worried at his delayed return. She kept telling herself that he'd said he might be gone up to a week and a half, depending on what he found, and she knew the weather would have made traveling much more difficult, but that was her head speaking. Her heart insisted on saying he was gone too long.

Turning back from the house, she headed toward the entrance to the canyon, following in the dogs' wake, trying to determine whether she could hear the hollow sound of hoofs on rock or the creak of the saddle leather.

Just as she'd decided that the dogs had sounded a false alarm, she heard the echo of voices. She stopped suddenly, and turned to look for Mark and Lindy. If it were O'Reilly coming down the canyon, he should be alone. She shouldn't be hearing voices.

Mark was coming around the side of the barn, carrying the egg bucket, eager to see where the commotion was coming from. Maggie quickly started toward him, motioning him to turn around, to get out of sight. Apparently her signals were slightly less than clear, since Mark continued to stand there, a confused expression on his face. Then his look focused on something behind Maggie's left shoulder, and he raised his right arm and began waving, excited.

"O'Reilly, you're back!"

Maggie whipped back around in time to see O'Reilly heading out from behind the last boulder, leading his pack horses. He looked up in the direction of Mark's call, then back toward Maggie, their eyes meeting. A grin spread across his face. Probably at the look of shock on hers, she thought sourly. Her heart was still racing, and she wasn't inclined to be charitable when considering his intentions.

Moving closer, O'Reilly lifted his left hand in greeting. "Honey, I'm home," he called out, a laugh in his voice. "And I've brought guests for dinner," he added, glancing back over his shoulder. Following the direction of his eyes she was just in time to see a group of strange horses round the boulder, and on them, four children; two girls and two boys.

Maggie felt as if she'd been nailed to the ground and her mind had turned to sludge. In spite of the evidence before her eyes, it took a moment for her to understand what it was she was seeing. Four more children. She craned her neck to see if anyone else was going to emerge from behind the boulder. For a brief moment she wondered if O'Reilly was some sort of pied piper who collected children every time he ventured out, and whether the entire town of Wikieup was going to be following behind him, listening to his tune.

Riding up beside her, O'Reilly stopped his horse and looked down at her shocked face, the grin on his features relaxing into a softer smile.

"I found them in Wikieup. There was no way I could leave them behind or send them back to the APZ, so here we all are." He looked back at the children where they'd stopped their horses, watching Maggie. His grin reemerged "Can we keep them, *pleeease?*"

There was a brown haired girl about fourteen or fifteen, another girl of about the same age, but appearing to be either Indian or Mexican, and two boys around Mark's age. All four sat quietly on their horses, as if waiting for an indication that it was okay for them to come closer.

Maggie looked up at O'Reilly, eyes narrowing. She was getting good at that expression, she thought.

"I am so *never* letting you do the shopping again," she murmured to him, then turning to the children lifted her right arm, beckoning them forward. "Come on in. You must be exhausted. Let's get your horses unsaddled and get you something to drink."

An hour later all the horses had been unpacked, unsaddled and turned into the pasture. The bundles still sat piled in the barnyard, and would need to be moved before the afternoon's rainstorm washed them into the next county. For now, however, the sky was blue and the group of eight sat in the shade outside the house, enjoying tepid sodas from the provisions that O'Reilly brought back from Wikieup.

Watching Christina talking animatedly with Mark, telling him about their adventures at the APZ, and the struggle to get to Wikieup, Maggie was amazed with the ingenuity of the children as well as the stupidity of the authorities who felt that they could control people's lives in this manner.

She remembered back to that night a month ago when O'Reilly bared his past, at least as far as the APZ was concerned. She recalled the emotion with which he'd spoken of Christina, his obvious connection with her, and his refusal to bring her into what he considered to be an unacceptable danger.

After meeting Christina, Maggie wondered at O'Reilly's belief that Christina would simply learn to "play the game" adapt and get by in the APZ. After twenty minutes of talking with the girl Maggie could have told him that this young woman would do no such thing. Christina Craigson might break, but she wouldn't be one to bend easily, especially if she felt that bending would require her to do something she felt was wrong.

Maggie had a more difficult time reading Alysa Thalman. She was very quiet and reserved, watching everything, but seldom voicing an opinion. When Maggie was first introduced to her, she had the impression that Alysa was a bit slow; a follower who needed to be told what to do. Quickly, however, she became aware of the level of respect the other three children afforded Alysa and realized that the girl's silence and meek manner secreted a quick mind and the ability to plan and make decisions. The two girls together would be a powerful team.

Maggie smiled to herself. O'Reilly was seriously going to have to get over underestimating the females in his life if Christina and Alysa were anything to go by.

The two boys reminded her of Mark at that age. They had obviously seen some terrible things, which affected them deeply. However, they seemed to view everything that was happening now as a great adventure. When Mark described to them the cave hideout, Nick and Ryan were immediately ready to set out to see this new treat. Occasionally Maggie would catch the two of them in some private communion that no one else was privilege to, but she chalked that up to being twins. They obviously made each other stronger.

"Well, guys," Maggie said, pushing herself to her feet. "We need to get the provisions inside and unpacked, and then we need to figure out sleeping arrangements. Mark, you, Ryan and Nick are going to move into the empty bunks in O'Reilly's room."

At O'Reilly's startled look Maggie held up a hand, telling him to wait. "Alysa and Christina, you're going to take the middle room, and Lindy and I will continue in my room."

"Why can't Nick and Ryan share my room, instead of all of us moving to O'Reilly's room?" Mark asked.

"Yeah, why?" echoed O'Reilly.

"Easy. O'Reilly's room is where all the extra bunk beds are. There's only one bed in my room, so there's no room for the girls. Lindy has her makeshift bed, which will last her a little longer." O'Reilly opened his mouth to start to argue, but again Maggie held up her hand. "Mark's room has a double bunk and O'Reilly's room has two double bunks. That's four beds in O'Reilly's room and four males to fill them."

"Okay, but I get top bunk!" called out Mark. "Hey, O'Reilly, looks like you and I are going to be roomies. You don't mind me taking the top bunk do you? Nick and Ryan can take the other bed."

O'Reilly looked like he very much would like to object to the plan, but one look at Maggie changed his mind.

"Don't worry, O'Reilly," said Maggie looking down at him laughingly. "It's only a temporary situation."

"And why is that, may I ask?" O'Reilly said with a slightly sarcastic note in his voice.

"Because tomorrow you and this crew of tough men here are going to start building an addition to the house. There's plenty of room under the rock overhang, and a fair amount of extra lumber in the barn, so it should be a piece of cake, right?"

"Can't argue with the lady," O'Reilly said to no one in particular, pushing himself to his feet. "Come on troops, we'd better get the packs inside and stored before the boss gets her tail in a twist." O'Reilly headed back toward the barn with the children in tow. Maggie stood watching him, a slight smile playing around her lips and eyes.

That night, after all the children had gone to bed, Maggie and O'Reilly sat out on the flat area immediately in front of the house that Maggie always referred to as the patio to O'Reilly's amusement. Rainstorms earlier that afternoon had cooled the air, leaving it fresh and clean smelling.

The newly expanded group had spent most of the afternoon unpacking and rearranging rooms. The children had come with pitifully few possessions, and Maggie was concerned that, with the rate Mark and Lindy were growing, in addition to four new children, they would soon be stretched hard to keep them all clothed. A seamstress she was not. The one time she'd tried to make Mark an outfit when he was a baby, she wound up with a creation replete with no neck hole and three arm holes. If they relied on her for their sartorial needs, things could get ugly fast.

Fortunately Christina was about her size, and Alysa a bit smaller, so some of the things that O'Reilly had picked up for Maggie would also fit the girls, at least for awhile. Meanwhile, Nick and Ryan could wear some of Mark's hand-me-downs. The prospect of a couture calamity was not yet imminent.

The breeze lifted, picking up tendrils of Maggie's hair. A stray lock, led by the wind, tickled O'Reilly's cheek as he sat next to her. Lifting his right hand he took the long strand, and turning, tucked it behind her ear.

Maggie momentarily stiffened at his touch, then relaxed again at its gentleness.

The silence grew longer and Maggie's eyes started to droop with weariness. Then O'Reilly's husky, gravely voice broke the spell.

"Are you angry about the children?"

"Angry? No, not angry. I'm worried a bit. How are we ever going to keep eight of us fed and clothed? I'm scared, I guess, but not angry. You couldn't have done anything else."

"There's something else you need to know, though."

A small jolt of adrenaline shot into her blood stream. "Why is it whenever you tell me there's something else I need to know, it's never a good thing?"

"Not always."

"Yes, always. Do you want me to list them?"

"No, I get it. I guess this might fall into that category, too. Did I ever mention to you that they were implanting all the residents of the APZs with microchips."

"Microchips? You mean like the identification chips they put in dogs so that they don't get lost, or rather so that they get found when they do get lost?"

"Yes, that kind, only with more information on them than the chips they implant into the dogs. These chips have your name, an identification number, your medical information, that type of thing." His voice had taken on a flat tone that caused more adrenaline to course into Maggie's blood stream. "The authorities said it was so they could track who was getting what, and making sure that no one was taking more than his share, you know, of food and clothing and things like that."

"It makes sense, I guess. With all the shortages of goods until they're able to get the food production reestablished and factories up and running, the government is going to need to be sure than no one is hoarding. I don't really like the idea of being implanted like a dog or a cat, but it would work, I suppose."

"Yes, it works. The thing they don't tell the residents is that each chip contains a GPS tracer, so that a satellite can track anyone, anywhere on the planet."

"I'm already not liking where this is going," Maggie said with an appalled expression. "I know you better than to think you brought the children here with those chips still in them. What is it you're trying to say?"

"I don't know how the children made it to Wikieup without being picked up. I know the techies were having problems with the tracking software before I left. The sudden demands on the system following the concentration overwhelmed it. I hope that I got the chips out before anyone got a fix on them, but there are no guarantees."

"See, I told you. Never a good thing. Next time you tell me there's something I ought to know, can't it be something like 'dinner's ready' or 'I've left you a million dollars in my will.'"

"I'll see what I can come up with," O'Reilly said with a unfamiliar note in his voice. "I'm sure there'll be something."

"So," Maggie continued, suppressing an internal quiver of fear, "What's the upshot? How much has this increased our danger?"

"I took the chips out of their arms soon after I met them. Then we destroyed the chips, so the furthest they can be traced is to Wikieup. Closer than I'd like, but no closer than the annihilation teams will be when they destroy the town. The rains would have washed out our tracks by now, so as far as they know the children could have headed in any direction from there."

O'Reilly turned his arm over in his lap, rubbing his finger lightly along the small white scar on his wrist.

"What concerns me more is that a captain in the Enforcers, Seth Rickards, connected me with Christina. He was questioning her about where I might be before she escaped. If they're able to track her to Wikieup, then he'll suspect that I'm nearby."

"What kind of guy is Rickards?"

"If you're on the force, he's someone you want at your back. If you're doing something you're not supposed to do, he's the guy you don't want tracking you down. He'll have seen my escape as a betrayal to the Enforcers and to the country. He'll know that I have information that could hurt the government, and he won't stop at anything to get me back."

"Okay, not great, but not terrible either."

"I wasn't sure what to do when I found the children, and if you say so, I'll take them and we'll leave. We'll go far away from here, maybe drop some clues so that Rickards doesn't look in this direction. I couldn't just disappear, though, and leave you wondering what happened to me."

"Yeah, that would have been a lousy thing to do. Not to mention the fact that we still don't have adequate skills to make a living out here." Maggie was quiet for a moment then suddenly said, "There's something *you* ought to know."

A snort of laughter escaped O'Reilly, and he turned to look at her, a grin stretching his tanned face white teeth flashing in the gloom. "Does this fall into the 'dinner's ready' variety, or the 'boogey man's hiding in the closet' variety?"

"Definitely the boogie man variety." Maggie answered with conviction. "A big, bad boogie man with slimy green skin, bulging bloodshot eyes and severe halitosis."

"Let's have it. Boogey men with bad breath are my speciality."

"While you were gone Emily had her calf."

"Yeah, I know. I saw them out in the pasture. I would have thought that information only ranked at the level of a two-inch tall boogey man with hiccups, if that."

"No that's not what you needed to know, though I will say that if you're gone the next time a cow needs a midwife, you better not come back, extra children or not!"

Maggie paused, considering her words. "The problem is that Emily had some difficulties, and I sent Mark to see if there was any information on delivering calves in any of the books we found here. He couldn't find anything, but I'd left my computer out on the table and he thought he'd log onto the Internet and find information that way."

The smile that had been resting on O'Reilly's face disappeared as he realized what was coming.

"He couldn't log on. The web required an authentication code. He thought it was my security code, since that's the computer I always used for work, and he came out to ask me the password. I shut down the computer as soon as I realized what happened. It couldn't have been more than a few minutes and it was nearly four days ago, but there it is. Christina may have led the Enforcers to Wikieup, but I may have led them directly to the canyon."

Both grew silent as O'Reilly apparently processed the information. Finally, after a few minutes so quiet that Maggie began to squirm, O'Reilly let out a huge sigh and said, "You're right. A big boogey man with halitosis and probably lethal levels of flatulence as well.

"It's possible that the computer wasn't able to be accurately traced in that amount of time." O'Reilly seemed to consider the options. "But in a worse case scenario, they now know you're out here somewhere, and Rickards isn't fool enough to believe that the kids heading this direction, as well as an unauthorized computer from the middle of nowhere are unrelated."

"Do we need to run?"

"You say it's been four days since the computer?"

Maggie nodded.

"And it's been three days since I met up with the kids in Wikieup. I'm afraid that if they're coming, they'll be close by now. If we're out moving across the empty lands - a group of eight - there's no way we'll go undiscovered.

"No, I think the only option right now is to make sure the caves are provisioned and get ready to hide. If they're coming I don't think we have much time."

All the warmth seemed to have been sucked out of the evening air, and Maggie shivered.

O'Reilly started to push himself to his feet. "It's getting late Maggie. We've got a lot of work to do tomorrow. I'm off to bed. I only hope my new roomies don't snore."

He put a hand on her shoulder, then suddenly leaned forward and brushed her cheek with his lips. "Don't worry. We'll get it all worked out. But I think we might wait a day or two before beginning your addition." Finishing getting to his feet, O'Reilly went into the house and closed the door quietly behind him.

Left alone in front of the house, Maggie hugged her legs to her chest and rested her chin on top of her knees; wishing she weren't alone, that O'Reilly had stayed out with her. She was scared. She wasn't ashamed to admit it. After everything she'd been through in the last year, she couldn't ever remember being so scared.

It was going to happen, then. They were going to have to fight to survive. Not just the elements, but people, too. She remembered back to the night O'Reilly told her about what was happening in the APZ; when he'd made her promise that if they came for him, she'd take Mark and Lindy and hide in the caves, and let him be taken. That they wouldn't let her live. That Lindy might be the only one that would come out of a direct confrontation alive because of her young age. Now there were four others that would die with them. Four others depending on them for safety.

She put hand to her cheek, where O'Reilly had kissed her. She felt a well of conflicting emotions bubbling up inside her, threatening to overwhelm and incapacitate her in the flood; fear, confusion, annoyance (plenty of that), frustration (even more of that, damn O'Reilly), mixed in with an unexpected amount of happiness and even love. It was an unpalatable mixture and it churned her inside like a blender.

Heaving in a huge sigh that caused Jack, who was laying nearby, to leap to his feet on the alert for what ever danger had crept up on him unawares, Maggie pushed herself to her feet and turned to head inside and to bed.

I hope all three of them do snore. Loudly.

30

Where the hell are they?

Rickards stood in the middle of Highway 93 near the front of his jeep, looking around at the empty buildings of Wikieup. Other than a few furtive dogs, sliding in and out between the buildings, as well as an impressive variety of bird life, there was no indication that Wikieup was anything but a ghost town.

"Captain, there's no sign of the children or of O'Reilly," Harlan approached from the south, where he and a group of other Enforcers had been conducting a door to door search of the town. "The team is continuing to look, but I feel fairly certain that there is no one in the town at this time. There are signs, however, that someone recently broke into many of the stores and cleared out the shelves of dry goods. It's impossible to tell if it's the people we're after or another band of ghosts, but I have trouble believing in coincidences."

"So do I, Deputy Harlan. But, if they're not here, then, where are they?" Rickards suppressed a tremor of annoyance at the man's officious tone.

"I'd pin my bet on the computer signal from northeast of here. That's wide open country, very rough, covered with canyons and washes, but there are a few ranches and camps scattered about. From what I've heard about O'Reilly, I'd guess that he chose one of them as his headquarters. Probably the most out of the way one he could find. It's too bad that we couldn't get here sooner and catch them before they went to ground."

"Yes, too bad indeed," Rickards growled, anger and frustration over the delay clouding his features as surely as the monsoon storms obscured the nearby mountains.

In spite of Rickards' intention of heading to Wikieup the afternoon they picked up the children's signal, things hadn't moved quite so quickly. Their primary problem had been transportation.

All of the vehicles assigned to the Enforcers, the fire department, and the medical department were kept in the same lot to streamline and carefully monitor supplies of gasoline, diesel and oil. When Rickards had radioed to the transportation yard, he was told that a shipment of gasoline had been diverted by a band of ghosts on I-40 outside of the Albuquerque APZ. Until a replacement shipment arrived, the entire Laughlin APZ would be running on fumes and under no circumstances was the transportation director about to let Rickards take a bunch of gas guzzling vehicles off into the backwoods of Arizona on a wild goose chase. Or words to that effect.

Rickards demanded. He threatened. He yelled. He even tried to cajole, something with which he had no skill, and which was frightening to watch, but to no avail. He found that Loveless, the grumpy fifty-something mechanic in charge of the motor pool lived up to his name and adamantly refused to hand over the keys. Rickards considered holding him at gun point. However, he realized that any vehicles released in such a manner still would have no fuel, and that such behavior would almost certainly mean his immediate removal from the Enforcers, followed by long term incarceration. Since neither would further his aim, he stopped short of such an action.

Ultimately it took two days before the replacement shipment of fuel arrived at the APZ and his team was able to secure enough vehicles to head after the children. During this enforced down time, the team researched the area to which they were heading, and tiptoed around Rickards.

Now they were in Wikieup, the small and only bump on Highway 93. Reference books identified 93 as what used to be Arizona's deadliest road. Now, after extensive renovations, it was simply a long road through the middle of some very rough country covered with brush and boulders. Regardless of all the information the books held, the one thing they didn't say was where the quarry was. All Rickards knew was that they were no where in sight.

"Have the techies back in Laughlin been able to pin down where the computer signal was coming from any closer than when we left?"

"No, sir," answered Harlan. "They'd need the computer to try and log back on to do that, and unfortunately that hasn't happened. Attempts to initiate a reverse log on have been unsuccessful as well. However, based on the coordinates that they gave us before leaving the APZ, we're looking at this area here." Using a red marker, Harlan indicated a large square northeast of their present location, somewhere in the box between Highways 93 and 89 and south of I-40. "I suggest we send out the seekers to these coordinates and see what we get. We can monitor the signal on the mobile station here, then if they pick up something, we'll know where to head."

"Sounds like a good plan, Harlan," Rickards said, nodding. "Get them in the air right away.

Harlan nodded and turned starting back toward the truck carrying four long range seekers. Stopping suddenly, he turned back to Rickards.

"Sir, there's another thing we're going to have to consider, even if we do find them."

"What's that, Harlan?"

"This time of year the roads in this area can be pretty bad. It's very possible that we won't be able to move the vehicles in, even with four-wheel drive, until the rains let up a bit. I've seen some of these remote ranches and camps socked in for several days or more during a wet summer or winter. It doesn't take long for the roads to dry if we hit a few days where the monsoon holds off, but going in when it's wet could be a disaster."

"Just find them, Harlan. We'll worry about the roads when we know where we're going." Rickards looked stormier than the skies. "I want those seekers up in the air within a half hour. The good news is that if we can't get in, they can't get out, so right now we just need them found."

"Yes, sir." Harlan hurried to the truck to relay his orders.

Rickards stood looking around the deserted town, as the thunder rumbled and the first large drops of rain began to fall.

Where the hell are they?

31

James O'Reilly lay on his bunk, listening to the soft breathing of his three new roommates and wishing he was elsewhere. Two rooms elsewhere to be exact.

The soft sound of the front door opening and closing followed by a second door opening and closing told him that Maggie had come in and gone to bed. He knew the next few days were going to be hard on her. Hard on everyone for that matter.

Raising his right arm and laying it across his eyes, he thought again about the wisdom of making a stand there at Hideaway. They could still saddle the horses tomorrow morning and make a run for it. If they were lucky, they might make it out of the area before the seekers arrived. The problem was, though, that if they hadn't gone far enough before the seekers started circling, they would be sitting ducks out in the washes and flats of the open range. Four of them might have been able to manage it. With eight, it was virtually impossible. In the caves their heat signatures wouldn't be picked up, nor would they themselves be seen.

How long did they have?

Not long if he knew Rickards. Of course, as he told Maggie, there was a slight chance that he'd removed the children's chips before anyone got a fix on them. That would be the best case scenario. If that were the case, they could take extra precautions for a few weeks, then return to life as normal, or what passed as normal these days.

It was almost certain that Maggie's computer had been tagged, but since no one would connect Maggie with him unless the chips were located, it could easily slip by without anyone taking immediate action, especially if things were busy elsewhere. A wry smile twisted his lips. With Christina, Alysa and the boys missing and their connection to him, he was sure that things were extremely busy elsewhere. Rickards was no fool, though, and if they had picked up on the kids' chips heading in this direction, the computer signal, whether or not it belonged to a known fugitive, would be seen as significant.

He didn't dare count on best case scenarios. Rose colored glasses would do nothing but get them captured or killed. He was relatively certain that seekers would be the first signal that someone knew where they were. However, should they be taken by surprise in this canyon, there would be very little possibility of making it to the caves and hiding undetected.

How long?

If Enforcers had arrived in Wikieup immediately after O'Reilly and the children left, they would still need to send out seekers to determine which direction the fugitives had gone. They hadn't seen or heard any seekers while riding, and even at night he'd sat up, standing guard, listening for the tell-tale whine of the drones' propulsion systems. It hadn't materialized. That should mean that Rickards was still at least three days behind them.

Should mean.

He knew Rickards too well to underestimate him. No, the best move would be to assume that within the next week Enforcers would descend upon this canyon in numbers that would do the invasion at Normandy proud.

Well, maybe not quite that many. The Laughlin APZ didn't have that kind of resources. But just as O'Reilly wasn't underestimating Rickards, he was equally sure that Rickards wouldn't underestimate him. If the captain believed that the kids had met up with O'Reilly, Rickards would stop at nothing to recapture them, and he would bring the manpower to do it.

A soft sigh and a murmur came from across the room. It sounded like the upper bunk. Was that Nick? Or Ryan? Hell, he couldn't tell the two apart and he knew they got a huge kick out of his continual mistakes.

O'Reilly made a fist with his right hand and brought it down to his side, hitting the mattress beside him with a soft thump. He'd been so careful since Sarah and Kay-Tee died to keep everyone at arm's length. How in the hell could he suddenly find himself in charge of the well being of seven other lives? God sure had a sense of humor.

It didn't really matter at this point whether he *wanted* to be responsible for other lives. He was, and he had to do his best for them.

Tomorrow morning they would need to split up in groups and prepare for a siege. The children should be put to work carrying more supplies to the caves. Maggie, Mark and he had put up enough to last for a week or more, but there were eight now, assuming he made it to the caves at all. The collapsible water containers he'd brought back from Wikieup would have to be filled and stored. More food would need to be carried, more bedding, more everything.

Meanwhile, he, and maybe Mark and Alysa, would need to take the extra horses and cattle and drive them up to the east pasture. He thought about simply opening the end gate and letting the animals drift out on their own, but quickly dismissed that thought. It would probably take them too long to move since the grazing was still good down here in the canyon bottom. A large collection of horses and cattle would be a sure sign to anyone monitoring the seekers that people were about, even if the machines didn't pick up the people themselves.

We'll have to take some of those water proof tarps, O'Reilly thought. *If we saddle all the animals, once we get to the top pasture, we can unsaddle and wrap the tack in the tarps and leave it under some brush or make a rock cairn. That way when Rickards comes, it will look more like we've made a run for it. Being turned out and not milked will probably cause Lizzie to start drying up, depending on how long we have to leave them there, but there's no help for it. A milking cow with no calf would be a dead give away to anyone trying to figure out if we're here or not.* O'Reilly sighed. Maggie wasn't going to like giving up the milk supply until Lizzie calved again, but she'd like living in the APZ even less.

While all this was going on, Maggie could be working in the house to make it look as though no one was living there. It wouldn't be easy. No dust would be a huge giveaway. Dust was a way of life on an Arizona ranch.

Job description: Low pay, hot weather, no moisture and plenty of dust. Obsessive-compulsive neatnicks need not apply.

Of course, being the monsoon season, the dust was not as prominent as it usually was. For this short time every year most ranch wives traded dust for mud. O'Reilly never thought that he'd miss the dust.

Maggie didn't need to make it look as though no one had been there in the past fifty years, though. Only that the fugitives were no longer in residence. If she could get everything essential hidden somewhere, that would add to the impression that they had bolted, realizing that someone would be looking for the kids.

223

Taking a deep breath, O'Reilly rolled onto his left side. Starting tomorrow night, they'd all better camp out in the caves, just in case Rickards decided to make a surprise nighttime or dawn attack. O'Reilly closed his eyes, and concentrated on slowing his breathing. He might as well enjoy the last night sleeping in a bed that he was likely to see for awhile.

From across the room, one of the boys began to snore.

The night air was peaceful, a light breeze playing hide and seek between the walls of the canyon and the outbuildings. Soft lunar light splashed the camp with silver. The windmill creaked into motion, then stopped. In the pasture the horses and cattle grazed quietly.

Gradually a high pitched whine built, causing several of the horses to twitch their ears, one tossing his mane and swishing his tail in annoyance. One of the cows lifted her head, a mouthful of grass hanging unchewed as she looked toward the sky. In the hen house Houdini ruffled his feathers and, confused about the time of day, emitted a crow, creating a rustle among the hens.

The whine swelled, then just as suddenly as it came, it began to recede. The cattle and horses returned to their moonlit grazing. In the hen house, silence returned. At the main house there was no indication from the humans that anything had changed.

The wayward wind again picked up and died, picked up and died. Everything once again was peaceful.

32

"We've got them! I think we've got them!" A young deputy, whose name Rickards couldn't remember, threw open the door to the van and was beckoning the captain over from where he was sitting with the rest of the team, drinking coffee.

Large panel LED lights operating off the oversized solar charged batteries stored in the jeeps surrounded the cluster of vehicles, drawing millions of small bugs to their deaths while illuminating the camping area set up on the edge of town. There had been some talk of taking over beds in some of the abandoned houses, but most of the men felt uncomfortable with that situation. In the end, everyone decided to stay together as a group, setting up tents and sleeping bags in the middle of the highway.

In lieu of a campfire, a small propane stove provided a hot meal and coffee for the team of ten officers. *A campfire would have been nice,* thought Rickards wistfully, *but try finding dry fire wood in the desert during the monsoon season.*

Fortunately for his team, Wikieup seemed nearly untouched by scavenger teams, ghosts, annihilation teams or any of the other groups of people who might have appropriated everything left on the shelves at the time of the disease and concentration. It was obvious that someone had been in the stores recently, presumably O'Reilly, but he'd left everything more or less intact, taking only what he needed to live in the wilderness.

At least that's what Rickards assumed. There did seem to be a lot of things missing for just O'Reilly and the four children, but the stores in no way resembled the trash pits usually left behind by early looters or later bands of ghosts.

At the deputy's shout, a flood of adrenaline shot through Rickards' system. *I've got him*, he thought. *Finally I've got the slippery son of a bitch.* Rising hastily to his feet, Rickards walked swiftly over to the van that was acting as the mobile tech station. Inside the young deputy - *Martin, no Martinez*, thought Rickards - was sitting at a computer screen, busily typing on his keyboard.

Climbing in and taking a seat in the second chair, Rickards looked over Martinez' shoulder, studying the screen. The night vision sensors on the seekers rendered the landscape in shades of blue and gray, giving it an otherworldly aura. Rickards had some experience in translating the ghostly scene sent by the seekers into real life, but he saw nothing in the view in front of him that made him think the fugitives were anywhere near.

"What have we got here, Martinez?"

"Seeker 2 has just passed over an area approximately forty-three miles to the northeast of here. It's a deep canyon with a wide area containing some buildings and a small stream. Probably a ranch camp. Here, let me roll back the footage." Martinez tapped a few keys on the keyboard and the picture on the screen abruptly changed, showing the land unraveling underneath the seeker as it moved along. A digital readout in the upper left corner indicated that the seeker had passed over this terrain only a short time before.

Abruptly the land dropped away as the seeker floated out over what appeared to be a deep canyon or wash. The seeker dropped altitude, maintaining its programmed height of sixty feet.

A number of fuzzy blue-gray blips appeared in the phosphorescent blue-gray landscape. The resolution of the cameras in the seekers wasn't perfect, but he could swear that these blips were livestock, not people.

"Are those cows?"

"Yes, sir, and horses. See, there and there?" Martinez indicated several blips that had a definite equine appearance as opposed to the bovine aspect of the other blips. Rickards squinted his eyes, trying to see if he was missing anything.

"This is ranch land, Martinez. One would expect to see horses and cattle. What makes you think the fugitives are nearby?"

"The location for one thing. There's a high concentration of livestock in this one area in conjunction with buildings... See, there," Martinez pointed to a large shape in the background. "That's a barn and that's a windmill over there," the deputy indicated another tall stick-like shape that had a barely discernible set of blades at the top, spinning slowly in what appeared to be a gentle breeze.

Rickards studied the pictures. The blue-gray landscape showed the buildings and the livestock that Martinez indicated, beyond doubt. What he still wasn't sure of was why that meant that the runaways were hiding nearby. The last thing he wanted was to send his team on a wild goose chase while the fugitives made good their escape from another direction.

"Surely there are ranches scattered all over this land. Why should it be unusual to find them?" Rickards queried, continuing to study the landscape as it slowly passed on the camera feed.

"We sent the seeker around the perimeter of the area and found fences with gates closed. It's been months since everyone either died or was concentrated. Even if this area has good grazing, it wouldn't have supported this number of horses and cattle for that long, and you can see that there is still plenty of grass."

Rickards leaned forward, looking closely and indeed he could see that there was plenty of growth of some type. A vantage point sixty feet in the air made it difficult to tell exactly what kind it was. Martinez, realizing the captain's difficulty, tapped a few keys, causing the scene to zoom in closer giving Rickards a sudden feeling of vertigo. The tall grass growing in the pasture became instantly visible, though he wasn't sure if he'd have known what it was if Martinez hadn't pointed it out.

"Any sign of human habitation?"

"Other than the structures, which were obviously there before the reorganization, we're not seeing any humans."

"Well, then..." Rickards started, a frown creasing his face.

Martinez hurried on, interrupting his superior in his haste to clarify his statement. "We did, however, find a large overhang in the cliff wall. It's coming up in the video feed in a second." Martinez paused, staring intently at the screen. "There, you see." He pointed at a large dark area staining the bottom of the monitor.

Examining the undefined shape in front of him Rickards could only take Martinez' word that it was an overhang in the cliff wall.

Martinez continued, tracing the shape with his finger and pointing to minute smaller light areas within the general darkness. "We think there is a structure built under this overhang, using it as walls and roof, similar to the Anasazi and Sinagua cliff dwellings. We can't get any heat signatures from inside, but that could be due to the thickness of the walls if it's made of adobe or rock and the people are at the back. It's hard to tell, but it is late, and anyone living here might be asleep."

Martinez stopped and looked expectantly at Rickards.

Rickards continued to study the screen, silently pondering his choices. If he sent the team out to this remote canyon and found nothing but cows, he could miss his chance to apprehend O'Reilly. However, the reverse was also true. If he failed to send the team, and it was O'Reilly hiding out in this camp, he could be giving him the chance he needed to make good his escape. Even with the seekers it would be a miracle if O'Reilly could be tracked for more than a short distance. O'Reilly knew how to avoid the seekers, and how to take them out if the chance arose. Rickards team didn't have enough seekers to continually send ones out just to be destroyed.

Finally, taking a deep breath, Rickards turned to Martinez. "Tomorrow, if the roads are dry enough, we head for this canyon... what's it's name?"

"The maps say it's a place called 'Adobe Canyon."

"We head for Adobe Canyon as soon as possible. Use this time to plan our route. Understand? And just in case this isn't O'Reilly, maintain the current search pattern. At least for the next few hours."

"Yes, sir." Martinez nodded assent and turned back to his screen and began furiously tapping on the keyboard and scribbling notes on a nearby pad of paper.

Rickards pushed himself out of his chair and stepped down out of the van. The other Enforcers seated in the circle became silent as they realized that Rickards had returned. They watched him expectantly as he studied each of them in turn.

"Everyone needs to turn in," Rickards stated, holding up his hand to forestall the questions that began to erupt from the deputies.

"The seekers have found a site that looks probable. If the roads are decent we will head out in the morning, first light." Thunder rumbled again in the distance, causing everyone to look northeast in the direction of the storm. Rickards grimaced. "If the roads are impassable for vehicles, we will send out scouts on foot and proceed as soon as we get the all clear. Understood?"

The team nodded, a few of the men voicing their approval and understanding.

"Good. Hit the sack then. Be ready to move at first light."

As the men began to pick up their things and head for their assigned tents, Rickards turned away and strode beyond the reach of the lights. Standing in the darkened road, studying the barely discernible landscape, lit intermittently by the moon as it passed from behind the clouds, he contemplated the next day's activity.

If all goes well, by this time tomorrow I could have O'Reilly in custody, Rickards thought. *We take him by surprise, trap him in the canyon and finish it one way or the other. He's only got four kids for back up and we've got an entire team, so it should be a piece of cake.*

A persistent niggling feeling in the pit of his stomach made him doubt that it would be that easy.

33

With every step, the jug of water felt like it added five more pounds. Of course, Christina thought, if the two-gallon jug weighed about seventeen pounds to begin with, and it added five pounds every step, she'd be carrying well over a thousand pounds by now, which was impossible. Still, the container seemed like it was unbelievably heavy, even though when she'd started it hadn't seemed so bad.

Christina stopped and set down the large plastic bottle, then with hands on hips took several deep breaths. She tilted her head back, trying to catch the breeze to cool her hot, sweat soaked face. Everyone had been hard at it since early that morning, one day after arriving at Hideaway. Moving, carrying, hiding, O'Reilly and the woman, Maggie Langton, had been in a frenzy of activity. Christina was sure it was because of her, her brothers and Alysa. From all indications, O'Reilly, Maggie, Mark and Lindy had been living here quite comfortably - well maybe not comfortably but safely - with no concerns of being found. Until Christina and her group arrived, of course.

A twinge of guilt washed through her, quickly suppressed. It wasn't her fault that everyone was in danger. No one could expect her to stay at the APZ, with the exception of the Enforcers, of course. How was she supposed to know that the chips that were implanted in everybody's wrists actually enabled the residents to be tracked if they ran away?

Not that anyone seemed to blame her. Maggie was kind, telling her she was glad they were there. Mark was just a neat kid, a lot like her brothers. There was something bothering him that no one talked about, but just like everyone else, he'd probably been through a lot in the last few months. Lindy was a sweetie, although Christina had never had much use for little kids. You couldn't talk with them, really.

At Wikieup, when O'Reilly told them about the micro chips, and how those little chunks of silicon would enable the Enforcers to find them if the software was working, he seemed concerned, but not angry that they came. When they told him about their escape, he actually appeared pretty impressed that they had managed to outwit the authorities and make it all the way to Wikieup on their own. He certainly didn't act like he blamed her or the others for putting him in danger.

Her fault or not, though, things seemed to be quickly entering siege mode.

"Hey, Christy, are you coming?" Nick and Ryan were walking ahead of her, both holding a handle on a water jug, carrying it between them. Nick had turned back and was looking at her expectantly.

"Yeah, I'm coming." Christina took in a deep breath then bent to pick up her vessel again and started trudging through the long grass after the boys.

It had been so nice to sleep in a bed last night, instead of on the ground. Then, this morning after being woken at an unbearably early hour by a psychotic rooster they called Houdini, everyone was told to pack their blankets and carry them to the caves. O'Reilly explained that they would be spending the next few days or weeks sleeping in the caves in case the Enforcers had been able to trace Christina and her group to Wikieup and decided to send out seekers over land to determine if they'd gone in this direction.

Just a precaution, he said. No need to worry. Besides, it would be good practice.

Yeah, right.

Christina understood, but she was sure going to miss that old creaky bed tonight.

Then there was that look that passed between O'Reilly and Maggie, and Mark's obvious discomfort. While O'Reilly was telling them the reason for the temporary move, Mark started to speak, but a sharp look from O'Reilly and a sudden move from Maggie caused him to lapse into silence. Something was going on there, but she wasn't sure what, and it made her uncomfortable.

It really didn't matter, however, what the actual reason for the move was, Christina decided. It was the results that counted, and the results of the move were that Alysa and Mark were assigned to help O'Reilly shift the cattle and horses up the canyon and to the east pasture. Christina, Ryan and Nick were set to work carrying water, food, bedding and other supplies to the caves. Maggie, after showing them the way to the caverns, was busy in the house, trying hard to make it look as though no one had been there for awhile.

If it was just a precaution, it sure was an elaborate one.

34

For nine months out of the year you can't get enough rain to put out a cigarette, Rickards thought morosely, watching the clouds build to the east as they had every afternoon for the past two days. The towering thunderheads portended another afternoon of impotence, just as much as it foretold another afternoon of rain.

They'd hit one of those periods during the monsoons where the rain had been exceptionally heavy and widespread. A rain gauge they found in a yard in Wikieup measured nearly three inches yesterday alone, turning the small forest service and ranch roads around the town into a soupy mess. The steep forest service road that would take them to the top of the rim was especially hard hit. On top of that, it appeared that lightning struck their seeker, making it impossible for them to keep track of what was happening in the canyon until they could get there.

The National Weather Service, one of the few national organizations that was on the priority list for the government to keep up and running, reported a hurricane had ventured across the Gulf of California, punching up a massive load of moisture before making landfall in northwestern Mexico. That moisture was quickly funneled into a trough between a high pressure system parked over the four corners area, and the low perched off Baja California.

Results: huge amounts of rain in a short amount of time for much of the Southwest.

Yeah, tell me about it, thought Rickards as he'd read the weather reports earlier that day.

The only sun on the horizon, so to speak, was that the weather gurus were now predicting a drying period, beginning tomorrow while the highs and lows were busy readjusting themselves. With good luck, he should finally be able to get the full team to the canyon by the end of the day after tomorrow. Hopefully the rain had done its job on the fugitives as well, and they were holed up and completely unsuspecting.

He *had* been able to get scouts out today, but the brief radio contact they'd been able to achieve indicated that the going was slow and arduous. Even the ATVs liberated from several homes in the area had bogged down several times. The scouts had only managed to travel half of the distance to the canyon the seekers found, winding up spending the night at a small ranch camp, identified on the maps as Eagle Camp. Maybe tomorrow they'd be able to complete the journey. Depending on how much rain fell today.

The scouts had discovered two trucks and stock trailers, loaded with supplies a few miles from town near the base of the steep rim escarpment lining much of the east side of Highway 93. Rickards was convinced that O'Reilly, having scavenged the stores for essential supplies, had stored them in the trailers and moved them out of town so that the annihilation teams wouldn't discover and confiscate them. With the trailers safely out of town, he would be able to come back and collect the goods at his convenience.

The discovery of the supply trailers parked along the road to Adobe Canyon convinced Rickards that his team was on the right trail, and that they would find what they were seeking in that small, secluded valley.

We've got to get eyes in that canyon.

Where the hell is the desert we're supposed to be living in? Lately Rickards felt as if all of Arizona had been transported to some tropical island. Feeling a sharp sting, he slapped at a mosquito feasting off the blood in his neck.

Damned rain, he thought as he stared at the building storm clouds.

35

We're ready, thought Maggie, hands on hips as she surveyed the front room of the little house. It didn't exactly look the way it had when she and Mark had arrived several months ago. Only time would achieve that charming dilapidated, abandoned look that had greeted their eyes upon first surveying their new abode. However, the house no longer appeared as though people had been living there in the past week or so.

Hopefully when they get here, if they get here, they'll think we hit the road as soon as we realized that the computer was traced. Maggie grimaced, remembering Mark's recent withdrawal. In spite of her assurances that everything would be okay, and that sooner or later this situation would have arisen, especially with the arrival of the other children, Mark seemed to be trapped in a well of self blame.

O'Reilly had also tried to talk with him while driving the horses and cattle out to the east pasture yesterday morning. He told Maggie later that during the entire ride up, and the long walk back he'd attempted to break through Mark's self imposed shell, feeling as though he was beating at a brick wall with a feather.

Then, just as they were at the gate to the home pasture, Mark turned to him and said, "It's okay, O'Reilly. Honest. You don't need to lie to me to save my feelings. I know that getting on that computer is what's causing all this. They could have only traced the others as far as Wikieup. I brought them straight here. I understand that. There's no way I could have known the computer was dangerous. It was an accident, but that doesn't change anything. I just wish everyone would stop pretending that it didn't happen." With that, Mark turned and walked across the pasture, leaving a stunned O'Reilly standing in the gateway, hands hanging at his sides, feeling helpless.

As O'Reilly described the encounter to Maggie later, she could still see some of that feeling of helplessness lurking in his eyes, vying with an expression that Maggie could only describe as admiration.

He shook his head, then looked her straight in the eye. That moment was frozen in Maggie's memory, like a snapshot taken at a key moment in time. It was yesterday evening. The children and dogs were all bedded down in the cave and Maggie and O'Reilly had ventured back out to the main entrance to watch the evening rain and lightning show.

"You know something," O'Reilly said, a rueful expression on his face, "When my wife and daughter died, I would have given anything for someone to face the truth the way Mark did."

"It's not the same thing," Maggie protested. She looked at O'Reilly with a startled look on her face. Other than the one mention of a daughter weeks ago, O'Reilly had never talked about a family, other than that of his childhood.

"Maybe, maybe not. Mark's thinking he's pretty much given us all up, and he's not fool enough to believe that we've made all these precautions even though there's no danger. No, I'm pretty sure that Mark's aware that lives may be at stake, including yours. He's dealing with it, and not letting it cripple him, and I envy him that strength. He's struggling, sure, but he'll figure things out."

O'Reilly took a deep breath, held it for a moment, then blew it out.

"It's not that I personally caused Sarah's and Kay-Tee's deaths, but it was because of me that they were on that road at that time."

"You mean they didn't die from the disease?" Maggie was surprised. So much death had happened recently due to the virus that she'd never considered that his briefly mentioned daughter, and never mentioned wife, had died in any other manner.

"No. It was a car accident. Four years ago. Drunk driver ran them off the road on that steep part of I-17 between Cordes Junction and Phoenix."

"I'm so sorry," Maggie said. She stared at him, watching the different expressions flit across his face.

"The worst part is that they were only driving home that night because of me. Sarah had taken Kay-Tee down to see her mother on New Years. I was supposed to go, but wound up taking an extra shift that day. Sarah wasn't very happy about it, but she didn't complain. She never complained." O'Reilly paused, staring out at the rain.

"Sarah planned on staying the night at her mother's, but I asked her to come home instead. She agreed, and because of that she and Kay-Tee were on the road at the same time as the drunken bastard who ran them off."

"You couldn't have known," Maggie protested, reaching toward O'Reilly's hand.

"You're right, I couldn't have known, but the fact was that I did put them on the road at that time. It was an accident. Nothing more. But having everyone constantly tell me it wasn't my fault ate at me. It made me hold tighter to the idea that it was my fault. Mark's right. It's easier if people don't deny things. You just face up to your share of responsibility, no more, and move on." O'Reilly gave a little, humorless laugh.

The two of them sat in silence, watching the rain ebb as the storm moved off to the east.

Now, as Maggie thought back to last night, and the flood of emotions she saw washing through O'Reilly as he recounted the tragedy of his wife's and daughter's deaths, she thought she began to understand the toll that the current situation was taking on him. If he felt that he let his wife and daughter down; if somewhere inside himself he still felt as though he caused their deaths, as he apparently still did, then that guilt had almost certainly shaped his reaction to having other lives dependent on him now.

O'Reilly's initial aloofness made sense, too. It wasn't, as she'd first thought, that he'd resented being thrust into the role of babysitter for a bunch of greenhorns. From the way he'd described his earlier life, he'd done a pretty good job of isolating himself from anyone whom he might care about, and who might care about him. It must have been overwhelming, not to mention frustrating, to suddenly find himself in charge of seven other lives. It also explained a lot about why he'd left Christina behind, in spite of the way he felt about the APZs.

Maggie shook her head as she turned her back on the empty little house and walked out, carefully closing the door behind her. The challenge, as she saw it, would be to make sure that O'Reilly didn't sacrifice himself needlessly because he was afraid of letting someone else down. Her stomach turned at the thought of O'Reilly captured... killed.

The irony of the situation suddenly hit her, causing her to stop short. Here was someone fighting for all he was worth to keep from opening himself to anyone lest he be hurt, or cause hurt, again, and he'd told her most of his secrets. Yet, she couldn't remember a time where she'd bared her soul to him about her past.

Granted, she thought wryly, resuming her walk to the barn, her past hadn't been nearly as exciting as his, apparently. Downright boring, when you thought about it. But still, she'd been guarding her memories of Mike carefully, never discussing her loss with O'Reilly as he'd told her about his. Maybe it was because since running into the ranch lands, she'd been busy just trying to keep Mark and herself alive. Maybe there were other reasons.

She snorted. *Fine pair O'Reilly and I are,* she thought. *When all this is done, and we've lived through it, he and I will have to have a serious talk. All the skeletons out of the closets and the ghosts banished.* A smile flitted across her face as she realized that she was already thinking of the future, as though the battle had already been fought and won.

Maggie headed on, humming as she went, a bounce in her step.

36

The clouds parted, allowing the light of the three-quarter moon to splash down on the small side canyon, illuminating parts of the narrow cattle trail where it wound through brush and juniper down toward the main course of Adobe Canyon. The soft rattle of stones and thud of boots announced the advancement of Rickards' team.

A sudden yelp from midway through the procession brought the entire group to a halt, scrambling for their weapons in the half light. There was a pause as everyone waited, looking suspiciously around for the unseen assailant.

Nothing moved. The only sounds were distant thunder, and some not so distant, but very proficient, whispered cursing.

"Who's that?" Rickards barked in a strangled half whisper.

"Donner, sir," came the disembodied voice approximately fifteen feet behind Rickards.

"Well, what the hell happened, Donner."

"I bumped into a goddamned cholla cactus, sir. My damned jeans are nailed to my ass." A snort of laughter from elsewhere in the line was quickly choked off.

"Get 'em un-nailed, then, and get quiet. I won't lose the element of surprise because of some damned cactus."

They'd finally been able to make the break from Wikieup yesterday morning, using the four-wheel drive Jeeps and ATVs to traverse the muddy roads, leaving the electronics van and two men in Wikieup. Several times the field team was held up for hours while freeing a stuck vehicle, but in spite of the delays, they'd made their final approach to the canyon earlier that afternoon.

Rickards had decided that they should leave the vehicles at least two miles away from the canyon's rim, fearing that the engine noise would alert O'Reilly that they were coming. It was imperative that they take the fugitives by surprise.

The initial pass of the seekers had identified a second route out of the canyon. If the fugitives were using horses, as Rickards was sure they were, it would be possible for O'Reilly to take the children and make a run for it, establishing a good head start before Rickards could get vehicles to the far side of the canyon, either by coming down from I-40 or over from Highway 89. Of course, when the new seekers arrived, they should be able to find O'Reilly, but things would still be much easier if he was surprised in his hideout.

Scouts discovered this small trail leading down into the canyon, and it was decided that the team would wait for the cover of night, follow the trail to the canyon bottom, and establish themselves at either end of the valley while the residents were sleeping. Then, as the sun came up Rickards' team would make their attack, capturing the fugitives as they were rising.

The moon was sinking toward the rim of the canyon and the sky was silvery-dark, speckled with bright stars, when the band of Enforcers reached the point in the canyon where it opened up into the meadow they'd seen on the video feed sent from the seeker. Rickards held up a hand, signaling the men to halt while he inspected the valley. The barn and windmill glowed softly in the lunar light. In the shadow of the cliff wall, where the seeker's image had shown varying degrees of darkness, a house of a sort was now evident.

Rickards watched the house and barn for a few minutes, listening carefully for any noises from the buildings that might indicate where O'Reilly was. A low squeak caught his attention and he tried to pin point the source.

There it was. The windmill was turning slowly in a light breeze. Nothing more.

The house was silent, the windows dark. O'Reilly and the children must still be asleep. Looking at the peaceful scene, Rickards felt an unexpected twinge of remorse.

The setting was idyllic. Maybe not exactly Norman Rockwell, or

Wyeth, but it definitely carried the same sense of peace. Compared to the chaos of the APZ, this small, secluded valley seemed like paradise.

Still duty demanded, and Rickards had always followed his orders.

For a moment longer Rickards watched the meadow aware of a slowly growing disquiet and ignoring the shuffling and fidgeting of the men behind him until a sudden touch on his shoulder jerked him back to reality.

He shook himself, as though waking from a dream and turned back toward the owner of the hand. It was Harlan, looking past Rickards toward the barn and the pasture beyond.

"Any sign of the fugitives, sir?"

"No. No sign of movement. They must be still asleep." Rickards glanced back at the peaceful scene that drew him in.

Giving himself a second mental shake, Rickards turned again to the group of officers following him.

"Okay, lets put the plan into action. Harlan, you take Stevens and Martinez and go to the far end of the meadow. Station yourselves so that you have eyes on the exit, but are also close enough to get back here pronto should need arise. I don't think there'll be a fire fight, not with the kids there, but you never know.

"Larson, you watch this end of the canyon. Take cover in those rocks. If O'Reilly makes it through us and heads this way, take him out."

"Yes, sir."

"Johnson, you, Gomez, Peters, Donner and I will move to the barn area, and from there closer to the house where we can take O'Reilly and the children as they exit."

Before leaving the vehicles, the team had discussed at length the best strategy for capturing the fugitives. Rickards felt it would be wiser to attempt to apprehend O'Reilly outside the house, presuming that the dark area the seeker had shown was actually a residence of some type. The consensus of the team was that O'Reilly would be less likely to have ready access to weapons outside of the building. It was to be assumed that he hadn't come to the valley unprepared, but hopefully he would be feeling safe enough in his little hidyhole that he wouldn't be carrying a gun with him when he came out to do the morning chores. If he did have a weapon on his person, at least he wouldn't have easy access to any others.

The plan was to wait for him, and hopefully the children, to leave the house. Two people stationed at the side of the building would quickly move to block his retreat back inside. The others would come at him from the front. If he could be taken alive, that was preferred. Rickards wanted to know exactly what it was about the information O'Reilly had discovered that had driven him out of the APZ. However, if taking him alive was impossible, then elimination was preferable to escape.

The horizon to the east above the canyon rim was beginning to pearl as the men moved into position, Gomez and Donner crouched down at either side of the door, while Rickards, Peters and Johnson secreted themselves among the outbuildings.

All was silent except for the slight creak of the windmill as it continued to turn in the gentle breeze.

It was shortly after 4:45, the sky overhead was lightening and Rickards was beginning to wonder how long O'Reilly and the children were planning on sleeping - didn't farmers get up early to do chores and things like that? - when suddenly all hell broke lose.

Donner was crouched to the right of the door, when without warning, a raucous screech erupted from the large deep-set window over his head. He startled, fell backward, and in doing so, released a burst of gunfire. Gomez, on the opposite side of the doorway was apparently struck, because he let out a yell that could be heard in Kingman, and fell backward gripping his leg in both hands and dropping his gun causing it to discharge.

Rickards yelled to Johnson and Peters to move and all three raced toward the house, rifles aimed at the front wall, where yet another belligerent blast of noise caused Donner to scramble away from the wall where he'd been crouching.

Rickards skidded to a stop and panned his weapon, pointing it at the dark opening in the structure's wall. With another harsh crow, a ball of feathers erupted out of the open window, causing Rickards to reflexively pull the trigger, the bullet shattering the window. The rooster, barely identifiable in the predawn darkness, hit the ground ten feet out from the house, ruffled its feathers, scratched the ground several times, then strutted off toward the barn to the amazement of the five men.

What the hell... thought Rickards. Suddenly he became aware of a chatter of voices in his ear.

"What's going on...?"

"Captain, what's happening, report...?"

"...hear shooting, do you need help?"

Pulling himself back together, Rickards touched the send button on the radio at his ear. "It's all right. We were surprised by... by an animal attack." Rickards couldn't bring himself to admit that they were thrown off guard by a chicken. The story was bound to come out, and be laughed about for years to come, but at this point he felt he needed more distance before he could see the humor in the situation.

"All is secure here but we have one man injured," Rickards glanced at Gomez, where he sat, rolling up a pant leg so that Johnson could see where the bullet had creased the flesh. "No sign of the fugitives."

No sign at all.

Rickards studied the house intently. *Why isn't there a sign? We've made enough noise to wake the people living in Laughlin.*

Pulling his rifle back up to his shoulder, Rickards approached the front door. He signaled Johnson, Peters and Donner to back him up. Slowly he reached out his left hand to take the knob, keeping his gun at the ready.

With a sudden thrust, he pushed the door inward, only to realize that, in spite of the growing light outside, inside the house it was still dark as midnight. He tensed, waiting for an attack from the gloom. When it didn't materialize, he fumbled at his belt for his flashlight.

Slowly he panned the light around the inside of the room. It wasn't large. On one side was a small kitchen area. On the other side, a table and chairs, a wood stove. A small couch was under the window. Along the back wall were four closed doors.

No sign of the quarry.

No place to hide, except behind those doors.

Rickards motioned to his men to follow closely. Cautiously he approached the door on the left. He quickly threw it open, standing back to the side in case someone opened fire.

Again, nothing.

Stepping inside the room, Rickards again panned his flashlight. It was a small room, with no windows or other possible exits.. The roof was the stone of the cliff, apparently eroded when the river was higher. The floor was a conglomeration of stone and concrete, though Rickards noticed a few horse shoes and pieces of various types of pottery in among the rocks. The only furniture was an old bed with a bare mattress, a scarred chest of drawers and a battered foot locker. Nothing in the room boasted of anyone staying there recently.

Turning, Rickards nodded to the other three men at the doorway, and headed for the second door. The gnawing uneasiness which had begun in his gut when there was no reaction to the foul-up outside began to grow into a more acute discomfort.

Approaching the second door, Rickards again signaled his men to wait. He threw that door open as well, again stepping back out of the line of fire.

A second failure.

Entering the room, Rickards saw a space similar to the first, except that the bed in this case was a set of double bunks. Several crates were stacked along one wall. Once again there was no sign of immediate occupancy.

Likewise, the next room contained nothing but two sets of double bunks, and a few chests.

Rickards turned for the last room.

They have to be here, Rickards thought. The tension was becoming unbearable. *Relax,* he ordered himself, *relax. If a mouse squeaked under your feet you'd probably shoot a toe off.*

"O'Reilly," Rickards called from the doorway. "O'Reilly, come out unarmed and you and the children won't be hurt. You have my word on it."

Rickards paused, listening. No sound from inside the room.

They have to be here. But, why was there no sign of people in the other three rooms? Why would they all be hiding in the one room? The Gordian knot in Rickards gut was growing to mammoth proportions. *They couldn't know we were coming.*

Taking a deep breath, Rickards reached for the final door and threw it open with a bang.

37

Maggie exploded out of a deep sleep to a cacophonous eruption from the front of the house outside and below the cave where she and the others were sleeping; Houdini, the rooster, making his daily announcements, gunfire, a man screaming.

Gunfire. Screaming.

Maggie scrambled upright, desperately looking around the dark cave, trying to see the other inhabitants. A low growl issued from the corner of the cave where Lindy's bed was located, and a whimper indicated that Lindy herself was awake.

"Maggie," a low whisper sounded several feet off to her left. "Get over there and make sure Lindy and those dogs keep quiet."

"Christy..." Tremulous voices, scared.

"O'Reilly, where..." Christina's voice sounded from across the cave.

"Quiet," O'Reilly's sharp command caught everyone's attention and the panicked voices died down rapidly.

"Maggie, take care of Lindy," O'Reilly began to rap out orders in a hoarse whisper. "Mark help your mother with the dogs. Christina, go to your brothers. Alysa, help Christina. Everyone keep quiet. Whisper if you must talk. No flashlights. Whoever is there might be able to see the glow.

Maggie crawled over to Lindy, bumping into Mark on the way. Lindy's whimpering stopped as she cuddled into Maggie's arms, head tucked firmly under her chin. The sounds had ceased outside, but the dogs continued to growl quietly in spite of Mark's efforts to quiet them.

Maggie could see the outline of the opening, illuminated by the paler gray of the early pre-dawn sky. Silhouetted against the lighter pearl gray was the shape of O'Reilly as he carefully tried to determine the source of the noise.

After what seemed like ages, O'Reilly turned and slowly made his way back over to where Maggie was waiting.

"I can't see down to the house, but it appears that there are several men there. One's on the outside and may have been shot, or injured somehow. I'm guessing the others are in the house. There are probably a couple up near the north end of the valley, and I'm betting that there will be at least one or two more at the south end."

"Who are they?"

"I think we'll have to assume that they're Enforcers," O'Reilly said. "I suppose it could be a band of ghosts that just came across this place, but they tend to hide out nearer to supply lines. When the sun comes up we'll be able to get a better idea who they are, and their numbers."

The light from the opening was gradually increasing as dawn moved toward day and Maggie could vaguely see O'Reilly's face about a foot from hers. She could feel his breath brushing across the skin of her face. His eyes closed for a moment and he shook his head gently.

"I'm sorry, Maggie, I thought for sure we'd have more warning; hear a seeker or something. I guess one might have passed in the night and they simply thought this was a place to check out. Maybe the barn and windmill made them nervous. I don't know." His eyes opened again, glinting faintly in the ever increasing light.

His expression lightened briefly. "Actually, your nemesis may have proven to be our only early warning system.."

"What do you mean?" Maggie asked. She was acutely aware of Mark several feet behind her with the dogs, listening to everything that was said. She could hear soft whispering from the other side of the cave where Christina, Alysa, Nick and Ryan had been sleeping. Apparently Christina and Alysa were comforting the boys, keeping them quiet.

"I think that Houdini must have surprised the men, causing at least one of them to open fire. You may have to rethink your chicken pot pie plans."

"Did they kill him?" Maggie asked, but before O'Reilly could answer, a crow wafted in through the outside opening, announcing to all that Houdini was still alive and flapping.

"Better luck next time," O'Reilly said with a chuckle in his voice, patting her shoulder gently.

"It would be a whole lot easier to be grateful to him if I didn't know the next time I walked into the chicken yard I was going to have my shins beaten black and blue," Maggie said ruefully. "I would be more than happy to give him his medal of honor posthumously."

"Yeah, right. Face it. If Houdini had died, you'd be feeling pretty guilty right about now."

"I'd live," Maggie grumbled.

O'Reilly leaned in closer, dropping his voice lower. "When the sun comes up, we'll watch to see what happens. If they are Enforcers, and I'm pretty sure they are, and if they begin an extensive search of the valley, we need to be ready to move."

The day before O'Reilly had cornered Maggie in the barn with adjustments to his escape plan that, while she didn't like them, unfortunately made sense, if anything did these days. In the updated plan, they would need to find a large, relatively flat stone, not too heavy, but large enough to cover the entrance to the small cave where they were hiding; about two or three feet by three feet.

Assuming that the Enforcers found the valley and managed to find the entrance to the caves, Maggie was to keep the children and dogs in the hideout. O'Reilly would slide the rock over the opening. Then he would head back toward the mouth of the caves. There was a small side cave about a hundred yards from the entryway. Several rock falls had left piles of debris along the walls where he would hide until the Enforcers passed, heading further inside the mountain.

After they went by, he would emerge and head for the entrance. Once there he intended to make a noise of some type designed to get his pursuers to turn around and chase him. His idea was that he could lead them out of the caves, and up the canyon toward the north where he would hopefully lose them in the brush and rocks. If he was successful, they would think he'd made a run for the north of the state after having sent the children on ahead.

As Maggie pointed out, there were a number of serious drawbacks to O'Reilly's plan. They needed to find a rock small enough for Maggie to move from inside the passageway leading to the cave, yet large enough to cover the entrance fully. Should O'Reilly be captured or killed while leading the Enforcers on a wild goose chase, it would be up to Maggie to get everyone out once danger had passed.

"Besides," Maggie stated, "How likely is it that they won't fully check out every nook and cranny on the way into the caverns? Or post a guard at the entrance? You know damned well that the likelihood of you making it out of the caves is not very high." She looked O'Reilly in the eye, daring him to refute her analysis.

"It's a chance we'll have to take," O'Reilly answered, meeting her stare. "If I'm captured, I will try and convince them that I've sent Christina and the other children on ahead on horseback and I stayed behind to delay pursuit. They don't know that you, Mark or Lindy are here, so they'll only be looking for the four children. Since Alysa's family is from the four corners area I'll try and get them to believe that the children are heading in that direction."

Maggie bowed her head, eyes closed. The thought of losing O'Reilly tore at her and she wasn't sure she had the strength. She swayed slightly and suddenly O'Reilly's arm was there, holding her upright.

Opening her eyes she faced O'Reilly again. Chin tilted upward at a stubborn angle, she demanded, "Why can't we just all go into the cave, pull the rock over the entrance and stay there until the Enforcers leave the way we originally talked about?"

O'Reilly's hand dropped away from Maggie as he looked at her with sadness in his eyes. "Face facts, Maggie, it wouldn't work. Even if we could pull the rock fully over the passageway from the inside, there would be no way to erase the signs of it being moved. Any halfway thorough search of the caves would find it and we'd all be sitting ducks. Hell, all they'd have to do would be sit outside and wait for us to be forced out from starvation or thirst. This is the best chance we have of getting you and the kids out alive."

"What about going deeper into the caves?" Maggie offered, unwilling to give up so easily. "You said the network goes on for miles. Pull the rock over the opening, then head further back."

O'Reilly shook his head slowly. "We can't afford having the Enforcers spend too much time in the caves. Even with the rock, if they take their time searching, they're bound to find the opening. A careful eye will see that the signs of our passage end at this one cave. Besides, I wouldn't have time to erase my footprints if I head deeper into the caves. They'll follow and there's a good chance I'll be trapped in a dead end. I'd rather take my chance in the open. I know this land much better than they do and there are many small canyons and other caves to hide out in outside Adobe Canyon."

O'Reilly stopped and watched Maggie intently.

"You promised you wouldn't sacrifice yourself," Maggie insisted, an angry sob in her voice.

O'Reilly reached out toward her, but she threw his hand away furiously.

"I promised I wouldn't sacrifice myself *needlessly*." O'Reilly said. "Believe me, if I thought there was any other way that had as much chance of success, I'd take it." He reached out and pulled her braid lightly. "I don't want to leave you either. All things considered, I'm not sure Arizona can survive if I leave you loose on the land." He attempted a smile, which Maggie didn't return.

The silence between them stretched into minutes as Maggie mulled over the proposition O'Reilly had just laid in front of her. Finally, taking a deep, shaky breath she said, "Okay, we'll do it your way. But I swear if you get captured I will hunt you down and..."

"Rub hamburger in my hair, douse it in A-1, stake me in front of a mountain lion's den and give him an engraved invitation?"

Maggie choked on a laugh and began coughing so violently that O'Reilly began to look concerned. Eventually Maggie caught her breath and looked up at O'Reilly. "I will not only stake you out for the mountain lions, but I will invite the coyotes and vultures to clean up whatever's left."

"Fine, we've got a deal," O'Reilly said, nodding, "Now that we have the dining arrangements made, lets go look for a rock."

Ever since O'Reilly presented his plan to her, Maggie had worked hard to convince herself that none of it would be necessary. Either the Enforcers wouldn't find the canyon, or, if they did, they wouldn't find the entrance to the caves.

In spite of her diligent positive thinking, things were rapidly moving in the wrong direction.

Maggie watched as O'Reilly moved back over to the opening in the outer wall of the cave. Outside the daylight was steadily growing. Soon the sun would leap over the horizon and illuminate the hole in the cliff face. The wall was thick, however, and it should be possible for O'Reilly to keep an eye on most of the valley without danger of exposure.

As O'Reilly maintained a watch on the canyon, Maggie began checking on the children, making sure that everyone was all right following their abrupt wakening. They were all looking calm, but frightened. Nick and Ryan were sitting huddled together, with Christina and Alysa nearby. Mark was sitting at the back of the cave, near the passageway, petting the dogs. His eyes followed Maggie around the cave as she got everyone jerky and water for breakfast. Several times as she passed by she placed a hand on his shoulder or head, giving him a reassuring smile, which he tried to return.

The children had been deliberately left in the dark regarding the particulars of the plan to avoid capture by the Enforcers. Maggie and O'Reilly both agreed that it would be better not to burden the younger members of their new family with the knowledge that O'Reilly might be forced to put himself at risk to save everyone else. The kids knew there was a plan, and that it involved hiding in the cave, covering the entrance with a rock, but that was all they knew.

With all the older children settled, Maggie gave Lindy to Mark, whereupon she promptly crawled off and began playing with Gypsy and Jack. Maggie softly approached O'Reilly where he stood watch.

"Have you seen anything yet?" she asked quietly.

"A bit. From what I can tell, there are seven or eight men. Maybe more, I'm not sure."

"What are they doing? We haven't heard anything for awhile now"

"It's hard to tell with the house being right below. I don't dare lean out in case someone sees me. It appears that the largest group of men is investigating the house. Someone is injured, probably shot when Houdini surprised them. It also looks as though they've posted several men at the north end of the canyon," O'Reilly nodded in the direction of the far end of the valley.

A shot of adrenaline coursed through Maggie's system. "Have they found the caves?"

"It doesn't appear so. At least they've been pretty quiet from what I can tell. I think they were just sent there so that it would be impossible for us to make a break for it in that direction. I'm guessing there are at least one or two stationed at the south end as well."

"Do you know who it is yet? Is it that captain you spoke about; Rickards?" Maggie tried to look out the opening as well, careful not to lean too far.

"I can't say for sure, but I can't imagine Rickards sending men out here without coming himself." O'Reilly stared out into the valley. "I'm sure that if they're Enforcers, then Rickards is leading them." O'Reilly looked down at Maggie and the next time he spoke, his husky voice was even softer so that it wouldn't carry to the back of the cave.

"We can't wait too long. It makes me nervous having those men so close to the main entrance. It may take them awhile to get up this high in the caves, but I must have time to get the rock across the entrance, wipe out signs of it being moved, and make it to the side cave. If I wait too long I'll get trapped and caught for sure."

"No, we agreed to wait until we knew for sure that the caves were going to be found."

"I don't think we have that sort of time. It'll be okay. I won't leave the caves. I'll hide in that small niche just as we agreed. If they don't find the caves, no harm, no foul. I'm just uncomfortable with those men already up at the northern end of the meadow, poking around."

Maggie's shoulders slumped as she gave into the inevitable. "You're right," she sighed. "I know it's the smart thing to do. I just don't like splitting up like this."

"Don't worry," O'Reilly said with a grin. "I have no intention of becoming lion poop."

The sound of a slamming door drew their attention. Four men emerged into view from below the opening in the cliff face. The leader, a tall muscular man, paused for a moment, the others waiting behind him for a signal of some type. From Maggie's bird's eye perspective, it was impossible to see any of the men's faces.

At the sound of the door, one of the dogs at the back of the cave let out a soft bark, followed by a growl.

Without turning from the opening, Maggie whispered back over her shoulder, "Mark, I need you to quiet the dogs."

When there was no answer, Maggie turned from the opening. "Mark, I asked..."

Mark was nowhere to be seen.

38

Rickards threw open the last door and stepped into the room.

Again, nothing. The fourth door hid a small pantry, shelves built into the rock wall. Several metal garbage cans sat on the floor. Inspecting them, it was obvious they'd held flour, rice and other staples at some time in the past. Now nothing but white dust covered the bottoms. O'Reilly and the children were not here. He'd failed and O'Reilly won. Again.

Rickards turned and stormed from the room and the house, coming to a stop outside the front door. He stood there, head bowed, breathing deeply. He was aware of Donner, Johnson and Peters approaching from behind, but didn't turn to acknowledge them.

Minutes stretched out until finally Rickards raised his head and looked forward into the gradually increasing morning light. Taking a final deep breath, he turned and looked at Gomez. "How's the leg?"

"It's just a flesh wound. Bled like hell, but I'll live. It's a long way from the heart." Gomez grinned up at Rickards from where he was sitting on a large rock on the edge of the flat area in front of the house.

"Guess we'll have to get Donner to work on his aim. At that distance he should have scored a better hit."

A snort of laughter from behind Rickards indicated appreciation for the comment from someone. Probably not Donner.

Rickards turned to look out into the valley again for a moment, then said, "Okay, it's obvious that someone has been here recently. There were cattle and horses here only a few days ago, and they're not here now. Someone had to be taking care of the chickens. So, we're going to search this entire valley to see if we can find where they've gone. Look for tracks, trails, anything that might give us a direction.

He turned again to Gomez. "Can you walk?"

"Yes, Captain."

"Good, I want you to head back out of the canyon."

"I'm fine," Gomez protested. "I can join the search."

"I need someone to get back to the rim and radio the vans to get seekers into the air as soon as possible. North and south of here. We need to determine if O'Reilly made a run for it on horseback, and get men up in front to capture him if he did."

"On it, Captain." Gomez struggled to his feet and began to make his way toward the southern entrance to the valley.

"Gomez," Rickards called after him.

Gomez turned.

"Send Larson here when you pass."

"Yes, sir." Gomez continued making his way out of the canyon.

Rickards touched the send button on the radio at his ear. "Harlan, you, Stevens and Martinez begin sweeping the area at that end of the canyon for hiding spots, tracks or any other indication where the fugitives might be."

The radio in his ear crackled to life with a "yes, sir."

"We'll be moving down from this end of the canyon and we'll meet you there. Let us know immediately if you find anything."

"Yes, sir," came Harlan's reply.

Where are they? Rickards thought again as he and the other three men worked their way through the barns and corrals, heading for the northern end of the canyon. *Where the hell did they go?*

There was no sign of the fugitives in the barn or pens, though the amount and condition of the manure present made it obvious that livestock had been kept there only a short time before. There were no saddles in the tack room, which seemed to indicate that they'd made a run for it on horseback. Still, Rickards was unwilling to trust the obvious. He knew too much of O'Reilly by now to make that mistake.

The only excitement came when Donner entered the chicken yard to check in the hen house. Out of nowhere a rooster, probably the same one that had been in the window, came rushing out, beating Donner in the shins. Donner tried to club him with the butt of his rifle with no luck. Finally, admitting defeat, Donner made for the door of the chicken coop as quickly as his feathered assailant would allow. He dashed through, slamming it behind him, only to find that the rooster knew how to get out of the chicken yard nearly as quickly as Donner did. The confrontation ended in a rout, with the damned rooster crowing his victory from the top of a fence rail.

The sun was well over the horizon when the radio in Rickards' ear snapped to life. "Sir, Harlan here. We've found what seems to be the entrance to some caves. There's no sign of footprints at the entry, but there are some prints further inside, through an opening into a second chamber."

"We're on our way, Harlan," Rickards answered. "Stand out and wave your arm so we can see what direction to head." Looking toward the far end of the valley, Rickards could see Harlan coming down a small slope from behind a tree and some rocks. At the base of the slope he stopped and began to wave.

"Johnson, Peters, Donner, with me. They've found something." Rickards and the other three began to jog toward the end of the canyon.

39

O'Reilly heard Maggie talking to Mark, then suddenly stopping in mid sentence. Then he heard her calling Mark's name, a rising note of panic in her voice. Realizing that something was wrong, he turned from the scene outside.

Mark was no longer sitting with the dogs. Maggie had moved to the center of the room and was agitatedly turning around and around as she scanned the cave, trying to determine where he'd gone.

Christina and Alysa looked up at Maggie's quick movement, a startled expression on their faces.

"Christina, have you seen Mark?" Maggie asked, fear in her voice.

"I'm sorry, I wasn't paying attention to him. I didn't see him go anywhere." Christina looked around the cave from her position near the wall of the cave as if expecting Mark to materialize out of thin air.

"Maggie, what is it?" O'Reilly came up behind her.

"Mark. He's not here."

"Where would he have gone?"

"There's only one place he could go." Maggie went to Lindy where she was playing at the back of the cave. "Lindy, where's Mark? Where did Mark go?"

Lindy stopped pulling on Gypsy's ruff for a moment and looked up at Maggie. Pointing at the passageway, Lindy said, "Mawk go there." Then she turned her attention back to the dogs.

The look on Maggie's face at Lindy's words twisted O'Reilly's gut. She headed for the passageway but O'Reilly's hand on her shoulder stopped her.

"Let me go, Maggie. I'll bring him back. Don't worry."

"Why would he go?"

"I don't know, Maggie, but you can grill him over it in a few minutes when I bring him back."

O'Reilly moved past Maggie, giving her shoulder a gentle squeeze, and crawled into the narrow passageway. He wriggled his way up the tight tunnel only to be brought to a halt by a wall of stone.

What the... Mark, he must have moved the stone over the entrance. Why would he... A chilling thought flashed through O'Reilly's mind. Yesterday, when he'd approached Maggie with the plan, he'd thought all the children were busy finishing the provisioning of the cave. What if Mark had overheard their plans? He'd been feeling responsible for bringing the Enforcers to the canyon. Was it possible that he'd decided to put himself in O'Reilly's position, throwing off pursuit? No. No matter how guilty Mark was feeling, there was no way he'd try and do something so foolish. He had to know O'Reilly would come after him, and the plan had ensured that Maggie could still get out of the cave. The rock wasn't that heavy.

O'Reilly moved closer to the rock, braced his feet against the side of the tunnel and pushed.

Nothing happened.

He brought his knees up further in an attempt to gain greater leverage and again pushed at the rock, trying to lift it off the opening, straining his muscles until he thought they'd explode. He was rewarded by only a slight shifting in its position.

O'Reilly couldn't understand what was happening. When Maggie and he'd chosen this rock, they'd made sure that Maggie could move it from inside the passageway. They'd practiced several times to ensure that she would not be trapped. Not to belittle Maggie's strength, but if she'd been able to move the damned rock, he should certainly be able to slide it aside with no problem.

O'Reilly slithered backward the ten feet into the cave, turning to find Maggie watching him. She was in control of herself, but he could see the tension in her movements.

"What's going on? Where's Mark?" Maggie asked.

"He's moved the rock over the entrance."

"Why would he do that?" Maggie asked, confusion clouding her eyes.

O"Reilly moved closer to Maggie, aware of the other children sitting on the far side of the cave listening to them. "Is it possible that he heard us talking about the plan yesterday?"

"No, he couldn't ... I... maybe, I don't know. I mean, we didn't exactly look outside the barn to make sure no one was there. All the kids were carrying stuff to the cave." Maggie stopped, head down, thinking. Finally, she raised her face and looked back at O'Reilly,

"What would it matter if he did hear. You don't think he's trying to take your place, do you?" New fear lit Maggie's eyes.

"I don't know, but he's put something extra on the rock. I can't get it to move much. I need something I can use as a lever. I've managed to get a small crack, but I can't get the leverage I need to move the stone the rest of the way."

Maggie looked around the cave and O'Reilly could see her mentally cataloging the items they'd hauled up. After only a few moments she turned back to him and shook her head.

"There's nothing here. I'm sorry. I didn't get the memo saying I needed to be prepared to stage a prison break."

O'Reilly could tell she was fighting hard to keep her fear under control and the weak joke was further evidence of her attempts to keep her emotions reined in.

"What are we going to do, O'Reilly?" Maggie looked at him desperately.

O'Reilly suddenly grabbed her arm. "Come with me," he turned and pulled her toward the passageway.

"O'Reilly, what are you..."

"Maybe if we're both pushing on the rock, we can get it to move."

"You've got to be kidding! There's no way we're both fitting in there." Maggie gave him a look that clearly said she thought he was out of his mind.

"Yes, we will. It'll be tight, but it's just wide enough. The extra muscle power may be just what we need to get the rock shifted. I'll go first. When we get to the end, I'll push myself back against the wall. You crawl up alongside me, then we'll both push."

O'Reilly began to climb into the opening. Turning his head, he beckoned to Maggie. "Come on."

Maggie turned and looked at the children where they were sitting on the far side of the cave, watching O'Reilly and her.

"Guys, I've got to go with O'Reilly for a moment. Christina, would you keep an eye out and let us know if something changes out in the valley?"

"Sure, Maggie." Christina got up and moved to the opening in the outer wall of the cave.

Maggie turned back to the tunnel and climbed in after O'Reilly.

After crawling the short distance to the entrance, O'Reilly turned on his right side, pushing his back against the rock wall of the tunnel. In the glow of the flashlight, he could see Maggie resting on her elbows, peering up toward him through the narrow space between his body and the left side of the passageway, a doubtful look on her face.

"Roll onto your right side, Maggie. Then slide up here in front of me."

He could hear Maggie muttering something to herself, but couldn't tell what. In spite of his sense of urgency, he couldn't help a small laugh. Whatever it was she was saying, he was sure it wasn't a compliment on his brilliant idea. Once again he had to admire her strength. He wasn't at all sure that he would be able to think clearly, let alone act, if it was his child who was missing.

Maggie rolled onto her right, and began a sideways wriggle up the sand floor of the tunnel, the narrowness of the passageway forcing her to press herself back against his knees and thighs. O'Reilly took a deep breath as she slithered further up his body. While his mind was occupied with finding Mark and getting him back to safety, other parts of his anatomy had separate interests. He was fairly certain that, considering the situation, Maggie would not appreciate any attention that was not focused strictly on retrieving her son.

An unfortunate blow from an elbow wrung a deep grunt from O'Reilly, and quickly refocused his attention on the task at hand.

"Sorry," Maggie gasped as she came to rest in front of him. "Now what?"

O'Reilly took several deep breaths before he trusted himself to speak with a steady voice.

"Uh... Okay. I'm going to get my hands through this crack." He indicated the small opening he'd managed to create on the right side of the rock. "You are going to brace your legs and push up on the left side of the stone as hard as you can while I try and move the it further in that direction. If we're lucky we'll be able to get past whatever it is Mark has wedged up there."

Maggie squirmed around, trying to get her arms above her head, and in the process endangering O'Reilly's newly regained focus.

"Got it," she panted. "Tell me when."

O'Reilly managed to get his arms above his head, and slid his hands through the small crack. Bracing his legs against the tunnel wall and floor, he counted, "One, two, three, push!"

O'Reilly's muscles bunched as he strained to move the rock. He could feel Maggie in front of him pushing upward on the left edge of the stone. With a grinding noise, the rock shifted several more inches to the left, and Maggie's side remained suspended a half an inch off the ground.

They both relaxed for a moment, breathing heavily.

"Okay, Maggie, one more time," said O'Reilly as he got ready to push again. Another count down, another muscle bursting assault on the blockage, and suddenly the stone at Maggie's end lifted into the air and O'Reilly's end shifted to the left a little over a foot.

Then refused to budge another inch.

"Again," O'Reilly said. Still the rock refused to move.

O'Reilly and Maggie collapsed together on the floor of the tunnel, muscles slack. The tang of sweat filled the air.

"What now?" Maggie asked.

O'Reilly was silent for a moment, thinking about the options. Taking the flashlight, he illuminated the blockage, and the crack they'd been able to open.

"Do you think you could make it out through that crack?" he asked Maggie, thoughtfully.

Maggie craned her head around, trying to get a good look. "I don't know. I might be able to. It would be a tight fit."

"Let's try. Switch places with me."

Maggie straightened her head, and O'Reilly could hear her muttering under her breath, "just switch places with me, he says. Crawling around in tunnels like a pair of snakes!" and he had to bite back a laugh.

They quickly determined that the first move was to have Maggie roll onto her left side, so that she was facing O'Reilly. Once that was accomplished, amid much grunting, and a few old fashioned, Anglo-Saxon verbs that had very little to do with the situation, O'Reilly began his move by sliding down onto his back, shrugging his shoulders as he inched his way over.

As his body took up more and more of the floor space, Maggie was forced to move herself up onto O'Reilly's chest, pressing her back into the roof of the passageway. O'Reilly found himself nose to nose with a flustered Maggie, and once again thoughts totally unrelated to Mark's rescue came unbidden into his mind. This time, however, it was an elbow to the solar plexus that brought him back to the here and now.

"Omph!"

"Sorry," Maggie said, obviously preoccupied with getting over to the other side of the tunnel.

"Maggie! For god's sake!" O'Reilly yelped as a knee descended on defenseless tissue.

"I'm so sorry! I didn't mean... there!" Maggie exclaimed as she finally rolled off of O'Reilly's chest and onto her right side as O'Reilly slithered over to the left. Both lay on their sides, facing each other once again.

"Okay, now see if you can make it through the crack," O'Reilly said, trying to ignore the throbbing pain in his assaulted body parts. He gave her the flashlight and watched as she wriggled and squirmed her way through the narrow opening.

Several times it appeared she wasn't going to make it, and once he worried that she was going to stick in the hole as tightly as a cork in a champagne bottle. Finally, however he saw her legs disappear into the pale glow the flashlight cast in the cave above.

Moments after her feet disappeared through the opening, her face came into view. "Mark's wedged some smaller stones around the main one. Just a moment and I'll move them."

Maggie's face vanished and O'Reilly could hear her moving rocks. Then, the flat stone covering the entrance was pulled back leaving him free to crawl into the cavern.

Maggie was standing in the middle of the cave, looking in the direction of the main entrance. As O'Reilly emerged from the passageway, she turned to face him.

"Mark's not here. If he overheard us talking about our plan, he must have headed for the small cave, planning on hiding there like you were. Let's go!"

"Wait, Maggie," O'Reilly reached out and grabbed her arm as she started to head for the main entrance. "You need to stay here. I'll go after Mark."

"Please, don't ask me..."

"You need to stay here. If we both go, it doubles the chance that someone will get caught. I'll bring him back. You need to wait here. If he shows up without me, get him into the cave. Try and get the rock back over the entrance. Wait there."

"They'll see the disturbance around the rock. They'll know where we are." O'Reilly could see Maggie's eyes wide with fear in the yellow light of the flashlight.

"Only if they make it this far. I'll do whatever I can to lead them off." He said soothingly.

"Jim, I don't like this. I should go with you. I...

"Maggie? O'Reilly?"

Both turned toward the new voice. Christina was at the mouth of the tunnel, head protruding into the small cave, looking anxiously between the two of them.

Great, thought O'Reilly, *Am I going to have every damned kid up running amok in the caverns when the Enforcers storm the castle? Why can't anyone stay where they're told?*

"Christina, what is it? You need to be back in the cave with the other children." O'Reilly snapped.

"Maggie said to keep an eye out and see what the Enforcers are doing in the valley. It's Rickards. He and the others are heading toward the entrance to the caves."

40

Rickards looked at the entrance to the cave Harlan had found. It would be easy to miss, hidden behind the juniper and boulders. Add that to an entry way clean of any prints except for those of his men, and it would have been very simple to overlook.

Have to remember to compliment Harlan, Rickards thought, looking back over his shoulder to where the men were waiting at the bottom of the slope. *Maybe in a year or two, when it won't give him such a big head.* It didn't matter how much time he'd spent with Harlan on this mission, he just couldn't seem to warm up to the guy. Rickards wanted to catch the fugitives as much as the next person, but Harlan's almost rabid eagerness was wearing on him, beginning to make him doubt his own motives.

Then there was this valley. Ever since they'd entered the canyon, Rickards had been struck by the peacefulness. Everything here, except for possibly that damned chicken, radiated tranquility, something that had been sorely missing in Rickards' life since the disease took his wife. He hadn't realized how much he'd missed it, until now.

Still, duty was duty. He had to believe in what they were doing. To doubt in his superiors, to doubt in the mission they'd accepted, would open the door to insanity. If he doubted, then he would begin to wonder why he'd sacrificed everything in his life that was important to him, including his wife. He couldn't afford doubt because in that direction lay madness.

Rickards turned and headed back down the slope to where his men were waiting expectantly.

"Okay, here's how it's going to work," Rickards started, fixing a stare on each man in turn. "I will lead. Harlan, you and Johnson next, followed by Peters and Larson. Donner, you will stay here at the opening and make sure no one gets by that shouldn't. You will, I repeat will, make positive identification before you open fire. Got it?"

"Yes, sir." Donner answered, obviously aware that he'd been left at the opening because of his dismal performance earlier at the house. No one wanted to go into dark caves, looking for a wily adversary, with someone who couldn't be relied on to hold his fire when necessary.

The men headed up the scree and into the opening, each man armed with a rifle at the ready, as well as a sidearm and a flashlight. It didn't take long before the flashlights were the only source of illumination, casting jumping yellow shadows on the walls.

It's a good thing we left Donner at the entrance, Rickards thought as he spun for the fourth time toward movement that turned out to be nothing more than a bounding shadow from one of the other men's flashlight.

"Check all the side chambers," Rickards ordered as the small group proceeded further into the labyrinthine caverns.

They moved deliberately deeper into the network of caves, moving carefully around rocks that littered the floor, apparently having fallen from the roof, or been carried down in floods. Every time they came to a new chamber, or saw a side tunnel, every possible hiding spot was thoroughly examined. Several times they thought they heard noises, but when they stopped and listened, there was nothing.

After the first fifty feet or so, they began to see some tracks, though it appeared that some effort had been made to erase them. In spite of the attempts at concealment, however, a footprint was occasionally evident next to a rock, or partially obliterated on the side of the main path. Not much, but enough to tell them that they were likely on the right trail.

That is, unless they were just exploring these caves, Rickards thought. *Place like this, tracks could remain for years virtually undisturbed. Who knows if they came up here to hide, or just out of curiosity.*

The men had been walking for a little over five minutes by Rickards' reckoning when a soft thump followed by a muffled rattle from ahead brought him to a sudden halt, causing the men behind him to stop suddenly as well.

Rickards signaled for silence. It was hard to tell anything, with the odd acoustics in the caves which distorted the sound of the breathing of the five men. After several minutes of listening, during which Rickards began to doubt that he'd actually heard anything, he signaled them forward, moving slowly.

Another thump-rattle. Once again everyone stopped, breaths held, rifles ready, waiting for anything further. Soft echos whisper-floated around the cave, making the men look nervously about. Finally Rickards signaled the men forward again.

They were cautiously approaching the conjunction between the cave they were in, and the next chamber in the chain, when a man stepped from behind a pile of debris. His features were distorted by the leaping shadows of the flashlights, but his voice was unmistakable.

"Hello, Seth. Been awhile," came the familiar husky rumble of James O'Reilly.

41

Where are they? Maggie thought anxiously as she paced back and forth in the small cave. It had been at least ten minutes since O'Reilly had headed out after Mark and she hadn't heard a thing. Christina had just poked her head out of the passageway again to let her know that the Enforcers had entered the caverns. It was only a matter of time. She was so nervous her stomach tied into knots, making her feel as if she were going to start puking at any moment.

O'Reilly's gun was missing. Before taking off through the tunnels he'd had Christina go back to get his holster, unwilling to face the Enforcers unarmed. But the weapon wasn't where it was supposed to be. Mark must have taken it. The idea of Mark racing off through the caves with a loaded gun made Maggie almost as nervous as the thought of him facing Enforcers period. O'Reilly seemed unfazed, and instead had Christina bring him his hunting rifle. Maggie supposed that having O'Reilly carry the rifle was better than nothing, but it did little to calm her fears.

She kept her flashlight shielded, so that if the Enforcers made their way this far, the glow wouldn't alert them. Immediately after O'Reilly left she'd pushed the rock back over the majority of the opening to the secret cave. If O'Reilly and Mark managed to dodge the Enforcers and escape through the main opening instead of coming back toward her, she had to be ready to protect the remaining children herself.

She figured if she heard or saw signs of pursuit, she'd quickly slide the rock the rest of the way over the entrance, erase indications of its existence with the juniper bough they'd been using, and run further up into the caverns. As long as the kids kept quiet, they should be safe, and hopefully she'd be able to avoid capture until the Enforcers left, or she was able to get behind them and make her way out of the caves to find O'Reilly.

When Maggie had first proposed going deeper into the caves instead of making a run for it, O'Reilly had rejected the idea, saying he didn't like the idea of being cornered and trapped if he was caught in a dead end.

Now Maggie was planning to use the idea he'd condemned as foolish.

When O'Reilly left Maggie standing in the middle of the cave, the most pressing thought in his mind was finding Mark as quickly as possible and returning him to his mother, whom, O'Reilly acknowledged, would probably then strangle him forthwith. *I might even help her*, he thought as he raced through the network of caves, scouring the side chambers with his flashlight.

He was sure that Mark headed for the small cave that O'Reilly planned on using as a hiding place, but he didn't dare take a chance that the boy lost his nerve and hid out closer to the secret cave.

Failure to find and return Mark wasn't an option in O'Reilly's mind. His own capture or death was acceptable, but he couldn't bear the idea of returning to Maggie without her son. The look on her face if he came back without Mark would destroy him as surely as a bullet to the brain.

As O'Reilly neared the main entrance to the subterranean labyrinth, he slowed. The last thing he wanted to do was to race headlong into Rickards and his men. Several times he stopped and listened. The caves distorted sound dramatically, but the third time he paused he was certain he could hear men's voices, echoing off the cavern walls. The voices sounded calm, and he was sure that they'd not yet found Mark, but as he hadn't found Mark either, and as he was getting closer and closer to those voices, he didn't find a lot of reassurance in that calmness.

Just as O'Reilly was beginning to wonder if Mark had headed further into the network of caves, rather than toward the exit, he spotted movement in a little side niche. Rocks, fallen from the roof, were piled along the side of this small half-moon chamber, leaving a two foot gap between them and the wall. As O'Reilly approached, he could see the ten-year-old boy huddled in that opening, hugging his knees to his chest, face buried in his arms..

"Mark," O'Reilly whispered.

The effect on Mark was electric. He shot out of his hiding spot, scrambling over the pile of rocks, knocking them hither and yon. He hit the ground poised to run when he realized that his attacker was really O'Reilly.

"You scared the crap out of me, O'Reilly!" Mark said, voice high and quavering.

O'Reilly signaled Mark to lower his voice, aware that the sounds coming from the distant caves had stopped abruptly with Mark's exclamation. The two held their breaths until they once again heard the murmur of voices. Alarm wasn't evident in the cadence or tone of the indistinct voices and O'Reilly felt sure that they didn't realize that Mark and O'Reilly were only a short distance away.

"If we had more time, Mark, I'd beat the living daylights out of you." Mark looked up into O'Reilly's face, uncertainty clear in his expression. "As we don't have any time, we just need to get you safely back to the cave."

"But..." Mark started to protest.

"No, Mark. It was brave of you to try and rescue us, but it won't work. I promised your mother I'd bring you back, and truth to tell, I'm afraid of what she'll do to me if I don't follow through." O'Reilly gave Mark a smile, trying to allay his fear. He could see he hadn't succeeded, however, and he could also tell that he hadn't succeeded in breaking through Mark's determination to be the sacrificial goat, either

O'Reilly set his rifle down, leaning it on the rock pile. Taking Mark's shoulders in his hands, he gazed down into the wide green eyes. "Mark, I know the man leading this group of Enforcers. You need to let me handle this. It's not your job."

Mark still didn't look convinced, but he could tell the voices were getting closer. O'Reilly gave him a soft shake and hesitatingly the boy started to move back toward the hideout cave. He stopped and turned toward O'Reilly again.

The volume of the voices suddenly increased as the searchers entered the adjoining cave. The soft glow of flashlights lit the chamber beyond the connecting passage. O'Reilly gave Mark an intense look and motioned sharply with his right hand, making it clear that Mark was to go. Mark turned to run and stumbled over the pile of rocks, then, collecting his balance, took off as quickly as he could in the low light.

As Mark raced off toward the hideout, O'Reilly bent to pick up the rifle. His heart sank as he realized that when Mark stumbled over the rocks, a number of them, some large and heavy, cascaded down over the weapon. Even without the flashlight, he could easily feel where the heavy stones had damaged the firing mechanism. He'd forgotten to retrieve his handgun from Mark, and now the hunting rifle was out of commission.

O'Reilly hadn't planned on an armed confrontation with the Enforcers in any case. He'd thought about it. It would be relatively easy to take the Enforcers by surprise in the caverns. However, others at the APZ would obviously know where the team was, and their failure to return would merely bring more officers down on O'Reilly's head. *Still, he thought, a gun of your own would certainly have provided some comfort when dealing with the armed officers bent on killing you or taking you in.*

O'Reilly turned back toward the advancing officers, who had again grown quiet at the noise created when Mark tripped over the rock pile. He had to give the boy time to get back to Maggie. There was no question of trying to hide until they'd passed, then attempting to draw them back toward the main entrance. He couldn't take the chance that Rickards would split his force, sending some men forward into the caves, and relying on others to go back after O'Reilly.

The only answer was confrontation.

And hope to hell that someone didn't open fire at first sight of him.

42

Maggie had just tripped over a large rock lying in the center of the cave for the fifth time when she heard the sound of running feet coming in her direction. Panicked, she raced to the passageway, and began shoving at the rock cover, desperately trying to move it over the entrance. It moved the final three inches just as the footsteps materialized into Mark as he rushed into the cave and skidded to a stop.

"Mark!" Maggie surged to her feet and rushed to her son, tripping over the damned rock for the sixth time. She grabbed him by the shoulders and pulled him to her. After a moment, during which she only felt gratitude that he was safe, and back with her, she suddenly held him out at arms' length and fixed him with a glare.

"What were you thinking!"

"Mom, it was my fault the Enforcers found us," Mark said. "You always say we should take responsibility for our actions. I was just taking responsibility."

"God, Mark, I don't know what I'd have done if I'd lost you. This wasn't your fault. It would have probably happened sooner or later. It's not your responsibility. O'Reilly..." Maggie's voice tailed off and a look of horror crossed her face. She looked up toward the entrance to the cave. "Mark, where's O'Reilly. Didn't he find you and bring you back?"

"He found me in that small cave near the main entrance. I guess I didn't hide very good." Mark looked up at his mother. "We were going to start back toward this cave, but the Enforcers came. O'Reilly said I had to come back and warn you, that he'd take care of things. He said he knew the guy leading the Enforcers."

Mark looked toward the rock covering the entrance to the

passageway. "He said we were to get into the cave, pull the rock over the opening and wait for him to come. He..."

Three shots split the air in rapid succession, echoing off the walls and roofs of the caverns.

O'Reilly stood facing Captain Seth Rickards and his men. *His possee,* O'Reilly thought wryly. *Just like sheriffs of the old west.* He studied their faces in the yellow flashlight glow. Dust floated through the air, giving the light a golden aura. He thought he recognized a couple of the men from the APZ, though he couldn't remember any of their names.

Rickards looked floored, the expression of shock on his face every bit as dramatic as O'Reilly had hoped for.

"Well, Seth?" O'Reilly continued nonchalantly when Rickards failed to speak. "I take it you're looking for me."

43

Rickards stood staring at O'Reilly, completely flummoxed.

The man looked completely relaxed, as if they had simply met on a street corner. Old friends who hadn't seen each other in a long time.

Rickards was aware of a rapidly growing annoyance as he stood watching O'Reilly, apparently at ease, meeting Rickards' glare forthrightly. Why the hell wasn't O'Reilly afraid? The man knew what was at stake. There was no way he could have deluded himself into believing that Rickards and the other Enforcers had just dropped by for a drink and a chat.

The annoyance gave way to anger, when O'Reilly gave him a lazy smile, and inquired what he could do for them. Rickards could feel the men behind him beginning to fidget, shifting their feet, making rustling, whispering sounds in the lose dirt and sand on the floor of the cave. He was conscious of Harlan moving up on his right shoulder, and knew that an explosion was imminent if something didn't happen to defuse the tension.

Deciding the best direction was to mirror O'Reilly's insouciant attitude, Rickards motioned his men back with a casual wave of the hand. Rocking back on his heels, he plastered a half smile on his face which he hoped didn't look as forced as it felt.

"You left rather suddenly, O'Reilly. Lot of us were wondering why." He tilted his head to one side, maintaining eye contact, striving to keep his body relaxed

"I decided that things in the APZ weren't quite to my liking." O'Reilly looked past Rickards to the men standing behind him. "I'm not sure whether you really want me discussing all the details in front of your crew there."

Damned arrogant bastard, thought Rickards, trying not to grind his teeth. He knew he'd made a mistake trying to bait O'Reilly in that manner. O'Reilly knew perfectly well that Rickards couldn't have him talking in front of the others. God knew what he'd say. Rickards was fairly sure that his men were loyal, but it was hard to say exactly what information O'Reilly possessed.

Rickards thought quickly, then decided to change directions and attempt a direct assault. "Where are the children?" He stood straight and looked O'Reilly in the eyes, casual smile banished from his face.

"What children?"

"Dammit, O'Reilly!" Rickards bellowed startling his men, but producing little noticeable effect on O'Reilly. "Where is Christina Craigson, her brothers Nick and Ryan Craigson and Alysa Thalman? We know they're with you. We tracked them as far as Wikieup and none of us are so stupid as to believe that they didn't meet up with you. Now where are they?"

O'Reilly slowly straightened, his eyes hardening. The difference was slight, but Rickards was encouraged by that indication that he'd gotten through with at least one jab. That O'Reilly wasn't unreachable.

His satisfaction didn't last long as he watched O'Reilly resume his studied casualness.

"They're not here," O'Reilly answered. "They headed out several days ago on horseback. We figured you'd track them here, so they decided not to stay."

"You don't really expect me to believe that, do you?" Rickards demanded. "They are kids... fourteen and eight year old kids. There's no way you'd let them head off on their own."

O'Reilly shrugged, adding fuel to Rickards' internal fire. "They made it to Wikieup on their own, didn't they?"

"They may have, but you wouldn't have sent them off on their own again. I know you better than that, O'Reilly. Where are they?"

"I said they aren't here. You're right, though. They didn't go on their own. There was someone else here when I arrived. I sent the kids with him."

The shift was so subtle Rickards almost missed it. Something about O'Reilly's eyes, the cast of his face. He wasn't sure what it meant, but something about the mysterious "him" caused a reaction in O'Reilly.

"Who is this person? You must have trusted him a great deal if you sent the children with him and stayed behind yourself."

"The kids wanted to go, and I'm basically a loner. It worked out for the best."

"Nonetheless, you wouldn't let them go if you didn't trust this man. Who is he? What direction did they head?"

"You don't really expect me to answer those questions, do you?" O'Reilly said. A slightly sardonic smile rested on his lips.

Rickards could feel Harlan moving closer to his shoulder, and held his right hand up, telling him to back off.

"I expect..." the sound of falling rocks interrupted Rickards' words, causing all the men to jump, looking for the source of the noise. Rickards looked quickly back at O'Reilly and was surprised to catch a flash of what looked like fear slide across his features, briefly replacing the cynical half smile that had been there only seconds before. Interesting.

O'Reilly quickly regained his composure and turned back to look at the group of men. Rickards studied his face, trying to determine the cause of the emotion he'd caught flashing through O'Reilly's eyes. Something further back in the caves worried O'Reilly. Something...

Rickards' eyes narrowed and his chin came up. "I expect you to do exactly what you have done, O'Reilly. You say they headed out on horseback several days ago? Then you won't mind if we check out the rest of the caverns before we leave. They're really quite... fascinating." Rickards began to move forward as if to begin his exploration.

"Feel free," O'Reilly stepped to the side to allow Rickards to pass.

Rickards felt a momentary flush of disappointment when he realized that O'Reilly wasn't going to try and block the Enforcers' intrusion. Then he caught that slight shift in O'Reilly's eyes again, and was positive he was going in the right direction.

"Peters, you and Larson watch him. Harlan, you and Johnson come with me. You'll excuse me O'Reilly if I don't trust you. If you don't mind, place your weapon on the ground."

O'Reilly held out his hands, showing Rickards that he held nothing. "What weapon?"

"Don't take me for a fool, O'Reilly. You wouldn't have come out to face us without a gun."

A sheepish grin, completely unexpected, and therefore vaguely troubling, crossed O'Reilly's face. "Yeah, well it won't do me much good anyway." O'Reilly bent over, reaching behind a pile of rubble to pick up a hunting rifle by the barrel. In the dim yellow light Rickards could see that the bolt handle was twisted, rendering the rifle useless.

O'Reilly held the rifle out and Johnson, slinging his own weapon over his shoulder, stepped forward to take it. Just as Johnson's hand touched the stock of the gun, O'Reilly swung his free arm around, and in one smooth motion gripped the barrel of his gun with both hands, and swung clubbing Johnson on the head. The man's flabby face took on a comically astonished look straight out of the cartoons before going blank. He fell swiftly to the ground, his flashlight spinning away into the adjoining cave.

O'Reilly immediately swung his makeshift club again, this time toward Peters, breaking his arm, causing him to drop his weapon. O'Reilly dropped to one knee and reached for the fallen gun as Larson took aim. Reacting instantly, O'Reilly swung the gun up, striking the barrel of Larson's rifle. A shot rang out, the bullet flying into the roof of the cave. Almost simultaneously Harlan and Rickards took aim and opened fire.

O'Reilly was thrown to the ground by the force of the impact, landing on his right side next to the pile of rubble near cave's wall.

Rickards maintained his aim on O'Reilly who was lying motionless on the ground in front of him the echos of the shots continuing to ring in his ears.. A spreading stain, black in the murky yellow light from the flashlights, testified to the accuracy of at least one of the bullets. Dust filled the air making breathing difficult, and a groaning sound gradually penetrated Rickards' concentration.

Rickards lifted his head, looking around in the dusty air as several small stones pelted his shoulder and head. He saw Larson and Harlan also looking around confusedly while small rocks and stones began to rain down around them. Peters was on his knees, hugging his injured right arm to his chest, and staring at the roof of the cave with a look of fear.

Johnson lay insensate while debris bounced off his body and dust clotted the blood oozing from the wound on the side of his head showing where the stock of O'Reilly's gun connected.

Coughing on air that seemed as thick as mud, Rickards started forward, trying to yell to the others to get out. Harlan apparently realized what Rickards was trying to say because he bent to grab Johnson by the arms and began pulling him away in the direction of the cave's entrance.

With a final rumbling groan the roof of the cave announced its imminent capitulation. Rickards dove for cover as larger stones and boulders rained down.

Pandemonium ensued.

44

aggie froze at the sound of the shots, her heart turning to ice in her chest. It seemed as if all the air had been sucked out of the cave and any second she would start flopping on the ground, gasping for air like a fish deposited on land by the angler's line.

She looked down into Mark's face and saw him staring back up at her, terror written across his face.

"Mom! O'Reilly! We can't leave him out there. He must be in trouble." Mark started to pull away from Maggie and head back toward the sound of the gun shots, trying to free himself from her tight grip on his arm. A loud grumbling roar stopped him and he looked around in confusion.

"Cave in!" Maggie said, hoarsely. "The shots must have triggered a cave in." She looked toward the outer caves as dust began to waft in toward them. Mark renewed his struggle to head back toward O'Reilly.

"Mark, stop it!"

"Mom, we've got to help him. He might be caught in the cave in. He might be hurt."

The panicked expression on Mark's face ripped through Maggie. She knew he felt responsible for O'Reilly being placed in danger, and that nothing she said would change his mind. She also felt a growing sense of panic in herself; that if she didn't do *something, anything* she would simply explode where she stood, raining down in little pieces all over the cave.

Maggie grabbed Mark's arm more tightly and began pulling him toward the stone covering the entrance to the hideout cave.

"Mark, you're going to go back into the hideout with Christina and the other children. I'll pull the stone over, then go find O'Reilly. Let me have the gun you took." Maggie reached for the pistol shoved in the waistband of Mark's jeans.

"But..."

"No buts. I can't be trying to find him and worrying about you at the same time. You'll be safe in the cave. If I can't find O'Reilly, I'll head deeper in the caverns until the Enforcers are gone."

"But, Mom, I..."

"Mark, we're wasting time." Maggie pulled the stone off the passage's opening, only to find Christina's frightened looking face staring back out at her.

"Maggie? We heard..."

"You heard shots. And the cave in. I know. Take Mark, Christina, I'm going to look for O'Reilly. He was out toward the main entrance when we heard the gunfire. We don't know where he is now, so I'm going to find out."

Maggie pushed Mark toward the opening, and Christina wriggled backward to allow him to slide in. After he was fully into the passageway, Maggie quickly pushed the rock back over the opening, and, using the juniper bough brought in for that purpose, quickly erased all evidence that the stone had been a center of attention.

Throwing the branch deeper into the caves, Maggie grabbed her flashlight and gun and headed toward the main entrance to the caves.

I can't breath! God, please let me breath! thought Rickards, as he choked in the dust from the cave in. Nearby he could hear the other men gasping for air and coughing. He felt as though he was going to deposit his lungs on the ground at any moment if he wasn't able to stop soon.

The air began to clear slightly, and he was finally able to draw a deep breath without gagging. He stood still for a moment, trying to calm his breathing and make sense of his surroundings. His flashlight had been smashed from his hand during the cave in, and now he found himself wallowing in a darkness so complete that he wondered briefly if he'd been blinded. Slowly kneeling down, he felt around his feet, hoping to come across the dropped light.

Rocks littered the floor around his feet, and he'd begun to despair when his hand grazed across the rough metal surface of the heavy flashlight. Retrieving it from where it lay in the debris of the cave in, he tried to turn it on. Nothing. Running his hand over the casing, he quickly discovered that the lens was shattered, and likely the bright LED bulb inside. The flashlight carried a spare bulb in the butt, but without a light, the likelihood of his being able to switch out the small bulbs was not good. He needed light.

"Harlan, Peters, Larson, where are you?"

"Harlan here, sir." The voice was muffled, indistinct, and Rickards couldn't tell which direction it came from.

"Larson. Peters. You there?"

"Yes, sir. We're here. Johnson's bad, though. He was caught in the cave in. A lot of rocks struck him." Larson's voice, Rickards thought.

"Do you have light? My flashlight was damaged in the cave in."

"Yes, sir. Just a moment and we'll get to you." Harlan, this time. At least he thought it was Harlan.

Gradually Rickards saw a lightening in the air at the far side of the tunnel. Apparently the cave in hadn't completely filled the passageway. There was a triangular gap at the upper right, and it was from here that the light was coming. He heard the clatter-tick of falling rocks as Harlan pushed his way through, over a the pile of rubble.

"Harlan, over here."

Harlan turned his flashlight in the direction of the voice, then made his way over to Rickards.

"How's everyone over there?"

"Peters and I have a lot of bruises. Larson's arm's broken from when O'Reilly hit him, and he took a hard blow to the head as well. Johnson's the worst. He's still breathing, but he was partially buried under rocks in the cave in. I don't know if he's going to make it."

Rickards thought for a moment. "First I need to change the bulb in this flashlight. Then I want you to take Larson and Peters and get Johnson back to Donner at the main entrance. I'm going to wait here. Wherever the children are, They had to have heard the shots and the cave in. They'll come to find out what's going on. I'm convinced of it."

"Sir, I don't like the idea of leaving you here alone."

"It will be fine, Harlan. O'Reilly's out of the picture," he nudged the body at his feet with his toe. "And I should be able to handle four kids. I'll leave the flashlight off until they get here, then take them by surprise. They'll give in without a fight, I'm sure."

"Are we taking them back with us, then?"

"It will depend on them," Rickards scowled. The dilemma of what to do with the children had been plaguing him for awhile. Christina Craigson and Alysa Thalman had already proven to be good at outwitting the authorities, and Christina had a lot of information that they couldn't afford to have spread around the APZ. Information that had gotten her put into isolation in the first place. The idea of having to kill children, though, did not sit well with him.

Duty versus conscience. Rickards wanted the freedom to make his own decision. Freedom that he wouldn't have if he kept Harlan nearby. There was no doubt in Rickards' mind which choice Harlan would make.

"At least switch flashlights with me. We can't fix the lens on yours, but since Larson and Peters still have theirs, it won't matter so much to me." Harlan held out his flashlight, exchanging it for Rickards' lensless one.

Then, still looking concerned, but following Rickards' orders, Harlan climbed back through the gap in the rock fall. As his light disappeared into the next cave, Rickards turned off his own flashlight, and faded back into the niche in the tunnel's wall, behind a boulder to wait for the children's arrival.

The air became thicker with dust as Maggie proceeded through the caves, leaving a nasty sensation in her mouth. *Feels as though I've been lunching on rocks,* she thought, spitting to try and remove the taste without success. Her sinuses felt as though they'd been filled with cement, and she briefly wondered if she would suffocate before finding O'Reilly.

There was a chance, she thought, that the cave in had totally blocked the cave, which would mean they were trapped there, the only way out through the small opening in the secret cave. Which was, she thought grimly, better than being trapped in these caves with no way out, but only marginally. Why hadn't they thought about the possibility of cave ins when they chose the caverns as a hiding place. Geez, she thought, with her over active imagination, she should have been picturing herself buried in rocks and spitting out stone dust a long time ago. All she'd been able to come up with were rattlesnakes, lions and the ghosts of dead prospectors, and those specters had been pretty much banished weeks ago.

As Maggie moved closer to the cave in, her flashlight took on an eerie yellowish glow, sending out visible beams as the light reflected on minute particles of rock suspended in the air. She stopped frequently to listen, fearful that she might turn a corner into the band of Enforcers, and find herself captured. Several times she started coughing, burying her face in her t-shirt to muffle the sound.

Just as Maggie was beginning to fear that she'd taken a wrong turn; that she would wander in this dust filled labyrinth for the remainder of her life, or at least until she went mad, she walked around a corner and was brought up short at the sight of the cave in.

The rocks and boulders filled nearly two thirds of the tunnel, leaving enough room to escape at the upper right of the cave. Maggie approached the blockage slowly, panning her flashlight over the rock fall. Other than the occasional rattle of falling stones, and the rasp of her breath, she could hear no other sounds.

Her light glinted back and forth over the sandstone, picking up an occasional flash from a larger piece of quartz or calcite. Just as she decided she needed to move on, the light fell on something that drove the breath from her body in a ragged gasp. Lying on the left side of the tunnel, half buried under dirt and rocks was a body. It was so covered with rock dust that it almost looked like a stone sculpture itself. A dark liquid glistened through the dust, winking and sparkling in the glow of the flashlight, almost beautiful in its contrast with the surrounding, unrelieved gray.

Maggie froze. Conflicting emotions took hold of her body. Part of her wanted to run the other way and take up permanent residence in the state of denial. But the rest of her had to know. Slowly she approached the man lying on the floor. He lay so still that it was impossible to tell if he was alive.

One step, pause. Another. The knot in her chest was taking on the dimensions of a basketball, pushing out all the air in her lungs. Each step was taken more quickly, until the last three were virtually at a run.

Letting out a soft cry, she dropped to her knees beside the body. With a trembling hand she reached out to wipe the dust from its face. Even coated in a thick layer of powdered rock, she could discern the clean cut features of O'Reilly. His skin was warm to her touch, and she leaned forward, close to his nose and mouth, trying to tell if he was still breathing. Unnoticed tears tracked through the grime on her face, plopping softly into the dust on his chest, leaving small wet pock marks in the dirt.

"O'Reilly, wake up!" She smoothed back the hair along his forehead. Her hand encountered a damp spot, sticky, and when she brought it up to her face, she could smell the blood mingled with the scent of damp rock dust.

"Oh, God, O'Reilly... O'Reilly, come on," she begged, reaching out to shake his left shoulder. "You can't leave us alone, you idiot. You know damned well we can't make it without you... I can't make it without you." She started to shake his shoulder harder, falling down a dark spiral toward panic.

"Is he alive?"

A voice, hoarse with dust, shocked Maggie, causing adrenal glands that she already thought to be on overload, to squirt another shot of adrenaline into her system. She shot backward, landing on her butt next to O'Reilly, and staring up into the dark niche where the voice had emanated.

A light blossomed, and Maggie could see a tall, barrel chested man, short cropped hair, turned white by the dust, dark eyes glowing out of the whitened face.

Kabuki actors, Maggie thought irrelevantly. *That's what we must all look like. White faces, dark eyes. Kabuki actors in a bad Japanese melodrama.* She stared at the man as he took a step forward into the glow of her flashlight, the two sources of illumination brightening the tableau in front of her, and leaving the rest of the cave in utter darkness.

"Is he alive?" the man asked again, gesturing toward O'Reilly. He was wearing an Enforcers' uniform, and carrying a rifle in his left hand, barrel pointed toward the ground. At his hip was a holster with a handgun. Maggie thought briefly of the handgun she'd dropped beside O'Reilly's body when she reached out toward him. No good. This guy would turn her into a sieve before she even got her hand around it. Better to play along for now.

"For the last time, is he alive? Please don't make me ask again." The man's tone was conversational, not threatening, but Maggie felt threatened nonetheless and it didn't sit well.

"I don't know," She answered him testily. "I can't tell, but if he is, it probably isn't due to your gentle care." She looked down at O'Reilly who'd remained silent throughout this exchange.

"Who are you?" came the hoarse voice again.

Maggie could feel a growing irritation as the adrenaline released by

281

her fear began to transform itself. "Maggie Langton. Who the hell are you?" she snapped back.

She was surprised by a snort of laughter, followed by a burst of coughing as the man tried to clear his lungs of the rock dust. He turned his head and spat a wad of mucus toward the wall of the cave.

Turning back toward her, he said, "Fair enough," his voice clearer, though still deeply resonant. "I'm Captain Seth Rickards from the Laughlin APZ."

"O'Reilly's mentioned you."

"He has? I'm surprised. What has he said?"

"He said that one would be lucky if you were on his side, there was no one better. But one didn't want you after him, because you wouldn't stop until you succeeded."

Rickards looked impressed, and flattered to some degree, but no less intimidating.

"Where are the children?"

"What children?"

Rickards took on a look of almost fatherly exasperation. "Come now. You know which children. The Craigsons, and Alysa Thalman."

Maggie started to answer, but Rickards stopped her with a raised hand.

"I already know that they met up with O'Reilly. He said he sent them on with some 'man' who'd been here already when he arrived. He didn't mention you, and I'm forced to the conclusion that this 'man' really didn't exist. So that means you probably know where he's hidden them."

"I..."

A soft groan issued from O'Reilly. Maggie looked down and was startled to see that he'd opened his eyes and was looking at her fuzzily.

45

Looking back, Rickards thought, it hadn't taken long at all for someone to come, though time passes slowly in the dark. The only sounds to keep him company were the occasional rattle of rocks as they tumbled off the pile left in the middle of the tunnel. He hadn't bothered to check whether O'Reilly was alive or not when Harlan was still there, and he couldn't tell afterward as he waited in the darkness. He doubted it. If the shots hadn't killed him, then the cave in probably finished the job.

Wrong again, apparently.

O'Reilly's eyes were open, and it was obvious that against all odds he was very much alive. Rickards stood looking down at the woman who'd come to O'Reilly's rescue and felt a growing sense of unreality. Why the hell didn't anything go as expected?

"Wha... what happened?" O'Reilly asked, trying to focus on the woman's face, apparently unaware that Rickards stood nearby, watching.

Where'd he find her? Rickards wondered. He'd have heard if someone else had escaped with O'Reilly or the children. He supposed O'Reilly could have run into her at one of the ranches, or out on the road. He gritted his teeth. How many other surprises was he going to get?

From what he could tell in the dim light she was attractive beneath all the dirt. Long hair, apparently dark blond, worn in a braid. She was undeniably filthy, as were they all, and tears had carved their way down her face, leaving darkened channels in the dirt. The eyes were what bothered him the most, looking at him with a haunted expression that struck a chord, though he couldn't pinpoint why.

"It's okay, O'Reilly. There's been a cave in, and you've been shot, but it's going to be okay." The woman, Maggie she said her name was, brushed her hand across O'Reilly's face tenderly, then looked back up at Rickards', her own features hardening.

A short burst of laughter, followed by a paroxysm of coughing startled both the woman and Rickards, causing them to break eye contact and look at the man lying on the floor. "You've got a damned strange idea of okay, if this is it," O'Reilly finally said, trying to catch his breath. "What does it take to make things not 'okay?'"

"I've just met your Captain Rickards."

O'Reilly's eyes sharpened, and he struggled to sit up, trying to follow her gaze. The movement wrung a groan of pain from him, and Rickards could see a fresh gush of blood from the wound in his right shoulder. Collapsing back on the ground, O'Reilly seemed to pass out briefly, then opened his eyes again, turning his head.

"I guess that would qualify. I..." O'Reilly seemed to drift out for a moment, then collected himself. "I don't suppose you had the decency to get pegged by a few rocks when the roof fell in, did you?"

"Sorry, not a scratch." Rickards answered smiling slightly at the jab.

"Damn," O'Reilly said softly. His eyes seemed to lose focus for a moment and Rickards thought he was going to lose consciousness again.

The woman was trying to use his shirt to staunch the flow of blood from the wound. Fear was written all over her face, but her actions were swift and sure. Once again Rickards wondered where O'Reilly'd picked her up. She seemed to be a handy type. Just the kind of woman you'd want to take with you when you were on the lam, if you could ignore the acerbic attitude.

Taking another step forward and dropping to one knee next to O'Reilly, Rickards spoke with intensity. "What made you run?"

O'Reilly's eyes shifted to Rickards, but he didn't answer.

"O'Reilly, what made you run? And don't give me any bullshit about not liking the food at the APZ."

O'Reilly let out a soft cough of laughter.

"Can't this wait," Maggie asked irritably. She'd torn off the bottom of O'Reilly's shirt, and was pressing it hard against his shoulder. "Can't you see he..."

"You saw the memos?" O'Reilly's voice was so quiet that Rickards almost didn't hear it.

"What memos?"

"The memos about the population consolidation across the globe? The ones that were accidentally sent with the census?"

"I found them, yes. Was that it? That the governments are planning to keep the APZs?" Rickards scowled. When the APZs were formed, he'd agreed with the governmental assessment that it was the best way to make sure that everybody received what they needed. When it became apparent that the APZs were here to stay, he had mixed feelings. It wasn't his job to evaluate the situation in the world and make policy to deal with it. His job was to carry out the policy set down by his superiors, and he'd done so to the best of his ability. He might not necessarily have agreed, but he followed through.

O'Reilly had drifted off again. Rickards reached out and grabbed his shoulder, shaking it sharply.

"Hey, stop!" Maggie reached out and hit his hand away. "What the hell do you think you're doing!"

Rickards ignored her, focusing on O'Reilly. His eyes were half closed, and Rickards wasn't sure how aware he was, but he tried again. "Was that it? The APZs?"

"What was phase one?" O'Reilly's voice was so low that Rickards nearly missed it.

"Phase one? What do you mean?" Rickards realized that Maggie was staring at him. She hadn't shown any signs of surprise at the conversation so far. No reaction when he'd said the APZs were there to stay. No shock about the memos. He must have told her. But this talk of 'phase one' was unexpected.

"The memos... one of them called.... called the APZs phase two. The consolidation of population." O'Reilly's voice was fading. His eyes were closed and Rickards wondered how much longer he could hold out. "It talked about a phase one. What was it?"

Rickards shook his head, even though O'Reilly wasn't looking at him. "I don't know what phase one was. I don't remember a memo talking about phase two. I didn't really read them. They were classified. I was told to destroy them. Which memo was it?"

For a moment Rickards thought that O'Reilly was gone, his stillness was so profound. Then he drew a shallow breath and coughed.

"Stop. Just stop," begged Maggie, still pressing the piece of material against O'Reilly's shoulder. A piece of material that was rapidly staining dark in the dim light.

Rickards looked at her, then back at O'Reilly. "Which memo was it?"

"Don't remember. I... don't remember." The last sounds sighed out of O'Reilly. The stillness returned and once again Rickards couldn't tell if O'Reilly was dead or alive. He looked at Maggie, who was staring back at him, wide eyed.

Rickards felt a disorienting sense of deja vu. He just couldn't put his finger on the source of the feeling. He closed his eyes, trying to think. The picture in his mind tickled the edges of his memory.

"It's not right, you know."

Rickards opened his eyes to see Maggie watching him. Those wide dark eyes filled with a strange mixture of defiance and pleading. She continued to put pressure on O'Reilly's wound, but her eyes were on Rickards.

"How can it be right to force people into the APZs?"

"How else can we make sure everyone is taken care of?" Rickards answered.

"Look at history." Maggie countered. "When has locking people into ghettos, internment camps or things like that ever been successful? How are the APZs any different, other than we're locking the entire population into them, rather than just select groups?"

At the mention of internment camps the picture that Rickards had been seeking flooded back into his mind. The dream the night they'd gotten a fix on the children. The girl in the hall, and on the train platform. The haunted eyes, begging him for help.

Rickards threw himself backward, staggered to his feet, and stared down at Maggie's confused expression.

The eyes, pleading for help. In his dream he hadn't been able to reach the girl in time. She'd had to get on the train. Even though she'd reached out for him, he hadn't been able to help her.

Maggie looked up at him from her place beside O'Reilly. Her eyes were eloquent.

46

Maggie stared at Rickards, startled by his reaction to her argument. He looked as though he'd seen a ghost, and for a brief, hysterical moment, Maggie wondered if the specter of that long dead prospector had materialized behind her.

She fought the urge to look over her shoulder, and maintained her eye contact with Rickards.

"Who are you?" Rickards said in a hoarse whisper, staring at her mesmerized.

"I told you. My name is Maggie Langton." Maggie felt confused. She wondered if maybe Rickards had hit his head during the cave in, and was just now showing the effects.

"How did you get here? I mean, how did you wind up with O'Reilly?"

"I'm a journalist. Friends in the Phoenix APZ got word to me what was happening there, so when my area was assigned to be consolidated, I took my... I left. I'd written about this ranch, so knew about the camp here in Adobe Canyon." Maggie was starting to get irritated all over again. O'Reilly needed attention, and there were limits to what she could do sitting here in the dirt. Of course, if Rickards decided to kill her, she wouldn't be able to do much anyway, so she tried to hide her annoyance. "I'd already been here a few weeks when O'Reilly showed up. He apparently grew up here."

"Did he mention this 'phase one' to you?"

Maggie was wary. If she said too much, Rickards could decide that she was a liability. That would very likely be deadly for her, and possibly for the children as well.

"No, he said nothing about any phases to me. He talked a bit about why he left, but he was a pretty secretive man." She glanced down at

O'Reilly, lying silently under her hand. The bleeding seemed to have stopped. Hopefully that was because the blood was clotting, and not because he was dead, she thought wryly. She didn't dare investigate too closely, however, because she needed to maintain her focus on Rickards. His agitation confused her and she was concerned she would say the wrong thing.

Rickards closed his eyes and turned his face toward the ceiling. Maggie watched him standing there. She briefly considered whether she should try to take advantage of his distraction to either attack or run. Just as she'd wound her courage up to the point where she thought she could take him, Rickards opened his eyes and looked again at her.

"What will you do if I leave you here?"

The question was so unexpected that Maggie just gaped at him, unable to think of a single thing to say.

Rickards, apparently impatient with her dumfounded reaction, repeated more sharply, "What will you do if I leave you here... alive?"

"Live, I guess. Try and figure out how to keep myself fed and clothed."

"And the children?" he asked.

Maggie realized that it would be foolish to deny the presence of Christina and the others. He was obviously aware that they'd met up with O'Reilly.

"They'll stay with me, of course. I'll take care of them."

Rickards closed his eyes again and breathed deeply. It was apparent that he was fighting an internal battle and Maggie could only hope her life would be on the winning side.

He opened his eyes again and motioned down at O'Reilly. "He probably won't make it. He appears to be badly injured. What if he dies?"

Maggie choked down the emotions that rose in her throat at the thought of O'Reilly dying. Still a quiver was evident in her voice as she answered Rickards' question. "We'll make it. I've learned a lot from him about living off the land."

Rickards seemed to be transfixed by what he saw in Maggie's face, heard in her voice. For a moment there was silence as he studied her. The moment stretched out and Maggie began to feel uncomfortable under the intense scrutiny. Finally, he spoke again. "I need to know that if I leave you here, you won't do anything that would threaten the well being of the residents of the APZs."

Maggie frowned, "What do you mean?"

"I have a duty to protect those people. Outlaws, attacking supply trucks, depriving the residents of things they need. I can't have that. I need your assurance that you won't join people like that."

"You have my promise. All I want is to be left alone."

Silence stretched out again until Maggie was ready to say or do anything, just to get some type of action. Finally, Rickards came to a decision. Slinging his rifle over his shoulder, he stepped forward and around O'Reilly. He stopped as he was passing Maggie and looked down at her upraised face.

"When I get to the other side of the cave in I'm going to have to let off several shots, make it sound like a gun battle. I'm afraid it may cause another cave in, but I don't have much of a choice. If I just return to my men, they'll wonder where the children are, and why I didn't bring them back with me. I'm going to have to convince the other officers that I ran into the children, they were armed, and I had no choice but to take them out. Do you understand?"

Maggie nodded mutely.

"I'm going back to the APZ, and I'm going to do the best job I can to protect the people in my care. I may not agree with all the decisions the government is making, but I have to believe that they're making these decisions to try and help the survivors."

"Will you look into the 'phase one' O'Reilly spoke about?"

"I don't know," Rickards voice took on a lost, forlorn tone that chilled Maggie more than anything else during this strange encounter. "So help me God, I just don't know." He paused for a moment then looked at Maggie one last time. "If you need anything, get word to me at the APZ. Rickards reached into his vest pocket, pulling out a small, handheld electronic device. "This phone is registered to me. You'll be able to send me messages without alerting the monitoring system. The address you need is in the contacts list."

Rickards dropped the phone onto O'Reilly's chest, then turned, walked to the far side of the tunnel, and crawled through the gap into the next cave. A few seconds later a cluster of both rifle and pistol shots rang out, then there was quiet.

The silence stretched out for minutes. Maggie looked down at the still form of O'Reilly in front of her. A flood of emotions washed through her with the violence of a tsunami. She put her forehead on O'Reilly's chest and wept.

47

"Hey, do you mind not being such a sadist with the iodine?" O'Reilly yelped. Ignoring him, Maggie scrubbed at the crusted blood and serum discharge around the wound in his shoulder, as she had every morning for the past four days.

Maggie bent low to her task. The bright morning sun illuminated the healing bullet hole as she poked at it with a clean finger, looking for signs of infection. When she bent lower to sniff at it, however, O'Reilly found himself protesting again.

"What *are* you doing?" he exclaimed, torn between irritation and laughter.

"That survival first aide book you brought back from Wikieup said that if an injury becomes badly infected or gangrenous, it gives off a distinctive odor."

O'Reilly's eyebrows shot upward and he fixed her with an offended stare. "Checking me for rotting meat, huh?"

"Yes," she said matter of factly. "And I can give you a clean bill of health, at least as far as putrefaction goes. Now, lets get the bandage back in place before the flies come out."

"Have I mentioned lately that you're getting entirely too much enjoyment from this?" O'Reilly demanded as Maggie began wrapping a clean dressing around the injured shoulder, fastening his right arm to his chest, effectively immobilizing it.

"Actually, yes, you have," Maggie answered distractedly, eyes fixed on the hot pink material she'd chosen for that morning's bandage, much to O'Reilly's horror. "And when you consider what you put me through back there in the caves, you should be glad I don't wrap this cloth around your throat and throttle you."

"Sadist," O'Reilly growled as Maggie finished fastening the

dressing. She shot him a raspberry, then picked up her materials and headed back into the house. He could hear the children down by the stream, cheerful voices in the distance, showing little evidence of the stresses of the past week. O'Reilly sighed and leaned back against the wall of the house, enjoying the morning sun and thinking about all the changes that they'd undergone.

Whispers, shadows, and questions. That's how O'Reilly remembered his time as the centerpiece between Maggie and Rickards. He recalled participating in the conversation, but couldn't recollect exactly how. Several concussive reports penetrated his fog, bringing him back to the surface of consciousness. Gradually he became aware of a weight on his chest. Reaching up with his left hand, he found Maggie's head, and ran his fingers lightly over her hair.

Maggie sprang upright, jarring his shoulder and wringing a groan from him. Pain swelled and ebbed, reminding him of waves washing up on the ocean shore. *Thank you God, I live in Arizona*, he thought, *I never want to see the ocean again. I never want to see a lake again. Nothing with waves. Not even a damned puddle.*

"O'Reilly! I'm so sorry. You're alive!"

"You're sorry I'm alive? That's one hell of a sentiment."

Maggie gritted her teeth, making O'Reilly smile weakly. "No, idiot. I'm sorry I hit your shoulder. I'm glad you're alive. But I may reconsider."

O'Reilly laughed, then winced at the explosion of sound in his head. "I'm glad I'm alive, too. And I hope you don't reconsider. Where's Rickards?"

"He's gone." Maggie hesitated. "I don't know exactly what happened, but he asked what would I do if he left us here... alive. I guess he accepted my answer."

O'Reilly frowned, trying to determine the meaning of Rickards surprise action. He wished the pounding in his head would go away. He wished the throbbing in his shoulder would go away. He wished the dust in the air would go away. He wished the feeling of exhaustion would go away. Just about the only thing that he didn't wish would go away was Maggie. Reaching out again with his left hand, he found her right hand on his chest and squeezed it.

"I'm so tired I can't think straight."

"O'Reilly, don't you leave me again. I swear I'll..."

"No, listen. Go back to the hideout cave. Check on the children."

"I don't want to leave you here in the dark.

"I'll be fine. It's not like I'm going to wander around and get lost." O'Reilly gave her a weak smile. "You need to make sure that Rickards and the others have left the canyon. Then we need to get out of here. You're going to have to check out this wound in better light, and it needs to be done soon. There's probably at least ten pounds of dirt in it, as well as the bullet, and it all needs to be removed before infection sets it."

Maggie stared at him appalled. "And you think I'm going do this?"

"Well, unless you want to run out and flag down Rickards, you're the one who's going to have to do this. I sure as hell can't."

Maggie pushed herself to her feet and glared down at O'Reilly. "You owe me."

O'Reilly, eyes beginning to drift closed again said, "Don't worry, next time you get shot, I'll be more than glad to dig the bullet out. Now go." He slid back into sleep before he heard her answer.

The trip out of the caves left a great deal to be desired, at least as far as O'Reilly was concerned. Walking out under his own power was out of the question, which left one woman, six children and two dogs. Not a good bet for a comfortable journey. Maggie finally solved the transportation problem by taking several blankets and tying them to two long boards retrieved from the barn following the Enforcers evacuation from the valley. She constructed a travois, then, with Christina's and Alysa's assistance, moved O'Reilly onto the sling. The three were then able to drag the contraption out of the caves and back to the house.

O'Reilly would swear later that they hit every rock and pothole along the path. Maggie was equally adamant that he would have to go on a diet, so that the next time she had to drag his butt half way across Arizona, it wouldn't be so heavy.

Of course, O'Reilly thought, the pain caused by the trip out of the caves was nothing compared to that which he was forced to endure after they reached the house. The bullet had entered high in his right shoulder, apparently deflected off a rib, headed upward and struck the collarbone, breaking it. The bullet itself was lodged in the muscle at the top of the shoulder.

It may have been a miracle, said O'Reilly, that at such close range he hadn't been injured more severely. In fact, upon later consideration, he decided that the head wound and corresponding concussion was more likely the cause of the fuzziness and blackouts in the cave, than the gunshot wound.

As miraculous as his escape from a deadly injury was, however, the greater miracle was that he survived Maggie's debut as a surgeon. The thought of that operation still twisted O'Reilly's guts. They'd had no anesthesia, and a razor blade had to stand in for a scalpel. Maggie was less than thrilled at her assignment, and spent the entire procedure muttering dire imprecations should he ever get himself shot again. O'Reilly, who had his teeth ground into a strap of belt leather in the true tradition of the old west, found very little opportunity to argue with her, particularly since every time he groaned, or allowed any other sound out of his throat, the threats became more animated, and more imaginative.

It took forty-five minutes, a quart of Betadine, and several yards of silk embroidery thread, brought by O'Reilly from Wikieup, before Maggie was finished, and by that point O'Reilly was beginning to think longingly of Rickards and a lifetime of incarceration. A three inch laceration over his left eye also received the gentle ministrations of the reluctant surgeon, and after studying the stitching in the mirror the next morning, he decided that it would be wise to cultivate his own sewing skills, lest he wind up without wearable clothing sometime in the future.

Now, four days later, O'Reilly was healing well, thanks to Maggie's diligence, as well as large doses of antibiotics, also brought from Wikieup. The danger from the Enforcers was in the past, the children happy and healthy, and Houdini was once again tormenting Maggie every morning at egg collection time.

Alysa and Mark trekked up to the east pasture to retrieve their horses the day after Rickards left, hunting for and bringing back Jenny, the calf, and Lizzie, the milk cow at the same time. Christina appointed herself chief gardener, working hard to restore the plants damaged by the Enforcers' march through the valley. Maggie continued to insist on daily schooling for Mark, now including Nick, Ryan, Christina and Alysa in the arrangement. Lindy continued to spend her time in pursuits of vital importance to two-year-olds, but unintelligible to everyone else.

The phone Rickards left behind was stashed safely in a spot known only to Maggie and O'Reilly. Maggie determined to check it and charge the batteries using her solar charger once a month.

In short, everything was returning to normal more quickly than anyone thought possible.

The spring on the door of the house twanged and squeaked as Maggie reemerged, milk bucket in one hand and the egg basket in the other. She paused briefly in the entrance, letting the screen door slam shut behind her. Setting the milk bucket on the ground, she raised her hand, shaded her eyes and studied the far side of the valley in the direction of the children's voices.

O'Reilly watched her standing there. The honey blond hair pulling loose from her braid as usual, floating around her face, drifting in the warm morning breeze. The sun turned the strands into a golden halo. A slight frown wrinkled her forehead as she scanned the distance, looking for Mark or one of the other children.

O'Reilly felt a strong reluctance to disturb the picture but finally said, "The boys are down by the pond. I think they're planning on catching us some fish for dinner."

"Damn. The girls?"

"Alysa wanted to take Christina down to gather reeds from around the stream. I think they're planning on trying to weave some baskets like the ones they saw in that book on crafts." O'Reilly grinned up at Maggie. "Off to collect eggs?"

"Yeah, I wanted to get it done before it gets any hotter. I'll be so glad when the monsoons are over and things start cooling down." Maggie sighed. "I guess it's up to me." She stooped and picked up the bucket and started to head down the path toward the barn.

"Hey, wait." O'Reilly struggled to his feet, trying to avoid jarring the injured shoulder.

Maggie stopped and turned, "What are you doing? You don't need to come. I can handle it," she protested.

"I'm getting tired of just sitting around being a drain on society," O'Reilly answered, panting from the effort of getting to his feet while bound up like a mummy. He walked over to where Maggie was waiting. "Besides, you faced Rickards for me. Performed heroic surgery. Checked me for rotting meat. Least I can do is guard your back when you do battle for my breakfast."

"Actually, I sort of had my heart set on that addition to the house, and a real bathroom, but I suppose I'll settle for a bodyguard." Maggie smiled up at O'Reilly as he stood looking down at her. Stepping forward, he slid his left arm around her shoulders and bent to kiss her lightly.

"I'm thinking I'd like to be more than a bodyguard, though I can see that the house addition would be an integral part of the deal. What do you say?"

Maggie pulled away and headed toward the barn, swinging the basket jauntily. She glanced over her shoulder, her eyes lit by mischievous laughter.

"I'll let you know once I see the addition."

48

Few people were present in the Enforcers' main office as Captain Seth Rickards entered at midnight four days after his encounter with O'Reilly and the Langton woman. The team had finally made it back into town late that afternoon, filthy and exhausted.

The trip over the ranch roads had been difficult, especially when several more monsoon thunderstorms turned the heavy clay soil into a snot-slick mess. Several times they found themselves struggling to dig out vehicles that became mired.

The men were subdued. No one had questioned Rickards upon his return to the cave's entrance, but it was obvious that some were uncomfortable returning to Laughlin with no visible evidence of their success. Harlan especially seemed unsure about the outcome in the tunnels. Twice he suggested they bring O'Reilly's body out and take it back with them.

He only stopped at Rickards' insistence that the body would be an unnecessary incumbrance as they tried to make their way out of the canyon on foot, and that carrying a dead body in this heat in the summer would be somewhat less than pleasant. Besides, as Rickards pointed out, they already had Johnson, with his head injury, and Larson with his broken arm. Not to mention Gomez with his gunshot wound. They didn't need any more burdens.

All in all, the trip back to Laughlin had taken nearly four days and the team was worn out. Rickards fully intended, after seeing to the injured, to return to his apartment, take a long shower, fall into a dry bed, and sleep for at least a year.

All went according to plan, too. At least until he'd fallen into bed. As he tossed from one side to the other, he couldn't free his mind of O'Reilly's last question. *What was 'phase one?'* Finally, after trying to fall asleep for an hour, and failing miserably, he angrily threw aside the blankets and rose. Pulling on jeans and a shirt, he headed down the silent corridor.

At that time of night it only took five minutes to reach the main office. He nodded at two deputies manning the desks, but avoided becoming involved in any conversation, instead aiming straight for the door to his private office. Once inside, he turned on a light and reached for the top drawer in the black filing cabinet behind his desk.

The file was where he'd left it. Far at the back of the top drawer, labeled memos. Pulling it from its nest, he spread the contents on the desktop and sat. After O'Reilly left the APZ, Rickards found the memos on his desk in an unmarked file folder. Scanning them he'd quickly determined that they were part of a huge screw up on the part of the central control, and notified his superiors. They'd instructed him to shred the documents immediately, and he'd prepared to do just that. At the last moment, however, he'd changed his mind and placed the memos in the file folder at the back of the top drawer in the locked file cabinet.

Now he was glad he had. Carefully he reviewed the memos, turning over page after page outlining the progress with consolidation of the survivors in the various industrialized countries. He found what he was looking for on the seventh memo.

It obviously originated as a fax, and apparently the paper had misfed as it passed through the machine since the letterhead at the top was partially cropped, making it virtually impossible to tell which country issued it. In spite of the ambiguity of the sender, however, the message itself was clear and it thrust an icy knife deep into Rickards heart.

It wasn't a long memo. An introductory paragraph followed by a four item outline under the main title *United Country Action Plan for Global Realignment*. This was where O'Reilly had found his phases.

The first bullet jumped out at him and challenged everything in which he believed.

Phase One: Reduction of Population.

Also by Cheryl F Taylor

Amethyst Stone has come home to take care of her father's rock shop, Stone's Gems and Minerals, while her father, Nick, recovers from a broken leg. It's not long, however, before things go awry, as the her father's assistant is murdered, and Amy is suspect number one.

Amy and her new assistant, Jackson Wolf, have to unravel the tangled clues to find out who killed Carl, and why, as well as protect the shop itself from the Copper Springs town council which would like to see it condemned.

As Amy and Jackson dig deeper, they realize that there is a lot more going on than it appears on the surface, and multiple people have a reason to want Carl out of the way. They just have to figure out who actually did it before they become the killer's next victims.

This is book 1 in the Rock Shop Cozy Mystery series

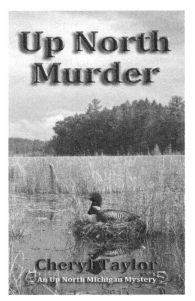

A phone call can change your life forever...

Abigail Williams gets that phone call. Gordon Dorsey, Abby's uncle and last living relative has drowned in the lake on his property, and Abby is his sole heir.

There are a few complications, however. Abby's inheritance is a trout farm in Michigan, but she's a city girl from Phoenix, Arizona.

In addition, Abby doesn't believe the official story of her uncle's death.

And the biggest complication... the four-legged furry owner of the farm who seems to have her own ideas about how things should be run.

Culture shock is the least of her worries.

This is book 1 in the Up North Michigan Cozy Mystery series

Made in the USA
Monee, IL
22 August 2023

41417126R00168